The Girls
OF NO RETURN

E R I N   S A L D I N

 ARTHUR A. LEVINE BOOKS AN IMPRINT OF SCHOLASTIC INC.

Saldin, Erin.

The girls of No Return / Erin Saldin. — 1st ed.

p. cm.

Summary: A troubled sixteen-year-old girl attending a wilderness school in the Idaho mountains must finally face the consequences of her complicated friendships with two of the other girls at the school.

ISBN 978-0-545-31026-0 (hardcover : alk. paper) — ISBN 978-0-545-31027-7 (pbk.) — ISBN 978-0-545-39253-2 (e-book) [1. Emotional problems — Fiction. 2. Schools — Fiction. 3. Frank Church-River of No Return Wilderness (Idaho) — Fiction.] I. Title.

PZ7.S1494Gi 2012

[Fic] — dc23

2011024214

10 9 8 7 6 5 4 3 2 1   12 13 14 15 16

Printed in the U.S.A.   23

First edition, February 2012

MAR - - 2013

For Rob

Epilogue

"Margaret called today."

Dr. Hemler shifts in his chair. "And did you speak with her?"

I shake my head, and blow on my hands. His office is always so cold. "She left a message. Something about a question." I act like I can't quite remember the message, as if it's not running through my head like the ticker at the bottom of a news screen. The pause between "It's" and "important." "I'll try you again," she'd said.

"What do you think she wants to ask you?" He picks up the remote control on his armrest and points it at the heating unit near the ceiling. There's a click, and then a soft whirring begins. "Will you call her back?"

"It's been over a year," I say. "I don't know what she could want to talk to me about."

He tilts his head. "Don't you?"

When I get home, I go straight to my room, shutting the door behind me, and sit down at my desk. I have that sickening, thick feeling in my stomach that I get whenever I have to do something terrible but necessary, like

1

apologizing to Terri or admitting I forgot some important event — my dad's birthday, for instance. Or telling the truth.

I can't put this off any longer. I grab a piece of paper from the fresh ream by my elbow. I grab a pen, and place an extra one nearby. And then I stop, terrified. I know I need to tell my story — our story — but I don't know how. Because the truth, see — it's a messy thing. Sometimes the only way to clean it up is to hurtle through each decision you made, trying to find the one that changed everything. Maybe then you can start to fix it.

"Tell it straight," Margaret commands from the back of my mind in that chain-smoking yogi voice of hers. "Leave nothing out."

"Easy for you to say," I want to tell her, but of course she's not here. None of them are. It's just me, here at the end, remembering how it all started and wondering if there was anything I could have done, even then, to save us.

CHAPTER ONE

BY THE TIME OUR BURGERS ARRIVED, I HAD HIS FOREHEAD memorized. I mean, down to the tiniest mole up near his hairline, catty-corner from the arch of his right eyebrow. When he's stubbed his toe, or when he feels as though the rest of the world is speaking an obscure tribal language that he can't possibly understand, he has a way of knitting his brows together so that his forehead resembles a children's science museum exhibit. Ancient Geologic Forms. The Landscape of Jupiter. Your Brain on Drugs. He was doing it now. He was talking too, though I can't say I was paying much attention.

"Look at me, please," he was saying (I think). "Would you please look at me when I talk."

I decided I'd finished with him. Without turning my neck, I shifted my eyes from his forehead and started in on hers. I wanted my study to be comprehensive.

"Ridiculous," he said. "A simple conversation."

"John," she said. "Let's not." And then from below what I can only describe as a perfectly taut canvas of pale skin, eyebrows

that never even jiggled with emotion, her voice chirped uncon-
vincingly, "Oh, look! Our burgers!"

The waitress laid our platters in front of us. I felt around on
my plate for my burger, touching my knife first. I wondered if this
was what it had been like for Helen Keller. Except that she
couldn't hear anything either. Lucky girl.

Because try as I might to shut out the sound, I could hear things.
The slam of glasses on the wooden counter behind me. Silverware
clattering against plates and teeth. A country singer crooning from
the jukebox about giving a penny for my thoughts, a nickel for my
heart. The waitress yelling over the crowd to a favorite customer:
"What'd ya catch me this time, Derek? An eighty-pounder?"

It was getting harder and harder to continue my study. I wouldn't
have minded seeing what an eighty-pounder looked like. What it
even was. I took a bite of my burger. The bun tasted like straw.

"Lida," my dad said. "Please."

I allowed my gaze to travel back over and down. His eyes were
round and a little moist, and I felt embarrassed for him. A grown
man should not cry in public, especially not in a roadside diner in
the middle of bear country. It's just unseemly. I blinked at him.

"How's your burger?" he asked hopefully.

I set it back in its red plastic basket and looked over at my stepmother. If she had been glaring at me before, she did a great job
of covering it with an indulgent smile.

"Flat," I said. "Boring. Kind of depressed."

"Your burger is depressed." She was almost glaring again. "Your
burger has feelings." She paused. "Really. Mine's just a burger."

There were virtually seismic shifts occurring on my dad's forehead. He put his hand on her arm and looked from her to me and
back again.

"I don't want to leave things this way," he said. He looked
straight at me. "Lida, you have the rest of the year to hate us on

your own time. Let it be for just this once." Then he turned and whispered something in my stepmother's ear, and she drew her shoulders back a little before whispering something in response. Meaning, she didn't agree with whatever he'd said. Meaning, he wasn't letting her off the hook either.

I looked around the restaurant. We were in Hindman, Idaho. Population: 148. Stoplights: 0. Diners named after the town: 1. Percentage of the town population that appeared to be in said diner on this nondescript June afternoon: 100. From what I could tell, percentage of the town who were men: about 99. Every table in the wood-paneled room was full. A chandelier made out of antlers hung over the bar, where big men crouched on stools like Ping-Pong balls on toothpicks. One guy in a camo jacket towered over the jukebox in the corner, rattling quarters around in his football-sized fist. Not the sort of place to start a fight, not without knowing who your friends are first.

"Did you hear what I said?" My dad tapped the table with one finger. "Lida, are you listening to me?"

"Absolutely," I said, turning back to the table and smiling at both of their foreheads. If my dad wanted to end things on a false note, that was fine with me. As long as it meant *she* had to play along too. "So," I said, picking up my burger again and giving it another go. "What do the two of you have planned for the next few months? Cooking classes? Couples' yoga?" Then I laughed, a short little trill that I had been practicing in the bathroom at home. Terri looked sharply at me and opened her mouth, but I soldiered on. This time I tried for sincerity. "No, I mean, really. Got any plans?"

My dad shifted in his seat. "I doubt there will be time for much besides the usual," he said. "The department is understaffed again this year, and I've agreed to pick up another class."

"Huh," I said. "Well, that's a surprise."

My dad is a professor of applied economics at Idaho State College, a Podunk institution in Bruno, a Podunk town in a Podunk state. He's always agreeing to pick up another class, and he always complains about it. Not that he'd know what to do with himself if he had any spare time. He'd probably just start worrying about me full-time, instead of the kind of part-time instructorship of worry that he's allotted for me so far. And nobody wants that to happen.

He looked back over at Terri, who gave him a little smile as if to say, *Well, why not?*

"We might find time to take a little vacation," he added, and shrugged apologetically. Now it was his turn to avoid eye contact. "Terri has — *we have* — always wanted to visit New York. Might be nice. Central Park in the autumn."

"Nice." *Don't care, don't care, don't care.* "You'll have to send me a postcard." I paused. "If I can even get mail up there."

"Lida, don't be dramatic," said Terri. "I'm sure you can receive mail. I'm sure you'll have everything you need at the school. It's not like it's the military or anything." She laughed weakly.

My dad leaned forward. "Well," he said hesitantly, "of course you can get letters from home. I think you can even write and send your own, once the subject matter has been approved. But there's no phone use, and no Internet. It's supposed to be rugged," he added, catching a glimpse of my face. "I thought we talked about this, Bun."

We had. We'd talked about it all spring. We'd talked about it when I stayed home from school. We'd talked about it on the weekends, when I was grounded and sitting with my back against my bedroom door, listening to the drone of his voice on the other side. We'd talked about it in my dad's last-ditch effort at family counseling, which was as useless as ever. And we'd talked about it after I'd gotten back from the hospital. We'd talked about it a lot then. Problem was, only my dad talked. I listened. And we all know how brilliant my listening skills were.

It wasn't going to be pleasant. This much I knew. I had spent the previous weekend packing according to a glossy list that the Alice Marshall School had sent in one of their brochures, the pamphlet entitled *Nuts and Bolts and Other Necessities*. The first page had a little disclaimer, stating that nuts and bolts were not actually allowed at the school. It was a figure of speech, the pamphlet said, and then it went on to list other items that were also prohibited. The usual suspects: guns, ammo, knives, cigarettes, drugs, fireworks, bows and arrows. (That one made me pause.) And then more things that I couldn't bring with me: candy, short skirts, stilettos (as if I owned any), combat boots, graphic T-shirts, tools and hardware (which explained the nuts and bolts comment, I guess), a computer and cell phone, and — this one was the worst — my iPod.

It was completely demoralizing, and I said so, yelling down the hall and into the kitchen, where I knew my dad and Terri were drinking their coffee. Terri yelled back that it wouldn't be the biggest loss, seeing as how I'd had my iPod taken away the previous week anyway. I slammed my door. Then I opened it and slammed it shut again, just for good measure.

There were two more lists, one much longer than the other, on the next page of the pamphlet. The first list (the longer one) included all of the things that I absolutely had to bring with me. *We Ask That You Bring Only the Exact Amounts Listed*, the pamphlet said. *Storage Space Is Limited, and We Frown Upon Excess*. "We frown upon excess"? I felt like I was on my way either to boot camp or high tea with the Queen Mum. Regardless, it was pretty stringent for a place that cost at least half of my dad's salary.

So it was up to me to choose which five T-shirts, which three sweaters, which two pairs of shorts, and which three pairs of jeans (*Of a Boot-cut or Straight-leg Style, Not Tight or "Skinny"*) I would bring. I'm not exactly a clothes hound, being more partial to hooded sweatshirts than glittery halter tops, but even I found the list to be restrictive. Into the bag went my four favorite gray T-shirts and a black one, three of my hoodies, and both pairs of jeans (I didn't have a third). I ignored the suggestion about shorts. To this sad collection I added seven pairs of underwear, six pairs of socks (I assumed that on the seventh day we would all go barefoot), my plastic rain poncho, a knit cap of my dad's that I quietly pilfered from the hall closet, a fleece jacket, tennis shoes, flip-flops, and the new hiking boots that Terri had bought for me the week before. I tossed in a swimsuit, the tags still attached, even though I knew there wasn't a chance in hell I'd be putting it on. It all barely filled my backpack. Bug repellant, a flashlight, my head-lamp (also new), and sunscreen finished the list.

I looked at my backpack. It was one of those hiking packs designed for long treks in the Andes or along the Appalachian Trail. My dad had said something about doing some hiking up at the school, and this pack was one of the necessities on the list. I picked it up with one hand. It was heavy. If they thought I'd be carting this monster around on my back, they were in for some serious disappointment.

I decided to bring as few items as I could from the second, shorter list. *Recommended Items*, it said. *For Personal Enjoyment and Downtime.* The pamphlet suggested books, journals, letter-writing materials, and playing cards. Enough diversions for a retirement home. I threw in the purple journal that Terri had left on my pillow that morning. (I knew it was from her because my father, at least, would never choose a book with a unicorn prancing across the cover.) No need to throw in paper for letters, I thought. There was no one to write to. I looked at the list again. Aside from

Solitaire, there weren't many card games I could play alone. And I definitely didn't intend on sitting around with some other lame, damaged girl, playing Speed or War or some shit.

I walked over to my bedside table and opened the drawer, pulling out the mess of loose paper and pens that I kept stuffed in there. At the bottom, underneath a copy of *How My Body Works* (guaranteed to prevent anyone from looking further), I found my pack of cigarettes and my X-ACTO knife. I wedged them both into one of the hiking boots, with a sock stuffed in for good measure. I quickly unpacked the clothes and put the boots in the very bottom of the bag before piling everything else on top again. I finished by cramming my sleeping bag in, and then I stepped back and looked at the pack. I was already looking forward to Downtime.

Now I wanted a cigarette. Desperately. I was surrounded by the clatter of the restaurant and the exuberant sounds of other people enjoying themselves, and I just wanted a smoke. It would look conspicuous, I thought, if I excused myself, walked out to the car, rummaged around in my pack before walking around the side of the building, and came back five minutes later with a breath mint in my mouth. My dad and Terri may be gullible and naïve, but they're not dead.

I sat on my hands and took a deep breath. One. Two. Three.

"Anyway," my dad was saying, "we'll definitely see you on Parents' Weekend, and that's not too far-off."

"September," I pointed out, "is in three months."

My dad smiled as though he'd caught me missing him before he was gone. "That's not so long, Lida."

Not long enough, I thought.

Terri looked toward the door. "Where is this woman?" she asked. "Do we even know what she looks like, this . . ." She rummaged in the pocket of her jeans, pulling out a slip of paper and reading the name. "This Margaret Olsen. How will we know her? How will she know us?"

"The sullen teenager you're sitting with might be a clue," I said. I was feeling very helpful.

"Lida," my dad said. "Please try. Just try up there, okay? Will you do that for me?"

I hated this. *This* is what happened near the end of every "conversation" I had with my dad. *This* was his ability to quietly — almost kindly, even — make me feel like an imbecile. Someone who can't get her shit together to save her life. Someone to be pitied, talked about in hushed tones, tiptoed around in case she gets pissed and does something drastic, like calmly pick up her water glass and drop it on the floor.

It shattered all over the rough wooden floorboards into shards the size of my palm, shards the size of my pinkie. A neat little river began edging its way toward my shoe.

"Jesus!" Terri was already out of her chair with a napkin, bending to mop up the water. She knelt next to me and dabbed at it fruitlessly. Her napkin was soaked. My dad just sat there, staring into his burger with a defeated smile on his face, like he'd just watched the tragic end of a movie that he'd seen twelve times before and was disturbed, but no longer shocked, when the heroine jumped off the cliff. The waitress was there too, with a broom and a long-handled dustbin, and she swept up the glass without looking at any of us.

"I'm sorry," Terri kept saying to the floorboards. "I'm so sorry." She was still just kneeling there, and she wasn't looking at anyone either, the soggy napkin lying like an embarrassing fact next to her.

"Nothing to apologize for," said a new woman's voice. "Water over rocks. Things break and come together. Nothing can be counted on, as Lida has so effectively shown us."

I nearly jumped when the husky voice said my name, and I looked up to find a tiny woman with a diamond stud in her nose, blond hair cut in a short pixie, and wearing a tank top and striped overalls that reminded me of a railroad conductor's uniform. She was shaking my dad's hand and saying "Margaret Olsen, nice to meet you," even before I connected the voice with the woman. She looked like a sparrow but had the voice of a chain-smoker.

My dad, to his credit, took it all in stride. He glanced at the nose stud, but generally maintained eye contact as he stood and introduced himself.

"And this, obviously, is Lida," he said, rocking forward on his toes once or twice. I couldn't tell if he was nervous or oddly proud. Maybe he was glad that I was "acting out," in case this Margaret Olsen had any doubts about my placement in the school. After all, the Alice Marshall School didn't take your run-of-the-mill good kids, girls with high GPAs and carloads of well-rounded friends. A broken glass was probably part of the entrance exam, and I had clearly passed.

"Lida," Margaret said, sticking out a delicate hand and grasping my own in a viselike grip. "Lida Lida Lida." She shook my hand in time with the words. "A name for a flower," she said, "or an exotic plant with medicinal properties." She narrowed her eyes at me then, just a little, and I wondered if this shaman act of hers was just a charade. "What kind of properties will you have, Lida?" she asked.

I looked toward the door. I stared at the moose head just above it. I examined that moose head like it was a stained glass window. I did not reply.

My dad chuckled anxiously. "Never knew her to be shy," he said.

Terri was standing by now too, assiduously brushing at the

knees of her pants. "I'm Terri," she said, holding out her hand to Margaret. "Lida's stepmother."

Margaret nodded. "I see." She angled her body so that she was standing slightly between me and my dad and Terri, and said in a low voice, "I'm not sure that we received all of Lida's personal information in her application packet. I don't mean to pry, but her mother is . . . ?"

"She's dead," I said.

Margaret turned toward me, so she didn't see the expression on my father's face. He opened his mouth and closed it again.

"I'm sorry," Margaret said.

"Don't be."

There was a long, awkward pause. My dad tried to catch my eye, but I looked away.

Finally, Terri broke the silence. "Well," she said, "as you can see, Margaret, we are quite done with lunch." She smiled at Margaret knowingly. I wouldn't have been surprised if she had winked.

"Ah," said Margaret. "Well. That's good timing. I have Bea waiting outside."

"Oh," said my dad, opening his wallet and throwing a few bills on the table. "You should have said something. We don't want to keep her waiting."

"No, we don't," said Margaret. "She's a temperamental old thing."

We trooped outside to the dirt parking lot in front of the diner. Across the street, I could see that the town's only store, a pawn-shop, was open for business. Other than that, the street was quiet. Mountains rose up on three sides of us. If this was going to be my nearest post of civilization for the next year, things were looking grim. It had taken us a good six hours to drive to Hindman from our house in southeastern Idaho, and as far as I could tell, the school was still miles away. This was not the kind of place you'd ever hitchhike out of.

We stopped in front of an old station wagon, rusted and black with a thick yellow stripe running around it. "What say you, Bee?" asked Margaret, and I got it, and smiled, and then erased the smile with a shrug.

"Ah," said my dad. "So this is the official school vehicle." He didn't look especially pleased. "I would have expected a van or bus."

"Oh, we have those, sure," said Margaret. "But I had some errands in town." She waved vaguely in the direction of the deserted street and patted the car. "Anyway, I thought I'd drive Lida to school in style. Less room to get lost in."

"Well. I see," said my dad, even though it was clear that he didn't.

"This should be everything," said Terri. In the approximately five seconds that we had been standing next to Bee, she had managed to bound over to our car and bring my bag back with her. "I'll just put it in the back, then?"

"I'll miss you too," I said sarcastically.

Terri gave me a look like I had just slapped her. She set the bag down heavily on the dirt and ran a hand through her hair. "It's a long drive, Lida," she said. "I didn't want to keep Margaret waiting."

"Sure," I said. "Whatever."

Margaret slammed shut the back door of the station wagon and dusted her hands on her overalls. My bag sat in the backseat like an overweight child. "Farewells take many forms. Luckily, we have lots of chances to practice in this life." She smiled at my dad and Terri, and rested one hand lightly on my shoulder. "Lida, it's time to go."

My dad walked over and engulfed me in a bear hug. I kept my shoulders stiff, but I didn't push him away.

"Be good, Bun," he said. "We'll be talking soon." He stepped back and looked up at the sky, blinking.

"Lida," said Terri, moving toward me. "I'll —" She stopped when she saw my outstretched hand. She shook it. Neither of us looked at the other.

Margaret opened the passenger door for me. "It might be hard to believe," she said, "but in the grand scheme of parent-child farewells, you are all behaving with impeccable decorum." She shook my father's and Terri's hands. "Lida will be safe and healthy at Alice Marshall," she assured them. "She may even be happy. That piece is up to her." She turned and smiled at me. "Ready?"

I nodded. I looked once more toward the dusty diner in the dusty town, the street that seemed to go nowhere at all, the pawnshop where people traded in their old hopes for chances at new ones. I took it all in, and then I looked at my father and Terri.

"Good-bye," I said to their foreheads. And then, in one fluid motion, I slid into the car and slammed the door shut.

CHAPTER TWO

HINDMAN BUTTS UP AGAINST THE SOUTHEAST END OF THE Frank Church River of No Return Wilderness Area, a two-million-acre maze of mountains, lakes, rivers, and impassable canyons, with the occasional forest ranger thrown in to make the place seem manageable, which of course it's not. The Frank, as some call it, or River of No Return, as others do, is at once as mystical and unpredictable as its name implies. Winding through it all is the Salmon River, with its various forks, tributaries, Class Five rapids, and a penchant for sucking in the occasional rafter and sometimes, but only sometimes, spitting him back. You may be going to the Church, but you may never come out.

This is what Margaret told me as we wound our way north-west into the mountains, Bee jolting mercilessly around potholes and rocks on the dirt road that seemed to get narrower the farther we drove. Her voice had lost all traces of new-age bullshit the moment we turned from Hindman's main street onto the wilderness access road. Now, she seemed to be speaking with a tour train conductor's excited chatter. I couldn't tell whether I should write her off as a fraud or applaud her for being such a skilled chameleon.

"Over five hundred and twenty-eight different species of wild-flowers, two hundred fifty types of wildlife, and more black bears per square mile than the San Diego Zoo," she said in her low voice, glancing over at me. "Harmless, of course," she added, "unless you piss them off. That's one of our rules up at Alice Marshall: Don't Piss Off the Bears." She laughed. "Problem is, with bears as with people, you don't always know what's going to get under their skin."

"I'll keep that in mind," I said, looking out the window.

"Here's my policy." Margaret continued as though she hadn't heard me. "Treat Them Like Trees. Only crazy people hug trees."

"So you're not just a crunchy granola," I said without thinking. My face turned red. I wondered if it was possible to get kicked out of school before you even got there.

Margaret glanced at me out of the corner of her eye. "I've found," she said slowly, "that parents need to hear one thing, and students need to hear another. Some books have many covers, Lida. But don't get me wrong," she added, swerving suddenly to avoid a chipmunk. "I've got more than enough hippy-dippy mantras and affirmations to go around. And they work." She grinned at the windshield, as if she'd just told a private joke.

"Great," I said.

We drove in silence for a while, Margaret murmuring to Bee and patting the dashboard every time we lurched over a bad pothole, me staring out the window at the increasingly dense vegetation, trees so tall and rangy that they almost blocked out the sun. I was trying not to think, and was finding it a strangely easy thing to do. Maybe the trend would continue. A year of not thinking. I could handle that.

Bee bounced past a small parking area by a trailhead with an outhouse next to it. No cars. There was a large mud-brown sign posted just past it on the road — courtesy, obviously, of the National Forest Service. DESIGNATED WILDERNESS AREA, it read. NO MOTORIZED VEHICLES BEYOND THIS POINT. The road beyond the sign had devolved until it was little more than two ruts, overgrown with grass and a fine coating of pine needles. I looked at Margaret, who kept driving.

"Um," I said. It occurred to me that she might actually consider the car to be a trusty old companion, like a dog or a horse. An extension of her legs. Certainly not something as *inhuman* as a motorized vehicle. I cleared my throat. "Um," I said again. "Shouldn't we park or something?"

"Oh, right," Margaret said. She was still driving. She smiled over at me. "That sign is for everyone else. This road here is just for us. It's our own highway to heaven."

She maneuvered expertly around a root the size of a giant's thumb that had sprung up in the middle of the road. Highway to heaven, my ass.

Margaret kept talking. "You're not going to have to worry about strangers up here, Lida. There's a fire lookout a mile up from the school, but that's about it. No one can live on this land but us."

It didn't seem like such a treat, this isolation. I may not have paid any attention to our neighbors in Bruno, but at least I knew that someone would hear me if I screamed, and that was a kind of comfort. "Pretty swanky," I said.

"You don't know the half of it," Margaret said, ignoring the sarcastic tone in my voice. "Give yourself a week. You'll see how blessed we are to be up here."

"If it's so fantastic, why haven't more people bought up the land?" I supposed I could see how the dark trees and the stillness outside the window might hold some sort of allure. I could imagine a golf course, full-service spa, maybe a meditation center.

"Because they can't," said Margaret. "Alice Marshall's father built the original school buildings in the late thirties, as a base camp for his fishing buddies. Legend has it that he was planning on turning it into a luxury fishing lodge, like they have up in Alaska. Died of a heart attack at age fifty-four, and Alice inherited it all. It's been a school since the mid-sixties. When Congress made this an official Wilderness Area in 1980, the buildings were grandfathered in."

"What does that mean?" I imagined a grizzled old man leading a small line of buildings, tiny as LEGOs, through the woods.

"Means that the school could stay open even after Alice's death, stay where it is, because it was built before the River of No Return became essentially sacred. We're the only ones who can drive in and out of here — even supply trucks have to meet us in that parking lot that we passed a while back. It means," she said, looking at me as we rocketed through another crater-sized pothole, "that the school is invaluable. Priceless."

Or worthless, I thought. Depending on how you looked at it, of course. "How long has it been a school for delinquents?" I asked.

"It's never been a school for *delinquents*." Margaret shook her head. "There are other schools out there that are much better equipped for extreme misbehavior." She caught sight of my raised eyebrows and said, "In the world of wilderness therapy schools, we're the equivalent of a misdemeanor. There are other schools that are more like felonies."

I didn't quite get the difference, but I didn't say anything. Was that all I was? A B-grade miscreant?

"Oh, you'll see what I mean, eventually." She paused. "In answer to your question, though, Alice Marshall was originally a boarding school for boys. In the early nineties, right before she died, Alice deeded it to her niece with the provision that it should be a safe haven for girls who find traditional schooling to be . . ." She paused, searching for the right word. "Challenging."

"She must have hated high school too," I said, and then catching myself, added, "or something."

Margaret nodded. "I expect she did."

The road became even narrower, so that it looked like a glorified hiking trail. Tree branches scraped against Bee's sides as we drove on, more slowly now. We were winding up, up, up through the forest, and every once in a while Margaret had to shift into a lower gear so that we lurched backward for one sickening moment and then finally forward again. Both of Margaret's hands were tight around the wheel. I thought it best not to talk.

We passed through an open cattle gate with two signs attached to its metal frame. One read NO TRESPASSING. The other read AMS. Of the two, the NO TRESPASSING sign was significantly larger. Its rusted red lettering and bullet-punctured, hanging-by-a-nail quality certainly had me convinced. A four-inch pine tree shot through the middle of the Alice Marshall sign, with the school initials kind of surrounding the tree in a Gothic font.

"Well," said Margaret. "Here we are. Home sweet rustic home."

About two hundred yards past the gate, the road ended abruptly in what was clearly a makeshift parking lot. Four vans were parked there, the same school crest as the sign on the gate painted onto their sides. There was just enough room for Bee. The trees surrounding the parking lot were huge and dense, and though I thought I could make out the shape of a building through the pines, I wasn't sure. Everything suddenly seemed very dark. Bee suddenly seemed very warm and cozy.

"It's not much to look at from inside the car," said Margaret, catching the expression on my face. "But if you stand outside for a minute, I guarantee you'll feel your soul expanding."

I wasn't convinced, but I got out. Not that I had a choice.

It was quiet. It was quiet and still, and it smelled like wood smoke, cider, and leather, and I won't say that my soul expanded, but it definitely didn't contract.

"There," said Margaret, pulling my bag out of the car. "See?"

I shrugged. I was very good at shrugging. If shrugging had been an Olympic sport, I would have at least made the team.

Margaret laughed, a throaty smoker's chuckle. "Let's go meet Bev." She handed me my pack and helped me wrestle it onto my shoulders. We headed down a pine-needle path toward two buildings that became slightly clearer the closer we got. One of them, set back among the trees, was a large rectangular structure. It had all the charm and personality of a prison. I pointed to it.

"Is that where we all sleep?"

"Goodness no. That behemoth is only used during Parents' Weekend." Margaret looked at me sympathetically. "Don't worry. The student cabins look nothing like this." She pointed through the trees to a small group of cabins that I could just barely make out beyond the dorm. "Those are the staff quarters," she said, adding, "and they're off-limits."

The smaller of the two buildings in front of us was a cabin, with a little log porch jutting out from the door. There was a windsock hanging off the side of the cabin that read WELCOME! in an embarrassing shock of pastels, but it wasn't a windy day, and the sock had sagged and folded over itself so that it said WEME!

"This is the director's cabin," Margaret said, before knocking on the door.

"Why are you knocking, then?" I asked.

Margaret looked at me strangely. "Did you think I was the school director?"

I gave another one of my award-winning shrugs.

"You really didn't read the pamphlet, did you?" she asked, just as the door opened and I stared into the much older, much stonier, much more intimidating face of the real school director. Her short brown hair was perfectly curled around her head in a tight helmet. Her pants were pressed and pleated into sharp arrows.

Even her shoes (brown loafers with buckles the size of collection plates) looked ready for battle.

"Beverly Cantrell," she said. "You can call me Bev." When I didn't respond, she shook her head. "And you are Lida. That much, at least, is clear." Her voice was crisp, and she enunciated every word precisely, as though in a spelling bee. She turned to Margaret. "I trust that the drive up was uneventful?"

"Everything was just fine," said Margaret softly. I was pleased to see that she was almost as cowed by this woman as I was.

"I'm glad to hear it." Her manner was so perfunctory that I imagined her clapping her hands twice, quickly, like an old-fashioned schoolmarm or maybe a drill sergeant. She gave Margaret a tight smile and turned back to me. "Lida, I'm not sure what Margaret has told you about the Alice Marshall School. Much of it you will have to learn on your own, but there are some aspects of living and learning here that I'd like to discuss before you get settled in."

Bev opened the door a little wider, motioning me and Margaret in. She followed us into a tidy living room that must have come straight out of an Eddie Bauer Home catalog — one where the models, all chiseled and perfect, frolic in the snow in their two-hundred-dollar coats before settling into the big room of their cabin for a night of board games and smoked salmon. The long leather couch was the color of caramel. It faced a coffee table that I could see was meant to appear just hewn by a local carpenter, even though the fancy carvings on its legs gave away its high-end furniture boutique pedigree. There were two large sitting chairs made out of a similar leather, with a pair of antlers emblazoned on the back cushion of each, like a rancher's brand. Watercolors depicting various stock western scenes were hanging on the walls. Probably by a famous artist, I thought, who was famous only because the people who made him so weren't from the West. In any case, this room was the perfect place to entertain the nervous parents of the school's inmates.

"By now you've read the informational materials," Bev said matter-of-factly, pulling me from my reverie.

I nodded. I could feel Margaret's eyes hot on my back.

"You can set your backpack here." Bev motioned toward the floor next to a chair before sitting in it herself. "Please make yourself comfortable on the couch."

I placed the bag down next to her and sat next to Margaret. I could already feel the tension in my shoulders as I tried to maintain a straight posture. I wondered if Bev had that effect on everyone.

"The first thing you must know, Lida, is that we are very pleased to have you join our community."

As Bev started talking, she casually unclasped the buckles on my backpack and opened the top compartment.

"Being a member of the Alice Marshall School is both an honor and a responsibility."

She pulled out my sleeping bag first. Then she grabbed my T-shirts, my sweaters, and my jeans, and set them in a careful pile next to the backpack.

"It is up to you to earn that honor, and it is up to us to encourage that sense of responsibility."

She pulled out the unicorn notebook. I blushed and played with the seam on one of the couch cushions.

"What's most important to us, however, is your safety. Only after that has been established can we focus on the areas of your personal growth."

She took out the underwear, the socks, the rain poncho, the flashlight. She took out first one hiking boot, and then the other. She took out the sock that I had stuffed in the second boot, and pulled out the cigarettes, and then the knife. These she placed in her lap.

A long, silent minute passed.

"We understand that you may have come here with old ways of being, old patterns of behavior, old habits."

Bev lightly tapped the cigarette pack with her index finger without looking down at it.

"But some behaviors are not appropriate for this environment, and will not be tolerated."

She picked up the cigarettes and, with an almost imperceptible flick of her wrist, pitched them cleanly across the room, where they landed softly in a trash basket.

"Other behaviors, those that might endanger yourself or others, are cause for immediate expulsion, if not also police involvement."

She held the knife in front of her face and stared at me until I met her gaze. It was unflinching. I nodded.

Bev placed the knife next to her on the chair and repacked my bag. Then she stood up and held out her hand. "Welcome to Alice Marshall," she said.

Margaret and I stood up. I cleared my throat. I was afraid my voice would crack, but I managed to shake her hand rather firmly. "Thanks," I whispered.

"Congratulations," Margaret said as we walked away from the director's cabin, my bag a bit lighter on my back. "You have successfully used up your Get Out of Jail Free card during the first bag check." She stopped suddenly on the trail and turned to me. "Listen, Lida. That really was your only pass. If we ever find anything even remotely like a knife in your belongings again, you'll be sent home before the excuse is even halfway out of your mouth."

"Okay."

"More than okay." Margaret was glaring at me, and I didn't like it.

"Fine," I said. "It was my only one, anyway."

"Good." She smiled. "Clean slate, Lida. Everyone deserves one at least once in their lives."

"Are there lots of bag checks?" I asked.

"Weekly," she said, "and unscheduled ones as well."

"Do you find things?" I'd felt pretty brave packing the knife. Apparently, I wasn't the only one.

"You wouldn't believe what we find." Margaret stopped walking and turned to me. "While Alice Marshall certainly isn't a school for delinquents — we're no prison, you know — the girls who live here have usually acted out in some way or another. Parents choose Alice Marshall because they know their daughter will be free from the dangers she faced at home — and those include the ways one can be a danger to oneself." She raised her eyebrows at me. "Everyone brings their own baggage," she said. "It's our job to help them unpack it."

"Okay," I said. "Whatever."

The path that led away from the director's cabin eventually opened onto a clearing where a number of larger structures stood clustered on a carpet of pine needles. Through the trees beyond, I could make out the inky blue line of a lake. Margaret led me past a group of buildings that looked exactly alike: dark wood siding, wraparound porches, a kind of Swiss ski chalet feel. She named each one as she passed, but I wasn't paying attention. I doubted I'd ever find my way around this place without some sort of guide dog or Sherpa.

". . . Math and Science Building," she was saying. "And over there's the Rec Lodge. That's where you'll find me most of the time."

"Why?"

"I'm the Outdoor Ed instructor," she said. "I'll be taking you on all of your backwoods voyages."

"Sounds great," I said. "Is there some way to test out of that?"

Margaret laughed drily. "Funny," she said. "No, there's not. Our most popular program at Alice Marshall involves a solo camping trip. The parents love it, and many of the girls look forward to it," she added, looking at my expression. "It's a chance to really test your knowledge of the woods . . . and of yourself."

"Jesus," I muttered quietly.

"It was all in the pamphlet," she said, her mouth curling up at one corner.

We passed the Bathhouse and the dining lodge ("also known as the Mess Hall," Margaret said), and then we turned left and walked through more pine trees (though never in a straight line, I noticed — this place must have been designed by a drunk) until we came to a cluster of nine or ten smaller cabins. There were noises coming from inside these cabins: giggles, whispers, coughing, talking, jarring exclamations. Whenever we passed a particularly noisy cabin, Margaret would rap once on the door and everything would go silent. The ground sloped down from the path for about sixty feet until it met a thin strip of sand and grass, and then the water. There was a fire circle next to the water, halfway between the Mess Hall and the first small cabin, and rough wood benches were placed neatly around it. From where we stood, I could see more mountains rearing up across the water to the north, all stone and granite and jagged corners.

Margaret stopped in front of one of the cabins, about three-fourths of the way down the line. "Good timing. It's Toes-Up."

"Toes-Up?"

"Heads down, toes up," said Margaret. "A period of rest and relaxation. You'll be able to meet your cabinmates all at once."

Lucky me, I thought. *Lucky, lucky, lucky me.*

Here's what the cabin looked like on the outside: rickety. Kind of weathered. Built from knotty pine logs that came together at the corners like the Lincoln Logs I used to play with. It didn't look big enough to fit any more than one or two people. It certainly didn't look like any place I would have ever chosen to live.

"Lida?"

"Right."

Margaret sighed. "Gets pretty cold here at night. You'll at least want your sleeping bag unrolled." She opened the door.

A word here about my hair. No, three words: stringy pulled pork. That's what it looked like to me, at least. Something you might find inside a rather unappealing sandwich that you bought at a greasy BBQ joint next to a rest stop along the highway. My hair was the end result of concentrated not-washing and a dedication to the art of fingercombing. It wasn't a masterpiece, not yet, but it had potential. What I'm trying to say is, it was my choice. I wanted it that way. Stringy pulled pork.

That's why, when Margaret pushed open the cabin door, my hand was stuck in my hair. I'd been twirling the strands with my right index finger (a nervous habit since sixth grade), and I guess I became overzealous, because I kind of twisted a knot around my finger and couldn't pull it out. So when that door opened and the faces of my new cabinmates turned toward me — not eagerly, exactly, but almost as if they had all recognized a disconcerting smell at the same time — I was jerking my hand around in my hair.

I'm not certain — I didn't have a stopwatch or anything — but I'm pretty sure nobody said a word for six or seven years.

"Oh," said Margaret, finally catching on to my predicament. "Here, let me."

As she reached over and started lifting strands of hair away from my hand, a low voice came from the back of the cabin like a slow-motion slap.

"Another genius joins the ranks."

There was laughter then, but I couldn't say if it was one person's laughter or four. My eyes were trained on the tops of my black Chuck Taylors, which were kind of shuffling back and forth of their own accord.

Margaret ignored the comment. Having freed me from my hair in less time than it took me to get stuck in the first place, and also having managed to usher both me and my bag inside, shutting the door behind us, she straightened and addressed the cabin.

"Folks, this is Lida Wallace. Please welcome her *kindly*."

I looked up.

Here is what the cabin looked like from the inside: pretty much as inspiring as it had from the outside. There was a set of bunk beds along each of the two sides and one along the back wall, with dressers at the foot of each one. From where I stood, I could see no chairs, no desks, and no pictures on the walls. Well, that's not exactly true. A calendar hung off the foot of the bunk bed on the right side of the room. The picture for the month of June, all neon blue and orange, was the outline of a man with a tail, playing some sort of flute. The days of the month that had already passed had been marked off with big, black Xs. I noticed that today's date already had one diagonal line drawn through it.

What else? Dirt. A shoe here and there. The room was pretty much empty, aside from a small pile of clothes in the middle of the floor.

And on four of the six beds, there were girls. I tried not to look too closely at their faces, but a swift scan revealed that yes, there were four of them and no, they were not smiling. At least not the ones I could see clearly. The light was angling in through the window in such a way that one of them was hidden in shadow on her bunk.

Margaret went on as though oblivious to the fact that the temperature had dropped about fifty degrees since we entered the cabin. "We've lost a couple of girls in the past few weeks," she said.

I wondered what she meant by *lost*.

"Andrea and Desiree had both been here for a year. They left within a week of each other." She smiled, as though to say *See? Not a prison!* I wasn't convinced. "Anyway," she went on, "this is one of the less-populated cabins right now, so you all have some extra space. Your bunk, Lida, is here." She walked over to the top bunk along the back wall, directly across from the door. Margaret patted the bare, plastic mattress.

Good, I thought. *I'll be the first thing anyone sees when they walk in. Maybe that'll keep the number of visitors to a minimum.*

"You'll share the dresser with Karen. Right, Karen?"

The girl lying on her back on the bottom bunk waved one of her feet in a lazy circle in response. I couldn't get a good look at her — she had draped one dark arm over her eyes — but her foot looked nice enough. Some sort of trail-running shoe. Small. Neatly laced.

Margaret began to walk back over to me, but stopped next to the pile of clothes in the middle of the floor. "Whose are these?" she asked. She bent down and fingered a T-shirt. "Gwen, are these yours?"

A small girl on a top bunk with black hair and perfectly razored bangs shook her head, just as the low voice, the one that had called me a genius, spoke up again.

"I wouldn't get too close, Margs. We're just starting our laundry pile, and Jules walked through some poison ivy yesterday."

It came from the bottom bunk on the right. I strained my eyes to see the girl behind the voice, which despite sounding bored and nonchalant nevertheless sent a chill across my shoulder blades. I could see now that she had her back turned to the rest of the cabin and was talking to the wall. I wondered how she had managed to braid her hair in such a long, even, black rope so that it stretched perfectly all the way down her back. More than that, though, I wondered how she knew what Margaret was doing without looking at her.

"Ah," said Margaret, rocking back on her heels and releasing the T-shirt. "I see."

"Thought I'd warn you."

Margaret straightened. She came over and stood next to me, placing one hand on my shoulder. "Well, Lida," she said, "I think you're in good company here. These girls —" She paused and looked at each girl on each bed for a long moment, staring longest at the girl with her back to us. She cleared her throat and started again. "These girls are strong, able, thoughtful, smart, and, though they might not want you to know it yet, kind. They're the best that Alice Marshall has. I'm sure they'll treat you how they would like to have been treated when they first got here." She kept staring at the girl's back. "I'm sure of it." Margaret took her hand from my shoulder and walked out the door.

There was a long moment of silence. No one moved; no one spoke. I shuffled my feet a little more and then shrugged. "Well, maybe I'll just . . ."

The door opened again quite suddenly, before I had even managed to pick up my bag. Margaret stuck her head in. "Two things I forgot to mention," she said to the room at large. "One. Lida, shower times are between six and seven in the morning, and between seven and eight at night. Bev expects you to shower at least three times a week, and she'll check up on you. Two. Whatever is under that pile of clothes had better be spilled, buried, scattered, or otherwise disposed of before Bev does her night rounds. That's all." She shut the door.

This time there was noise. A couple of groans, a long exhalation as though someone had been holding their breath, and a minor explosion of swearing.

"Shit," said the girl with the bangs — *Gwen?* — as she leaped down from her bunk. "Shitshitshitshitshit."

"At least she didn't confiscate it this time," said another girl. She was blond and a little chubby, with a sunburn on her forehead and nose. "At least she didn't report us."

"Not yet," said Gwen. She pushed the clothes out of the way to reveal a half-empty bottle of whiskey. From where I stood, still rooted to my spot by the door, I could see that it wasn't the cheap kind either.

Gwen shook her head sadly. "What a waste." She glanced over at the prone figure with her back to us. "Maybe if you hadn't said anything, Boone . . ." Her voice trailed off.

Boone? I thought. What kind of a name was that?

The figure stirred. Slowly, the girl turned over on her back and swung her legs over the side of the bunk. They were long legs, I could tell that much, and they were connected to an even longer girl. A girl with jet-black hair and cheekbones you could dive off of. Gray, steely eyes swept across the room, passing me by as though I was just another piece of furniture. She stood up and walked over to Gwen and the bottle of whiskey. I didn't even hear her feet hit the floorboards.

"What did you say?" Her voice had the same quality as thunder, like when you hear it rumbling in the distance and know you're in for it now, buster, that storm's gonna get you.

"I mean," said Gwen, faltering, "it's just that, you know, Margaret might have left it alone if we hadn't said anything." She looked sideways while she talked. It was clear that eye contact was out of the question.

"Right," said Boone. Her voice leaked contempt. "Sure. Then again, she might have just lifted up that T-shirt and found the bottle, and then she would have been obligated to turn it, and *us*, in."

Then she looked at me. She looked me up and down. Took in my sneakers, baggy cords, blue T-shirt, stringy hair. I felt like an old coat that had been hanging for some time in her closet. One that she was thinking about throwing away.

"You look terrible."

That was the first thing she said to me.

The second was, "How far did you crawl to get here?"

I shrugged. I had no idea what to say.

"What Boone means," said my bunkmate, Karen, who was now standing in a yoga pose on one leg with her arms above her head, "is that she'd like to know where you're from." Karen had dark mahogany skin and a head full of hair that cascaded past her shoulders in tight black ringlets. She fell forward so that her nose touched her knee.

"Bruno," I said. My voice came out high and scratchy, and I blushed.

Boone raised an eyebrow at me as Karen said, "Bruno, what? Is that a town in California?"

"No," said Boone. "It's here in Idaho. She's a local." She never took her eyes off me as she said it.

I guess I hadn't thought about it before, but with a price tag like Alice Marshall's, I should have known that a real, bona fide Idahoan would be about as rare as a yeti.

"Great!" said the girl with a sunburn, getting up from her lower bunk and stretching. "Maybe you two know the same people!"

Boone glared at her. "Doubtful, Jules. Idaho is hardly one big school cafeteria."

I hazarded a look at Boone's face. "Oh," I said, "are you from Bruno too?"

"No," she said, and her voice was falsely sweet, as if she was talking to a child. "I'm from no place you've ever heard of. At least, nowhere you'd want to go."

I opened my mouth to tell her I'd been to plenty of places, but was interrupted by the sound of a bell ringing monotonously. The girls from the top bunks swung down, and everyone shuffled toward the door. I didn't think anyone would miss me if I didn't show up to whatever torture chamber everyone was headed to now, so I was just turning back to my bunk when I felt a hand grasp my elbow and swing me around.

"Door's this way," said the sunburned girl (*Jules?*), a half smile on her face. "You might as well stick with us today. We're all you've got now." She pulled me outside.

The rest of the day went pretty much as you'd expect your first seven hours in a labyrinth to go. I couldn't find my way out of a shoe box. Every building was named for its function, which didn't help me since all the buildings looked the same from the outside. The only place I could reliably find was the Bathhouse, and I kept ending up there when we were supposed to be at the Mess Hall (a spacious room with round tables throughout for eating and an industrial-sized salad bar at one end), say, or the Rec Lodge. Usually it would be Jules who would come and find me, hissing, "Stay with the group! Follow me!"

And that wouldn't have been hard, if I'd known who was in my group. There were almost fifty girls at Alice Marshall, but we were grouped by age in our cabins as well as our classes. My cabin-mates and I were part of the largest group, studying with the other twelve sixteen-year-olds, but I had never been very good at discerning people's ages at a glance, and I kept wandering into class with the Fourteens, as they were called, or the Seventeens. Everything seemed veiled in dense fog. I felt every girl's eyes on me all day, and I knew that they were deciding that I was going to be the stock unattractive character in their own personal story of *My Time at Alice Marshall*. The dim one with dull hair and a poor sense of direction. What did I care? I didn't have any use for them either.

(Everyone else, it should be noted, was beautiful. Or at least, very nearly beautiful. Or at the very least edgy, with the potential for prettiness.)

Luckily, I only had the afternoon classes to get through. And dinner. (I sat with my cabin in the raucous Mess Hall, everyone talking about some guy named Bob, me holding the plastic silverware in my hand and staring at the swamp of mashed potatoes and gravy on my plate, deciding that I wasn't hungry for any of it.) And then the campfire, another drawn-out set of social customs that I didn't get yet and that involved not only singing but also acting, cheering, and holding hands in a circle as we stood around a five-foot-high inferno next to the lake.

Singing in unison has always embarrassed me. It's one of the reasons why I've never liked school recitals, the Pledge of Allegiance, or church. I was able to get a good look at the rest of the girls during the campfire, though, since no one could see me staring through the firelight. I have to say, watching them sing and clap, I had the distinct impression that I'd been sent to the wrong school. No one here looked capable of destruction, Boone aside. They looked more like they were trying for a merit badge at Girl Scout camp. I wondered when I'd see their other faces, the ones that would be more familiar to me.

By the time Lights-Out came around, I couldn't have been happier to see my new sleeping bag. While it had been fairly warm during the day, the cold had blasted in somewhere around dinner, and even my fingernails felt icy. Climbing up to my bunk was the sweetest thing I'd done all day.

Bev knocked on the door as she opened it. I supposed her job relied heavily on the element of surprise.

"Jesus!" cried Gwen, pulling her sleeping bag up to her neck. "I wasn't dressed yet!"

"Language, Miss Sutter," said Bev. She surveyed the room calmly. The pile of clothes (and the bottle) had been removed at some point during the day, though I couldn't say which of my cabinmates had found the time to do it. Now everything looked too clean, as bare and depressing as a homesteader's cabin.

Bev walked in a slow circle around the room, checking on each of us. I watched her eyes. She seemed to be looking everywhere at once. She stopped next to my bunk. "How are you fitting in, Lida?"

I attempted a smile, which crashed and burned. "Fine."

" 'Fine,' " she repeated. " 'Fine.' I can see that we'll have to work on your vocabulary." She turned toward the door and paused with her hand on the light switch. "Tomorrow is a new day," she said. "New challenges, new possibilities. How will *you* greet the day?" She turned off the light and closed the door behind her.

There was a snort and a giggle from one of the other bunks. Someone else whispered, "Shhh!" After that, it was silent for five or ten minutes, during which I fell into a state of almost-sleep and dreamed that my sleeping bag was being sewn up with me inside. Which is to say, I kept jerking awake and pulling the sleeping bag down around my shoulders.

Finally, when all of the sounds from outside had died down (cabin doors closing, Bev's clear voice saying "challenges, possibilities" over and over), someone, I'm not sure who, spoke up.

"The lady needs a new closing line."

"She needs to work on her material." Laughter.

" 'How will you beat the day?' "

"Or, 'Another day, another three hundred of your parents' bucks.' "

"How about, 'Have a nice sleep, and P.S., fuck all y'all.' " That voice, I thought, belonged to Boone.

There was more laughter, a joke or two that I couldn't quite hear, rustling and shifting as the other girls settled into their beds. I turned onto my side, clutching a fistful of sleeping bag and drawing it up to my face like a baby blanket.

"So, Lida." Boone's voice came at me from her lower bunk. "What's your Thing?"

Startled, I let go of the sleeping bag blankie and hugged my arms to my chest. No one could see me. "What do you mean?"

"Your Thing. Whatever you did that was bad enough to get you carted up here. What'd you do?"

"Everyone's got their Thing," Gwen piped in. "What's yours?"

The cabin was very quiet.

"I stole a car," I said finally.

"You stole a car," repeated Boone. "Whose car? How'd you wreck it?"

"I don't want to talk about it," I said. I was feeling rather brave inside my sleeping bag.

Boone laughed sharply. "Whatever," she said. "You'll learn to talk eventually."

Suddenly, the thought of talking, of explaining who I was and painting even the roughest picture of myself through one-liners and anecdotes, or — worse — through long, drawn-out conversations in which I bared myself, bared it all, for these girls who I would also have to learn in turn, like one learns a language or memorizes a song (laboriously, through repetition and mouthing "watermelon, watermelon, watermelon" when you don't know the words), just to get to a place where I felt like I knew the rules and could only *then* start playing . . . Suddenly, the whole thing exhausted me. I wanted to sleep for a month, preferably waking up to another life. I shut my eyes.

The last thing I heard before I fell into a deep, exhausted sleep was Boone's muted voice.

"Welcome to Alice Marshall, Townie."

When I woke up, they'd cut off my hair.

Epilogue

My dad and Terri don't know I'm writing this. Only Dr. Hemler knows, and I won't let him read it. I keep it locked in a vintage briefcase that I bought at Reruns Thrift and Save. I'm the only person who has the combination. Well, me and whoever donated the briefcase to the store with a small slip of paper tucked inside that said "1.8.3.3." (Underneath the numbers, the same person had scratched the words "Go to it." I love the shit you find at thrift stores.)

At least it's a healthier secret than the one I used to keep from my dad and Terri, though I don't know if they'd agree, if they read this. Sometimes I'm amazed when I think about how little they know of my time at Alice Marshall. They have the bare facts, and that's all they need. Parents are too easily frightened by the world their children live in. We have to protect them from harm, keep them safe as long as we can, no matter how we feel about them. It's our duty. I didn't know this going in, but I do now.

CHAPTER THREE

I TOLD BEV THAT I'D DONE IT. I TOLD HER THAT I NEEDED A change, and that I cut it with my nail scissors after everyone else had gone to sleep. I told her that I'd always wanted short hair, that this would be easier to manage, that I was sorry I hadn't cut it before I got to school.

She confiscated the nail scissors, which had been thoughtfully placed next to my backpack.

Of course, the truth was that it would have taken hours of meticulous snipping to chop off my hair with those tiny scissors. Whatever they'd used for the job had to have been more machete-like. What had been an easy-to-maintain, shoulder-length mess of pulled pork now resembled the waving, reaching tentacles of a sea anemone. Small tufts of hair sprouted from the top of my head, while the sides had been cut closer to the skull. They hadn't touched the back, probably because they couldn't get at it without waking me. So yes, that I *did* do. When I finally made it to the Bathhouse the next morning and saw what they'd accomplished, I took the nail scissors to the back of my head and cut straight across, hoping at the very least to save myself the humiliation of a PE teacher's mullet. The result was negligible.

What was amazing was that no one at the school seemed fazed by it. There were looks, to be sure, and even some poorly muffled laughter from a group of girls in the Mess Hall who looked like they'd walked out of an issue of *Teen Vogue*, but it felt as if I had crossed some threshold. Like, even though I still blended in as well as a pebble in pancake batter, they were willing to let me just sit there at the bottom of the bowl.

It was even more obvious inside the cabin. Almost since the minute I woke up in the chill morning air and reached up to scratch my head, the girls were nicer to me. Not *nice* nice, like they felt bad and took pity on me, but nice in the way that soldiers tolerate new recruits after they've gone through a hazing. I knew enough to understand that they'd done the worst they were going to do.

And I hated this. Sure, those first few moments staring at the bathroom mirror were horrible; I'm not going to lie. When I saw what they'd done, I rolled my fingers into fists and dug the nails into my palms, blinking back tears (though not fast enough). But when I returned to the cabin, they were all sitting there, kind of smiling, pleased with themselves but also a little embarrassed, like my dad had looked when he finally told me about puberty. No one mentioned my hair. But they didn't ignore me, and this was even worse than the hair.

"Breakfast time," Gwen might say, when we heard the morning bell ringing from across the school grounds. And then, as everyone scrambled to put on shoes and sweaters, Karen might turn to me: "You coming?" Jules was always nudging me and laughing at something or other, even though I never laughed with her. Only Boone didn't speak to me. She continued to act as though I was a fence post on the side of the road that she was passing at sixty miles an hour.

Frankly, I preferred her approach. It was embarrassing to see how the other girls just kept trying over the next few days, like watching the student body president dutifully show a transfer student around the high school. All that cheerful explaining — *Here's where your locker is! Here's the auditorium!* — while trying not to look at her watch. It had to be as terrible for them as it was for me. I knew that eventually they'd get it, and we could leave one another alone. And that would be a relief to us all.

Oh, I know: I wasn't the only girl to be new. Every girl at the school had, at one awkward moment or another, been the new one. That's what happens at a year-round school with rolling admissions, where new girls arrive every month or so with varying sentences. Four months. Twelve months — my own sentence. Fourteen months. (In that way, it was just like jail.) So I knew that they had all been in my position. Even Boone.

But I also knew this. Jules, Gwen, Karen — they all came from different stock. Clearly, there was something defective in them — otherwise, why would they be at Alice Marshall? But that didn't change the fact that they came from nice homes, freshly painted towns, schools in which they had friends to skip class with. Friends who called them every day, even when they were grounded. Hell-raising friends. Their *people*.

I came from a nice-enough house — a little bungalow near the college — but I'd never had any of the rest of it. Quite frankly, I wasn't about to start now. People, especially parents, *especially* my father, were always saying things like, "Oh, you'll make new friends," as though deciding what to bring to a potluck. *Terri will bring her famous coconut cake, and Lida will make friends.* Such a useless endeavor. I knew that, eventually, the girls at Alice Marshall would be able to sense what it was like for me (every word a mistake, every step a step in the wrong direction) and would leave me alone. They'd be grateful to have avoided *that* catastrophe.

39

But until then, I had to endure their lazy attention. And while it may have been painful, it at least allowed me to pick up factoids that I could squirrel away for later use.

Gwen and Karen were best friends, though they made an unlikely pair. Gwen was as Goth as a girl can be when her mother runs an exclusive hair salon in Beverly Hills. She dyed her hair jet black, but her bangs were impeccably even. She enjoyed death metal and televised skateboarding competitions, and poured equal amounts of milk and sugar onto her Grape-Nuts every morning. Gwen was always telling Karen about her Thing, which involved trashing the aforementioned hair salon and running away to Mexico for what turned out to be a very short weekend.

Karen was like a Joni Mitchell song compared to Gwen's Megadeth anthem. She was from a bucolic-but-forgettable town in Massachusetts, and she loved organic cotton, yoga, "natural" drugs, and meditation. Karen was prone to talking about herself in the plural first person, as in, "We're not sure that shirt is bio-ethical." It wasn't terribly surprising when I found out that she'd been caught selling peyote buttons to her friends at school.

Karen and Gwen spent all of their time together, so it wasn't hard to get them to leave me alone. A few curt replies to their questions, a grunt here or there when they addressed me . . . Girls like that didn't want to be around me anyway, and I sure as hell didn't want to be around them. They'd much prefer to sit around telling one another their stories, which were about as hard-core as pudding.

It was more difficult with Jules. Friendly and perpetually sun-burned, she was well adjusted, the picture of normalcy. Wore flip-flops and Keds. Really, the only odd thing about her was that she was at Alice Marshall, not twirling a baton on the dance line squad at her Denver high school. I was fairly certain that Jules didn't have a Thing. She wasn't capable of it. And that girl refused to take a hint. Jules could talk to a brick wall, I think, and never wonder why it wasn't responding.

On our way to breakfast, where we would be assigned our daily chores: "You never want Bathhouse duty. Try to have cramps whenever you get it."

To the Waterfront for canoeing lessons: "Always sit in the middle. You won't have to paddle as hard."

To biology: "Ms. Sterns is exactly that. Seriously. Don't mess around during Lab, and never fall behind in the reading. She'll have your ass."

She didn't appear to notice that I never responded to her little attempts at chitchat.

And then there was Boone. Boone didn't like anyone. It just wasn't in her nature. Everything she wanted you to know about her life, she told you herself, so obviously, I knew very little. I tried to keep my distance from her, which is hard when you both live in a shoe box.

Annoying as I found their attention, I guess it was at least a relief not to walk around with the constant fear of being clotheslined or shanked or whatever else they might do. My first week at Alice Marshall was tough enough as it was. For one thing, the school was big — the grounds covered over sixty acres, with only a few of the buildings situated next to the lake for easy navigation. I eventually got the whole thing mapped out in my head, but for the first few days, whenever I found myself alone, I had to walk down to the gravelly beach, stand directly in front of the docks, and look for the giant bell next to the Mess Hall in order to orient myself.

For another thing, our schedules weren't the same every day. Our classes consisted of math, history, English, biology, and wilderness education. If you went to math on Monday at two, you might think, *Same time, same place* on Tuesday, right? And then you'd show up to what you'd thought was the math building to find a group of sullen Fifteens awkwardly discussing *The Sun Also Rises*. Eventually, I started writing down the schedule on the first page of my purple unicorn journal. This meant, of course, that I was constantly opening my purple unicorn journal in front of the other girls. I don't think I need to elaborate. (Thank you, Terri. No, really. Thank you.)

There were only a few activities that remained constant, day in and day out. First, the morning exercises. Commonly referred to as "Morning Ex." Led by Margaret, of course. She said that the focus was on creating clarity and purpose, but I thought that she was just stalling for time while the kitchen staff finished grilling up the pancakes or bacon. We gathered in front of the Mess Hall after the breakfast bell had been rung, sluggishly touching our toes or dancing in place or doing jumping jacks until she told us we could go inside. Usually, at least one girl would balk and say it was bullshit, refusing to play. And then she'd have a choice: Walk in circles around the Mess Hall, or go back to her cabin without breakfast. Margaret was no softie. Morning Ex was a real highlight of everyone's day.

In the afternoons, we had Toes-Up and Waterfront Hour. Rain or shine. Some girls basically spent Toes-Up praying for the sun to come out. Not me. I hoped that it would rain all year. No way was I putting on my swimsuit and parading around the dock.

The other constant was more pleasurable. Mail Call. Margaret would stand on a table near the front of the Mess Hall after dinner, calling out names and pitching our letters at us before we had time to take them from her. I think she enjoyed this task as much as teaching. When that tiny woman called your name in her husky voice, it was like a starling had accidentally flown into the Mess Hall and landed on the table, roaring like a lion.

Finally, there were names for things I didn't know — or, to be more precise, things I thought I knew turned out to have different names. For instance, they called the lake Bob. Don't ask me why. "Gonna go sit by Bob," someone would say, or "Bob looks like hell this morning." I thought Bob was one of the part-time groundskeepers, the only men to grace Alice Marshall with their presence. I almost asked, and then was glad I hadn't when I finally figured it out.

So I started, slowly, to understand the language of this surreal place. Bob. Things. Morning Ex. And the group of girls who I kept seeing around the grounds, the ones who looked like runway models, or at least less emaciated, angrier versions of tabloid celebrities? They were called the I-bankers.

On Tuesday morning, about four days after my arrival, I was walking behind Boone when we passed a group of manicured and pressed girls hugging a slightly less attractive, younger girl, who nonetheless appeared to be wearing the same leather Pumas as the rest of them.

"Another merger for the I-bankers," Boone said, shaking her head.

I glanced behind me. There was no one else around. She must have been talking to me. Even so, I had to admit that I had no idea what she was talking about.

"What?" I asked, but she didn't say anything else, and I didn't press it.

I decided to suck it up and ask Jules about it later that day, as we walked through the trees to yet another mystery class.

"What's up with the 'I-bankers'?" I asked, in what I thought was a nicely offhanded way. It was the first time I'd initiated a conversation with any of my cabinmates, and I wanted to get the tone right. Nonchalant and cool. "I mean, you know, Who and Why?"

Jules beamed at me, clearly delighted that I'd finally spoken to her of my own accord. "Oh, that's Boone's word," she said. "It pretty much sums up all of those girls who come from New York.

Most of their mommies and daddies are investment bankers anyway, so it makes sense."

"Do they mind?"

"Mind what? Being called what they are? It's fitting." Jules shrugged. "And besides, what are they going to do? Take it up with Boone? I don't think so. Boone's been here longer than any of us. She personally 'welcomed' each and every one of them to school." She winked. "With a little help, of course."

"Oh." I touched my hair. "So it's always something."

"Yeah, it's always something," Jules said. "But it's different for every girl." She wrinkled her nose. "For instance. The I-bankers just got little things, you know, because they're in different cabins. Mice in their sleeping bags, replacing the two-hundred-dollar makeup in their luggage with little jars of honey and mud . . . easy stuff that still drove them crazy. But the girls in our cabin? Different story."

"Like?" I wanted to stop asking her questions — I knew she'd probably take this as a sign that we were BFFs or some shit — but I had to know.

"Gwen packed too much — she brought, like, eight wardrobes' worth of black shirts. We were on campfire duty a couple of times that week, and Boone would bury two or three of Gwen's T-shirts underneath the kindling while she was building the fire." Jules smiled sadly. "Gwen was upset, you know, but what could she say? She'd packed too much."

A chipmunk darted across the path in front of us and scurried up the side of a pine tree, chittering madly.

"What else?" I said.

Jules thought for a minute. "Karen has a retainer. She was always clicking it in and out of her mouth, and it drove us crazy. It's been 'missing' for months. Not that she cares. She'll just go back to the orthodontist and get a new one when she gets out of here. And let's see . . ." She chewed her bottom lip.

"What'd she do to you?"

Jules looked at the ground for a minute. Then she met my gaze. Her eyes were too bright, and her face looked redder than usual. "She cut up the only picture I had of Westy."

"Who's Westy?" It was a strange name for a boyfriend, I thought.

"My terrier. I only had the one picture. It was terrible." For a moment, I thought Jules was going to cry, but then she cleared her throat. "It took almost eight days for my parents to send me another picture. They FedExed it, but it still took forever."

"Oh," I said. I didn't feel like mentioning that it would take a lot longer than eight days for me to get my hair back. Somehow, I didn't think she'd get it.

"Anyway," she said, "you passed. At least you didn't freak out."

I thought about the way the tears had fallen sloppily down my cheeks while I stood in the Bathhouse in the early morning light, and I thanked myself again for pulling my shit together before I walked back to the cabin.

"So Boone just . . . gets away with it?"

Jules threw me a sideways glance. "No one says anything about the things she does," she said quietly. "Maybe it's just a rumor, but —" She glanced around quickly. "Well, Andrea — she left before you arrived — she told me that Boone stabbed a girl, long before she came here. Everyone knows about it. She wasn't caught, or maybe they just didn't have enough evidence."

"Not even the girl's testimony?"

Jules looked at me. "Dead people can't testify," she said. "So in answer to your question, no. No one mentions her little tricks."

I remembered how Margaret had described Alice Marshall to me. *We're the equivalent of a misdemeanor.* Misdemeanor, my ass.

We were almost to the Rec Lodge. I could see a few of the younger girls and a couple of Seventeens clustered by the door. If they had been smoking, they would have looked exactly like a picture I'd seen once of poor farmers huddled around the employment office during the Depression. The girls all looked bedraggled and hung dry.

"Time for Circle Jerk, you idiots." Boone walked up between Jules and me and laid a hand on each of our shoulders. Her fingers dug into the bone. I tried not to flinch.

"She means Circle Share," said Jules, "and I don't mind it."

"You only go for the coffee." Boone rolled her eyes skyward.

Jules shrugged nervously. "Well, yeah. I guess I do like the coffee."

The mystified expression on my face must have been clear enough, because Boone sighed.

"Circle Share," she said, glaring at me. "Where you reach deep inside yourself and dig up your worst with a bloody trowel. Then you show it to the rest of us." She released my shoulder and marched inside.

That didn't particularly help.

"This is where you talk about your Thing, if you want," translated Jules. "But only if you want to."

"Does anyone ever want to?" I blurted. I couldn't imagine a scenario in which I would ever, ever, ever want to open myself up to a bunch of strangers, all of whom had good haircuts and friends in the room.

Jules laughed. "It's a free-for-all in there," she said. "You'll be lucky to get a word in."

"Where are the others?" I asked. I hated to keep talking like this, but I hadn't seen Gwen or Karen yet.

"They're in another session," said Jules. "Bev likes to keep the different years mixed up in Circle Share." She lowered her voice. "Oh, I think we're about to start."

We edged ourselves into the lodge after Boone. The room was filled with about fifteen girls from all four years. Some of them were still milling about, but a few had taken their seats already on the folding chairs that were spaced evenly in a half-moon around the fireplace. Friends sat with friends in tight little strings, scooting their chairs closer together and giggling. I slowed down so that I wasn't walking with Jules, and tried to find a seat next to no one. That was impossible. I settled for sitting down next to a girl with a red scar across her neck, who didn't even glance at me. Across the circle from me, Jules and Boone sat next to each other, not talking. Jules raised a hand to try to catch my attention, but I looked away quickly.

"Welcome, ladies." A matronly woman who looked vaguely familiar seated herself next to the fireplace. She was short and round and had an inviting air about her, kind of like a beanbag chair. "Make sure you get a drink if you want before we get started." She gestured across the room to a makeshift coffee station where a small tower of Styrofoam cups perched next to a couple of industrial thermoses. I could've sworn I'd never seen it there before. The woman glanced over at me and smiled. "Welcome, Lida."

She already knew my name. This wasn't a promising start.

"I'm Amanda," she said. "I mediate these sessions. I think you'll find that there's great potential for healing in Circle Share." She nodded at everyone in the circle. "Great potential."

Why did every adult at this place sound like a motivational Book on Tape? Just when I thought it couldn't get any more ridiculous, the whole group started speaking in unison.

"We are kind to others; we are kind to ourselves. We honor the Circle of Truth."

I closed my eyes for a moment so that no one could see me rolling them.

After the incantation or whatever was finished, Amanda went on. "Today I thought we'd have an open discussion," she said, her voice almost hypnotic. "Last week, it seemed as though many of you were ready to share, and I was disappointed that we ran out

47

of time. So today, we're going to open the circle. Anything goes."
She smiled beatifically.

I wasn't about to share anything with this transcendental nun,
but I guess I was alone in that. Almost immediately, girls started
talking over one another, and Amanda had to finally insist that
we take turns. Take turns, indeed. I was happy to wait them
all out.

And oddly, as the hour dragged on, the whole thing started to
feel slightly professional, like the chairs should have been leather
and I should have carried a nice pen. A handful of the girls talked
about their Things, the rest of us listening like a compassionate
interview committee, and I was lulled and comforted, in a strange
way, by the familiarity of what they said. While I knew the girls
(aside from Jules) could be sarcastic and snide in other classes,
they kept it to a minimum in Circle Share. Maybe it was the way
Amanda listened. I will give her this: She was the only counselor
I've ever seen who could pay attention without getting that smug
"I'm just waiting for you to finish so that I can tell you what
you're *really* thinking" look on her face.

Whatever it was, it worked. The girls brought their baggage
into the Rec Lodge, unzipped it, and dumped every kind of
drama onto the floor. There were the usual cases: drugs, mother-
punching, small fires in the school library, suicide threats and
sometimes an earnest attempt at follow-through. Knifing, stab-
bing, spitting, blackmailing, bullying, hating, hating, hating:
Those were our Things.

Two girls talked about their Things like they were discussing a
track meet — how long, how fast, how their feet pounded. I
guessed they did this because they couldn't *not*, couldn't leave
those Things in a dank cubby behind their eyes. They thought
that by taking them out and airing them, they'd get a little cleaner
each time.

"It's like I needed to say it, you know?" A girl with a cheerleader's face and a tiny barbell piercing her eyebrow had just finished talking about how she used to steal her mother's diamonds and sell them at the antique mart so that her boyfriend could buy meth. She wiped her eyes and took a deep breath, letting it out slowly. "It's like . . ." She paused and started again. "It's like, talking about it now, it doesn't seem so bad." She caught Amanda's eye from across the circle. "What I mean is, no, it *was* bad. But now that I've talked about it, I can see that it's not, like, irreparable."

Yes, it is. The sentence popped into my head with such force that I was afraid I'd said it out loud, and I glanced around to see if anyone was gaping at me. But only Boone was looking at me with narrowed eyes. Could she see what I was thinking? I wouldn't put it past her. She was still staring at me when I looked away.

Eventually, Amanda looked at her watch and sighed. "I'm afraid we're out of time," she said. "I'm sorry." I don't know what she was apologizing for — that hour had lasted forever. She may have said something else, but I wouldn't know, since I was the first one out the door. I could already tell that Circle Share wasn't going to be my favorite class. Eventually, they'd all expect me to open up and add my Thing to the ratatouille of crap that the other girls had already prepared. And it wasn't going to happen. They'd have to cut the truth out of me.

CHAPTER FOUR

LUCKILY FOR ME, CIRCLE SHARE WAS ONLY A WEEKLY TOR-ture session, and I skated through the first two without drawing attention to myself. That was my plan in general: Get through the next year without notice. It had worked before, and it was starting to work at Alice Marshall too. Gwen and Karen had begun shooting each other glances every time I walked into the cabin. Fine with me. Boone kept on ignoring me unless she was pointing out some flaw. Even Jules stopped being *quite* as aggressively cheerful after two weeks of my grunted responses to her lame questions. Things were beginning to feel a bit more familiar.

We were working on knots in Outdoor Ed, and Margaret had asked us to practice tying them during Toes-Up one afternoon. I didn't mind Outdoor Ed, actually. Margaret was interesting to listen to, and she didn't take any bullshit. The only time I'd raised my hand was to ask when we were going to learn how to whittle, and she'd looked at me, blinking slowly, for a long minute.

"No knives."

Thought as much.

Then she added, "But I like the challenge. Perhaps later in the year we'll all try to whittle without knives. Maybe we'll use rocks, instead." She nodded. "Very pioneering of you, Lida."

Everyone else had groaned. Did I know how to play to a crowd, or what?

So anyway, I was lying on my bunk during Toes-Up with a short length of rope in hand, listening idly to Karen and Gwen as they chatted about some girl named Mariah whose boyfriend sent her a case of wine and didn't even try to camouflage it as something else. Gwen was lying on her bunk too, and Karen was sitting on the ground in a V, her legs stuck out at an angle I had only seen accomplished during Cirque du Soleil performances on TV.

"What an ass."

"I bet Bev had a nice dinner that night."

"Yeah. Pasta and Chianti."

The slip-hitch knot wasn't going well. The rope kept sliding out of place every time I thought I had it. I'd pull it tight, and the whole thing would fall apart. I remembered what Margaret had said about tying knots: "It's like anything in life. If you try to force it, you'll end up with a tangled mess." Every activity here was supposed to elicit some sort of Zen experience. I tossed the rope onto the floor. *Meditate on that, Margaret,* I thought.

I couldn't see her from my bunk, but I knew that Boone was crouched in the back corner of her bed, reading a magazine and bringing a small flask up to her mouth every so often. Boone had a way of producing a bottle of liquor out of nowhere whenever she wanted to, like a delinquent magician.

Jules flounced into the cabin dramatically, chewing on a Red Vine. She stopped in the middle of the room, ripped off a piece of the licorice with her front teeth, and said, "There's a new girl. A Seventeen."

This bought some interest.

"Excellent," said Karen. She stretched forward and wrapped one hand around each foot. "Anyone know where she's from?"

Jules shook her head. "Some of the Fifteens were talking about it in the Bathhouse while I was in the stall. Apparently, she's from all over. Her dad does something top secret, like in the Special Forces or CIA or something."

"Sure," said Boone. There was a pause while she took another sip. "Just like my brother is off 'on assignment' instead of locked up in the state pen."

"You don't know," said Gwen. "He might be."

"My brother? I hardly think that killing a redneck in a bar fight constitutes a special assignment." Boone's laugh was hollow.

"No," said Gwen patiently. "I mean her father. He *could* be Special Ops or something. He could be a dignitary. It wouldn't be the strangest thing. My friend Hannah's mother was a spy for the government when they lived in London. It happens."

"Bullshit," said Boone. "People who claim to be spies when they're at work are usually *only* who they are when they're at work. Butchers. Postal carriers. Substitute teachers."

"Anyway," said Jules, "she's really pretty, but in, like, an interesting way. And Tara said she'd seen her bags when she came back from Bev's —" She paused for effect. "And they were about half as full as they'd been when she went in."

"So Tara must have seen her before she went into Bev's, then." Boone's voice was sarcastic. Tara was an I-banker who seemed to digest gossip as voraciously as an owl, regurgitating it in the form of little pellets of dubious information. "Tara really gets around, doesn't she? Bullshit bullshit bullshit."

Jules was undeterred. "Whatever. One of her cabinmates told me that Margaret had to pick her up at Runson Bar, because she *flew* in." The airstrip at Runson Bar had been utilized a time or two by the I-bankers, though it wasn't generally thought of as an elegant way to arrive at the school. For one thing, the chances were pretty good that whatever back-country pilot you'd hired would crash the plane into the craggy mountains that rose up on all sides of the two-foot-long landing strip. "She was smoking as she stepped off the plane. Right in front of Margaret. And did I say she's pretty? She is."

"Oh, for the love of Christ," said Boone. "She's not going to get any uglier if you stop talking."

Jules looked hurt. "Fine," she said. "Be that way. You'll see what I mean soon enough."

And we did. The entire school seemed to be present on the beach that afternoon during Waterfront Hour. Usually, half the girls would be asleep on the docks, even if it was cold out, and the other half would be curling their hair or talking furtively in the Bathhouse. On the day I came to Alice Marshall, for example, there weren't too many girls at Waterfront, and I sat on the sand by myself, staring across the water and trying to look as though I was thinking of something extremely important. Clearly, no one had been that curious about *me*.

But on the day the new girl arrived, everyone stood around in small groups, or took their time getting the gear for the canoes. Even Boone was leaning against the lifeguard stand, her arms crossed in front of her, staring out at Bob like she didn't have anything better to do. (Normally, I wouldn't even see her at Waterfront. I wasn't sure where she went during that hour of each day, but it was clear that Boone never swam.)

It was a gray day, but warm, a slight wind shaking the tops of the pine trees so that they whispered to one another from thirty feet overhead. Even though I was far from an expert at canoeing, I planned to take a boat out by myself. I held my paddle in front of me and stood by the canoe on the beach. I was pretty sure I had forgotten something, so I was looking around, trying to remember what it was. But who was I kidding? We were all waiting for the Seventeens to troop down from their cabin.

Which they did, with a little more pomp and circumstance than usual. I'd only been at school a couple of weeks, but I was already used to the Seventeens' posturing. As the oldest girls, they felt entitled to ignore everyone. They felt entitled to pretty much everything. They marched down to Waterfront in a line, with their prize — the new girl — in the middle. Then they stood casually in a circle on the beach, talking to one another as though they didn't realize that everyone was staring at her. It was like her cabinmates had already had her appraised and knew exactly what she was worth.

And yes, okay, she *was* pretty. Jules was right. But she was pretty in a strange way, like the composition of her face had been sketched by a different artist than the one who finally molded it. She had almond-shaped eyes and a jaw that was angular and sharp, but even though she walked slowly, she seemed always to be moving her head, so that it was hard to get a good look at her face. She was tall with graceful arms, and skin that looked like it had been cut from white plaster. She was wearing a very cool vintage leather jacket and straight-legged, scuffed jeans. Her hair was so blond it was almost white, and it hung down the length of her back, catching the light as she turned to listen to what one of her cabinmates was saying. Sure, she was pretty. But I didn't see what the big deal was.

I pulled a life jacket from the shed where they were kept and buckled it on. As I grabbed the prow of the boat to pull it into the water, I looked back at the cluster of Seventeens. One of them must have said something witty, because most of the girls in the circle started laughing. But the new girl — she just tossed her head once, like a pony. Reached up and flicked a piece of hair away from her face while the other girls laughed and gradually fell silent. Then, and only then, a smile passed so quickly across her face it could have been a wink.

Such a small movement, you might have missed it if you weren't paying attention. But it was a smile with a thousand stories behind it. In that split second, I saw what everyone else had already seen, and I felt the heat even from where I stood.

Georgina Longchamps. A French name. It wafted around the Mess Hall that night at dinner as we all watched her eat her food slowly, delicately. *Longshawm*. It was a mouthful.

"Apparently, she goes by Gia," said Gwen, darting her eyes over to the Seventeens' table and back again.

Jules was thoughtfully chewing on a piece of broccoli. "Gia's a beautiful name," she said. "She must have a beautiful mother."

"Why?" asked Gwen.

"I think beautiful people pick better names for their kids," Jules said. "They want their names to match how they look." She nodded, as if confirming this fact to herself.

"Jules," said Boone, "I swear to God. Sometimes you are just so full of shit."

Jules just speared another piece of broccoli and brought it to her mouth. "Ishchrue," she said as she chewed.

"Where was she before coming here?" asked Karen.

"Unclear," said Gwen, who had bribed a Seventeen with a couple of American Spirits to get the little information she had. "I think somewhere abroad. Boarding school? Her cabinmates don't seem to know the whole story."

"Hard to keep a secret at this place," Boone said.

I had been cutting some butter for my baked potato and I paused, the clear plastic knife in my hand. Had Boone just glanced at me? I stared at my potato.

I think everyone was wondering how Gia would be welcomed — what Boone would do to her to make her enrollment at Alice Marshall unofficially official. Gia already seemed somehow exempt, but I knew Boone didn't see it that way.

We got our answer the next morning during Circle Share. It was another hot day, but the sky was pocked with dark clouds. The Frank's weather patterns were as comprehensible as Sanskrit. I was getting great use out of my hoodies, carrying one with me everywhere I went in case the clouds won and it started to rain, but I was tired of it. Even though I wouldn't be caught dead in a bikini or a wraparound sari on the beach, I still longed for direct, unfiltered sunlight.

We filed into the Rec Lodge once again. While I still didn't want to participate in Circle Share, it had proven to be an innocent form of gossip. Sure, the things you heard around the circle couldn't be spoken of outside of the Rec Lodge, but while we were in there, it was open season on the deliciously terrible Things we had done.

I got my coffee and sat down, careful not to look around. Eye contact meant an invitation for a smile, a joke, a brief conversation. From there, it was just a short jump to "And why don't you tell us a little about yourself, Lida?" I still wasn't in the mood for self-disclosure, so I stared at the ground.

Which is why I didn't see Gia come in. She was already sitting down by the time I even noticed that the chatter in the Rec Lodge was more subdued than usual. When I looked up, she was directly across from me in the semicircle, and she was looking straight at me. She wasn't smiling, exactly, but she had this . . . *questioning* . . . look on her face. Her eyes were soft and kind. It was the strangest thing — I felt as though her gaze was touching me with feathery fingertips. I blushed and looked at my lap.

"Welcome back, everyone." Amanda glanced around the circle, trying to make eye contact with each girl. She did this every week. When she got to Gia, she smiled and nodded but didn't say anything.

I mumbled as the other girls' voices marched through the incantation, and then we all waited for Amanda to speak again.

"I see you've all gotten comfortable," she said. "Anyone have anything to share? Any thoughts come up in the past week?"

There were some nods. A few girls shifted around in their seats and glanced at one another, wondering who would go first. There was a long pause, and then a girl with dark hair cleared her throat. Her name was Katia. I'd seen her eating sullenly with the other Fifteens. She always looked like she was about to slap someone.

"I, uh, I heard from my boyfriend," she said, smiling sadly. "His parents are moving him to Pittsburgh. So he, well, he said not to wait, you know? He said . . ." She stopped, and I could see that she was picturing the letter in her mind, making sure she remembered every word exactly as it was written. "He said that *it's probably better to just go ahead and cut our losses.*" Her eyes had filled with tears, which she brushed away with the back of her hand. She glared at her lap. "What fucking losses?"

There were supportive murmurs from the circle. *Screw him. What a loser.*

"He'll come crawling back," someone said, and I tried to picture it: a scrawny punk with safety pins in his jacket and tight black jeans, trying to crawl through the woods and up the mountain. He wouldn't get twenty feet.

"I see," said Amanda. Her hands were folded calmly on her round belly. Nothing ever fazed her. "And he was important to you?"

"Of course," said Katia defensively, glaring at Amanda. "I mean, he wasn't my first or anything like that, but he *got* me. He had this van, right? And he put a bed in the back — not like just a dirty mattress or anything, like a real bed with a down comforter and satin sheets. So whenever my parents were getting on my case, he'd just roll up and we'd take off for San Francisco or somewhere. He was always looking out for me."

Amanda put her hand up to keep Katia from saying more. "That doesn't sound like he was taking care of you, Katia. It almost sounds like he was keeping you from taking care of yourself. What do you think?"

"Not true," said Katia, but Amanda just sat there quietly, letting what she'd just said sink in. This was her way. She would just sit there like Mother Nature, all comfortable and easy in her chair, and wait for you to get it.

Finally, Katia spoke again. "There was only one pillow on his bed," she said. "And he never offered it to me. What kind of guy only buys one pillow? Bastard."

She talked some more, and other people joined in, adding their stories of manipulative boyfriends and hurried, selfish sex.

I didn't speak up. Obviously. My experience with guys was limited to a nasty kiss in the parking lot of the 7-Eleven with an older guy who'd agreed to buy beer for me. He was losing his hair and his teeth were coated with a film like they hadn't been brushed in a week. He tasted like menthol cigarettes and overripe fruit. Not a romance worth talking about. As always during these conversations, I felt like I was missing some key hormonal confluence that would allow me to identify with the others. I'd never felt that way about some guy, never thought I'd die without him, never wanted to pull my hair out by its roots if he didn't touch me again. I just didn't get it.

I could see that I wasn't the only one bowing out of the discussion. Across from me, Gia sat quietly, her long legs stretched out in front of her and crossed at the ankles. She was still wearing her jacket, which must have been made in the seventies or early eighties: light brown distressed leather, with so many zippers running up and down its front that I imagined hidden pockets, secret stashes. A half smile played across her lips. She seemed mildly entertained, like she was watching a PeeWee Baseball game. Her thoughts were as obvious and familiar to me as though they were my own. *Bullshit.*

I watched her cautiously for a while until I became aware that someone else was watching her too. I can't say how I knew, but I did, and I looked around the room for the reason. Boone was leaning forward, her eyes fixed on Gia. She wasn't trying to be subtle. She was staring at Gia like she was just waiting for the other girl to look back. But Gia didn't meet Boone's gaze.

I looked at Boone and Boone looked at Gia and Gia looked at no one in particular until the hour was up and Amanda told us we were free to leave.

I rose quickly from my chair, hoping to get out of the Rec Lodge before anyone tried to talk to me. Amanda walked out and I followed her, as the rest of the group slowly got up and chatted with one another. I'd made it to the porch of the lodge before I heard someone near me say, "Here it goes," and I turned and looked behind me.

Boone was standing next to Gia by the doorway, her hand out with its palm turned up, as though she was waiting for Gia to put something in it.

"I wonder if you'd let me try it on," she was saying. "Walk around with it. Just for a few hours."

This was a change. As I understood it, Boone's "welcomes" were accomplished while the new girl was asleep or otherwise occupied. This was more direct. I wondered why Boone was playing it this way.

Gia glanced down at the jacket she was wearing. Then she looked up at Boone, her bleach-blue eyes calm and noncommittal. "I'd prefer to wear it myself," she said in a strange accent that was somewhere between Britain and Baton Rouge. Her gaze traveled up and down the length of Boone's body before she added, "I'm not sure it's your style."

It happened before I had time to imagine it happening. Boone slammed Gia up against the door frame, her ear just inches from a rusted old nail that was protruding from the wood. Boone held her there, the pipe bone of her arm pressing into Gia's neck. Boone's voice was low, but I could still hear her even as she leaned in and locked eyes with the other girl. "Prep school reject." She leaned in closer. "East Coast whore."

Like I said, it happened so quickly that no one had time to act. And it was over as soon as it had started. Boone stepped back politely and shook her arm out while Gia felt at her throat with delicate moth-wing fingertips. Then Boone asked for the jacket again. She said she felt sure that Gia wouldn't mind giving up her *accoutrement* for the sake of friendship. *Accoutrement*. A French word, naturally.

One finger still on her neck, Gia stroked the hollow of her throat as if restructuring it, and then she smiled. She shrugged the jacket off like a kimono, like she was practiced at letting things slide off her. It fell to the ground behind her. Without a word or another glance at Boone, she adjusted the sleeves of her shirt so that they came evenly to her wrists, and then she turned. She stepped heavily on the sleeve of the jacket, leaving a dark, almost black smear of dirt in the form of a footprint. She didn't look at any of us, but she threw back her shoulders a little as she walked away.

No one picked up the jacket. Boone just stared down at the ugly smudge curving down the sleeve before wiping her nose with the back of her arm and walking away too. Nobody said anything as the group slowly dispersed.

I knew one thing, though. From then on, I would always glance at that rusted, protruding nail in the door frame whenever I passed by it. I would glance at it like I wasn't really looking, but I would memorize every shadow on its sharp, jagged end.

CHAPTER FIVE

WHAT BOONE WANTED, SHE GOT. YOU WERE LUCKY IF SHE bothered to ask. No one had ever defied her before. So after the incident with Boone, Gia became legend.

What we knew about her was nothing and everything. She had gone to school in Switzerland/India/Las Vegas/Maryland. She received daily, coded love letters from her German/Spanish/Icelandic/Colombian boyfriend — who was, everyone suspected, a freedom fighter, nationality notwithstanding. She could swear in three or nine languages, had escaped from a boarding school or detox center, and — despite Bev's thorough search — she managed to smuggle in both cigarettes and weed in the lining of her pillow.

I watched Gia. In the Mess Hall, around the campfire, walking toward the Waterfront. There was something about her that seemed bright and hard, like a star. It made me want to keep looking. So I did. And I began to notice things.

She cut her oranges in half and spooned the flesh out like she was eating a grapefruit.

She never sang, and spoke only when spoken to.

She walked languidly, hips first, as if daring her legs to catch up.

When she caught me watching her, she would close her eyes for one beat, two, and then open them again and look straight at me.

I was not the only girl staring at Gia. But I was the only girl she stared back at. Sometimes she would nod at me, as though we were two travelers on the same road.

Still, I couldn't bring myself to talk to her. I mean, why would I? What could I have to say to a girl like that? More important, what could she have to say to me? I was better off not even trying.

Margaret had been teaching us about orienteering in Outdoor Ed, and we spent a lot of time wandering around the school grounds with our compasses out, trying to decipher whether the Mess Hall was north or south of Bev's cabin. But compasses wouldn't get us very far, Margaret told us, unless we knew how to read maps.

"Maps are an accessory to movement," she said one morning as we all lay stretched out on our bellies in the Outdoor Ed classroom, studying the five or six copies of a topographic map of the Wilderness Area that she had spread out in front of us. "They can keep you grounded to a particular place, but they can also lead you on other journeys. Once you know how to read a map, you will know how to root yourself so that you can stretch and grow. It's good to have a point of origin to wander away from."

I saw Gwen raise her eyebrows at Karen. Her look plainly said *More new-age bullshit*, but I liked what Margaret was saying. "Point of origin." I liked the sound of it.

"But more literally," Margaret said, "a topographic map can

show you not only where you are, but also how far above sea level you are, how to get to a major road, where the nearest town lies, what rivers you might fish in if you get hungry. Maps can save your life." She let that sink in. "You've all noticed that each time I lead you on a hike, no matter how short, I have a map and a compass with me, right?"

There were some halfhearted nods. A good three-fourths of our Outdoor Education classes had consisted of hiking into the woods that the school backed up against and following a series of trails, some better maintained than others.

"This is because it's easy to get lost on even the shortest hike. If I know how to read a map, know north from south, I can get us home. Simple as that." She walked over to a group of I-bankers, who had set up a little makeup display on their map, and who were tensely trading pots of blush and eye shadow in much the same way that their parents traded stocks. "Darcy," she said, tapping one of them on the shoulder while sweeping the makeup off the map with the side of her shoe, "what do the brown lines mean?"

"Fuck!" said Darcy, diving for her makeup. Some other girl had gotten to it first, though, and the little pots were gone in an instant. "Damn it, Chandler, that was —" She started to complain, but then she saw Margaret's expression and stopped. "I don't know," she mumbled. "How am I supposed to know?"

"Good question." Margaret was unfazed. "Paying attention will help." She moved over to where I was lying near Karen and Gwen and Jules. "Thoughts?" she asked the four of us.

There was a long silence. Karen closed her eyes as though she was thinking, and Gwen stared at the map, intense concentration clouding her face. Jules looked at me.

"No clue," she said.

"Lida?"

I sighed and scooted closer on my belly. I looked at the map carefully. There were little numbers written alongside some of the brown lines, which often took the shape of circles within circles. The smallest circle in the middle always had the highest number. "Elevation?" I asked.

Margaret smiled at me. "Pretty much," she said. "Those are called contour lines. They show the shape of the land, as well as the elevation. Each line typically represents a hundred feet. If you can 'read' them, you can pinpoint the exact elevation of any given place in the wilderness."

"And why would we want to do that?" Darcy wasn't about to play along.

Margaret crossed her arms and looked up at the rafters of the Rec Building. She got that Zen look on her face that I had slowly come to recognize as the expression she wore when she'd rather be swearing at someone or worse. "Ah, Darcy," she said, "once again, you have gotten to the marrow of the question."

"What?"

Margaret continued as though she hadn't heard her. "It may seem hard to believe now, but winter closes in quickly here. You might want to know if the hike you're about to take in, say, November, is going to lead you straight into avalanche territory. Closer to home, you might want to figure out how far you'd have to walk, and over what kind of terrain, if you were thinking about leaving the school." She smiled at Darcy, who I'm pretty sure had been wondering that exact thing.

We spent the rest of the morning identifying rivers, finding the school on the map, guessing at elevations, and figuring out how far it was from one place to another. Answer: far. In the River of No Return Wilderness Area, nothing — and no one — was close by. Even the airstrip at Runson Bar was a good twelve miles away, and that's as the little toothpick plane flies. We counted the lines around Bob, and realized that we were sitting exactly seven thousand feet above sea level. I pretended to be as disinterested as the other girls, but secretly, I kind of liked looking at the map. It was like trying to learn a language, but without past participles and future conditionals and all that. I would never speak French. I knew that much. But I thought I might be able to speak Map.

"Boone," Margaret said toward the end of the class, "can you find Elk City on that map?"

Boone had fallen asleep on top of the map she was studying. She'd been drooling, because I could see the faint imprint of a river on her cheek when she raised her head.

"What."

"Elk City."

Boone stared at Margaret for a minute, her eyes hard. "Why don't you just ask Meriwether Lewis over there?" she said, jutting her chin in my direction.

I blushed.

"Boone." Margaret placed a fist on her hip and stared her down.

"Fine. Elk City," Boone repeated. "North Pole?"

Margaret sighed. "A brilliant guess," she said, "but not a place that you have on the map in front of you."

Boone stared at the map as though she was looking for Elk City, but I knew she was just trying to look busy. She may have even known where the town was, but she wasn't going to say, and Margaret knew it.

"Okay," she said. "I see how it's going to be." She paused. I could picture the cogs turning in her head, and I knew she was about to throw something new at us. "It just so happens that you're in luck. We're going to try something different. Approach this from a different angle. You all have journals, right?"

We stared at her. This didn't sound promising.

"Good. We're going to begin a long-term project," she said. "The whole school is doing it, actually: Mapping Your World."

Mapping Your World, as Margaret explained it, meant that we had to think of creative and interesting ways to depict our lives and the world we lived in. Our maps didn't have to have pictures. They didn't have to be true to scale. They could have contour lines, she said, but we could distinguish between the lines however we wanted. Counting the years instead of feet, for example. Letters to people we knew, stories, pasted-in photographs, poems — we could put anything we wanted on our maps. All they had to be was true to us. "This is your chance to be creative," Margaret said, as though no one in the room had ever used her imagination.

I thought about the different ways I'd wielded my creativity, but I didn't think they'd represent well on a map.

So that's what I was attempting to do when Gia finally talked to me: Map My World.

I had quickly realized that most of the other girls at Alice Marshall smoked too, and most nights, after Bev finished her rounds, I followed the others down to the beach behind the cabins, where Gwen, Karen, and a handful of others perched on their heels and formed a wavy line in the sand, staring out at Bob. Sometimes Boone sat there too, holding her cigarette tightly between her thumb and forefinger like it was a joint. Most times, she stayed away. I learned that cigarettes were mailed inside of care packages: hidden in hollowed-out books, boxes of tampons — even, in one particularly brilliant maneuver, inside of twenty fat mechanical pencils, their lead removed. The rule was that whichever lucky girl had gotten the goods distributed them evenly, and no one argued. Nobody seemed to mind that a few of us didn't get care packages and never added to the till. Then again, there was never a lack of cigarettes.

I never sat with the other girls, and they never talked to me except to offer me a cigarette (and even that was done silently, by holding the pack out in my direction and nodding). It was an easy kind of camaraderie, one that asked nothing of me. I always made sure to stub out my cigarette before the others had finished theirs. Then I would walk through the dark, no flashlight, listening to the muted night sounds. My feet scuffing against the ground. A twig snapping under my shoe. In the woods beyond, the muffled movements and inarticulate rustlings of the forest at night. Other girls felt frightened by the noises. I felt enveloped.

Gia had been coming down to the beach since the very first night she arrived at Alice Marshall. She smoked a French brand of tobacco that she rolled herself into tight little bullets. Oddly enough, no one ever asked her to share. She would listen to the chatter of the other smokers and laugh when others laughed, although she didn't contribute much to the conversation.

I was surprised, then, when she asked me a question, almost two weeks after she arrived at Alice Marshall. I was sitting on a log, away from the group. Gwen was nearby, talking with a Fourteen about tattoo designs. Boone wasn't there. And I was mapping my world, kind of. At least, I had a stick in my hand, and was drawing pictures in the sand. The stick pushed through the dark, damp ground, and slowly, images began to emerge. *Here* is an outline of my house. *Here* is where the bathroom is. *Here* is the sink, the drawer underneath, the plastic dividers that hold a selection of beauty utensils. Tweezers. Nail clipper. Cuticle scissors. Razor.

I hadn't seen Gia come down until she was sitting right beside me, the sleeve of her sweater brushing up against my windbreaker.

"Nice artwork," she said. "Paint-by-number?"

It took me a full minute to respond. First, I looked around. There was no one else she could be talking to — I mean, who else was drawing in the sand with a stick? Also, no one seemed fazed by the fact that we were having a conversation. Potentially, that is. It wouldn't be a conversation unless I said something and broke what was threatening to be a humiliating silence.

"Just doodling," I said, running the tip of my shoe over my drawing in the sand and smudging the pictures. "Margaret says we have to map our worlds." *Margaret says?* I sounded like a third-grader. *Margaret says everyone is wearing their hair in French braids.* Pathetic.

"Yeah," said Gia. "She told the Seventeens that too." I saw her smile out of the corner of my eye. "It's an impossible task. She might as well ask us to make stained glass windows depicting our lives from birth on."

I considered the bizarre image of a church full of our windows. "Half of them would probably be broken," I said, surprising myself.

She shook her head. "I mean, it's embarrassing enough that we have to sit around the fireplace sharing our feelings like we're in some knitting circle. Now it has to be a craft project?" Her laugh was low and throaty. "Do we get a badge for it?"

"The Emotional Vomit badge. I can pin it next to my Knot-Tying and Bullshitting badges."

"Oh, that's good," she said. "You seem to know what you're talking about."

"I was a Brownie in kindergarten. I took notes."

"Ah."

We were quiet, listening to the chatter around us, the water as it licked the shore. I was nervous talking to her like this, but she didn't seem in any hurry to leave.

"Anyway," she said, "what's your story . . . Lida, right?"

"Yeah," I said. I liked the way she said my name, clipping the consonants so that it sounded like she was running over my name on her tiptoes. "No story, really."

"Impossible. You can't be here without a story." She nudged me with her shoulder. "It's a prerequisite." Her smile was warm.

"Oh," I said. "Yeah, I guess you're right." I laughed — something between a chuckle and a cough. "Well," I tried again, "what do you want to know?"

"What's important?"

"I guess I have a terrible stepmother."

"The oldest story."

"And my dad's kind of a lost cause."

"Of course."

Gia was staring at me like she was waiting for me to tell her something honest and true, but I didn't know what else to say or how to say it.

And then I did. "Sometimes," I said quickly, "it feels like the situation with my stepmom and my dad is only the exclamation point."

"Exclamation point to what?"

"I don't know for sure. Something more real than my stupid home life." I shivered and hugged myself.

"Where's your mother?" she asked.

"Dead."

"Oh," said Gia quietly. "How terrible."

I kicked at the sand. "Whatever. I didn't know her." And before she could ask, I added, "Cancer." It never failed to halt further questions in their tracks.

"It doesn't matter if you didn't know her." Gia spoke softly. "A mother is a mother. You lose your mother, you lose yourself. Everything else is just confetti."

Her voice was sad and sure. She knew exactly how I felt. It seemed suddenly too quiet on the beach. I glared at the ground, willing my eyes dry.

Gia was watching the side of my face. I saw her nod, as though agreeing with something she had just thought.

"You're not the only one, Lida," she said. "You're not alone."

Gia put her hand on my shoulder and pushed herself up. She left her hand there for a second after she stood, and then she took a couple of steps.

I didn't want her to leave. "Hey," I said. She turned. "What about you?"

"What about me?"

"Well, um, what's your story?" I was trying to play it cool, but I couldn't stop myself from leaning forward, ready to catch anything she might say.

But she laughed instead. "Storytime's over," she said. "We'll have to save it for another night." Gia ran her fingers through her hair. "I'll see you around?" It was dark, but I could still see that she was grinning at me with her eyes.

"Yeah," I said, "sure."

I stayed there on the log for what might have been ten minutes and might have been two hours. There were hundreds of questions cartwheeling through my mind, not one of them with an answer. How had she known the way I felt about my mother? I hadn't even told her everything — I hadn't told her anything, really — and yet she still seemed to understand. And what if she was right? What if my mother's absence defined me? What if I was destined to always be just *partial*, like some half-finished sketch of a girl: a misplaced eye, part of an ear, one long arm at a wrong angle?

I felt this strange connection to Gia, like we were tethered together with the finest string. I hadn't felt this way with any of the other girls who'd tried to strike up a conversation with me. They were all too settled in their delightfully delinquent lives. Even their Things fit them too easily, like old sweaters that they'd worn every day for years. Not Gia. She didn't seem to want to be settled. There was nothing easy about her.

Later, I lay on my bunk and imagined how Gia probably brushed her hair before bed: rhythmically, methodically, the hair falling in a soft white current over her hand and the brush. How it must have felt to be that hand, that brush.

I didn't fall asleep until the sky had lightened to pearl gray and the first birds had begun their impatient song.

Epilogue

Dr. Hemler tells me I can call him by his first name. "Call me Hank," he says, for what must be the thirtieth time in the year I've been seeing him.

"No thanks," I say. I remind him, probably also for the thirtieth time, that some people are just born looking like forty-year-old men, and that my guess is he was one of them. "Sorry. You'll always be Dr. Hemler to me," I say, and he laughs, I think. Sometimes his laugh is more of a choking sound. Then he smiles.

He's always smiling, this guy. Smiled the first time he met me, when I was about a half step away from throwing myself off a bridge. Smiled through my tears, my rants, my long silences. And he's still smiling now, sitting across from me in his mauve wingback chair, casually holding the yellow legal pad on which he compiles his notes about me, week after week. Dad and Terri must be paying him a bundle to keep that noncommittal grin on his face.

"Margaret called again," I say, and then, before Dr. Hemler can ask, I add, "but I didn't talk to her."

"You'll have to talk to her eventually," he says.

"I know."

He jots something on his legal pad. "Have you started writing it down?"
he asks, and I nod, glancing away. "Good," he says, and makes another
mark with his pencil. "That's a start."

I've been keeping a journal ever since I left Alice Marshall. For the first
ten months, all I wrote about were feelings. Sadness, anger, annoyance, guilt,
little winks of happiness. I wrote about emotions like they were characters in
a story, friends with whom I had long talks on Saturday nights. But, as
Dr. Hemler so thoughtfully pointed out, I never connected them to anything
real. I never wrote about what happened back there in the woods, never gave
these feelings any context. They were characters without shoes, freckles with-
out faces.

Now he says, "How have you found the process of writing about your
experience so far? Difficult? Easy? A little of both?"

"Dr. Hemler," I say, crossing one leg over the other and settling back into
the couch where I sit every Thursday from four to five, "it's always easy
at the beginning."

CHAPTER Six

FOR THE NEXT FEW DAYS, GIA WAS EVERYWHERE. YES, THE school was small. Yes, there were only fifty of us, give or take. But there were girls whose names I still didn't know and probably never would. I never saw these girls, even though they might have been standing next to me every night as we brushed our teeth in the Bathhouse.

With Gia, though, it was like I had a heat sensor right between my eyes. Whenever she was around, I knew it long before she even came into view. Sometimes, when she walked into the Rec Lodge or Mess Hall, or when I rounded a corner on the path between the school buildings and saw her standing quite still by a tree, she would already be looking in my direction, like she was expecting to see me. Then she'd smile, so quickly I would almost miss it, and we'd each keep on in our own way.

At first, I wondered why she didn't say anything. But it didn't take me long to realize that her silence was protecting me. Because, nine times out of ten, if I was walking anywhere, it was with my cabinmates. And that meant Boone.

Gia and Boone hadn't spoken to each other since the scene outside Circle Share, but the way Boone looked at Gia said more than enough. If the imaginary sensor between my eyes could track everyone's heat, I'm pretty sure it would have melted from the rage that practically sizzled off Boone every time she passed Gia on the school grounds. Boone hadn't said anything about what had happened, and no one in my cabin had dared ask.

So, Gia and I didn't talk during the day. And for almost a week, we didn't talk at night either. There were shadowy evenings when I practically sprinted down to the Smokers' Beach, only to find her talking to another Seventeen — usually one of her cabinmates. She'd raise her eyebrows in my direction in a kind of facial shrug — *what can I do?* — and then she'd look back at the Seventeen, bored but polite. There were other nights she didn't come down to the beach at all.

But I was there every night. Waiting. And eventually, it worked. I felt her coming this time, so it wasn't a surprise when she sat down next to me on my log, grabbed my hand lightly, let it go, and said in a John Wayne voice, "Well, you old so-and-so, how the hell are you?"

"Fair to middlin'," I answered, my own western twang matching hers.

There were only a couple of girls on the beach that night. In Outdoor Ed that afternoon, Margaret had taken us on another grueling flower identification hike, pointing out blue lupine and pink bistort, which looked like sticks of old-fashioned rock candy, and my cabinmates had practically fallen asleep before the door shut behind Bev. It had been a struggle for me to slip on my shoes and come down to the beach — my sleeping bag had never been so inviting — but I'd done it. And now I was glad I had.

"Not smoking tonight?" Gia glanced pointedly at my hands, which were folded on my lap. "That's quite a prim posture you've got going."

I unfolded my hands quickly. "I'm practicing for Parents' Weekend."

She laughed. "Shouldn't we all." Gia reached into the pocket of her jacket and pulled out her tobacco pouch. "You ever roll your own?"

I shook my head.

"Want to learn?"

Did I ever.

"Okay. So first, take a rolling paper. Here." She held out a small rectangular package, and I pulled out a paper as thin and translucent as an old woman's skin. "Make sure the crease is sharp. Then grab some tobacco and roll it up tightly."

I reached into the pouch and pinched off what I thought was a small amount of tobacco.

"Whoa," said Gia. "You don't want to give yourself lung cancer all in one night, do you? A little less."

So I tried. I took less, placed it on the paper, rolled it up. Unrolled it. Tried again. And again. By this time, the paper was looking more like a failed origami project than a cigarette. I couldn't get it right. "Shit," I said, blushing. "You make it look so easy."

"Here," she said, "let me." Gia reached over and lightly pulled the paper from between my fingers, dumping the tobacco back in the pouch. Slowly, she smoothed the paper on the knee of her jeans, and then folded it back along the crease. "Waste not, want not." She reached inside the pouch and pulled out a new knot of tobacco, rolling it between her fingers as she dropped it onto the paper. Then she ran one finger over it all, making sure it was even. "The last thing you want is a lumpy cigarette," she said to herself. "Never good."

Then, holding the paper between index finger and thumb, she rolled the paper again and again in a seesaw motion. She waited until the shape was tight before rolling it one last time and quickly running her tongue over the paper's loose end. Then she pasted that down with her thumb and looked up. "Victory."

"That was amazing. How'd you learn to do it so well?" Her flawless execution had made my attempt look even more pathetic, and I was glad for the darkness, which hid the red splotches that were traveling down my neck.

"Practice." She handed me the cigarette. "We'll get you there."

"Thanks."

She quickly rolled one for herself and passed me a book of matches that said *Skyline Lodge* across the front. "I collect them," she explained, "from my travels."

"Nice."

We smoked quietly together, the air filling with smoke that smelled of leather and spice, the silence punctuated only by my rasping cough whenever I inhaled too forcefully. Smoking Gia's cigarettes taught me the true meaning of the term "breathing fire."

I had so many questions I wanted to ask her, but they all seemed stupid when I put them into words in my head. I wanted to know where she was from, why she was at Alice Marshall, what her life was like when she wasn't hidden away near some subalpine lake; in short, I wanted to know everything about her.

But I settled instead for saying, "You really threw Boone for a loop."

"Who?"

"Boone." She *had* to know who Boone was by now. "You know, the girl who tried to take your jacket?" Everything I said was starting to sound more ridiculous by the second.

Gia tossed her hair out of her face. "Oh. *That* girl." She stared out at the lake. "It seemed to me like I messed up her little ritual in some way — like I read my lines wrong." She looked at me. "I mean, what? Would everyone else have just given her the clothes off their back?"

I smiled. "Pretty much."

"This place is strange."

"Well, you're famous now," I said. "Resident badass." I wanted to lean over and nudge her with my shoulder or something, but I didn't feel steady. Sure, she was talking to me now — but how long would that last before she realized her mistake?

"I'll take that as a compliment," she said. "And here's one in return: I have a feeling that you're something of a badass yourself."

"Not really," I said, though I wished it were true.

She considered her cigarette, which had burned down to about a centimeter of glowing ember. "Maybe not in the traditional way," she mused, "but on a much more . . . intrinsic level. Like you're wounded but fierce. No. Like your wounds *make* you fierce. I've watched you," she added. "You don't seem to want to have much to do with the other girls around here." Then she paused. "Not that I blame you. They all seem so — well, *tame*, I guess." She laughed. "Does that even make sense?"

"Yeah, it does." I paused, and then kept going. "Their problems are all so obvious, you know? It's a little ridiculous."

"Yeah. They're trying too hard." Gia ground what remained of her cigarette into the sand and then flicked it out toward the lake. "So, hey," she said, "you told me about your mother, but you didn't tell me too much about your dad. Let me guess: You're nothing like him, are you?"

"Not hardly," I said. "He's . . ." *He's what?* Good with numbers? A practical man? Just plain oblivious? "I think he thinks I'm an alien."

"That's what I thought," Gia said, smiling. "Some people take after their parents. Some people are *reactions* to their parents. I think you and I are in the second group." She dusted her hands on her thighs.

A reaction. That sounded about right. "What's your dad like?" I asked.

"Dave?" Gia shrugged. "He's not a bad guy, really. Just busy."

I'd always wanted to call my father by his first name, but he didn't like the idea; he refused to answer when I tried, and told me that, as far as I was concerned, his legal name should be "Dad Wallace." I loved that Gia got away with it. "Does he have to travel all the time for his work?" I asked. "I mean, he's probably got some top secret clearance or something, so can he even tell you where he's going?" I imagined Gia's father's passport, unintentionally left on a table. Gia flipping through it, taking notes.

Gia stretched her arms in the air, and then hugged herself. "Yeah, he travels. But my guess is there's no place that mystifies him as much as his own house," she said, and yawned. "There's nothing more frightening to a man than a daughter."

I'd thought I knew what she was talking about, but suddenly I wasn't so sure. "Why?" I asked.

"Oh, that sounded too dramatic." She laughed lightly. "I meant to say that even the best parents can't understand their own children. You know?"

I nodded. "We're not even on the same page as them. We're not even reading the same book."

"Right."

We sat quietly together for a minute or so. I tried to think of things to talk about, but everything sounded childish in my head, so I waited for Gia to keep the conversation going. She didn't say anything, though, and when I glanced at her from the corner of my eye, she was staring out at the water as though she could see precisely what was on the other side. Then she stood up. "Man, all this philosophical talk has tired me out. I'm exhausted." She held out her hand formally, and I shook it. "Good night, you old so-and-so. Pleasure doing business with you."

I laughed. "Good night." I watched as her shadow receded toward the cabins. Then I stubbed out my own cigarette. I held the butt in my hand for a few moments before flinging it into the water.

Our nightly smoke breaks were one of the reasons why everyone looked forward to Mail Call so much. We didn't hold out much hope for our letters; Bev read through each one with a Sharpie pen, and she carefully blackened out anything that had to do with drugs or sex or good times in general, so there was only a slim chance of getting any real gossip from the outside world. (She also crossed out anything that would wound us, cruel messages from family or friends we might have hurt before we came to Alice Marshall.) Any gossip we did manage to get was passed around the school like a joint. We had no TV, no radio, and no iPods, so we were hungry for news of any sort. But gossip was a rare and unpredictable commodity. What everyone really wanted, what we looked forward to the most, were the care packages: candy, smokes, maybe a real letter hidden in the fold of a book's jacket flap.

There were no care packages coming in for me, not even straight-up, honest ones with writing paper and gummy bears, pens with their ink cartridges still intact. My father sent me, instead, twice-weekly postcards that he obviously bought at the college bookstore. On the backs of photos of "The Student Union," "Sunset Over Main Campus," or "Bruno at Night" (just a black, blank card), he would write messages so mundane it was as if he were challenging himself to lower the bar.

I never wrote back.

I got perhaps the best card a few days after Gia taught me how to roll a cigarette.

Hot summer in Bruno so far. Terri's mowing the lawn, says hi. I might put shelves in the dining room. Nothing on TV. Thinking about you. Dad.

His greatest work yet. It was strange, but my father had somehow figured out a way to imply that the very last thing he would do, after all other options had been meticulously exhausted, was think about his daughter.

It warmed my heart. It really did. It warmed my heart so much that I kind of snorted through my nose.

"What's so funny?" asked Gwen. She had just drained a glass of milk with her dinner, and I could see the faintest white mustache on her upper lip.

"Nothing," I said.

"Hand it over," said Boone.

"It's nothing."

"Give it." She wasn't going to ask again.

I tried to look bored as I handed her the postcard. She passed the card around the table, letting the other girls read it. I snuck a look over at Gia's table, where she was quietly eating a fruit salad, spearing each piece individually with her fork.

"Is this what we have to look forward to in middle age?" asked Jules, putting the postcard facedown in the center of the table.

"If so, then shoot me now," said Gwen. "It's a classic — one for the archives." She looked again at the postcard. "Who's Terri? Your mom?"

"Stepmother," I said. I ran my fingers over the plastic knife by my plate, feeling its dull ridge against my thumb.

"Where's your mom?" Gwen was apparently suffering from a bout of curiosity.

"Dead. And no, I don't want to talk about it," I snapped.

The table was quiet for a minute. Gwen blushed, and she looked at Karen.

"Well, anyway," said Karen quickly, glancing at the card again, "why did he put a period after his name? Does he think he's worthy of his own sentence?"

"Seems fine to me," said Boone. "At least he knows how to spell."

I looked at her as she pushed her chair back and rested her feet lightly on the edge of the table. As far as I knew, she had only received one letter since I had arrived. She had walked around for days with it folded evenly in the back pocket of her baggy jeans. Almost the entire letter had been blackened out.

"Girls." Bev was standing by our table. No one had noticed her walking over, and we all sat up a bit straighter. Jules handed me my postcard silently and then stared down at her plate. Bev looked at Boone with a blank expression on her face until Boone sighed heavily and took her feet off the edge of the table. There was a crack as her chair's front two legs hit the floor. "Thank you," said Bev. She glanced around our table. "I just came from the Bathhouse," she said.

Boone groaned.

"I suppose I don't need to elaborate, then," said Bev. "Boone, thank you for volunteering. Lida, you may assist her. I'll check it again before campfire." She turned and walked back to the teachers' table.

"Christ," said Boone. She glared across the table at me. "I hope you have an inner Mary Poppins, Townie. That place is a sty."

This was going to be just wonderful.

The morning chores were doled out daily by cabin, according to a chart on the giant dry-erase board that hung next to the doors of the Mess Hall. We rotated throughout the week between trash pickup, kitchen patrol, campfire prep, Bathhouse duty, Waterfront maintenance, and the general upkeep of the classroom buildings, which usually just meant throwing away candy wrappers in the Rec Lodge and sweeping the porches of some of the other buildings. Of these chores, Bathhouse duty was the worst. Obviously. We did our chores directly after breakfast, and there was nothing less appealing than pulling the rubber mats from the shower stalls and hanging them outside in the cold morning air, fingers like icicles and the heavy mats slapping against the front of our jeans as we wrestled them over the railing that surrounded the Bathhouse. We felt dirty even before the day had begun.

The beauty of it was, if Bev didn't like what she saw as she roamed the grounds throughout the day — if she found stray life jackets on the beach or the salt and pepper shakers hadn't been refilled in the Mess Hall — she "selected" a couple of girls from the assigned cabin to finish the job right after dinner. The randomness of her selections, coupled with the blaming and cursing that followed in the negligent cabin, ensured that we did our chores thoroughly and efficiently.

The only problem was the Bathhouse. If Bev wandered in after canoe lessons or Waterfront Hour finished, she was likely to find the wreckage of a tsunami. And even though she knew, she *knew* that the mess had only just been made, she would still force two girls from the cabin who had cleaned it so impeccably that morning to go back in and "finish" the job.

While cleaning the Bathhouse twice in one day was unsavory, it wasn't nearly as disturbing now as the fact that I'd be doing it with Boone. Alone. On a good day, she was intimidating. I couldn't imagine what she'd be like when she was irate. And I hadn't yet been alone in a room with her.

Boone and I made our way to the Bathhouse after dinner, each of us carrying a bucket. Boone had the mop and a box of trash bags. I had the toilet scrubber and an assortment of yellowed and flaking sponges.

Inside, the Bathhouse looked like the "aftermath" scene in one of those B-grade horror movies, the one where the psycho comes into the peaceful summer camp and wipes everyone out with a single breath, and they never have time to clean up the mess they were casually making right before they died. The bench in the middle of the room had been tipped on its side. One of the sinks was dripping, and there was toothpaste forming a little beard around the faucet of the other one. The toilet seats had paper stuck to them in places, or they hadn't been flushed. And the floor — well, let's just say that the floor was about ready to birth its own organisms.

Boone shook her head. "What an embarrassment." She walked to a corner of the room and picked up a soggy towel, letting it drop back onto the floor with a wet thud. "Little rich girls don't know how to clean up after themselves," she said to herself. "They need a lesson in personal hygiene."

I didn't know if she was including me in this group, and I didn't want to ask. I had the feeling that some of the messiest girls — I-bankers, for the most part — were going to find gum in their hairbrushes and mousse in their shoes by morning, and I didn't want Boone to think I was one of them.

That's why, when she growled, "You gonna help me clean this craphouse, or what?" I let out the breath that I'd been holding and jumped into action.

We started cleaning, both of us focused on getting the job done as quickly as possible. Thank God we had gloves. After about thirty minutes, we could see that we'd made some progress, but it was still this side of disgusting.

"Makes me want to wear socks in the shower," I said, and Boone raised her eyebrows.

"Where I'm from, you'd be smart to wear socks in the shower all the time — in the shower, in bed, even in the public pool."

Where I'm from. I'd heard her mention "the mill" a few times while we were all eating in the Mess Hall, so I had an idea where she was talking about. Still, I don't know what emboldened me to ask.

"Are you talking about the old lumber mill in Minster?" It was the only mill I'd ever heard of. "Is that where you're from?"

Boone looked up from where she was mopping out the shower stalls, and I was suddenly afraid she'd come at me with the blunt end of the mop handle. But the words were already out there, humid and suffocating in the air.

"You want to know where I'm from," she said.

I nodded, though not very convincingly.

"Well, Townie, get this: I'm from a joke," she said. "I'm from a mill town without any mill. Do you know what that does to a place?"

I shook my head. I vaguely remembered hearing that the Minster lumber mill closed down a few years before, but I hadn't thought any more about it since then.

"Take your average mill town," Boone explained, leaning the mop up against the sink and drawing a large circle in the air with her hands. "You've got your tract houses, you've got your over-grown ball field, you've got your trailers and churches and drunks. Right?"

Her description sounded real enough, so I nodded again.

"Now imagine the town, only take away the mill. Take away the houses, the field, the churches, the jobs. What have you got?"

"Trailers and drunks?" I answered nervously.

"Trailers and drunks." She pointed her finger in the middle of her imaginary circle. "And it's so goddamned pathetic that it grabs you by the throat and chokes you." Her voice was husky. She turned and picked up the mop again. "Unless you choke it first."

I stood there dumbly, the toilet scrubber dangling from my hand. Suddenly, the Bathhouse seemed dark, the other girls very,

very far away. I walked over to one of the stalls and knelt, trying to look busy.

But Boone heard the question I was too afraid to ask.

"Whatever," she said. "You'll hear about it in Circle Jerk, anyway. The lumberyard office," she said. "I burned the bastard down. I waited until old Lenny the caretaker left the counter for a smoke break, and I torched it."

"So, um, what. Like with gasoline?" I imagined Boone heaving a jug of kerosene toward a run-down building. I imagined the lighter in her hand. The way her eyes must have lit up.

"Nosy, aren't you," she said. "Simpler than that. Matches and empty cigarette cartons. I built a little campfire in the middle of the office. It didn't take long to burn. An hour, tops."

"It's always over too fast," I said without thinking.

"Yeah." Boone was staring at me now. "That's right. But what do *you* know about it?" She took a step closer to me. "You've been to some dark places," she whispered, "haven't you?"

The door to the Bathhouse suddenly opened and two I-bankers flounced in, giggling wildly. They stopped when they saw us. Boone pointed the mop handle toward the door, and they hustled back out, but the moment had passed. I was saved.

That's the thing about secrets. Sometimes you have to keep the sharpest things hidden.

Later, when we walked out of the Bathhouse and into the waning light, the ground around us smelling fragrant and full, Boone swept her arm out in front of her, taking it all in: the pines, the dried needles on the ground, the stumps of fallen trees that were still beaded with sap, the splinter of Bob that we could see from where we stood. "You know," she began, "the only reason I'm here and not in juvie is because some Mormons took pity on the poor Minster delinquents — *Mill Casualties* they called us — and set up a fund with the Department of Juvenile Corrections to send us to places like this. Can you believe it? All of this," she said, "for one hour's work. Now that's what I call efficient."

"You like it here?" I asked. This was surprising.

"Who wouldn't?" she said. "It's our own Eden up here. You'll see. Colder, sure, and the snakes don't talk. At least, not the ones with scales."

She raised her eyebrows at me and flicked her tongue out from between her teeth, hissing. Then she laughed and walked away.

CHAPTER SEVEN

AS THE DAYS WORE ON, I DIDN'T KNOW WHAT TO MAKE OF the conversation I'd had with Boone in the Bathhouse. She hadn't mentioned the girl she'd killed, and I'd been too afraid to ask. I was starting to sense that there were layers to Boone's anger, her potential for harm. I hoped that our talk had kept me somewhere near the topmost layer, where I was safest.

With Gia, though, it was different. With Gia, I wanted to dive to the depths.

I was used to the general transparency of high school. Girls like Jules, Karen, and Gwen were as familiar to me as cutout paper dolls: the Cheerleader, the New Ager, the Goth. Boone was a special case, but I was beginning to feel like I had her number too. I would say that I had a five percent chance of guessing what she'd do or say at any given moment, and that was a huge improvement from the way things stood when I first got to Alice Marshall.

But Gia. Everything she said was new and unexpected. It was like I was being offered a delicate gift every time she spoke. And she *got* me. I saw that the first time we talked. When she said she sometimes felt like she was narrating her life, like she was standing outside and watching herself, I knew what she meant. And when I told her I felt vacuum-wrapped, she understood what I meant too. Sometimes, late at night as we rolled cigarettes next to each other on the beach, we'd be speaking so quickly, interrupting each other with words that overlapped and blended — almost into their own language, it seemed — that I felt light-headed.

We still didn't hang out during the day, though. Gia was always surrounded by her cabinmates and a loud group of Fifteens who clearly idolized her, and I didn't want to crowd her. Plus, I thought she was probably still shielding me from Boone's wrath. For at least a month, Boone and Gia did a pretty good job of managing, aside from meals and the occasional campfire, to never be in the same place at the same time. It was quite a feat, really. The only time that they were forced to be in the same room together was during Circle Share, which gave our particular session the gritty allure of a Spanish bullfight.

They never spoke to each other, but sometimes they would say things to other people that sounded like thinly veiled messages. Once, while a girl named Sara was talking about how her mother clearly preferred her sister, Boone interrupted. "It sounds like your sister's a prissy little bitch," she said, looking directly at Gia. "Does she think she's better than you? She's not. We all walk the same road."

"Sara," Gia interrupted smoothly, "I would worry about your own issues, not your sister's. Envy is an unattractive accessory." She looked at Sara sympathetically when she said this, and Sara blushed, worrying the frayed cuff of her jean jacket.

This kind of skirmish didn't happen every day, and it was subtle enough that Amanda never knew what was really going on. Those of us who were looking for it, though, could see exactly how much Boone hated Gia. It was palpable: a heavy, humid hatred that practically radiated from her skin. I wasn't sure how Gia felt.

Sure, she gave back everything Boone threw at her, but her voice held less vinegar, her eyes less fire. Sometimes, it seemed like she couldn't care less. And that was the most impressive thing of all.

The nail that Boone had pushed Gia up against on that first day was still sticking out of the wood by the door, like those historic battleground markers you pass on the side of the road. I never saw Gia look at it, but I caught Boone staring at it once from across the room. Her look was hard, like she was accusing the nail of failing her in some way.

It was early August, that time of the summer when it's not yet dark at dinner but no longer light as you brush your teeth before bed. Dusk stretched across the grounds for hours, bathing everyone in a gray that was sometimes murky, sometimes luminous. On the evenings when the light around us was clean and the shadows were kept at bay, Margaret would involve the whole group in a post-dinner game of Capture the Flag or a scavenger hunt. The days would shorten quickly, she said. We had to take our nights while we could still get them.

Sometimes, our nightly activity would include wish boats. Since Alice Marshall had rolling admissions, girls came and left at various times in the year. Whenever a girl was going home, we'd all fashion boats out of bark, decorating them with moss and tiny pinecones. Then we'd gather at the beach and send our boats drifting, along with a silent wish for the girl who was leaving. (I have a feeling that most of the wishes sent out on the water had nothing at all to do with whoever was escaping, but more to do with an expected care package, a letter from a boyfriend, maybe a silent hope that charges wouldn't be pressed after all.) In the past, Margaret told us, they used to glue candles onto each boat, but they stopped when they realized how much they were littering. I imagined thousands of birthday candles washed up on Bob's far shoreline and nestled in the dark belly of the lake. I wondered what the birds and bears and fish thought of these candy-colored twigs.

So when Margaret stood up at dinner one night and told us to grab a fleece and our headlamps and meet her by the docks in twenty minutes, I assumed that there was another good-bye ceremony, though I couldn't figure out who was leaving. But when we arrived at the dock nineteen minutes later, our fleeces bundled in our arms, we could see an armada of canoes on the beach, the paddles resting atop each red boat, a life jacket on each of the seats.

"We're going on a little water excursion," said Margaret. "There's something I think we should see."

I saw Gwen and Karen look at each other. It was forbidden to be on the water at night.

"We'll be out there a while, so there won't be any campfire tonight." Margaret waited while a couple of stragglers joined the group, and then she started again. "First things first. I'm going to need a volunteer to be my canoeing partner."

Some hands went up, though we knew the drill by now. Margaret never picked people who raised their hands. She already knew exactly whom she would choose.

"Boone," she said, "thank you for volunteering."

Boone scowled from where she stood near me, her hands stuffed in her pockets. I could tell she didn't mind, though, by the way she rolled her eyes, like it was almost harder to smirk than to smile.

"The rest of you, please get in pairs and get your vessels in the water. We'll reconvene at the end of the dock." Margaret paused. "And people. Life jackets. They aren't seat cushions. Wear them like a second skin."

There was the sudden commotion of girls yelling at one another, claiming each other as you would a seat on a bus. Jules caught my eye and smiled, motioning me to come over to where she was standing near an older canoe. I sighed, but was about to step toward her anyway when I felt a hand lightly graze my forearm. Gia was standing next to me. She didn't have a fleece with her, but was instead wearing a black, long-sleeved shirt with an Indian silk scarf wound loosely around her neck. I looked toward the water, where I could see Boone's back in the canoe as she and Margaret started paddling away.

"Ready, sailor?" Gia asked, and it was settled. We walked slowly toward the water together, me matching my steps to hers. I took off my shoes and walked into Bob's shallows, pulling a canoe behind me. Gia stepped in lightly before the boat was entirely in the water, and I pulled it a little farther before grabbing the sides for balance and getting in. I was sitting in the front, but I looked back at the shore before I sat down. Jules was just grabbing a canoe with Lucy, a sullen Fifteen whom I didn't know she was friends with. She caught my eye in the dimming light, but I couldn't tell if she smiled.

Gia and I sat on the bottom of the canoe, our backs resting against the hard edge of the wooden seats. The sides of the boat came up almost to our armpits, and I felt cradled, defended. We lifted the paddles from the water and moved them in graceful arcs through the air before dipping them down again and breaking the dark shell of the lake. A thin stream of water wound its way down the length of the boat, dampening the seats of our pants. We didn't say anything as we paddled — it was enough to listen to the sound the boat made as it cut through the water, following the faded yellow light of Margaret's headlamp in the gathering dusk as she and Boone glided across the lake in front of us. The canoes gradually started to spread out the farther we got from the shore, so that we must have looked, from above, like a scattered cluster of dots — a paper marked in red by an overly zealous teacher. The dark seeped in slowly, and now the outline of Buckhorn Peak rose up like a woodcut to our right.

My arms were starting to ache with the strain of paddling by the time Gia finally spoke. "God, this is beautiful." Her voice washed over my shoulders and ears like a soft wave. "I love the lake at night. No electricity, no nothing." She paused. "It gets dark like this in other parts of the world," she said. "Places where the light never seems to shine. You'd like it, I think. Travel. You'd make a very savvy foreigner." She laughed quietly.

I listened to the sound the water made, like a splitting melon, as my paddle plunged down into it once again.

"Have you traveled much?" I could hear water dripping from Gia's paddle each time it arced through the air.

"No," I said. "I mean, you know, just Seattle and Portland. Salt Lake, of course."

"What's in Salt Lake?"

"Nothing. Terri took me there a couple of times for back-to-school shopping. I hated it."

"Ah. Terri."

I'd told Gia all about my stepmother: how she married my dad when I was nine, how having a ready-made sullen daughter hadn't exactly been her plan, how she and I fought constantly when we weren't ignoring each other.

"But," she went on, "why did you hate Salt Lake? I mean, I don't know much about it, really, but I skied once in Park City, and that's nearby, isn't it? It was gorgeous."

"Well," I said, resting my paddle across the boat and letting us float, "we never went anywhere exciting." I paused, remembering. "There was this hotel that we stayed at, on the outskirts of town. We just lay in our beds after a day of useless shopping —"

"Why useless?"

"Nothing ever fit or looked right. Anyway, we'd just lie there on those beds and click through the cable channels, not saying anything, not even smiling in time with the laugh tracks. Just lying there, propped up by pillows. For hours."

"What a nightmare."

"It was," I said. "Everything, absolutely everything, was beige. And it was like Terri tried to match all of her outfits to the room:

beige khakis, beige blouses. She even had these sensible, cream-colored canvas shoes. Like she was trying to kill me with monotony."

"Oh my God." Gia laughed, and I was filled with a warm glow. I loved it when I made her laugh. "She sounds terrible," she said. "Typical evil stepmother syndrome. They're always jealous of the daughters. They pretend to try, but it's all just an act."

"Yeah," I said slowly, though I was remembering something else: me, nine years old, playing alone in my bedroom with Raggedy Ann, whom I knew I was too old to love but loved anyway. I was sitting on the floor, following Raggedy Ann as she waltzed through her day, shopping for groceries, going to a dance. There was a knock on my bedroom door, and Terri opened it. She was smiling — uncertainly, I could see now — and she had a small plate of cookies in one hand. *Oh, hello, Ann*, she had said to my doll. *I wonder if I might join you and Lida.*

I shook my head.

"What's wrong?" asked Gia.

"Nothing," I said, as I tried not to remember what happened next: the expertly aimed throw, the doll making contact with the plate, the cookies falling like fat tears onto the carpet, the door swiftly shut, the footsteps receding. "She's always been a bitch," I said.

"Sounds like it. Hey" — Gia's voice dropped lower — "I never asked. When did your mother die? I mean, how old were you?"

I focused on the distant orbs from the other girls' headlamps. "Eight," I said. "I had just turned eight." I held my breath, glad she couldn't see my face.

"Wow," Gia said. "That must have been hard."

I nodded, hoping she could see the back of my head. I didn't trust my voice.

There was quiet in the canoe as I took first one breath, then another. We rocked from side to side. The other canoes were ahead of us now, and I knew that we had to start moving or risk Margaret's wrath. I picked up my paddle and dug into the water again. Behind me, I heard Gia do the same.

"Hey — you don't have a stepmother, do you?" I said. Gia had never mentioned anyone in her family but her father, and even that had been in passing. We usually stuck to safer subjects: Alice Marshall, the other girls, Terri, strange things she'd seen during her travels. I never pressed her to talk about things she didn't want to go into, and she normally afforded me the same courtesy. She couldn't have known how her last question had affected me.

"I used to," she said. "I've had a couple, actually. They never last."

"Oh," I said. "Why not?"

"I guess Dave finally sees the light. Or something." There was a pause, and then she said, "One of them was okay, I guess, Leslie. She used to let me wear her jewelry."

"What happened? Why'd she leave?"

"Why does anyone leave? She was a bad fit. She just wasn't right for us," Gia added, something sharp in her voice. "Dave said that if she couldn't control —" She stopped talking.

"What?" I wondered what about Leslie had been so wrong that she wasn't worth keeping. I cleared my throat. "What did your dad say?"

"Nothing. He told her to leave, that's all." Her voice sounded distant.

"Were you mad at him?"

"Mad at him? Why would I be? He always does what's best for the two of us." I could almost feel her nodding in agreement with herself. "I'm his highest priority."

"You two must be close," I said, but I guess she didn't hear me, because she didn't say anything after that. We drifted on, edging closer to where the other canoes were now clustered near the northern shore of the lake, directly across from the school.

Margaret was already talking by the time we joined the group, twenty canoes bobbing silently on the still water. We pulled up in the shadows, and I could only see Boone's outline behind Margaret. I doubted she could see who was in the canoe with me, if she even looked.

"We would have hiked here," Margaret was saying, "but, as most of you know, Bob's circumference is not entirely navigable. I don't think that the school's insurance policy covers scaling the cliffs on the west side of the lake."

She paused while a few girls giggled. It was well known to everyone there but Margaret that one girl had scaled those cliffs in order to dive off them into the deepest part of the lake, and that girl was sitting right behind her in the canoe.

"It has occurred to me lately that we tend to forget to be surprised in life," she went on. Her voice took on the musing quality that it often had when she was thinking out loud. The giggles immediately died down. "Surprised by anything — the mundane, the beautiful, even the wicked. We think we can see everything coming our way, don't we? That it's already planned out, like a road map. And then the surprise, when it comes, is unwelcome." Margaret reached up and turned on her headlamp's high beam. "My challenge to you all this week is to welcome the surprises that come your way — both good and bad. If you can, even embrace them." She turned, shining her light on the rock wall behind her. We turned our lamps on too.

At first, it just seemed like the rock was wet, glistening and gray in the light. Then more lights were turned on, and suddenly the whole waterfall was visible, cascading down from what could easily have been the very top of the mountain. This was no trickle; the water coiled and rolled through deep crevices and out over the bare roots of trees before thinning near the bottom and slipping easily into the lake. Flowers jutted out of the rocks that lined the waterfall, their colors more vibrant in contrast to the inky night around them: blue columbine and pink monkey flowers, shining moss of the deepest green.

There was, I'll admit, a fairly audible collective sigh, followed by uncomfortable laughter. My face flushed with pleasure. We were just across the lake from the school, and not one of us had known the waterfall was here.

Margaret was right. It was a surprise. A beautiful one. And yes, I was delighted by it. But I was also delighted by the flaxen-haired girl in the boat with me, and by the prospect of the long ride back to shore. I wanted to stay and stare at this thing that had been here all along, graceful and lovely even before it had been seen, but I equally wanted to turn the boat and steer away from it, out toward the middle of the lake where I could be alone once again with Gia.

"Pretty cool, huh?" Jules and Lucy had drifted next to us, and Jules reached over and grabbed the side of our canoe, holding on to it with one hand so that if one boat moved, the other followed. Our headlamps were still on, pointing in unison at the waterfall, but the other girls had started whispering and laughing among themselves.

"Yeah." I swung my head around to look at Jules. The light from my headlamp hit her in the eyes and she ducked her head down until I turned it off. Lucy sat in the back of the canoe, glaring down at her life jacket. "I'm surprised no one knew about it," I said, wondering how long we'd have to endure this conversation.

Jules laughed. "Maybe Boone did," she said. "Maybe she swam over here after she jumped off the cliff."

"I highly doubt that," said Gia softly from behind me. She hadn't turned her headlamp on when the rest of us did, and her voice came from shadow.

No one said anything for a moment. Jules played with the strap on her life jacket with one hand. "Hey," she said finally, "you should come over to our cabin sometime, Gia. Sneak in during Toes-Up or something, you know?"

Gia didn't say anything. Lucy's scowl deepened, and as though Jules could feel it hitting her back, she added, "You too, Lucy, of course." The scowl relaxed. Jules kept going. "It just seems like, if we all just hung out a little more . . ." She let her voice trail off.

Then what, Jules? I wanted to ask her. *What do you think will happen? Gia and Boone will become bosom buddies? We'll all sit around singing "Kum-ba-yah"?*

In the distance, I could hear Margaret telling us to head back in. "It's the witching hour, ladies," she said, the words seeming to echo over the water.

Gia's voice came from behind me again. "Thanks for the offer," she said, "but I try to stick with places where I'm welcome." Her voice was friendly but firm.

"Yeah, but —" Jules started in again.

"Jesus, Jules, take a hint," I said sharply. "You're not, like, a genie. You can't just snap your fingers and make everyone get along. Don't be simple."

Jules let go of our canoe suddenly as though it were a scalding pan, and rubbed her arm. "Oh," she said, "I didn't mean . . ."

Lucy sighed with resignation and thrust her paddle in the water. The two of them started to float away toward the school with the rest of the group.

"Forget I said anything?" Jules's voice was small.

Gia waited until they were out of earshot before she spoke again. "She doesn't get out much, does she?"

"Clearly not," I said.

We turned the canoe around, and our boat moved slowly across the lake, at least five lengths behind anyone else. Bats swooped around us, skimming the water before lifting off and veering away. I had slipped into my fleece and buckled my life jacket over it while we were looking at the waterfall, but the slight wind that we created as we moved still seemed to seep through, tickling my skin.

"What'd you think of the waterfall?" I asked finally. I'd been enjoying the quiet camaraderie, but I wanted to hear her voice.

"Oh, that?" Gia laughed softly. "Very inspirational." She shifted in the boat. "Sometimes this place is a little too touchy-feely for me, you know?"

"A little too *Sesame Street.*"

"So many lessons —"

"So little time."

We laughed together.

"You'd think they'd get it by now," she said. "This place isn't a rehab clinic. It's not even one of those hard-core wilderness schools where they practically chain you to a tree until you discover your oneness with nature. It's just a way station."

"That's an attractive thought," I said. Truth was, I thought it might be a bit more than that. Truth was, I kind of liked the waterfall. But I wasn't about to say that.

"Oh, you get it, don't you, Lida? We're all just waiting here, inert — like mail that's being held at the post office while the homeowner is on a trip."

I smiled to myself. "Who are the homeowners?"

"Our parents, of course." I could hear Gia breathing heavily as she paddled and talked at the same time. "I think Dave's hoping to keep me out of the house until I'm too old to return."

"Oh no. I'm sure he —" I started to say, but she cut me off.

"Kidding," she said. "That's not what I meant."

"Okay." But I wondered what she *had* meant, if not that.

Gia changed the subject then, and started talking about some guy from Ireland who'd sent her a letter earlier in the week. I tried not to listen too closely. I couldn't keep track of her admirers, and frankly, they didn't interest me that much. Gia could quote entire letters to me — she had a photographic memory, she

99

said — but sometimes I wished she'd get a letter from a crazy aunt or a famous politician. Anyone but these love-struck boys.

We were the last ones to pull our canoe out of the water and hang our life jackets up in the ramshackle boat shed. Everyone else had already gone back to the cabins. We rushed to the Bathhouse, passing the rest of Gia's cabinmates as they headed toward their cabin, and brushed our teeth quickly and silently. The last thing either of us needed was Bev's steely eyes taking in our empty bunks during Lights-Out.

As we were finishing, two Fifteens came in. They'd clearly thought they'd have the Bathhouse to themselves, because the taller one had her arm slung around the other's shoulder and was whispering in her ear as they walked in. The girl being whispered to was blushing, and she was reaching up to grab the taller one's hand when she saw us.

"Oh," she said, dropping the hand. Without even looking at each other, the two girls whirled in unison and walked back into the night.

"What was that about?" I asked Gia. I rinsed my toothbrush and zipped it back into my plastic shower kit.

Gia smiled impishly. "I think we interrupted a bit of a rendez-vous," she said.

"What, like — ?" I looked at the open Bathhouse door, and the darkness beyond.

"Yeah, *like*." Gia shook her head, still smiling. "Young love. You've noticed what goes on around here, haven't you?"

I shook my head.

"But of course you've seen the 'couples' around school. Right? Holding hands at campfire, sneaking off from the Smokers' Beach late at night? Tell me you've seen them." She was laughing at me, and I blushed. "Don't worry. It's just playacting. As soon as they get out of here, these girls will go back to their lives and boyfriends and random hookups. But while they're here . . ." Gia shrugged. "Anything goes."

"Oh," I said. I stared down at the sink.

Gia elbowed me in the side. "Don't worry about it, Lida. It's as real as dreams." She winked, and was gone.

I gargled some water and spit it back into the sink before turning off the lights and walking back to my cabin in the dark. Were the two Fifteens out there, waiting for me to leave? Probably. I closed my eyes. I stood still, seeing one hand reaching for another, feeling the charge like static between them as they touched, and then I opened my eyes again and kept walking.

By the time I got back to the cabin, the other girls were already lying in their sleeping bags with books or journals.

"Damn," I said. "Has Bev already been by?"

"Bev's giving us the night off," Gwen said, her voice sleepy.

"No nighty-night bedtime kisses," said Boone.

"Good," I said.

"Hey, Lida. Where were you?" asked Karen. "I didn't see you out on the water. Did you escape to the Smokers' Beach?" A copy of *David Copperfield* was resting facedown on her stomach.

"I was out there," I said gruffly. I pulled myself up onto my bunk and swung my legs onto the mattress.

"I can vouch for her." Jules spoke cautiously, as if deciding upon each word as she said it. "She was there."

I knew that now she would tell everyone who I'd been in a canoe with, about the conversation she'd had with me and Gia, and I would have to explain myself. Maybe the other girls wouldn't care, but Boone would. I closed my eyes and waited.

But Jules didn't say anything. She yawned and turned over roughly in her sleeping bag. The rest of the girls took her cue. Gwen stood and turned off the light, and I heard the sounds of books being shut and dropped on the floor, sleeping bags zipping all the way up. I grabbed the flannel pajamas that I kept under my pillow and undressed in the darkness on my bunk. But I couldn't sleep. I felt off-balance, almost seasick. No matter how hard I tried to think of something else, I could hear the laugh that seemed to lie just underneath Gia's tongue as she talked about the Fifteens we'd seen. *Playacting.*

CHAPTER EIGHT

SATURDAYS WERE OUR ONLY FREE DAYS, AND EVEN THEN WE weren't exactly free. We still had our morning chores, still had Waterfront Hour, still had a campfire at the end of the day. The only things missing were our classes. (Even on Sundays, we had to attend shortened versions of math, science, and English. Thirty-minute sessions instead of an hour. Then, in the afternoons, there was usually a schoolwide workshop on self-esteem or communication skills, for example. Total waste.) Considering that we hardly had any homework as it was, our classes weren't the burden that they could have been.

Still, I felt unshackled on Saturdays. It always surprised me how everyone else knew just what to do with their free time. Some girls would write letters, paint, play horseshoes next to the Mess Hall, strum one of the few guitars that always seemed to be on hand. Sure, there were a few catfights, curses lobbed across the school grounds like footballs, someone arriving at the infirmary with a cigarette burn on her arm that she refused to explain — the natural results of unsupervised time. But for the most part, on

Saturdays, Alice Marshall seemed more like a finishing school for debutantes than a place where hard girls went to soften. Gia usually spent Saturdays in her cabin writing letters, or hanging out with her cabinmates on the dock. She told me that she didn't want to alienate herself from the other girls in her cabin, and I said that didn't seem likely, seeing as how they practically struck up a band every time she smiled.

I hated Saturdays. They just highlighted my inability to do very much with myself. I suppose I could have read — Alice Marshall had a tidy little collection of bookshelves in one corner of the Rec Lodge — but that seemed beyond pathetic. I could have hung around the other girls, like Jules (who was usually in the cabin with a notebook or a deck of playing cards), but the idea of making small talk was exhausting.

So I wandered instead. All over the school grounds. In and out of classrooms, around the Waterfront, winding a slow path through the cabin area and over to the Mess Hall. I would sometimes stop there and pick up a cup of coffee to take with me; I drank more coffee on Saturdays than the rest of the week combined. Sometimes I collected sharp rocks as I walked, dropping them into my pockets, only to shake them out later. I might see if I could glimpse the doe and fawn that sometimes napped in the dusty shade of the hall's slightly raised deck. From the Mess Hall I would walk down the subtle incline past the bell and toward the beach. Then I would turn around and go back toward the cabins. I could keep up this wandering for an entire afternoon. I just made sure to never stop moving.

I found myself doing just that a few days after Gia explained Alice Marshall's version of the birds and the bees. It was a bright day — the sun was just grazing the tops of my arms and shoulders. Some of the I-bankers had optimistically put on tank tops in the morning, though by lunchtime their arms were goose-pimpled and red. Margaret said that this had been a bizarrely rainy and cool season for the Frank. Still, the blue sky was promising. It had to start feeling like summer *sometime*, and this was the closest it had gotten so far.

I was doing my regular thing, wearing a nice groove between the Mess Hall and the Bathhouse with my feet, trying to keep my eyes simultaneously on the ground in front of me and on the look-out for Gia, when I ran into Margaret near the Bathhouse.

"Lida," she said, walking toward me. I always thought Margaret was taller than she actually was, and so was constantly surprised every time she came near enough for me to feel like I was towering over her. She stopped when she was a couple of feet away. "We haven't gotten much of a chance to talk lately. How are things? How're you settling in?" She was wearing a faded T-shirt and baggy jeans, and she scratched absentmindedly at a mosquito bite on her arm as she talked.

"Peachy," I said. "Lots of personal growth, lots of inner harmony."

"Sarcasm, sarcasm." Margaret shook her head, smiling. "Be careful, Lida. You might just find yourself growing harmonically when you're not looking."

"Pretty sure I'd notice," I said.

"Hmmm." Margaret stared at me for a minute, just long enough to make me feel uncomfortable. It was a real skill of hers. "Stranger things, Lida," she said, before walking away. "They've been known to happen."

Margaret headed toward the Mess Hall, and I turned to continue my pointless pacing. Boone was watching me from the doorway of the Bathhouse. She looked outfitted for combat: Her long braid was pulled tighter than usual, and she was wearing a pair of hiking shorts that appeared to be made out of canvas. It was the first time she'd worn anything besides her jeans, and I could see now that Boone had long legs as dark and smooth as river rock.

"Hey," she said, frowning at me. Ever since we'd cleaned the Bathhouse together, Boone had been looking at me like I was an exotic insect that she was about to name and pin to a wall.

"Hey." I looked again at her outfit. "Uh, going somewhere?"

"Hike."

"Oh." Boone was the only girl I knew at Alice Marshall who hiked for fun. She took what I'd been doing every Saturday and made it into something respectable: an outing. I shuffled my feet a little in the dirt.

She stuffed her fists into the pockets of her shorts. "Fine," she said, as though I'd asked. "Come on. Your scrawny ass could use some exercise."

I looked down at my legs. I always wore long pants, and that day was no different; I had on a pair of jeans that were almost dirty enough to pass as camouflage. Boone was right. I wasn't muscular. In fact, my legs resembled winter branches. "Um," I said, "I wasn't planning on —"

"What are you, an idiot? You're coming with me, Townie. Let's go." She spoke as though I had no choice in the matter, and frankly, I don't think I did.

"Okay," I said cautiously. "Let me just get . . ."

"Now," Boone said, jutting her chin toward the curtain of trees beyond the Mess Hall. "We're going."

She took off, and I took off after her, trying desperately to match my own clunking gait with her graceful one. I wanted to ask where we were going as we practically sprinted through the school grounds and into the trees. Once we hit a well-worn trail that led away from the school and up the side of a mountain, however, I knew exactly where we were headed, and I suddenly regretted having come.

Everyone said that the hike around Buckhorn Mountain, on the eastern side of Bob, was the easiest and most traveled trail in the area around Alice Marshall. The peak had a higher elevation than the mountains around Buckhorn, but the trail itself — if you were in good condition — could be scaled in a quick hour-and-a-half "jaunt." After all, you were *only* climbing about twelve hundred feet from the lake to the turnaround point. The path wound up and around the side of the mountain until it curved and started back down at the timberline. There were a few breaks in the trees where you could look out and see Bob and the school laid out prettily like some Swiss alpine resort — it's where I guessed most of the photographs for the brochure had been taken.

Personally, I had always thought that if Buckhorn was the easiest trail, then there was no way I would ever try to hike any of the others. I'd been on it a handful of times already in Outdoor Ed. Hikes don't get easier the more you do them: The incline stays just as steep, the rocky part just as forbidding, the footholds as elusive. The only thing that might change is the way your lungs contract and wheeze, and since I started my nightly pilgrimages to the Smokers' Beach, my lungs had definitely changed — just not for the better.

But we didn't take the usual path. Boone and I followed the Buckhorn trail at first, saying little to each other, scrambling in places and walking slowly in others. She seemed to float over the trail as though she didn't even notice what it was doing to her legs and chest. The subalpine fir trees and whitebark pines started to thin the farther we got.

When we reached the curve in the trail that switched back across the timberline and swung down to the school, Boone didn't turn. She marched straight ahead through the trees toward a rocky outcrop.

"Where are you going?" I called after her, but she didn't answer. I craned my neck, still panting from the climb, but I couldn't make out where she had disappeared to in the rocks. I stepped off the path and followed.

The outcrop that I'd seen from the trail was actually a mess of stone slabs and knee-high boulders that wound all the way around to the backside of Buckhorn. Stepping onto one of those rocks and looking out was like walking through a magic portal. The entire perspective changed. I found Boone standing on a boulder, her hands in her pockets like she was waiting for a bus, and I scrambled up to join her. From where we stood, there was no Alice Marshall. No Bob. No tiny specks of girls like little black ants crawling across the dock or beach. All I could see were endless, boundless mountains. Granite ridges; dark, knobby peaks; and almost everywhere, a green so deep and steady that it blurred my vision. Wrapped along the side of a mountain range in the distance was a swath of charcoal and nutmeg, where it seemed as though a painter had once brushed a forest fire across a canvas.

"Damn," I said quietly. "I didn't even know this was here."

"Seriously?" Boone laughed. "Where did you think we were living — a movie set?" She stared hard at the mountains in the distance. "There's the rest of the Frank. It's always been here. Always."

I had a hollow, sweet feeling in the pit of my stomach like I got when I imagined stepping off a plane into another country, another life. Giddy, and a little scared. Such immensity. I swallowed.

"So this is what you do, then, during Waterfront Hour," I said. "You just come up here and sit?"

"Hell no," said Boone. "This is only a rest stop. But don't worry," she added, glancing at me, "we're almost there."

We picked our way across the side of the mountain, stopping every few steps to look out at the view. It slowly became clear to me that we were following a crude path through the rocks of a talus slope, though it was barely discernible and absolutely confusing: sharp, right-angled turns, figure eights around boulders, and all the time, walking with one hand on the side of a rock in case we lost our footing and slipped.

The path crossed the backside of Buckhorn and turned before climbing steadily upward along the mountain's spine. It had gotten windy, the kind of wind that, when you're scrambling across a ridge with no buffer between you and either edge of the mountain, seems particularly insistent. I was already wondering how long we'd been out and how we were ever going to get back. I was also wondering if this had been a good idea. I mean, Boone could have just reached out and pushed me off any one of those boulders. Wouldn't have taken much. Just a flick of the wrist, really.

"There," she said, stopping next to a large rock and pointing above us. "The height of civilization."

And that's when I knew where we were.

I had seen the fire lookout from the school grounds. Everyone had. If I stood on the corner of the docks and craned my neck, Buckhorn Peak held court above the other rocky ridges off to the east, and on top of the peak, perched so precariously that it must have been held there by magnets, was what looked to be a tiny little shack. I never thought that (a) anyone could possibly live there, and (b) I would hike all the way up the peak to find out.

But indeed that's what I had done. We were standing maybe fifty feet below the shack now, and I suddenly understood what science teachers had been trying to tell me all along: Objects appear smaller from a distance. The shack was no paper hut — it was a large, octagonal wooden house with a thin deck attached to each of its sides. It still looked like it might topple over and crash down the mountain with the slightest puff of wind, but it was at least big enough to live in.

And someone did live there. I may not be a genius, but I do employ certain powers of deduction. As we made the final push up to the lookout, I was able to see quite clearly that this place was inhabited. Clue: A couple of socks were knotted around the deck's guardrail, drying in the sun. Clue: The air smelled of fried bacon. Clue: A man walked out the door of the lookout, waved to Boone, and said, "Elsa! Glad you made it!"

Elsa. I had never imagined that Boone had a first name. But here it was, ringing clearly in the air, and Boone gave me a warning glance — *Yeah, so what?* — before heading up to give the guy a hug.

"I brought someone," she said, pulling away from him and punching him lightly on the arm. "Lida."

He stepped forward and held out his hand. He must have been in his early twenties. Tall, rugged, wearing cargo shorts and a ratty T-shirt. The kind of good-looking that it's hard not to notice: floppy hair, perfect jaw, et cetera et cetera et cetera. I already assumed he was an asshole. But then he smiled, and I relaxed a little. His grin was just goofy enough to make him appear normal, even if only for a second.

"Ben," he said, grabbing my hand and shaking it. "Glad you came up here. I don't get many visitors."

"Thanks," I said, and shook my head. What was I thanking him for? Being lonely?

"You're welcome," he said, laughing. "Well, shit," he said. "I had better entertain you all, hadn't I? Either of you hungry?"

I glanced at Boone, unsure of how to answer. She had already walked out onto the hut's deck like she owned it, and was leaning over the railing. She looked over at Ben and nodded. "It's not like the food at school's gotten any better," she said. "It's still just congealed grease."

"Grease is good," Ben said, holding the door open for us. "It's nature's lubricant."

Boone rolled her eyes. "You are a sick man."

The inside of Ben's place looked like a ship captain's quarters. It was really just one big room with a cot in the corner and a

110

table in the middle that was piled high with books and papers and a couple of coffee cups. There were windows on all eight sides, with telescopes positioned on ledges under two of them. The little wall space between each window was taken up by what I recognized, thanks to Margaret, as topographic maps. I walked over to one of them and put my finger on Buckhorn Peak. Near it, I saw the watery dot that I knew must be Bob. I counted the contour lines from sea level to the top of the peak. "Eight thousand, six hundred feet," I said under my breath.

"Roundabouts," said Ben, surprising me. I didn't know he was standing close enough to hear. "That school of yours is at, what — seventy, seventy-one hundred? You know your way around a map, don't you," he said, handing me a cup of coffee. "Milk? It's powdered."

"I'll take it black," I mumbled. No wonder I was exhausted. We'd just climbed fifteen hundred feet.

"Good choice," said Ben. "I've been here for a couple of months, and I still can't get used to the taste of powdered milk. It's like chalk."

Boone was spooning the milk into her mug. "You just have to grow up with it," she said. "Then you won't want anything else." She continued heaping it in.

Ben turned on a small gas burner that was set up in one corner and cracked some eggs into a frying pan. "You guys don't mind a little midafternoon breakfast, do you? I just made the bacon this morning." He waved his spatula toward a plate on the table that was covered with thin strips of bacon.

"Sounds great," Boone said.

"You ever been to a fire lookout?" Ben asked me as he flipped the eggs over.

"No," I said.

"Ben can spot a match being lit from two hundred miles away," said Boone.

"Not quite, but I do have a view of a forty-five-mile radius from up here, and with my trusty maps, I can pinpoint the location of a puff of smoke to within half a mile. If something lights up, I'll be the first to catch it." He pointed the spatula at Boone accusingly. "Each time you all light up on that beach of yours, I have to hold my breath." ˙

She turned to me. "He's all-seeing, all-knowing. Just like God." Her voice was deadpan, but a smile winked at the corner of her mouth. It was as though, walking into this cabin, she had shed some coarse, rough coat and was stretching out her arms, comfortable in her skin. She lounged against one of the ledges beneath a window, smiling and chatting as though she had never thought to burn a building or cut a girl's hair as she slept. Or stab someone.

"Right," said Ben. "Just like that." He shook his head at Boone. "Little heretic."

I wandered over to the table, where the books were stacked unevenly. "Nice library," I said.

"Yeah," said Ben, "I keep meaning to build some bookshelves, but I always seem to be too busy." He laughed. "It's not like I'm overwhelmed with work here, but the hours do pass, you know?"

"What do you do, then, besides watch for fires?"

"He surfs the Internet," interjected Boone. She was having a good time. "Watches porn on the Playboy Channel. Goes out for drinks with friends."

"On the money." Ben divided the eggs onto two plates and laid some bacon across the top of each one. He handed the plates to Boone and me, and we dug in. "Well, I hike around in the early mornings, when there's less chance of a spark. I look for mountain lion tracks."

I stopped chewing. "Excuse me?"

"Pumas, cougars, mountain lions," he said. "It seems like every state has a different name for them." He laughed. "They're the most elusive of the forest creatures. You'll likely never see one.

But don't worry — they *could* eat you, but they *probably* won't."
Ben patted me on the back. "Not with all these delicious deer
running around everywhere."

"Oh." Mountain lions had definitely not been mentioned in
the Alice Marshall School brochure.

Ben shrugged and went on. "I read. I meditate. I chat with the
rangers down in Hindman on my walkie-talkie. Sometimes visitors hike in." He smiled at us. "Mostly I just sit around waiting
for Elsa to come break the silence."

Boone blushed and looked down.

"It's a nice enough way to spend five months," Ben said, "if
you can handle the isolation."

"I could handle it," said Boone, putting down her empty plate
with a clatter. That girl could sure eat quickly. "I'd love to not
have to deal with everyone else's shit."

It was exactly what I'd been thinking. Except I was also thinking that I wouldn't want to have to deal with my own. All that
time alone? It could be dangerous.

"Yeah, you'd do great up here," said Ben. "I wouldn't be surprised if you started talking to the animals." He turned to me. "I
don't know if you know it, but Elsa understands more about these
mountains than most geologists."

"Right. I'm a regular Annie Oakley," Boone said with a laugh.
"Shut up, Ben. Lida doesn't want to hear your crap." She was
trying to cover it with gruffness, but even I could see that she
was practically glowing with pleasure.

Ben raised his hands in surrender. "Okay, okay," he said.
"What about you, then, Lida? You think you could live up here
for a season? Get your supplies packed in on a mule? Learn how
to use an ax and a saw? Take bucket showers and use a latrine,
wait for the bears to come a-knockin'?" He picked up a book and
set it down again. "Are you a natural woodsman, like Elsa? Or
are you a city girl at heart?"

"Don't know," I said. "Neither, I guess." But that wasn't exactly true. When I'd looked out over the wilderness from the back of Buckhorn, I'd felt at once lighter and stronger. I'd sure as hell never felt that way in Bruno.

Ben eyed me for a moment. "Well, man, you'll have to work on that." He gestured to Boone. "You spend enough time with Elsa here, you'll quickly learn how you feel about nature."

"Yeah," I said. "I guess so." I felt strange, like I was watching two people who had always only spoken English suddenly begin speaking in Swahili to each other. But in this case, I was one of the people talking.

"Damn," said Boone suddenly, looking out the window at the sun. "It's already four." She shook her head at me. "I didn't count on the extra time it would take to climb up here with Townie. We have to go."

"Oh, so that's how it is. I can already see what you'll be like when you're older," said Ben. "Love 'em and leave 'em." He winked at both of us. "I wouldn't want you to get in trouble, though. Better get a move on."

Boone and I made our way to the door.

"Oh, Elsa," said Ben. "I almost forgot. I finished a book that I think you'd like." He picked up a hardback novel with an orange cover and handed it to her, glancing over at me. "*The Dharma Bums*," he explained. "Kerouac wrote it right before going to live in a fire lookout all summer. It's his best one." He winked at Boone. "I'll be interested to hear what you think."

Boone took the book without a word and wedged it in the waist of her shorts so that it lay flat against her back. She nodded.

"Thanks for coming," Ben said to us. "Lida, I hope to see you again. Maybe you can join the book club that Elsa and I have got going here."

"Sure," I said.

"Come on, Lida," said Boone, "hustle."

We hiked quickly away from the doorway of the lookout, where Ben was waving at us. I could see now that it had indeed gotten later; the sun was resting atop one of the peaks in the distance like it was trying to decide whether or not to go down. And so we hustled. Boone marched quickly ahead, and I scrambled after her, stumbling over the rocks when we got to the outcrop and sliding a little as we made our way down Buckhorn's switchbacks.

I didn't think we'd talk on the way back down, and was silently concentrating on not twisting an ankle or tripping on a log when Boone spoke.

"You're kind of funny, Lida," she said over her shoulder, "when you're not acting like the world's asking you to donate a kidney." She kept moving, though she slowed down enough that I caught up with her. "I've noticed the way you are with Margaret," she went on. "You're different with her. Sharper. You talk back." She kicked a rock off the trail. "You can be pretty sassy for a church mouse."

I blushed. I knew what Boone was insinuating, and what she was asking. She wanted to know why I was so outspoken around Margaret and so silent around her and the other girls. And I wanted to tell her. *Because there are two of me*, I wanted to say. *Because one Lida can crack a whip across her father's back with a single sentence and the other can't even look you in the eyes. Because that's how I've always been: one part nail and one part glass.*

But I just kept walking. "I guess I don't usually have that much to say."

"Right," she snapped. "My guess is that the things you don't say could fill a book." There was a pause, and then she chuckled, almost as though she was laughing at herself. "Whatever. Who am I to judge? Stay curled up behind the pew, little mouse. It's probably safer there, anyway."

All in all, our descent took less than half the time it had taken to climb up in the first place. We reached the base of the trail just as we heard the dinner bell start ringing. I started to sprint toward the Mess Hall, but was jerked back by Boone, who had grabbed hold of my sleeve.

"Not a word," she said. "And you don't go up there without me." The old Boone was back suddenly, her eyes glinting with the promise of broken arms, black eyes, sharpened blades.

"Okay," I said, and then continued boldly. "Hey. Are you guys . . . I mean, are you and Ben like . . . ?"

Boone stared at me as though I had suggested she check the dullness of a knife by drawing it across her own neck. "Don't be stupid," she said. "Ben is twenty-five. Besides, did you even see him? You think he looks twice at anything less than total perfection? Forget about it. He'd never even consider —" She shook her head at me angrily. "Seriously. Forget it." Boone let go of my sleeve and swung away from me, running toward the sound of the bell.

I would have run after her to tell her that her secret was safe. Maybe I would have even told her that I knew what it felt like to stand next to a sculpture and feel like a rock. But I didn't. I saw Gia instead.

She was resting against the front of the Mess Hall with her arms crossed. There was no one around her for once, since everyone else had already rushed in for dinner, and the way she looked off toward Bob intently, as though searching for a cloud that she'd misplaced, made her seem sad and a little vulnerable. Then she turned slowly and, seeing me, smiled. She was wearing a thin T-shirt with a feather reaching across it. Her hand rose in a half-wave and she left it there in the air, like a salute.

I walked over to her. "Hey. Cool shirt."

"Hey yourself." She tilted her head and smiled slightly. "I thought maybe I'd find you at the Waterfront, but I didn't see you." She shrugged. "Too bad. I wanted to go canoeing."

I tried to compose my face into a suitable imitation of her

expression: part nonchalance, part irony. I coughed to cover up the blush that was spreading down my neck.

"Sorry," I said. "I had this thing."

"I bet." Gia laughed. "Whatever. I found other ways to occupy my time." She stood there for a long, delicious moment, smiling at me with that look on her face that felt like a promise. "Well? Shall we?" She nodded at the Mess Hall door.

"Sure," I said, and followed her in.

We hung out at the Smokers' Beach that night, and the night after that. It felt like there was a perfect silver ring that encircled us whenever we were together, and I didn't want to tarnish it. But every night as I walked away from the Smokers' Beach, the taste of cigarettes heavy as soot on my tongue, I wanted more.

Yes, I wanted more. I wanted to raise my eyebrows at her whenever Boone got into one of her moods and said something sharp. I wanted to pick the locks on the Mess Hall windows at night and push her through, arms first; I'd wait out there in the cold, hugging myself and keeping watch, whispering the same song lyrics over and over to myself until her head appeared in the window and she dropped an armload of Triscuits and cheese, yesterday's cake, a can of whipped cream at my feet. I wanted to sit next to her around the campfire and hold her pale hand during the last soulful songs. But even more than that: I wanted her to give me something I could use in our friendship, like an orienteering tool — a compass or a thermometer, at least — something to give me direction, to gauge the meaning of her laughter and her silence. I wanted to hear her say *best friend*, to watch her mouth form each perfect word.

But these things didn't happen. The closest I got — the closest I would ever get, it seemed — to really knowing what Gia thought of me were the little comments she dropped like jewels for me to pick up and slide in my pockets surreptitiously. Calling me her old so-and-so, a name so strange it was almost sweet. Telling me I was a badass. And one evening, late, walking with me to my cabin and saying in a half whisper, "I've been around the world two or three times, Lida, but I don't think I've met anyone like you."

It was enough. For the moment, at least.

Epilogue

I'm writing this for her, of course.

Really.

No, really.

Now see, just as soon as I wrote that, I read it over again, and here's what I said to myself, loud enough to slap myself in the face with it but not loud enough to wake my dad and Terri: "What utter crap."

Am I writing this just for her? Impossible. If I'm being honest (and admit it, it's time to be honest), I'm writing it more for me than for her, since she'll never read this anyway. I'm writing it for the things I should have said but did not, and the things I should have done but could not.

I can hear you now. "But, Lida, it's been over a year. Can't you, um, just move on?"

Answer: I can. I have. Kind of. To those who watch me (Dad, Terri, Dr. Hemler), I'm doing well. Better than that, even: I'm doing extremely well. Impressively well. And most of it's real. I knew what I needed to do to survive when I left Alice Marshall; I knew that if I didn't reach into the world, I wouldn't make it a week back in Bruno. So I reached. And there

were hands to grab on to, and voices urging me forward — and I did move,
step by step, into a life that has sheltered me so far from my memories.

I was able to hold them at bay for a long time. But ever since Margaret
started calling, things have changed. Now, sitting up in bed in the middle of
the night, my sheets tangled around my waist, I am caught by my memories,
which rush at me with accusing fingers and leave me shaken and helpless.
I've begun to worry that the past year and a half has all been a ruse, a castle
on a fault line, the earth's plates shifting at any moment, even now.

So, yes. I write it for her. But oh, oh, oh, I write it for me.

CHAPTER NINE

BOONE AND I DIDN'T TALK ABOUT THE HIKE TO THE LOOKOUT;
she didn't mention it, and I was afraid to. I couldn't figure out
why she'd taken me up there, and the Elsa who chatted comfortably with Ben was nowhere to be found at school. Once we
got off the mountain, she was the same unpredictable Boone.
Same anger bubbling under the surface like hot tar. Same ability
to shut a person down with a single look. The only difference I
could see was in the way that Boone treated me when we were
alone together. If I found her in the cabin before the other girls
came in, or if we were alone on the beach at the tail end of
Waterfront, Boone would make the occasional joke, looking at
me like she knew I'd get it. Sometimes, she would even laugh. It
was subtle, but it was there: an acceptance, even — maybe — a
grudging regard.

Boone couldn't have known about the time I spent with Gia; if
she had, she would never have invited me on the hike. She would
definitely not be making jokes with me. So I certainly wasn't
about to bring it up. I learned that lesson soon enough.

We were sitting around the table at lunch. Karen and Gwen were talking about something having to do with shampoo, maybe hair spray, and Jules was smiling around hopefully. I was trying not to look over at Gia's table. Boone was shoveling down a bowl of disgusting chili, but she looked up sharply when she heard Jules say, "I would give anything to have hair like Gia's. It's just so silky. What kind of conditioner do you think she uses?"

"Next subject," Boone said, narrowing her eyes at Jules. "You're ruining my appetite."

Jules looked swiftly down at her plate. "Sorry," she said.

"Why do you hate her so much?" The words were out of my mouth before I had a chance to take them back.

Boone leaned over and spat on the floor before answering, which should have been a sign.

"What's there to like?" she'd said. "I know her kind. She's worse than the I-bankers."

"I don't think —" I started, and she raised her hand swiftly in front of my face, either an innocent Stop sign, or the beginning of a slap. She narrowed her eyes.

"You got a horse in this race, Townie?" she asked.

I shook my head.

"Then shut the hell up."

Circle Share continued to meet once a week, and it wasn't until mid-August that I had to decide between Gia and Boone. It was a hot day, the kind of glaring hot that sinks all the way through your skin, and everyone was moving more slowly. It felt like it was going to rain, but so far, the only moisture I felt was that of my own sweat. I was washing my face in the Bathhouse, pretending that I was submerged in the chilling depths of Bob. Since I refused to go swimming, even though I love it, this was as close as I got to feeling the relief of cool water. I could have stayed there forever, which is why I lost track of time. I was a few minutes late getting to the Rec Lodge.

The transition from the brightness of the afternoon sun to the dim, shaded interior of the building was disconcerting, and I blinked rapidly, trying to focus. Almost everyone was there already. The worst part was, they were apparently waiting for me. I started toward the group, scanning for an empty seat, and then I stopped. There were only two open spots. One was next to Boone. One was next to Gia. I swallowed.

"Welcome, Lida," said Amanda. "Take a seat wherever you like."

I took an uneasy step forward. If I sat next to Gia, Boone would declare war on me too. This was no child's game. My hair would be the least of it. But if I chose Boone, would Gia speak to me again? My breath caught in my throat. She could pick any girl at the school to spend her time with — any of them. Why would she waste her energy on someone who was too weak-minded to pick a goddamn place to sit?

Amanda tilted her head. "Is something the matter?" She gestured around the circle. "Don't worry — we haven't started yet. We were just about to begin."

I took another step forward, my feet moving in slow motion. But maybe Gia would think that I hadn't seen the place next to her. Or, if I did, that I wouldn't think it was for me. And was it? Really, who did I think I was? Why did I think she would even want to sit next to me? Of course she would assume that I would sit with my cabinmates. It's what anyone else would do.

I walked quickly to where Boone was sitting and plopped myself down, bending over to retie the laces of my shoes. When I sat up again, Amanda had begun the incantation.

"We are kind to others; we are kind to ourselves," we said in unison. "We honor the Circle of Truth."

I studied my lap, raising my eyes briefly to look at Gia. She sat tall and regal in her chair, staring straight ahead. On the seat next to her was a small notebook that she sometimes carried around. I exhaled the breath that I hadn't known I was holding. Had the notebook been there all along? If so, that seat had never been mine.

Amanda began the session by talking about the idea of centeredness, of having a place within yourself to come back to, again and again, even during the difficult times. As she finished speaking, the other girls started adding their own voices, everything blending together in a monotonous, calming drone.

Slowly, I let my mind wander away from the room and its inhabitants. I pictured the cafeteria of Bruno High School, the parallel rows of long, white tables that always seemed to be claimed by bands of girls who waved their friends down from across the room. The tables all had their own groups of people — speaking their own languages, it seemed, like small, proud European countries. I had always eaten in the hall. Now I added another white table to the room, with a girl sitting on each end of it, both of them waving to me.

I kept that image in the back of my head as I listened to a Fifteen talk about how, after she'd broken into her parents' wine bar and stolen their money, she felt calm, at peace. Boone agreed with her and then sat back, clearly done talking for the day. Another Fifteen named Crystal chimed in with her own Thing: running away to Santa Cruz with a group of high school dropouts. She began to relate it to what Amanda had said, but I wasn't paying attention. It was all lies, anyway, everyone rewriting their stories as they spoke so that all of the insight that they had since adopted was available to them back then, even as they broke windows and panhandled on the boardwalk. I didn't need to listen to this crap.

". . . To think about not just *what* you've done, but *why* you've done it."

I snapped back to attention when I felt Amanda's eyes on me. I may not have said a word in Circle Share, but I spent enough time halfheartedly listening to notice the way Amanda talked about our Things. And it was clear that, right now, she was talking about what I called our Sea Level Things.

The Sea Level Thing. The place from which your Thing (or Things) sprang up like a jagged mountain. Because, see, even though most girls were sent to Alice Marshall for one specific thing that they did, a final straw like robbing a wine bar, our Things were more complicated than that. They were as layered as the contour lines on a map. You got to the summit of one Thing, only to realize that there was a steeper, craggier Thing looming above it — something else you'd done that no one knew about, for instance. And another one above that. And one above that. And lying there at the base of them all, the line that encircled all of the other Things somewhere around sea level, was usually a word. *Loneliness. Fear. Rejection. Failure.* It was embarrassing to realize that everything that felt so utterly complicated could be summed up in a word. It made me feel simple, like I'd been staring at a math problem for years that a first-grader could just walk up and solve.

"Lida," Amanda said now, "how do you feel about what Crystal said? Does any of it sound familiar to you?"

"What?" I asked.

"Maybe you would like to share some of your own experiences," she said. "We haven't heard much from you."

I looked quickly at my knees. "Oh," I said, "that's okay." I waited for the moment to pass, as it always had whenever Amanda singled me out.

But Amanda didn't say anything else, and when I finally looked up again, she was still staring at me. Everyone was. Even Boone looked mildly interested. She had her head cocked to one side, and she was smiling at me as though encouraging a toddler to walk across some railroad tracks. Gia knit her eyebrows together and gave me a sympathetic frown. Everyone was waiting, and this time, they weren't giving me an out.

Think. Think. Think. Think. The word kept repeating in my head, silencing all the other sounds around me. It was as though I was watching the word march from one side of my brain to the other and then back again. *Think.*

I stood up so quickly that I almost knocked my chair over. I steadied it and pushed it back from the circle. "I . . . I'm sorry," I said. "I don't feel very well."

Amanda raised her eyebrows. "I see."

I placed one hand on my stomach and one hand on my head. I knew I must look like a preschooler or a clown — *Now pat your head and rub your stomach!* — but I couldn't think of what else to do. "Really," I said. "I think I'm going to be sick. May I go to the restroom?" I was using my most courteous voice. I was almost unrecognizable. I stepped around the chair and nodded my head toward the door.

Amanda sighed. "Sure," she said. "Take all the time you need." As I walked out, I heard her say, "Now, Shandra, what about you?"

I couldn't walk away fast enough.

And the funny thing is, I thought I'd gotten away with it. I hid out in the cabin for the rest of Circle Share, scratching my initials into the side of my bunk with a pen cap. I lay on my bunk during Waterfront, pretending to be asleep. I even sat with my cabin at dinner without being asked about my "illness," though Boone did pull me aside as we walked into the Mess Hall and whispered, "No one leaves Circle Share, you idiot." I hoped perhaps that no one besides her had noticed that I left so abruptly. Or that no one cared.

I was so wrong.

Margaret caught up to me as I was walking with Boone and Jules out of the Mess Hall. She was wearing her train conductor overalls again, and had tossed a knit cap over her spiky hair. "Lida," she said. "A minute, please?"

"Sure." I shrugged, and turned to follow her. I looked back in time to see Boone smirk at Jules and mouth something indiscernible.

Margaret and I headed through the trees toward the beach. The sun had just set, and Bob had the blue-black, forbidding darkness that it always got that time of night. It had never rained, but once the sun went down, a familiar chill had descended over the school. We walked out onto the dock, and looked across the water.

"Let's talk," Margaret said, and paused. "I hear you were sick during Circle Share."

I was quiet. The dock rocked under our feet in time with my own breath.

"I get the feeling that you think talking is an elective at Alice Marshall." She spoke softly, so that I had to strain to hear her. "Lida, it's not. You'll come away with nothing if you don't open up and share. You've been here for almost two months. It's time to start participating." She looked at me and sighed. "Whether you admit it or not, your past actions have affected others. Including yourself." She said it like it was something I owned and had neglected, set aside on a windowsill and forgotten about. *Your Self.* "You still need to repair those relationships."

"How?" I asked. I wanted to explain to Margaret that my Thing was a relentless series of events that I couldn't change and would never escape. How could I repair relationships when I didn't have any relationships to begin with?

Margaret pulled her knit cap down farther over her ears. "These Things don't happen *to* you, Lida. You *choose* them. Or if you don't choose them, you at least choose how you react to them.

127

Once you accept that you are responsible for your happiness, you'll begin to work on the things that could make you happy. Family. Friends. Yourself."

She said *yourself* again in that way of hers. Only Margaret could do this. Only Margaret could sound like Yoda and yet also like a rock star.

I swallowed. If I looked carefully, I thought I could just see the peaked roof of Ben's lookout.

"Lida," Margaret began again, but I interrupted her.

"I can't," I said.

"Can't what?"

"Can't talk about my Thing." I was breathing quickly now, and my face felt hot.

Margaret looked at me steadily. "You can," she said.

"No, I can't."

She didn't take her eyes off me. "You are no different from any girl here," she said. "Your problems are no greater and no less important than anyone else's. The only difference that I can see, Lida, is that you're unwilling to do the work of healing." She spoke matter-of-factly, unsympathetically. The Margaret I knew was gone, replaced by someone who sounded just like Bev, just like every guidance counselor and therapist I had been dragged to see in the past year.

"Healing?" My voice was loud and sharp in comparison. "What healing?" I took a deep breath and continued. "Am I supposed to tell everyone what happened? If I just say it, will it be like — windshield wiper, it's erased?" I waved my arm mechanically in front of my face, half laughing, half shouting. I felt unhinged. "No, thank you." There were tears in my eyes, and I blinked quickly, hoping Margaret hadn't noticed.

"Lida," Margaret said more softly, "I understand how you're feeling. You're afraid that you'll expose your pain and that nothing will change."

One tear rolled down my cheek, and I swiped at it angrily with the cuff of my hoodie.

Margaret continued. "But I can promise you: Telling your truth makes all the difference in the world. Some of the girls here will be grappling with the consequences of the things they've done for years. Some of them have already been to juvie, you know, and some will end up going back. But they will be in a different place when they do. It's not what they've done that changes; it's how they relate to it."

There was a slight wind coming off the lake, and I hugged myself.

"Look," she went on. "Why don't you start by writing it down. You don't have to show anyone. Just get it out somehow. Start at the beginning. Leave nothing out. Can you do that?"

I nodded once.

"Good." Margaret turned to go. With her back to me, she said, "And, Lida, this isn't a suggestion. It's a requirement — if you want to stay here, that is." She walked back down the length of the dock, her footfall as gentle and quiet as a cat's.

That night, after Bev had checked on our cabin, I pulled my headlamp out from under my pillow and put it on. I opened my unicorn journal in the weak light of the beam.

"What are you doing?" asked Jules from across the room.

"Mapping my world," I said. "It's very therapeutic."

"Good luck," said Boone. "If you figure out where you are, let us know."

"Ha-ha," I said.

We'd been Mapping Our World for a couple of weeks now, though I didn't have much to show for it. A few doodles of trees and flowers; one rough sketch of a woman, her hand resting on a doorknob.

The cabin was quiet. I turned to a fresh page in the journal. *Start at the beginning*, Margaret had said. *Leave nothing out.*

I stabbed at the journal swiftly with my pen. It poked a tiny hole through the paper. *There,* I thought to myself. *That's* what it was like. I stabbed at it again. And again. And then I started writing.

My mother's not dead.

I put the pen down and looked at what I'd written. I could see the letters, but it was strange — they didn't seem to work together to make a whole word, a complete sentence. So I grabbed the pen and wrote it down again.

My mother's not dead.

Now they started to make sense. I kept writing.

She's not dead, but I don't know where she is.

It was so hard to keep my hand steady as I wrote. I was shaking, and I knew it was just a matter of time before the tears started to fall, so I wrote faster, the words starting to resemble scattered twigs across the page.

It'd be so easy to say it doesn't matter. To say, maybe, that an eight-year-old can't know her mother that well anyway, and that kids heal, they're resilient, blah blah blah — all the things I said to the family therapists that my dad and Terri dragged me to those first few years.

Deep breath.

But I did know her. I knew her in fragments.

Making up a new recipe on a Sunday morning, laughing as we threw eggs and flour and basil and celery into a pan and watching it bubble through the clear oven door.

Walking around the neighborhood together when I couldn't sleep. Summertime, the evening still light enough for me to see the outline of her hands, stuffed in her pockets. Her voice a perfect monotone as she answered my stupid questions about flowers and trees.

Waiting for her inside the school after everyone else had been picked up. How she ran in, her apology too loud. How, in the car, her face had dis-solved into someone else's face. Why didn't you remind me. You have to remind me next time. *She was only wearing one earring. She'd forgotten her shoes.*

Watching my birthday cake sail into the backyard, landing upside down in the rhubarb.

Dancing in the living room to an old ABBA record. Her arms like propellers. Her head like a hammer.

And this one, again and again: Standing next to her at the kitchen table, waiting for her to look at me. How she'd reach over and touch my head absentmindedly from time to time, like she was reminding herself that I was still there. Still a burden. Still the one wrong thing in her life that she couldn't get away from.

Until she did.

If my father knows where she is, or has heard from her over the years, he's given no indication. He's never talked about where the divorce papers came from, though I saw them once in an envelope on the kitchen table. I didn't ask, because I didn't want to know. Even then, I understood that there's never going to be some great drama in which I finally meet my mother again and ask her why she left and it turns out that she worked for the mob, or had a tragic past that was about to catch up with her, or even that she just got lost one day and never found her way back. That's not what happened.

And sometimes, I can even convince myself that I'm okay without her. Okay with not knowing why she left, or why she hasn't come back, not once, to see how I've grown. But other times, I know that her absence means everything. *Then I feel this canyon inside of me, and I know that, somewhere at the bottom, is her reason for leaving. And that reason was me: something I did, something I said. Or maybe everything I ever did or said — all of it wrong, from the very beginning.*

I reached up and angrily wiped my face with the back of my hand. I turned more toward the wall so that no one could see me crying if they woke up.

Oh, Dad tried, at first. He said everything the child psychologist told him to, like it wasn't my fault and I still had him, and my mother loved me even though she left. Then he ran out of steam, and I stopped being eight. We never mention her anymore, and if we do, it goes something like this:

Me: Why the hell would you ever buy a compost bin, if you don't like vegetables?

Dad: I didn't. That other person did.

Terri: Who wants some coffee?

Me: Fuck off.

That other person. It's what we've always called her. As in, that other person in the checkout line, that other person in the emergency exit row, that other person in the room right here, right now, every single day, breathing in my ear, looking past me, telling me good-bye.

There it was — my Sea Level Thing, my pain. I hoped that my cabinmates couldn't hear me crying, my breath coming out in harsh bursts. I was suddenly so tired. I wanted nothing more than to put the pen down and go to sleep, but I knew I couldn't stop now. I was done lying — I'd shared the beginning. Now I had to share the rest. I had to write about what I'd done.

And so I kept writing. I wrote until the cabin's windows started to shimmer with the approaching dawn. I wrote until it was all there, every contour line accounted for, what happened that day in the bathroom, what happened at the hospital. I put into words, for the first time, what I'd done and why I'd done it: my Thing. And then I slept soundly, filled with a peaceful exhaustion that I hadn't felt since I was seven.

Epilogue

I know I look terrible. I didn't sleep last night, because I was up writing, collecting the words from somewhere in the back of my mind and setting them down again. It was the second night in a row that I haven't slept, and my hair, which hangs below my shoulders now, is greasy and tangled. Normally, I wouldn't go to school with it looking like this, but some things are more important than glossy, cascading locks. Besides, the BHS Telegram is meeting later today for the last time before graduation, and nothing says "literary magazine" like poetically disheveled hair.

I'll never forget how it felt to write in that purple unicorn journal. I've done a lot of work over the past year and a half, hard work involving expressing and explaining and dialoguing and internalizing and externalizing — all words Dr. Hemler has thrown at me (and with good reason). But nothing I've done can compare with what it was like to write down my Thing for the first time, to just put it on paper and make it real. It seems so clear to me now, but I didn't even know what my Sea Level Thing was until I started writing.

And now I'm doing it again. Therapists are smart, but they don't always ask the right questions. Dr. Hemler might say: "Have you made your peace with what happened, Lida?" and I would say, "Yes." But if he were to ask me, for instance, if I've forgiven myself, I would have to say, "I'm trying. I'm really trying." And then I'd pick up my pen.

$\mathscr{C}$HAPTER $\mathscr{T}$EN

"YOU'LL NEED YOUR SLEEPING BAG, OF COURSE," MARGARET was saying. "And your raincoat. We wouldn't want to forget *that*."

Margaret had told us that the rains in central Idaho usually stopped by early to mid-July, but it was the fourth week of August, and it just seemed to be getting worse. After a spell of hot weather, the clouds had moved in and taken up permanent residence. Rain wept down the windowpanes of the Rec Lodge. We were seated around the fireplace, listening to Margaret as she paced around us, ticking items off on her fingers as she talked.

"Headlamp, some sort of hat, lots and lots of extra socks." She paused. "I don't think I have to tell you how important those will be."

Our shoes were lined up behind her in front of the fireplace, drying. I looked around at the other Sixteens. We were all wiggling our toes in soggy socks, trying to warm up.

"I'll be bringing plastic bags to tie around our shoes, in case we get caught in another downpour like today on the overnight."

Someone groaned — Gwen, probably, or one of the I-bankers. I touched the toes of my right foot. The sock was still cold, clammy as a wrung-out washcloth.

We'd spent the morning hiking up and around Red Dot Trail, over toward the cliffs, working on our "elevation sprints," as Margaret put it. Elevation sprinting apparently meant scrabbling up slick boulders and down again (muddy hands, the knees of my jeans soaked through), and hiking uphill whenever the opportunity arose, even if it meant going back up the way we'd come if we'd just walked downhill. We were all pissed off and exhausted, not to mention unbelievably dirty, like a motley crew of plumbers and mud wrestlers. I couldn't imagine what we'd look like after the overnight, if it meant enduring two rainy days like this one.

"Fine," said Margaret finally. "I can see that whatever I say now will be lost on you lot. Go get showers. Get warmed up before lunch. We'll finish planning the overnight tomorrow."

Someone cheered, and there was a smattering of applause as we scrambled to our feet and rushed out the door toward the Bathhouse, only a few of us pausing to put our shoes back on as we went.

The scene in the Bathhouse was as chaotic as it was every morning about five minutes before the breakfast bell was rung. The I-bankers had taken over the sinks with their professional hair dryers and Gucci makeup bags. Clothes were strewn everywhere, dropped on the rubber mats in muddy piles and hung carelessly over the sides of the shower stalls where they dripped in the increasing steam. Boone, Gwen, and Karen sat on one of the wooden benches in the middle of the room, hunched together, whispering. I planted myself in front of them, mock-soldier style.

"Some hike," I said, and watched as Gwen blinked twice at Karen before smiling at me. I knew they weren't sure what to make of my rather sudden desire to actually make conversation; to be honest, I didn't quite know what to think of it either. I only knew that, ever since writing down my Thing the week before,

I'd felt lighter, easier. It wasn't some miraculous transformation, but it had started to feel like more work to ignore them than to talk to them. So maybe that *was* a miracle.

Boone looked up. She was sitting on her hands to keep them warm. "That's not even the half of it," she said. "Wait until Margaret's got us loaded up with food and camp stoves and we're hauling ass up the side of some canyon."

"That woman loves a good walk," said Gwen.

"I wonder what kind of New Age bullshit she's going to spring on us this time," mused Boone.

Gwen giggled. "Remember the last hike? How she made us lie on our backs at the top of Bernard Mountain and contemplate the term 'common decency'? What was that gross book she was reading from?"

"*The Plague*," said Karen, "and we liked it."

"*We* would."

"Fuck off."

Boone laughed. "Time before, she had us writing love letters to ourselves. That was a mistake. Some of the letters were, uh, quite *intimate*."

Jules stepped out of one of the showers, wrapping herself awkwardly in a large flannel shirt. She sat down next to Karen, held her jeans out in front of her, and looked at them balefully. "Cold, wet denim," she said. "This is gonna be good." Jules glanced behind her at the empty shower. "Anyone want it? Lida? Grab the shower now, before someone else does."

I wrapped my arms around myself and was about to make some excuse about not wanting to warm up just to get cold again or something, when I was saved by another Sixteen, who practically threw herself into the shower stall.

"Shit," I said, hoping my voice sounded sufficiently disappointed. "So anyway," I went on, "have you all been on an overnight before?"

The four of them nodded.

Great. I was going to be the only one out there without a clue.

"Don't worry, Townie," said Boone, smiling mischievously, "you won't be alone out there. This isn't the Solo Trip that Margaret keeps yammering on about — that comes later." She stood and, with an expertly aimed throw, tossed her towel over the side of one of the shower stalls just as another Sixteen walked out, clutching her own towel tightly around her body. "I'm calling that one," Boone said loudly enough for the room to hear. She turned back to me. "And anyway, you're never *really* alone in the woods. Bobcats, mountain lions, bears . . ." She let her voice trail off as she stepped toward the shower. "And if that's not enough," she said over her shoulder, "you've always got your shadow."

"God, it's tenacious," said Gia, shaking her head. "I mean, this rain is just *enduring.* It kind of reminds me of monsoon season," she added. It was Waterfront Hour, and the two of us were seated in the Mess Hall, drinking hot chocolate and watching some of the Fourteens as they wove lanyards and gossiped. It was clear from the way some of them held the completed ropes between their index and middle fingers, gesturing while they talked, that they'd much rather be sitting on the Smokers' Beach, holding something else.

Gia and I had started hanging out during our free time, usually sitting somewhere quiet where we could talk and not be disrupted. Gia never approached me when I was with Boone and the others. She always stared past Boone in the Mess Hall or around the campfire, her expression blank, just like she was looking through the window of a fast-moving train. Because we never spoke while I was around my cabinmates, the time I spent with Gia still felt precious, like a jewel sewn into a pocket.

"Monsoon season?" I asked.

"Bali, remember?"

"Oh, right." It was hard to keep track of all the places she'd been. "When were you there?"

She waved her hand in the air. "A couple of years ago."

"Oh. Sorry."

"That's okay," she said.

Even in the rain, even with a giant bronze raincoat draped around her shoulders, Gia looked glamorous. She'd put her hair up in a messy knot, and a few pieces fell around her cheeks like tinsel. I self-consciously touched the matted tips of my hair, which was at what I believe is commonly called "the awkward stage": still too short to pull back, but just long enough to hang in my eyes and swing into my food while I ate. It didn't help that, when it rained like this, my complexion resembled that of a dead fish, one that had been floating belly-up in the lake for some time. Not Gia. If anything, the dark skies outside only provided contrast to the brightness of her eyes.

"— but he wasn't quite how I imagined," she was saying, and I realized that she'd been talking the whole time I'd been staring at her hair, her eyes. I hadn't been paying attention when I should have. This had been happening more and more often.

I nodded, but not before Gia saw my jolt of guilt and surprise. Her voice was quiet. "I'm boring you," she said.

"No, you're not."

"I guess I probably do talk about the same things over and over." She looked down at her lap. "Maybe it does get kind of boring."

It was true that I'd heard these stories before, but I wasn't bored — it wasn't that, exactly. There was nothing she could say that would *ever* sound monotonous to me. But how could I tell her that I wanted the stories beneath the stories, the things she wouldn't say in a room full of girls, things she might tell only me? I felt like I was trying to take a bath in a few inches of water. I couldn't settle into the conversation like I wanted. I could almost see the right words — any words, really — float away before I could grasp on to them. So I just shook my head.

She must have seen my discomfort, because Gia reached across and laid a warm hand on my arm, squeezing lightly. "Sorry. Forget about it; I think I'm just sensitive." She quickly changed the subject, and started talking about her cabinmates. Something about a boyfriend in Australia or Austin, I wasn't sure.

Wasn't sure, and didn't care. All I cared about right then was my brain. My fuzzy, cotton-swabbed, frisked, and addled brain, good for very little besides directing me into, and out of, awkward situations. I wondered if there was some way to vacuum it up, clean out all the dusty corners and make it shining and bright, all hard surfaces and gleaming appliances. But nothing seemed to work. Lately, whenever I was with Gia, I couldn't focus on what she was saying; I could only focus on her gestures, her eyes. My thoughts were either electrified and brilliant or sluggish, tangled in dreams. I knew I needed to get it together before she tired of me, decided I wasn't worth her time.

Luckily, the bell rang before Gia could notice that I had lost the thread of the conversation again.

"Shit," she said as we stood and gathered our things. "Nap time. Sorry, I mean math time. Where are you off to?"

"An overnight-planning session with Margaret," I said. "The Sixteens are hiking to a couple of different lakes this weekend."

"Oh." Gia pulled the hood of her raincoat over her hair, and for a moment, I couldn't see her face. "I didn't know that."

"I thought I told you." I felt anxiety descend like an ice pack on the back of my neck. Hadn't I?

"No," she said. "You didn't tell me." She paused. "When do you leave?"

"Day after tomorrow."

"Right," she said. "I guess I just wasn't aware of that." She turned her back to me and headed toward the door. "You do what you need to do."

She was going to walk out. I'd done something wrong, and she was going to leave. My chest felt tight. "I'm sorry," I said.

Gia paused by the door, her hand on the knob. I thought for a moment that she hadn't heard me.

"I'm sorry," I said again.

Gia laughed. "Why are you apologizing? I was just surprised, that's all. Have a good time, you old so-and-so." She stepped out into the rain, and was halfway across the common area before I had my jacket zipped. She yelled something back at me, something about Jennie and Meredith, two other Seventeens, but her words got lost. She was gone by the time I stepped out the door.

I knew pretty much what to expect when we got to the campsite. Margaret had held a camping skill review the night before we left, and I had tried to memorize everything I could about the fine art of Leave No Trace Camping. Or, as Margaret called it: LNTC. Or, as the rest of us knew it: Leave Nothing to Chance. (The threat of black bears was high, and while grizzlies hadn't been seen in the Frank in decades, we weren't sure they weren't about to make a glorious comeback that summer, like a down-on-their-heels football team that wanders in at the last minute to massacre the opposition.)

Here are the basic rules of LNTC, as Margaret told us:

1. Leave no trace that you've been in the wilderness. Seriously.

2. This usually just means digging a "glory hole" for your private business, and carrying out your toilet paper and Snickers wrappers in a Ziploc bag.

3. Various methods of LNTC should be spoken of with reverence and respect. You should be able to say things like "Can I borrow the glory shovel? I need to start digging," without busting into snorts of laughter.

4. If you do laugh, that's okay. Just as long as you dig the damn thing.

Here are the basic rules of LNTC, as I understood it:

Leave no evidence that you ever left the comfort of your bed to struggle through the woods with the sole intention of eating starch and beans and lying on your back on a rocky and downward-sloping campsite while you stare at the ceiling of your tent and listen to the sounds of a variety of carnivores as they rustle around outside. Leave no evidence that you are scared shitless, that every movement terrifies you, even the quiet scratching that you will realize in the morning must have been chipmunks. Leave no evidence that you are afraid you didn't dig your glory hole deep enough and that you used twice as much toilet paper as everyone else. Leave as little evidence as possible to indicate that you are the most incompetent camper to ever set foot on the trail.

Needless to say, it was my first time camping.

It had stopped raining the night before, and the sun was shining with a vengeance, but the ground was still muddy and slick, especially in the places where our path was covered in shadow. Margaret had given each of us a map of the four-mile hike, and I stopped from time to time to mark our progress. I was surprised by how easily I could identify creeks and streams as we crossed them, how quickly the map had become familiar. The trail followed switchbacks up through a dense forest of lodgepole pines and subalpine fir, the occasional blue wink of lupine visible in the underbrush. Once we reached the peak and started to descend toward a cluster of tiny lakes, my knees wobbled and I struggled to keep from pitching forward and knocking over the girl in front of me. I was exhausted at first by the constant zigzagging; my pack settled more heavily on my shoulders with every turn. Eventually, though, I found myself hiking in a steady rhythm of breath and footfall. Time passed easily, and I was able to enjoy counting the blue gilia flowers that crowded the edge of the trail.

I had to hand it to Boone, though: From the very beginning of the hike, she walked with a step so light that she surprised a family of mule deer around one bend. We hiked for four hours, and she never once stopped to use the bathroom. And it was no different once we got to the campsite. Margaret had paired us with one another before we hit the trail. Boone and I would be sharing a two-person tent. That alone made me nervous enough; it didn't help that the tent — in its bag at least — looked big enough to house only a small rodent. I turned around for a minute to pull the tent out of its sack, and when I looked up, Boone was gone. Two minutes later, she was back with an armload of dry wood.

"Where did you find that?" I asked. As far as I could tell, every stick in the forest was soggy and wet.

She didn't answer me. "You ever built a campfire?" she asked instead.

I looked at her. The answer was obvious.

"Useless," she said to herself. Then: "Come over here."

I got up slowly from where I'd been kneeling, reading the tent instructions, and walked to the middle of the large campsite, where the fire ring sat empty.

"Kindling first," said Boone. "Small stuff: pinecones, dried moss, little sticks."

That was easy enough. The place was littered with that sort of thing.

"Now," she continued, "build a pyramid of medium and large pieces of wood over the pile of kindling." She paused as I wrangled the wood into place. "Good. There you are. You might not have died on the Oregon Trail."

"Thanks," I said, brushing off my hands on the sides of my pants. The truth was, I'd enjoyed making the fire. I liked the feel of the wood in my hands, the sense that I was doing something useful — no, more than useful: necessary.

"All we have to do later is light it," Boone said.

"I'll leave the fire starting to you," I said, and swallowed heavily. I hadn't meant it to come out that way.

"I wouldn't, if I were you." She stared at me.

The I-bankers were setting up their tents around us. Since our year was so large, we had split into two groups for the overnight. The other group, with the rest of our cabinmates, had set down their packs a mile back at Infantry Lake. Margaret, Boone, and I, along with a pod of six grumbling I-bankers, were making camp along the banks of the creatively named Soldier Lake, a body of water about the size of a suburban backyard. From the top of the peak, before our descent, it had looked like it was swaddled in yellow lint. From up close, the algae didn't seem so concentrated. It was almost pretty, with the gabled cliffs rising behind it and clusters of water lilies breaking the surface.

"I wonder how Miss Flynn's getting along," I said. Margaret had cajoled the math teacher into chaperoning the other group of girls.

"She's going to make them sit around the campfire tonight singing songs about their common denominator." Boone smirked.

We heard a high-pitched, silly laugh from nearby. Two of the most outlandish I-bankers, Chandler and Macy, were setting up their tent on a patch of cleared ground near ours. Chandler was from New York, and carried a Louis Vuitton purse around the school like she was planning to pop over to Bloomingdale's right after her canoe lesson. Macy, the one who had laughed, was smaller and not as pretty as auburn-haired Chandler, but she wore full makeup every day, and I must say, it helped. It also appeared as though she had brought her artillery with her; I spied an open Chanel toiletry bag next to the packs.

"Sorry," she squeaked. "I couldn't help but overhear."

Boone continued as though she hadn't heard her, and I saw Macy blush crimson and glance nervously at Chandler. "In any case," Boone said, "we got the long end of this stick. At least Margaret knows what she's doing up here." She paused. "Even if we *are* accompanied by stupidity squared."

I didn't even look to see how the two I-bankers responded to that.

It surprised me how much energy it took to set up camp. First, there were the tents to set up and secure to the ground with sharp, tapered stakes. Then we had to gather even more wood for the fire, and pump lake water through our filters into the collapsible buckets that we packed in, and designate a bathroom area far enough away from the lake that we wouldn't contaminate our drinking water. Only then was it time to light the fire and prepare supper. By that time the sun was casting its last feeble rays over the lake.

The nine of us sat on large rocks or pieces of broken wood that we'd pulled around the campfire. We ate mac and cheese out of the pot, passing it to one another and scooping up the noodles with pieces of flaky pita bread. Macy warmed water over the fire, and we drank hot Tang and felt it fizz on our tongues. It was the best meal I'd ever tasted, and I surprised myself by saying so.

Chandler swallowed a large bite. Some cheese oozed out of the corner of her mouth, and she casually wiped it away with the back of her hand. "Better than anything I've eaten at Adriano's," she said. "The New York culinary scene could take some tips from you, Margaret."

"I've found that the best meals are the ones I've worked for," Margaret said. "Plus, I think altitude makes a great seasoning."

She placed her tin cup on the dirt by her feet. "You can make this dinner when you return to New York, Chandler. It may not have the same dried pine needle garnish, but I bet your family would like it."

"Not a chance." Chandler flicked her hair over her shoulder. "Unless I spiked it with Xanax, I don't think Mumsy would approve. Plus," she added with a laugh, "old dog, old tricks. It's back to the high life for me." While the I-bankers could probably pass as dutiful daughters at their parents' hoity-toity church meetings and cocktail parties, we all knew what lurked under the cleanly pressed façade.

Margaret let her arm sweep out toward the lake, which was black and still in the moonlight. "The ancient Idaho batholith," she said. "All of this used to be glaciers one hundred million years ago." She paused for a moment, looking out at the dark water. "What have we learned here, if not the possibility of re-creation?"

"Rocks don't have juvie records." Boone was sitting off to the side of the fire, away from the heat.

"You own it, and then you leave it behind," Margaret said.

"Easy for you to say." Boone stood up. She walked over to our tent and stuck her torso in, emerging with her hand clasped around something. "Glory time," she said, and sauntered off into the woods. She didn't even take a flashlight.

"She's like an Eagle Scout or something," Macy whispered to Chandler. She sounded a little breathless. "Don't you think?"

"Yeah." Chandler looked admiringly at the dark curtain of woods that Boone had disappeared into. "She's fierce."

She's fierce. The phrase kept running through my head as I helped the other girls clean up, washing the pots and cups with boiled water, storing everything neatly in our packs, hanging the food sack over the high branch of a tree. *She's fierce.* Of course I had noticed the grudging respect with which even the I-bankers treated Boone, but I thought it was a respect born out of fear — not approbation, and certainly not envy. Now I saw that I was wrong. These girls came from money, or at least the appearance of it. The Chandlers and Macys of the world would mess up, get sent to someplace like Alice Marshall or even nicer, release some demons in Circle Share, make some art projects to show their parents, go home, and do it all over again. And they would keep doing it all over again until they graduated from high school and got accepted at an equally swanky, artsy college that didn't believe in grades and thought that their high school escapades were evidence of some latent genius.

I had always figured that the wealthiest girls had the least to lose. What I didn't understand until then was that they knew it too, and were ashamed. It didn't matter to them that Boone probably didn't walk out into the woods to squat near a bear and dig her hole in the pitch-black night — that she probably sat comfortably with her back to a fallen log and smoked the cigarette that I thought I'd seen tucked behind her ear as she went. They knew as well as I that Boone could leave Alice Marshall and return home to a locked door. For that reason alone, she was a warrior. What had Gia said once? *Your wounds make you fierce.* If that was true, then Boone must have been born wounded.

Nights were always cold at Alice Marshall, but we weren't prepared for the chill that descended like an ice storm around our campground as soon as the fire got low. It went straight through to the back of your skull, this cold, until you couldn't think about anything other than getting in your tent and pulling the warm bonnet of your sleeping bag over your head.

"Morning comes early here, girls," Margaret called from inside her bivy sack — really just a sleeping bag that zipped entirely shut like a cocoon, with a mesh screen over her face for her to breathe through. She didn't use a tent. (It looked like my idea of hell, but Margaret swore that there was no better way to commune with nature than by placing as few obstacles as possible between yourself and the ground. She said that she was so comfortable in her bivy sack that she could sleep through an earthquake.) "The sun is our natural alarm clock."

"Great," I mumbled. Boone and I were already in our sleeping bags, knocking hips, shoulders as we shifted around, trying to get comfortable. "As if we're even going to fall asleep." The tent, which had seemed small during the day, had apparently shrunk even further when the sun went down.

"Speak for yourself," Boone muttered. "I'm already asleep." She flung herself over onto her stomach and tightened the drawstring around the opening of her bag.

I attempted to find some way to position myself so that I wasn't lying directly on top of the sharp rocks that we apparently hadn't seen when we set up the tent. I knew my hips and legs would be spotted with inky bruises by morning. Finally, I gave up trying, and lay quietly in the dark. I was about to start counting sheep or mosquitoes when Boone unzipped part of her sleeping bag and flung it off.

"This is impossible," she said.

"Yeah."

"We're never going to sleep," she said. "We might as well have brought some knitting to keep us busy. Make a blanket for show-and-tell."

I laughed at the image of Boone clumsily trying to create anything, much less a blanket, out of a large skein of yarn. Then it was quiet again for a few minutes. I listened to her breathe, and compared the tenor of our breaths.

Boone suddenly propped herself up on one elbow so that she was turned toward me. "So, Gia, huh." Her voice was flat. It was too dark to see her face, but I could feel her watching me intently.

"Gia?" I said, trying to sound like I hadn't been thinking of her all day. It was only too easy to picture her hanging out in a cabin with the other Seventeens, laughing with Jennie and Meredith, realizing that they were so much more her kind of girls than I was.

"You've been following her around like an embarrassed cat." A fact, not an accusation.

"Bullshit," I said, but I wondered how she knew. Had Boone seen what no one else had seen? The way I hid my face behind my coffee mug in the Mess Hall during breakfast, believing that Gia wouldn't notice me staring, wouldn't notice that my coffee had long grown cold? I watched her even when I didn't think I was; I would come out of what felt like a trance, only to realize that I'd been following her every move. If I hadn't been able to notice this, how had Boone? And what else had she seen?

"Fine," she said. "Whatever. It's your life. Waste your time on that bitch if you want to." She didn't sound as angry as I'd imagined she'd be, and her calmness scared me.

We lay in silence for a while. I crossed my arms and stuck my hands in my armpits, warming them. A couple of the other girls giggled from within their tents. The night gradually fell still.

"Only," said Boone suddenly, "it's just that you're too smart for this." She spoke in careful, even tones, and I could feel without looking that she was leaning forward, as though she was delivering a secret message or code. "You're too smart to get wrapped up in someone else's blankets."

"What blankets?" I asked. "What are you talking about?"

"Blankets, covers, stories, lies. They're all the same thing."

"You've read her wrong," I said. I was thinking about the way Gia had looked at me when I told her that I was leaving for the backpacking trip. I'd hurt her, I realized suddenly. She hadn't known I was going away for the night, and her feelings had been hurt. I was filled with the sweetest sort of shame. She *wanted* to be around me, perhaps even as much as I wanted to be around her.

"Jesus, Lida," Boone said, and her calm evaporated. "What do you think is going to happen? Why do you think she needs you?" Her voice was rising now, and she shook her fist in front of my face. "Haven't you seen the way she ——"

Boone was interrupted by the sound of heavy footfalls, as though someone — or something — was walking slowly through the campground. A twig snapped. There was a huffing, woofing sound, as though something extremely large and hungry was trying to pant and breathe and sniff at the same time. A muffled gasp erupted from one of the other tents.

"Quiet," I whispered needlessly. Boone and I were both frozen in our bags.

The steps shuffled around one of the tents, seemed to walk away, came back.

"Christ," Boone said under her breath. She let her fist fall back by her side.

We listened as whatever was out there took one step, two steps, stopped, and then approached our tent. I could hear every breath it took as it came closer and closer.

"Boone ——" My voice cracked. *Where* was Margaret?

There was pressure on one side of the tent. Something was pushing against the nylon. I watched as a patch of the wall started to sag toward us.

Boone sat straight up in her sleeping bag. "That's IT!" she yelled, and clapped her hands three times. "THAT IS IT!"

There was a loud snort of surprise, and the side of the tent sprang back into place. It sounded like entire trees were being snapped in half as the animal crashed into the woods behind our tent. It was gone before Boone had even stopped clapping.

"And stay the fuck away!" Boone shouted.

There was a smattering of applause from the other tents, some semihysterical laughter, a few exhalations that carried a curse or two with them.

"Ladies." Margaret's voice carried across the campground. It was as calm as ever. In fact, it sounded . . . sleepy, like she'd just woken up. "Just an interested neighbor, I expect, coming to check out our lodging. Nothing to worry about. Go back to sleep."

"An interested neighbor?" I looked up at Boone, who was still frozen with her sleeping bag around her waist. She looked like she was listening for any sound of the animal's return. "Was Margaret going to do anything? Or was she, like, just going to wait for it to nose around her bivy sack and then offer it some crackers?"

Boone shook her head. "I think she slept through it. Nothing fazes that woman," she said, and I could hear the admiration in her voice.

"Ladies." This time, Margaret spoke firmly. "Good. Night."

Boone slowly lay back down again, but the rigid way that she held herself suggested that she was ready to jump back up at the slightest sound. She sighed. "I guess we should get some sleep."

"Okay," I said. "Okay." We both knew that sleep, or even a vague approximation of it, was out of the question.

We didn't speak again that night. And I was grateful, in a way, to whatever it was that came into our camp. Boone and I had been about to enter into a conversation whose contours and ridges were unchartable, and I felt the relief of having escaped it, even if just for a while. I remembered the outline that her fist had made in the shadows of our tent, and wondered how close it had been to my face.

CHAPTER ELEVEN

WORD TRAVELS FAST AT ALICE MARSHALL. I DON'T KNOW how, but the whole school had heard about Boone's "conversation" with a bear before we even got back. All of the Sixteens returned from the overnight after breakfast while the other students were cleaning the grounds, and as soon as we were in our cabins, delegates from the other years started pouring in. They'd leave their chores unattended, mops and brooms and sponges still in their hands as they leaned against our cabin walls, offering their own versions of the story before Boone even said a word. I didn't see Gia, but a couple of her cabinmates came over, so I knew she'd hear all about it soon enough.

"I hear you got out of your tent and fought back with a stick."

"Shut up. It was a rock."

"A rock she'd carved into a knife."

"Did you get to touch the grizzly's fur?"

"It wasn't a grizzly, stupid. It was a cougar."

"A black bear."

"A jaguar." (Everyone paused at that one, and then the girl who said it blushed and added, "I mean, bobcat?")

Boone played to the crowd, shrugging her shoulders and saying things like, "You do what the situation calls for," and "I wasn't going to let that bastard interrupt my beauty sleep." She never actually corrected any of the girls, and none of the other Sixteens we'd camped with at Soldier Lake did either.

Because I'd been sharing a tent with Boone, I experienced (for the first time in my life, I need not add) what it felt like to have the spotlight of fame brush over me, even if just peripherally. "What did you do, Lida?" the girls would ask. "Did you help Boone? Weren't you terrified?" And Boone would save me before I had to answer, saying, "Lida stayed strong. She held down the fort." Which was true in a sense, if by "fort" you mean "tent," and if by "holding down" you mean "lying in your sleeping bag, immobile with fear."

As a result of my newfound popularity, I didn't talk to Gia for a couple of days. It wasn't that I didn't want to, but she kept her distance while Boone and I were fending off the multitude of questions about what was increasingly being referred to as the "Bear Attack." I caught her looking in my direction once or twice in the Mess Hall, but I couldn't be sure she was looking at me. Even if she was, there was no way to know what she was thinking. Was she upset with me? Or had I imagined that our conversation before the overnight had been laced with tension?

Finally, Circle Share rolled around. I got there early and took a seat by myself — no way was I going to risk having to choose where to sit again. I didn't have to worry; Boone came in with Jules and sat next to her, like she always did. A Fourteen sat on her other side. Gia walked in with one of her cabinmates, and the two of them sat down together, the other girl chattering on.

Amanda settled herself in her chair, holding a cup of coffee in one hand.

"Good morning," she said. "Let's start with our incantation."

That morning, the group seemed less enthusiastic as we mumbled through the words.

"Good," said Amanda. "Why don't we begin this session with an open discussion." She smiled.

For some reason, no one wanted to talk.

"Does anyone have anything to share?" Amanda asked.

Crickets.

"No one?"

Nope.

Amanda sighed and sat back in her chair. "Well, this is a surprise," she said. "Normally, almost all of you have *something* to say." She looked around at the rest of us. "Hmmm."

I shifted in my seat. When Amanda made that thoughtful sound, it was never good. She and Margaret were alike in that way. You didn't want to give them a chance to come up with a new activity; it would usually involve some heavy lifting of the soul.

"Okay," she said finally. "Let's try this." She was sure looking pleased with herself. "I think we all know how good it feels to share what pains us. Right?"

This time, a few girls nodded.

"I know it's hard," Amanda added. "And sometimes this circle can seem too big for something so personal. Sometimes I think we need a smaller audience, maybe just one person's ear. Is that right?"

A few more nods.

"Okay." Amanda closed her eyes, thinking. Then she said, "Okay," again, and opened them. "I hear from Margaret that you've all been 'Mapping Your Worlds.'" She made air quotes with her fingers. "Now, I'm not sure exactly what constitutes a map of one's world, but Margaret assures me that you've all had the chance to be quite creative with your maps. Yes?"

Only a couple of nods this time.

Amanda sat up straight and pointed at us, swinging her finger in an arc. "This is what we're going to do. It'll be our session for the day. Pick a partner — anyone — and share what you've mapped of your world so far. Go somewhere private, if you like. Give each other feedback." She paused. "*Positive* feedback."

We all stood and began to move sluggishly around the Rec Lodge. Most girls attempted to look amused by the whole thing, but really they just looked nervous. I looked down at my lap. I hadn't written anything in my purple unicorn journal since the night Margaret had told me to get it all down on paper. That was as far as I'd gotten in Mapping My World. Now I wished I'd made some silly drawing of a house and a tree, smoke curling out of the chimney, a stick figure waving from the window. Shit.

"Let's get this over with, shall we?" Gia had drifted over to my chair and stood above me, looking down. "Otherwise, Amanda will probably force us to light sage and lemongrass and wave it around in some cleansing ritual."

I laughed and got up. "Sounds good," I said, trying to sound casual. I was listening for any hint of anger in her voice, but there was none. She appeared to have forgotten all of my missteps in our previous conversation. I allowed myself the briefest sigh of relief.

As we walked out of the Rec Lodge, I saw Boone watching me from the other side of the room. She shook her head. I glanced away.

We met up on the dock after each going to our cabins to get our "maps." I could see Gia already sitting on the farthest edge of the dock as I walked over from my cabin, and my breath caught. If her map was anything like mine, I was going to learn about her Thing. Finally, finally. It would draw us closer together, a secret bond that we might not speak of but would both *know*, the way you know things about a sister or a lover that you don't need to mention because they're just understood. I was going to understand her. I quickened my step.

Gia had swung by the Mess Hall on her way back, and she had brought two cups of black coffee with her. I settled myself on the dock. We sat cross-legged, facing each other. There was water on either side of us, and it rocked the dock gently from side to side. On the beach, a couple of girls sat in the sand, large pieces of poster board between them.

Gia took a sip of her coffee. "I hear you killed a bear, skinned it, and hung it by the fire." She smiled mischievously. "Well done."

"I know," I said. "The, uh, story has gotten a little out of hand."

"That's what I thought," she said. "Whatever. It gives the other girls something to fixate on for a week or so. Some of these girls are just famished for drama."

"Yeah," I agreed.

"Not you, though." She smiled at me, and I felt any residual tension of the past few days evaporate.

"Thanks. I learned it from watching you," I said, and we laughed.

"Oh yeah, I'm one cool cucumber. Hey," Gia added, "so you had to share a tent with Boone." She shook her head. "My apologies."

"Yeah," I said. "But I'm here, aren't I? So I guess I survived." I smiled awkwardly.

"Congratulations." Gia glanced at my journal. "Well," she said, and took another sip. "We might as well start this lovefest. You go first."

"That's okay," I said. "You can go, if you want."

"If I wanted to, I would," she said, and laughed.

I looked down at my journal. Suddenly, the words I had written seemed foolish and contrived. "It's stupid," I started to say, but Gia reached over and grabbed the journal from me.

"I'll be the judge of that," she said. She glanced at the cover, where the unicorn glittered and pranced. "Interesting. Not your purchase, I'd imagine." She opened it and began flipping slowly through the first few pages, where I'd started out doodling.

I pulled my knees up to my chest and hugged them. I was sitting facing the east side of Bob, and I squinted, attempting to focus on Ben's lookout. I tried to think of other things to keep myself from watching Gia. I couldn't imagine what Boone would have done with her map — drawn a picture of the Minster mill and set the paper on fire? What about the others? How much did I really know about Jules, for instance? She never mentioned her own Thing in Circle Share, though it seemed like she was always talking, speaking up in support of one girl or another. It was odd to think that what any of us knew of one another was only the smallest fraction of what our lives actually looked like. It was only in Circle Share that we even glimpsed one another's pain, and even then, it was still a fragment. I sat there, trying to picture everyone else's maps — trying to think of anything I could besides the girl who was now pointing to the first page on which I'd scribbled my story.

She looked first at the tiny holes I had stabbed into the paper, and then she glanced farther down the page. "Here?" she asked, and I nodded, miserable.

"Margaret told me I had to —" I tried to explain.

She held up her hand to silence me. She started reading. Immediately, she looked up again sharply. "Your mother's alive?" Gia let one finger fall in the middle of the first page, holding her place. "You told me she was dead."

"I know I did," I said. "She's . . . It's . . . I just don't like to talk about it, you know? It's just . . . too *big* to explain."

"Is it?" she asked. Then her expression softened. "Okay," she said. "But you didn't have to lie to me. You never have to lie to me. You know that, right?"

"Yeah," I said, "I mean, I wouldn't. I won't."

She kept reading, past what I'd said about my mother. She read about the things I'd done to myself and why I'd done them. She turned each page carefully, as though she was afraid of ripping the paper. She read it all. Then she closed the journal and handed it to me. She looked out over the lake, focusing on something just out of sight. We sat like that for a few minutes.

Gia finally broke the silence. She tilted her head. "What about friends?" she asked.

"What do you mean?"

She tapped the cover of the book lightly with her index finger. "I mean, you don't mention any friends in here, not even before you started to . . ." She cleared her throat. "Didn't you ever have any?"

My face flooded with embarrassment. "I thought maybe you could tell," I said, lifting my palms up helplessly. "No friends."

"That's hard to believe." She reached up and squeezed my shoulder. "I mean, I knew you didn't feel at home in high school, but — none? Really?"

"None." I'd always felt that, in high schools and junior highs across the country, it's as if there's an unmarked date in the school calendar by which time everyone needs to have found their people. Unmarked because unspoken. And if you miss that date, if you're absent, say, and you don't know that the deadline for finding people is *today*, then that's it. You're shit out of luck.

And I must have been absent that day. Oh sure, I knew a few other gangly and awkward girls to nod to in the halls, could even sit silently near them while I ate my lunch, trying not to make any noise when I took my sandwich out of its plastic wrap. But that was as far as it went. I never found my people. No one ever found me. And who are you, if you're no one to anyone?

I knew that it was normal to feel awkward and out of place in high school. Made-for-TV movies and sappy books with water-color paintings on their covers assured me that everyone goes through this, everyone thinks they don't belong at some point. But I knew something else. I knew that, after a minor public humiliation or two (a de-pantsing in gym class, the wrong outfit on School Spirit Day), the heroines of all those movies and books found their place. They found their people. They looked back on the hell that had been their lives and realized that they had *learned* something from it. They were better people for having been outcasts.

But what about the girl who was so forgettable that her own mother couldn't remember to call? The girl who was so wrong, so incongruous with the world that the woman who *made* her had to leave?

Gia stared at me intently for a long minute. Finally, she set the journal down between us. "Can I see?" Her eyes traveled down the length of my body.

"No," I said quickly.

"Okay, Lida." She reached over and touched my hand, which was still wrapped around one of my knees. "I had no idea."

The water slapped against the dock more insistently, and I peered across the lake at the dusky cloud that was just edging over the granite cliffs. I shivered. "Oh, you know," I said, "maybe I was just bored." I tried to keep my tone light. "Or fucked-up."

"No." Gia tapped the journal again. "This is real pain." She stared at me, blinking, and then she shook her head lightly and smiled, letting me off the hook. "Well, you definitely tried, didn't you? That takes imagination, at least. It's pretty impressive."

Her hand was still on mine.

"Thanks?" I laughed nervously. "Actually, I think it's kind of embarrassing. It's not like I *did* anything, really. Now, it just seems a little silly."

Her gaze was level, probing. "There's nothing silly about it." She squeezed my hand once and let go.

I let out a long, relieved breath. "Sorry," I said, talking quickly. "I don't know why I'm so nervous. It's just that I've never told

159

anyone about it." I paused. "Hey — don't tell anyone, okay? I'm not . . . It's not . . . something I want to share."

"It's in the vault," Gia said, pointing to her chest. "Where all secrets stay hidden." She grinned.

When Gia smiled at me like that, my whole body heated up a few degrees. "Okay," I said, hoping she didn't notice the ridiculous blush that I could feel spreading down my neck. "Now you."

"Sure thing." Gia rocked forward and reached into the back pocket of her jeans. She pulled out a single sheet of paper that had been folded into a perfect square. Slowly, she unfolded it and set it on the dock so that the pencil drawing was facing me.

It was a sketch of the school grounds. The cabins were little boxes wearing lopsided, triangular caps. Gia had drawn pointy waves where Bob was supposed to be, placed symmetrically around a long rectangle that I assumed was the dock. Each tree looked exactly the same as the next: a child's rendition of a Christmas tree. It was the picture I had wished I had drawn when Amanda first told us to share our maps: a picture of nothing.

"You didn't expect me to take this seriously, did you?" Gia said. She laughed at my silence. "Look, Lida, I think it's great that you listened to Margaret and mapped your world." She put her hand on my knee. "I really do. It's just not quite my style." She sat back and studied me. Raising an eyebrow, she said, "Don't be upset."

I stared at the picture. I had the urge to rip it up and throw each tiny shred in the lake. Instead, I said, "Why would I be mad?"

"I don't know," she said. "Look — I don't want to demean what you've done." She pointed to my journal, which lay on the dock between us like a gaudy, embarrassing hat. "If I had something like that to tell, I would. Believe me, I'd tell you."

"So do it anyway," I said, surprising myself. "Tell me something about your world." I wadded up her drawing in my fist and pitched it in the water.

She watched as the ball of paper bobbed on the lake's surface, slowly absorbing the water until it began to sink. She tilted her head, her eyes half-closed. When the paper was no longer visible, she opened them again and looked at me. "You already know everything."

I don't know anything, I thought. "Tell me something I don't know." I sounded belligerent, almost angry. I felt stupid. Stupid for writing everything down, stupid for sharing it with Gia. My little story was probably as dramatic to her as a trip to the grocery store, all of it printed so carefully in that goddamn purple unicorn journal.

Gia looked back at the beach, where the two girls were pointing at something on one of the poster boards and laughing. "Something you don't know." Her eyes shifted from side to side, as though she was sifting through images in her head. "It's not like I have any one Thing," she said slowly, choosing each word carefully. "So there's not much for me to talk about. What particularly do you want to discuss?" The voice of a mother, humoring her difficult child.

"I don't know," I said, fumbling. I took a deep breath. "Okay. Easy. Why are you here?"

Gia smiled. She stood up and stretched her arms to either side of her, turning toward the lake. "It's beautiful here, isn't it?" She looked down at me and then squatted so that her face was only a foot from mine. "Fine. Get ready to be amazed." She laughed. "I'm at Alice Marshall because the other schools I attended were bad fits. They couldn't give me what I needed."

"What couldn't the other schools give you?" I met Gia's gaze, pressing on. "What did you need?"

"Oh, you know. An adequate education, for one. Not that I'm getting that here." She smiled and shook her head. "I don't know — all the other girls had these *issues*, you know? Teachers too. No one took the time to get to know me. It was kind of like the thing with Boone. Making assumptions before they even met me." Gia shrugged her shoulders. "Nothing huge, Lida. No big crisis. They were just bad fits. Sorry to disappoint." She jostled me with her elbow.

It was all I was going to get. I shouldn't have been surprised. The funny thing was, Gia might have thought she was really telling me something about herself. But these stories didn't tell me anything about the way she felt at night, when she stood completely alone on the beach and looked toward the thin black line of shore that rimmed the other side of the lake. Or how she felt when she came upon a rabbit's delicate bones on Red Dot Trail, bleached and picked clean by other scavengers. Or what images filtered through her mind just before sleep, when the body has little resistance to the memories and desires that are kept at bay in the waking hours. And that — *that* — was what I really wanted to know.

I sighed, defeated. "Can you tell me anything else?" I asked, trying one last time.

Gia pointed to her chest and smiled at me. "The vault, Lida. The vault."

The bell rang, signaling lunch, and I stood and dusted off my hands on my knees. I grabbed the journal and stuck it in the waistband of my pants, like I'd seen Boone do.

"Well," I said lamely, "lunch."

Gia laughed. "Astute observation."

We started down the dock. I turned to head toward the Mess Hall when I felt Gia's hand on my arm.

"Hey," she said. "Wait. I have something for you. Come with me." She walked briskly toward the cabins, and I followed.

All of the cabins at Alice Marshall looked exactly the same: one room, nondescript bunks, splintered dressers. But when Gia turned on the light in her cabin, I recognized her bed, on the bottom of one of the bunks, immediately. She didn't have a sleeping bag. A luxurious silk comforter lay across it, with three thick pillows propped up along the wall as though it was a couch or a daybed. Next to the head of her bed, she had set up a little nightstand out of an upended apple crate, where I could see a hairbrush, a notebook, and a tiny framed photograph.

"Nice thinking," I said, walking over and touching the nightstand. "Where did you get this?"

Gia waved my question away. "Let me find what I'm looking for." She walked over to one of the dressers and started rummaging around, pulling out each drawer and rifling through them. It was clear that she had an entire dresser to herself.

I picked up the framed photograph and studied it. The picture had been taken in front of the Eiffel Tower, in Paris, from a far distance. Two people stood at the base of the tower. They were both wearing black. One of them was Gia — it was clear from the blond hair that, even at such a long distance, managed to take up so much of the frame. The other person, slightly taller, was more indistinct. Was it a man or a woman? The more I looked at the photo, the blurrier it became. I set it down.

"Here." Gia held something out to me, grinning. "I just think it would look better on you."

It was one of her T-shirts, the one I'd noticed early on. I'd complimented her on it since then. The shirt was dark green and sheer, with a large gray feather falling diagonally across the front. It had looked fantastic on Gia — a little rock and roll, a little "Who the hell cares?" — and I had said so. Now she was holding it out to me.

"I can't," I said. "It looks so good on you."

"Take it, Lida. It's just your style. Besides," Gia added, "if I *really* miss it, I can always go back to the store later and get another, can't I?"

I took the shirt and held it in my hands, running my thumb over the thin material. No one had ever shared clothes with me before. "Thanks," I said quietly.

"Forget about it. It's yours." Gia looked at me and shook her head, smiling. Then she walked back to the door of the cabin and held it open for me. "Come on. We're going to be late for lunch." She winked at me. "And I wouldn't want to get you in trouble."

CHAPTER TWELVE

I SPENT THE NEXT COUPLE OF WEEKS ALTERNATELY MEETING up with Gia on the Smokers' Beach and stepping carefully around Boone. I still didn't want to hear what she had to say about Gia. Also, I didn't want to have to admit to her — or anyone — that Gia didn't tell me *anything* when we shared our maps with each other. I tried to muffle the drumbeat of anger that sounded every time I thought about Gia's drawing: those boxy houses and chicken-scratch trees.

Luckily (or not so luckily), something else was coming up that kept me from dwelling on it too much. Parents' Weekend. An event as tantalizing as used Kleenex. A weekend when, according to the girls who had been here the longest, the school transformed into a sort of rustic dude ranch where no one meant anything they said. I knew if I said anything at all, even if it was a lie, my dad and Terri would probably be ecstatic.

Not everyone's parents could visit, of course; some of the I-bankers' parents were tied up in important business transactions in tall steel buildings somewhere. But, as is usually the case with relatively wealthy, neurotic, fearful, overly concerned parents, there was sure to be a good turnout. What parent could resist seeing her troubled teen making progress in the form of art projects and journal entries? Who wouldn't pay to hear how their daughter is "coming along nicely," even if she isn't, just so that they can go home and sleep soundly in their comfortable, well-appointed beds, made all the more comfortable because their daughter — well loved, cherished — is not with them and won't be for a long time still? As Boone put it, "They come for the relief of leaving."

Preparations for Parents' Weekend were intense. It appeared to carry the same weight for Bev and the teachers as would, say, hosting the Olympic Games. In the week leading up to the "Yuppie Incursion" (Boone's words again), cleaning the Bathhouse became a three-hour ordeal, and basic cabin upkeep was supervised by Bev herself. On both Thursday and Friday, classes were canceled so that we could spend our time sweeping one last time and making sure that our "personal items" were in "neat and tidy array," including two random bag checks. For me, all of this meant stuffing my purple unicorn journal into the foot of my sleeping bag and lining up my hiking boots next to Karen's underneath our bunk. Also, taking off the black hoodie that I had been wearing for a solid week, and putting on a fresh, clean, gray one. Also, brushing my hair.

The parents were due to arrive between noon and three on Saturday. A few had cleared it with Beverly and were driving all the way in, but most people would come in one of the five large vans that were picking up passengers in Hindman. Bev found it in her heart to let us sleep in on Saturday morning, so we didn't see what the teachers had done to the school until we all wandered into the Mess Hall for a late breakfast.

Whoever had made the dude ranch comparison had not been exaggerating. Our dining room, which would normally be described as industrial-cheap-with-wood-accents, now resembled a hotel banquet hall that had been decorated for a Wild West–themed wedding. The color scheme was Southwestern Chic, all muted rust and soft turquoise. Streamers fell from the ceiling, and there were cowboy hats and horseshoes tacked up to the walls. I half expected Margaret to walk into the room dressed in buck-skin and holding an emcee's microphone. The tables were covered in vinyl tablecloths with a cowboy boot pattern, and each place setting had a wooden napkin ring in the shape of a sheriff's badge. (The silverware had changed too, I noticed. Bev had gathered up all of the plastic utensils, and replaced them with polished forks and shining knives.)

"You should see the Rec Lodge," Jules said. "It's just as gaudy." We had walked through the breakfast buffet line and were sitting outside with our disposable plates, eating sausage sandwiches and apples in the cold morning sun. No way was Bev going to risk any of us messing up her perfect design before the parents even got here. "I peeked in. They've thrown some sort of bearskin rug down on the floor."

"Sounshcherble," Boone said through a mouthful of breakfast sandwich. She swallowed. "The parents can see right through it."

"Mine won't," I said. "It's probably what they've been imagining this whole time. They'll just be disappointed that there aren't any horses."

Boone laughed. *"Au contraire,"* she said. "Ponies there will be. Bev brings them in for a Sunday morning trail ride."

"Seriously?"

"Seriously. Didn't you know? Alice Marshall is actually a rodeo training ground. You won't see the woman in anything other than a plaid flannel shirt all weekend. She must raid every Goodwill store in Idaho for her collection. The theme of the weekend is 'Good Clean Fun.'"

"It's true," said Jules. "There's a Parents' Weekend every four months. Mine came the last couple of times, but they're coming back anyway, just because they had so much fun. They think this place is a resort. My mom actually said she was jealous of me."

It surprised me to hear that Jules had been at Alice Marshall that long. I wondered what she could have possibly done to warrant such an extended sentence. And — not for the first time — I drew a blank. I just couldn't imagine her doing anything remotely *bad*.

Gwen reached over and grabbed the sausage off Karen's plate. "At least the weather is nice," she said, taking a bite. "I don't think Bev has a rain plan."

"Oh God," said Boone. "Think of all the sharing of feelings we would have to do in the Rec Lodge. One giant Circle Jerk. There would be an avalanche of insincere remorse."

I laughed with the others. "So, what *will* we do?" I asked. "I mean, am I supposed to spend the whole day leading my dad and Terri around on a tour? That won't take very long." I chewed on a fingernail, doing the math in my head. If we all went to bed at nine and woke up at eight, the whole weekend would amount to . . . about fifteen hours of awkward silence.

"No, there are plenty of activities planned." Jules leaned forward excitedly. "Canoeing, hikes, some crafts in the Rec Lodge, a bonfire at night . . ." She thought about it. "Last time, we tie-dyed T-shirts. That was pretty fun."

"Don't forget the one-on-one meeting with Bev," Boone said. "Everyone has to do it. Even those of us who don't have the honor of hosting our parents here. It's Bev's equivalent of an end-of-term evaluation. You might consider telling your parents to turn back now."

"Oh God," I said. "This is worse than I thought."

"There is an upside." Karen spoke up cheerfully. "There's nothing like meeting everyone's parents and seeing where we all come from. It's a real window into the soul, you know?"

"Yeah," agreed Gwen. "It can explain a lot." She laughed.

"Whatever," said Boone.

"No, really," said Karen. "It's kind of fun, in a weird way."

Boone stood up. "Yeah, I'm sure it's totally great," she said. "If you're a sadist, that is. You won't find me spying on all your dysfunctional family reunions. No thank you." She crumpled her paper plate in one hand. "You all have fun, though. I'll see you at the end of the weekend." She walked off in the direction of our cabin.

"What's wrong with her?" I asked.

"Her parents have never visited," whispered Jules, even though no one else was sitting near enough to our group to overhear. "Some parents, you know, only come once, but hers never have."

"I don't think she has parents," said Gwen. "I think it's just Boone and her brother, and he's . . . you know. Incarcerated."

"She's lucky." I said it without thinking.

Gwen and Karen frowned at me, and Jules shook her head and looked down at her plate. My face turned red. "I mean she's lucky not to have visitors. This weekend is going to be excruciating."

That wasn't what I had meant at all, of course. The only communication I'd had with my dad and Terri in the past three and a half months had been in the form of my dad's informative postcards. I hadn't ever written back. The most recent card, a picture of the Statue of Liberty with Mickey Mouse ears Photoshopped on her head, had been postmarked *New York*. So yes, I *was* envious of the girls whose parents couldn't make it. I wondered what it would be like to go through life without my dad and Terri there at every turn like critical, nervous, disappointed shadows. In some ways, I thought, Boone had it easy.

As I was walking back to my cabin for last-minute sweeping and scouring, I saw Gia. She was headed quickly in the direction of Bev's cabin.

"Hey!" I called.

She turned, saw me, and waited while I caught up to her. "Hey yourself." She reached over and picked a piece of lint off my shirt.

"This is going to be some weekend."

"Undoubtedly." Gia seemed preoccupied.

"So, is your dad coming?" I asked. I wondered what he would look like. I thought he might arrive by helicopter.

"Yes," she said, glancing back toward Bev's cabin. "He'll probably be late, though. He always is. When you're as busy as my father is, you don't catch a bus with the other parents. You make your own schedule."

"Well," I said, "I can't wait to meet him."

"Oh sure," Gia said. "I think there'll probably be time for that." Her smile was evasive. "Why don't we play it by ear? Listen, I have to go. Bev has a telephone message for me."

"Sure," I said, and watched as she walked away. *Play it by ear?* Just when I thought that Gia and I had some sort of understanding, she made me feel as though I was asking her for a favor. I could have just as well asked for a slow dance or a raise.

The vans were supposed to wait in Hindman until all of the parents were there, so we expected that they would arrive around three or three-thirty at the earliest. But the vans rolled into the parking lot, one by one, at twelve-thirty. It was only fitting; these were the kinds of parents who relied heavily on the element of surprise in their relationships with their daughters: "forgetting" to knock before entering a bedroom; arriving a half hour early to pick them up from parties, hoping to catch them drinking or smoking or worse; showing up at school on a Friday morning, just to make sure that they were actually attending class. These parents were used to the satisfaction of learning that their suspicions were well founded. Of course they would show up early.

Someone rang the bell. There was a general frantic scramble toward the Bathhouse for one last glance in the mirror before we all headed toward the vans, which were releasing their cargo in a steady wave of beige slacks, polo shirts, and pearls.

I hung back. I watched Jules as she squealed and made a beeline for a woman who looked young enough to be her sister and an equally tanned, silver-haired man. The woman was carrying a little terrier in her arms, and Jules leaped toward it, practically smothering the poor thing. She picked it up and twirled around, the terrier yapping excitedly. The man and woman laughed, and I wondered again how it was that a girl like Jules could end up at a place like Alice Marshall. As far as I could tell, her family was perfectly, blissfully normal.

Gwen and Karen had each found their parents too. Gwen's mother had peroxide-blond hair, which contrasted nicely with her daughter's jet-black locks. They made a striking pair, even if they weren't smiling. I didn't see her father, and then remembered that her folks were divorced. Karen's parents looked like aging hippies. Her dad was short, with round glasses that perched fitfully on his nose. Her mom looked a lot like Karen, though she wore a large silk shawl and the dazed expression of someone who may or may not be high. I remembered then that she was an artist. They looked around at the other parents, wide-eyed, as though they were children who had accidentally been seated at the adults' table. Karen spoke to them patiently, probably explaining where they were and why.

I couldn't see Gia anywhere.

I saw my dad and Terri before they saw me, which was good, since it gave me a chance to compose my face in a suitable expression of equal parts ambivalence and exhaustion. They were standing next to one of the vans, and Terri looked like she was about to climb back inside. I think she even had one hand on the door handle. My dad was looking around worriedly. I wonder if he thought I might have run away. After all, how would he know? He hadn't heard a word from me in months. I thought about turning around and leaving, hiking up Buckhorn and hiding out until the weekend was over, but then my dad caught my eye and smiled so widely that I couldn't help it: I smiled back.

"Lida!" His voice boomed over the noise of the crowd, and a few girls turned and stared as I made my way over. He engulfed me in a bear hug, wrapping his arms around my shoulders and head so that my face smushed up against the pocket of his T-shirt. I let myself breathe in his familiar scent of Old Spice and soap before stepping back.

"You look fantastic!" he practically shouted.

"Hi," I said lamely. "You made it."

Terri stepped forward, though it looked like she had to pry herself away from the safety of the van door. "Hi, Lida. You do look well." She wisely did not try to hug me. "I like your shirt."

"Thanks," I said. I had put on Gia's shirt that morning. I'd been wearing it so often since she gave it to me that the hem was starting to fray, and I twisted it with my fingers. The noise around us had swelled. I couldn't make out what anyone was saying, and I wondered briefly if what seemed to be happy chatter might actually be forty stilted conversations. I took a deep breath. "You look good too."

Terri tried out a smile, which kind of surrendered halfway across her face.

"May I have your attention?" Margaret's voice cut through the group. She was standing on a large rock at the edge of the parking lot, a bullhorn in her hand. Even on the rock, she was only a few inches taller than some of the fathers. "May I have your attention?" The noise gradually subsided, and everyone turned so that they could see her. "My name is Margaret Olsen. I have met most of you before. I am one of the instructors here at Alice Marshall, and I am pleased to welcome you all to Parents' Weekend."

There was a smattering of enthusiastic applause, followed by the low growl of girls chastising their parents for clapping.

"I will be leading you all on a tour of the school grounds. While we're on the tour, some of our other staff will be taking your luggage to the guest dorm, where you will all be staying. If there is anything you'll need during the tour, please be sure to bring it with you now."

"That's the woman who picked you up in Hindman, isn't it?" my dad asked as Terri dove back into the van to retrieve her sunglasses and a water bottle.

"Yeah."

"She's quite a character."

"Yeah."

My dad smiled hopefully at me. "Are you two buddies?"

I just stared at him. We were off to a great start.

The tour was short but informative. Margaret led the way, sharing her litany of interesting anecdotes about the school, her voice raspy over the bullhorn. I learned, for instance, that Alice Marshall had never married, that huckleberries grew prolifically around the north side of Bob, and that girls who had attended the school went on to become ambassadors and air force captains. One even became a famous cartoonist whose little quips I had been accustomed to reading on Saturday mornings in the Bruno paper. (It was hard to imagine that a woman who now drew cuddly puppies with big, floppy ears and captions like, "I guess that's why they call it 'dog tired'!!!" ever sat around the Smokers' Beach, talking about the cigarette she put out on her sister's arm.) You had to hand it to her, though; Margaret did a great job of playing to the crowd.

I tried not to lose sight of my cabinmates as the tour continued. I wanted to see what they did with their parents: Were they making conversation? Fighting? Gwen and Karen were at the front of the group, so I could only see the backs of their heads. Jules was nearby, walking slowly with her mother and father and chatting happily. She caught my eye once or twice and grinned. Obviously, she was no help. I tried to stay as near as possible to my dad and Terri without being close enough to talk. It worked, for a while.

After the tour, though, we had an hour of free time before Bev's official welcome. I saw girls leading their parents toward the docks, the horseshoe pit, the area just outside of the Mess Hall that had been designated a smoking area for this weekend only. (Gwen's mom, I noticed, practically sprinted in that direction.) I stood next to my dad and Terri and shuffled my feet.

"Well," I said.

"Yes?" asked my dad. He looked like he was ready for anything — a game of hoops, an epiphany, a cocktail. He smiled at me eagerly.

"I guess I could show you my cabin."

"Great idea! We'd love to see where you hang your hat." Dad nudged Terri, and she nodded slowly in agreement. I wondered if maybe she had taken a pill or two to aid her in this journey. Her edges appeared to have been softened to the point of viscosity.

I hoped that Jules would be in the cabin with her parents, and that the adults could fill the hour with whatever it is that strangers say to one another once they own homes and shop at Costco. No such luck. When I opened the door, the only person there was Boone. She was standing at her bunk, busily stuffing a shirt, a book, and a bottle of bourbon into a backpack. She zipped it shut before my dad and Terri had time to see anything, slinging it over one shoulder and walking toward us and the door. She winked at me.

"Oh, um, this is Boone. My cabinmate," I said weakly.

My dad stuck out his hand so quickly that he almost hit Boone in the stomach. "Interesting name," he said. "Pleasure to meet you."

Boone took his hand and shook it once, twice, as though at a job interview. "Pleasure's mine, sir," she said formally, glancing over at Terri and taking it all in at once: the hair, the perfect skin, the beige slacks. "I've heard so much about you," Boone said to her. She turned to me. "Gotta jet. You know where to find me if you need anything." She paused. "You know, like a horse tranquilizer for yourself or . . ." Her voice trailed off as she looked Terri up and down. Boone winked again, and was out the door before Terri's cheeks had time to turn completely red.

My dad cleared his throat. "Another colorful character," he said. Terri's expression was shifting, as it usually did, from shock to fury, though I saw something else there as well — a wave of sadness so brief and so acute that it almost stung. She opened her mouth to say something, and my dad shook his head lightly, a pleading look in his eyes. She closed her mouth. My dad cleared his throat. "Well then," he said, "let's see this place." He walked around the cabin, taking it in. "Nice."

I have to admit, it was looking pretty good. Not inviting, per se, because a room with only bunk beds and nothing else doesn't exactly scream "creature comforts," but it was at least cleared of any signs of misbehavior. The smokes had all been packed back into their tampon boxes and dirty socks. Our diaries were hidden in their respective secret places. And Boone had just taken the only bottle of liquor with her. We had done a good job of making our lives here look as neutral as Terri's wardrobe.

Terri and my dad sat on Jules's neatly smoothed sleeping bag, and I sat across from them, on Boone's. We stared at one another.

"Lida, you really do look great," said my dad. "Really . . ." He paused, considering his options. "Sporty. It looks good on you."

Sporty?

"You cut your hair." Leave it to Terri to point out the obvious.

"Yeah," I said. *Quick, Lida. Think.* "It was for a play I was in."

My dad beamed. "An actor in the family! I always wondered if you might have some stage talent in you."

"What play?" Terri sounded interested, but I couldn't be sure. She might have been testing me.

"I forget," I said, my mind flipping through vague memories of various junior high and high school English classes as quickly as possible. "It was right after I got here. Shakespeare, I think. I played a boy."

"Of course!" My dad was almost bouncing in place, he was so excited to hear that I had finally picked up an extracurricular activity. "Just like they did in Shakespeare's time!"

Terri put a hand on his arm, probably to keep him from floating away on his cloud of happiness. "Honey, women didn't act in Shakespeare's time. The men had to dress up like the female characters." She looked at me.

Was she challenging me? Did she think I was lying? I mean, I *was* lying, sure, but did she have to say something? It had been so long since I had seen the two of them that I had forgotten how to read Terri's behavior. She was either really trying to piss me off, maybe even blow my cover, or she was just making conversation.

"Right," I said. "We're like an all-female troupe of Shakespearian actors." I met her gaze, expecting disbelief, but she smiled at me instead.

"That's neat," she said. "And anyway, it's growing out quite nicely."

It was just like her to smooth everything over with sweetness.

As though I couldn't hear what she was *really* trying to say. *You're a liar, Lida. And your hair looks like hell.* Still a bitch.

My dad started telling me about life in Bruno. Apparently, nothing had changed since I left. That was no surprise. Nothing ever changes in Bruno. Life in that town is as predictable as Tupperware: This goes here, and this goes there, and it's all sealed up nicely so that nothing ever festers or combusts.

"I guess you got our postcard," he was saying.

"Hmmm?" I hadn't been paying much attention.

"From New York. You got that, right?"

"Nope," I said, "I didn't."

"Oh." My dad rubbed his hand over his knee. "I guess it got lost. We did send you one."

"You went to New York?" I was all innocence.

"Just for a few days, earlier this month. You'd have loved it. What a great town."

Terri chimed in. "You wouldn't believe the food there. Anything you could ever dream of. What was it we tried that one night? Afghani kebabs?"

"No, I think the restaurant was Moroccan. Or maybe Malaysian."

My dad and Terri started giggling, sharing a moment. I wondered if Boone had been kidding about the horse tranquilizers, and if not, where she might keep them.

"Oh, you two," I said, sounding like a syrupy grandmother. I almost went on: *It must be so hard, when all foreign foods look and taste the same to you.* But I didn't; I swallowed my sarcasm. After all, I had been given a free pass with the hair. Why not give them a free pass with their trip? What can I say — I was feeling magnanimous.

The bell rang then, signaling the all-school introduction in the Rec Lodge, and we stood up to go. On our way out of the cabin, my dad put his arm around my shoulders.

"I've missed you, Bun," he said. And I didn't say it, but for the briefest moment I thought, *I've missed you too.*

After Bev's introduction, which was as boring and predictable as you'd imagine, the afternoon activities began in earnest. Jules was right: There was no shortage of family-friendly, noncombative, juvenile things to do. Some parents painted rocks and made wish boats in the Rec Lodge. Others played badminton with a net that had been set up on the beach. Dad and Terri and I canoed around the dock a few times until Terri's arms started hurting. Then we joined a small group that was taking a short hike up Red Dot Trail with Margaret. She took us on the portion of the trail with the least amount of elevation gain, and listed the names of trees and flowers as we hiked. Sometimes she would ask one of us girls to tell her what a particular tree or flower was called, so our parents could see what we were learning. She had already taught us to identify all the flowers in the Frank, even the ones that were no longer in bloom, and the words tripped off our tongues like the names of folk music trios: Jacob's ladder, whortle-berry, Indian paintbrush, Trapper's tea.

"Lida," Margaret said at one point, her hand gesturing toward a large, splintered log that was decomposing on the ground, "what do you call this?"

I met her eye, which was a steely challenge. There was no way I could get away with not answering. "Nurse log," I said dutifully.

"Good. Why?"

"Because it acts as a sort of . . . incubator for plants and fungus as it decays."

"Excellent." Margaret grinned proudly.

Even Terri smiled when I answered correctly. And I had to hand it to myself. I had a knack for this wilderness stuff. Long division stuck in my head for about the life span of a bee in a jar, but the intricacies of nature made themselves at home in my brain. I reveled in the odd habits of forest life. And yes, I'll admit I felt a small burst of pride that my dad and Terri could see this too.

The whole day was like that: quiet, respectable. Dinner was a slightly formal affair, with a meal so good I thought Bev must have made it herself. We sat in our cabin groups at tables that had been pushed together, and the parents talked to one another, trading information about mortgages, school systems, weather patterns. It couldn't have been more mundane, though it did give me a chance to examine each family. Gwen's mother had a husky voice and an intense way of maintaining eye contact while she talked. Jules's parents seemed to connect with my dad and Terri, and smiled broadly at all times. Karen's parents looked like they might have felt a bit left out; her mother said something about a farmer's market at one point, but they were otherwise quite silent. All in all, a disappointingly innocent meal. Boone had still not returned from Buckhorn, where I knew she'd gone, but no one seemed to notice. I wondered if Margaret had given her a Get Out of Jail Free card for the weekend.

The only odd thing that I noticed was Gia's empty seat at her table. I hadn't seen her all day. No helicopters had landed in the parking lot, and there hadn't been any planes skimming the lake. Not that I really expected this kind of dramatic entrance, but you never know. I wondered where she was. I wouldn't have admitted this to anyone, but I wanted my dad and Terri to see the kind of friend I had. Yes, it was juvenile, but I hoped that they'd get a chance to see that the coolest girl at school wanted to be around me.

I looked for her during the all-school campfire, but she wasn't there either. I sat sandwiched between my dad and Terri, singing songs that included words like "ha'penny" and "bushel." Even the music was meant to elicit a spirit of benevolence and wholesomeness. Our voices, rising in a crescendo and then falling again in harmony, insisted that we were good.

By breakfast on Sunday, however, the spell had been broken. We were bad girls; no one could have expected us to keep up the charade for much longer. In retrospect, I'm proud of all of us for having been so damn pleasant on Saturday. It couldn't have been easy for anyone.

When Jules and I walked to the Mess Hall to meet up with our parents, some Seventeen was standing in front of the building, screaming at a nervous-looking woman in an outdated pantsuit.

"Never going to happen, Joyce! NEVER!" The Seventeen flipped her mother off and stormed away. Her mother stood there, twisting her hands together.

I looked over at Jules. "Here we go," I said.

"I hope my parents didn't see that," she muttered as we entered the dining room. The scene that greeted us, however, washed away any hope that we could maintain our facade of normalcy. The air had shifted; it had a density that was unsettling, and I took a deep breath, preparing myself. One table was populated solely by parents. They spoke to one another in tight, worried whispers, shaking their heads and looking at the next table over, where their daughters sat together, discussing their mothers and fathers in something distinctly louder than a whisper. A Fourteen stood next to the wall, jabbing her finger at her father and crying. Other tables appeared to be fine — the girls and their parents sat in their proper places — but on second glance, it was clear that no one was talking, and that the tables were merely backdrops for the angry, measured, accusatory glares that were being passed around like bowls of fruit. It was as though everyone had dreamed about each painful conversation, each thrown glass, each slammed door, and had woken up with those memories sharp and jagged in their minds.

"This happened last Parents' Weekend," Jules said to me under her breath as we made our way to our cabin's table, where our parents sat looking like shipwrecked tourists. "The first day was fine, but the second day — no one could hold it in any longer. Explosions everywhere." She smiled at me. "At least you're not angry."

"Yeah," I said. I didn't tell her that I had dreamed of New York City, my dad and Terri hand in hand in Central Park, a small child walking in front of them, clutching a Raggedy Ann doll and kicking at the leaves with green rubber boots. I had woken up sweating, my nails digging into my palm, knuckles white.

There was no one else from the cabin at our table. Boone, having come back from Ben's lookout late in the night, had risen early and was gone again before any of us woke up. Karen and her parents were at their meeting with Bev. And, from where I sat, I could just make out Gwen and her mother as they stood outside, both of them smoking long, thin cigarettes. They didn't appear to be speaking.

"Morning, Lida." My dad nodded at me and then resumed looking around the room anxiously. No doubt he was wondering when I would break down and do something stupid, like pour syrup over my own head. I looked at the syrup bottle. I thought about it.

"Well, little ladies, it appears as though the tide has shifted." Jules's dad spoke in a fake western drawl, and he winked at me and Jules. "The natives are getting restless."

"Morning, hun," Jules's mom said, reaching over to pluck a stray hair from her daughter's shirt.

"Where's Westy?" Jules asked.

"He's in the dorm. You know that dogs aren't allowed in the Mess Hall." She looked truly apologetic.

"Not for lack of trying," her dad added. "That Bev is a hard nut to crack."

"Good thing she's not here, then," I said, looking pointedly toward the window, where we could all make out the plume of smoke from Gwen's cigarette. "I wonder what she'd say about *that*."

(The teachers who *were* in the Mess Hall were clearly pretending to have lost the gift of sight. I assumed that some parents, like Gwen's mom, were just as protective of their daughters' right to smoke as they were of their own right to, say, have a screwdriver every morning with breakfast.)

I sat next to my dad at the large round table. Terri was on his other side. I reached over and grabbed an English muffin from the cornucopia of pastries, pancakes, and assorted pork products that had been laid out in the center.

"This is not how we normally eat, you know," I said as I smothered each side in butter and honey. "I haven't seen this much food since last Thanksgiving."

"I'm sure it's not that bad," said Terri. Even this subtle reprimand seemed to lack its usual gusto. She must have slept quite poorly.

The three of us ate quietly, letting the ambient sounds of other people's arguments wash over us. Jules and her parents were talking too, but I didn't pay much attention to them. Having my dad and Terri at Alice Marshall was as exhausting as a ten-mile hike, and I was famished.

After breakfast, some of the parents and their grumbling daughters made their way over to the parking lot, where, true to Boone's word, a number of horses were stamping the ground in anticipation of a trail ride. Luckily, I was spared a humiliating encounter with a saddle. It was time for our meeting with Bev.

First, though, we had to stop by the guest dorm so that Terri could grab a sweater. That woman does not engage with the elements very well. She is always too cold, too warm, too tired. Too much. I was thinking about this as my dad and I waited outside of the dorm, our hands stuffed in our pockets because, really, it was a bit chilly.

"Lida." My dad interrupted my thoughts. "You do look well. I mean, you look happier. Well-adjusted. Terri and I have noticed that."

"Thanks," I said. "It must be the result of being surrounded by so many well-adjusted role models."

My dad appeared not to notice the sarcasm in my voice. "Well, whatever it is, it's working."

"Just a few more years here, and I'll be ready to reenter the world on a part-time basis."

"Don't be like that. You've made huge strides here. Lots of things to be proud of. The only thing I wish . . ." He looked away uncomfortably.

I sighed. "What?"

"I just wish that you would try a little with Terri." It was as though he recognized the futility of what he was saying as soon as he said it, and he shook his head sadly, closing his eyes for a brief moment.

"She doesn't —" I began, but he interrupted me.

"I don't need to hear about it anymore. I love you, Lida, but this has been going on for too long." His voice was weary, but he continued. "She is trying. She has always been trying. I wish you could see that and appreciate it. If you could just give her the chance to be the mom that she wants to be to you —"

"Whatever," I said. "Thanks for the input. I'll keep it in mind the next time I find myself in a Disney Channel miniseries."

Terri came out of the dorm then with a white sweater draped over her shoulders, and we walked the rest of the way to Bev's cabin without saying a word.

When we entered, Bev was sitting in the same chair that she had sat in on my first day at the school. After she stood to shake my dad's and Terri's hands, she gestured to the couch in front of her and we all sat down. Bev crossed one ankle over another. I could see that she was wearing argyle socks beneath her gray slacks.

"Mr. and Mrs. Wallace," Bev began, "thank you for coming to Parents' Weekend. I think it's important for the girls to reconnect with their families at certain times during their enrollment at Alice Marshall." She smiled in turn at my dad, Terri, and me, her head swinging between each of us like a metronome, and then she went on. "I believe that it offers the girls the chance to reexamine old patterns of behavior that may have been destructive or have had an otherwise negative impact on their home life. For those reasons, I thank you for taking the time to come here." She lifted a folder from the table next to her and opened it. "Before we begin, do you have any questions for me?"

My dad leaned forward and propped his elbows on his knees. "Only whether Lida is making progress," he said, "and whether she's enjoying herself." He laughed as though he had made some sort of joke.

Bev apparently did not think it was funny. "Don't worry," she said, "we will be addressing those concerns." She looked down at the folder. "Let's see what the teachers say, shall we? 'Lida is doing as well as can be expected in most of her classes,'" she read aloud.

As well as can be expected? What, did I have some strange disability that I didn't know about? As well as can be expected, given the polio. As well as can be expected, with the three arms and all.

Bev continued. "'Lida shows extremely strong orienteering skills and is willing to work as a team member.'" She glanced up. "All fine so far. Good, in fact. Not everyone is a team player here, as I am sure you can imagine."

My dad smiled uncomfortably. Terri did too, though because

she was always smiling uncomfortably, it didn't make that much of an impact.

"It says here that Lida has difficulty talking about her problems with others. That is certainly something that we insist upon, and while she hasn't been here for a great deal of time, it has been long enough that she should be participating in our larger discussion groups." Bev had a concerned expression on her face, the way a mechanic might look at a man who had just brought in a junker that he hadn't bothered to repair for a number of years.

"Lida?" My dad turned to me. "What's going on? Why aren't you participating?"

This was exasperating. Surely they didn't expect me to open up then and there, divulging my feelings like I had just been waiting to be asked. I reverted back to the tried-and-true shrug.

My dad shrugged right back at me. "That's your answer? That's not good enough." He was tensing up, I could see. Old patterns of behavior, indeed.

Bev interrupted. "Let's ask Lida to use her words."

Use her words? Well, if that's how they saw me . . .

"Bottle," I said. "Ga-ga." I stuck my thumb in my mouth, and took it out again. "Binkie."

"Lida Renee!" my dad said. Bev sat back, frowning at me. On my left, however, I heard a short burst of laughter that was quickly muffled. I looked over at Terri, who had a hand clapped over her mouth. She wouldn't make eye contact with me. Everything up to that moment had followed the familiar script that dominated all of my conversations with my dad. Terri's laughter, however? *That* was new.

Bev pointedly ignored Terri's outburst. She addressed me directly. "I know that these kinds of conversations can be uncomfortable," she said, "but they are a necessary aspect of your education here. Your refusal to participate in the discussion group is reflecting poorly on your performance at Alice Marshall. What do you think that means?"

My first impulse was to say something sarcastic ("I guess this means that I won't make Varsity this year"), but this was Bev I was talking to, not my dad. So I hedged my bets. "I don't know," I said.

"It means that we will have to deduce that you are not getting the skills you need in order to reenter your home life with confidence. It means that I have to encourage you to remain here until you acquire those skills." She addressed this last bit to my dad and Terri.

It was obvious that Bev thought this was a pretty good threat. She probably used it in most of her meetings, thinking that it would whip the girls into shape. How funny that, of all the people who worked at Alice Marshall, the director would be the most oblivious. Oh no! I would have to stay longer! I wouldn't be able to go home! *Why* did Bev think that any of us would ever want to go home? What did she think we were eager to return to?

Nevertheless, I made the requisite sad face, as though I had been hoping that this meeting would signal my release from the school. My dad and Terri made their sad faces too. They were probably just as relieved as I was.

We passed Jules and her parents as we left. Jules's mother was smiling and talking to Westy in a high-pitched baby voice as the dog ran in wide circles around their moving feet. Jules gave me a little wave as she disappeared into Bev's cabin.

We had some time before the vans were supposed to leave: two hours and seven minutes, not that I was counting. We got coffee from the Mess Hall (where a gaggle of ostracized mothers sat hunched over their mugs, speaking to one another in furious whispers), and then we stood outside looking at Bob, the bell, anywhere but at one another.

When Margaret walked by, my dad raised his arm in a jaunty wave. She came over to us, smiling broadly and adjusting the sleeves of her sweater. "Mr. and Mrs. Wallace," she said, "I hope you're enjoying your time with Lida."

"We are, we are," said my dad. "And are you —" He fumbled, clearly unsure of how to proceed. *Are you enjoying yourself as well? Are you having fun with Lida too?* He laughed at himself and changed the subject. "You teach the Outdoor Ed class, right?"

"Sure do," said Margaret.

"You don't know by chance where the English teacher is, do you? I'd love to hear more about the play Lida was in." If he'd been that kind of dad and I'd been that kind of daughter, I'm sure he would have given me one of those classic awkward-slash-proud side-hugs at that point. "Sounds like a fun project, though I have to say" — he chuckled — "I'm surprised that they took it so far, you know, asking the girls to cut their hair."

"Ah," said Margaret. She looked at me, a microburst of laughter in her eyes. Then she turned to my dad and smiled blandly. "You know, I think she went on the mail run. But yes, Lida does have a wonderful acting instinct, doesn't she?"

I looked away, trying not to laugh.

"Must run," said Margaret, gesturing toward the Mess Hall. "I'm on cleanup duty today."

Obviously, that included cleaning up our little white lies. We watched her walk away, her sweater hanging bulkily over her tiny frame.

"Great teacher, that Margaret," said my dad. "I was glad to hear Bev say that you're doing well in her Outdoors class." He had his hands in the pockets of his jeans, and he rocked back and forth on the balls of his feet while he talked. "You know, Margaret told me privately yesterday that you're her star pupil. She said you have a real facility for orienteering."

I stared at him. Margaret said that? "I just pay attention," I said. "You'd have to be pretty stupid to get lost with a map."

"Is that so." My dad chuckled. "I might beg to differ. You're looking at the most inept Boy Scout to ever set foot in the wilderness. I couldn't find my way out of a shoe box when I was your age." He shook his head. "You must have gotten your outdoor skills from your mother. She always knew just where to go —" He stopped suddenly.

There was a long moment during which my dad's face turned red and I looked above his forehead to the web of branches on an old pine tree. Had he really just said that? I thought about changing the subject, saving us from this awkward conversation, but I couldn't; I had to know.

"She did?" I asked, my voice scratchy.

He looked at me and spoke slowly. "She did. Your mother used to lead backpacking trips in Alaska before we got married. Didn't you know that?" Then he blushed and spoke softly, as though to himself. "Well. How would you?"

Whenever I thought about my mother, I imagined her in a series of black-and-white photographs that I'd never actually seen but had developed in my mind anyway. My mother and father, dancing on their wedding day. My mother at the sink in a farmhouse where I'm sure they never lived, washing tomatoes, her hair in a bandanna. My mother in the hospital, holding me in a blanket. My mother walking out the door, locking it behind her. To these pictures I now added a new one: a young woman with a backpack, standing on the crest of a mountain and holding her hand to shield her eyes as she surveyed the wilderness below. A young woman with shorter hair, a crooked smile. A woman who looked like me.

I glanced over at Terri, who seemed to have stepped back while my dad and I talked. I expected her to look uncomfortable, even annoyed that the dreaded specter of my dad's first wife was floating around the conversation. But she was just standing in her normal posture, looking out at Bob.

Dad cleared his throat. His voice was gruff. "Whatever your mother did later in life," he said, stumbling over the words, "whatever demons she may have succumbed to, she had good intentions for you, once." He took a breath. "She always talked about how she wanted you to grow up in the mountains."

"What else did she want for me?" I spoke quickly, afraid I'd lose my courage. Even so, I couldn't ask the question that was always in the back of my mind: *And why couldn't she stay to give it to me?*

My dad looked steadily at me. "She wanted so much for you, Bun. But she couldn't —" He stopped. Then he said, "Maybe it's time we started talking about some of these things. Maybe I've tried too hard to shield you." He shook his head. "Maybe I've been shielding myself. In some ways, I think, I've let you down."

I stuffed my hands in my jeans pockets. I noticed for the first time that my dad and I shared the same nose, the same way of scrunching our eyes almost shut when we were feeling vulnerable. "You did a good enough job," I said. "I'm not totally fucked-up." I smiled at him, just for a second. "Maybe there's hope for me yet."

The grin burst across my dad's face, and he stepped forward as though he was going to pick me up and swing me around. He settled for slapping me on the back and laughing. "Yep," he said. "I'd say there is."

And that was it. We didn't say anything else about my mother. I had a feeling that the conversation would continue, though, that we'd talk about her more when I left the school. It seemed like, having told me something about her, my dad had exhausted his reserves of good memories for the day. But he didn't stop smiling for about five minutes, and I wondered at the ease with which I could make my dad happy. Just saying "I'm not totally fucked-up" had sent him spinning off into giddiness and bliss; what would happen if I said something even kinder? Would he implode?

"Well," I said finally, "you guys probably need to pack. I should clean up around the cabin too." What a lie. The cabin was spotless. Quarantined rooms during a flu epidemic weren't as clean as it was that weekend.

"That's a good idea," my dad said. "Why don't I go back to the dorm and get our things together. Terri, you and Lida can work on her cabin."

"Oh —" I started, but he was already walking away, his shoes crunching on dried pine needles. I turned to Terri. "You don't have to help. Really. I've got it."

"That's okay," she said flatly. "It'll be fun." She sighed, and followed me to the cabin.

No one was there. Just my luck. Also, there wasn't anything to put away, aside from a beach towel that I had hung over the end of my bunk the day before. I peeled my hoodie from my T-shirt and took it off, tossing it on my bed. I wasn't hot, but I needed something to fold.

"Here, let me." Terri grabbed the beach towel and began folding it. She took her time.

I picked the hoodie back up and folded it. Then I unfolded it. Then I folded it again. I was waiting for her to speak. Surely there was a smug sermon coming my way.

Sure enough: "Lida, you are such a worry in your father's heart," Terri said. I was about to tell her that I didn't need to hear it when she went on. "But sometimes you are just so funny." She set down the towel on a dresser, her back to me, so it was hard for me to hear, at first. But Terri was laughing. "I mean, where do you come up with this stuff? 'Ga-ga.' That was price-less!" She kept laughing. "That Bev is a piece of work. Did you see her face? I mean, did you see her *socks*?"

This would have been the time for me to join her, the two of us giggling together like sisters, but I couldn't. I was in shock. So I just stared at Terri as she doubled over with amusement and waited for her laughter to die down. Finally, she held up one hand as though to stop me from saying something.

"Okay, okay," she said, catching her breath. "You don't see it. But I do. You're smart, Lida. Quick with words. Lord knows I've always felt one step behind you."

I didn't know what to say. I'd imagined a lot of things about the way Terri felt toward me over the years: angry, annoyed, resent-ful, jealous . . . But I'd never thought she could feel intimidated.

Terri was watching me closely. "I know that I was . . . hesitant . . . around you when your dad and I first got together," she said quietly. "I didn't have any experience with children, and you were just so . . . angry." She shook her head. "I can see now why you would be. After all, your little world had just shattered and I stepped in and — " She took a deep breath. "But that was a long time ago. Someday you're going to have to accept that your father and I love you. That I love you." There was a pause, and then she placed her hand on my shoulder and squeezed. "I don't know why that's so hard. But one of these days, I hope you see it."

She was waiting for a reaction, and this time, she wasn't going to let me off the hook. So I said the most truthful thing I could. "I'm trying." I looked at the rafters; I looked at the floorboards. I looked at Terri, and I nodded my head and said it again. "I'm trying."

She nodded. "So am I." We stood there, smiling self-consciously at each other until I broke the gaze and kicked at the floor with my shoe. Terri turned around and looked at the cabin.

"Well," she said, as though nothing had transpired, "why don't we get this place cleaned up? It looked pretty good yesterday."

I refrained from telling her that we'd just effectively cleaned it by putting away the towel, and I let her putter around the cabin, straightening the tops of the dressers, opening and then shutting the drawers more securely. She was still talking — had moved on to the scintillating topic of their new dishwasher — but I wasn't really listening. Who was this woman? Laughing at my jokes, telling me she loved me — not the old Terri, that's for sure. Had she been sent away to a school for resentful stepmothers? Had she been weaving God's Eyes and discussing her failings with the other parents? Or was this new Terri actually the one who had been there all along? No, that was impossible. If she'd been trying, I would have seen it. Right?

Oh, hello, Ann. I wonder if I might join you and Lida.

I closed my eyes. Saw the plate hit the door, the cookies strewn across the carpet.

I wonder if I might join you.

It was suddenly silent in the cabin, and I realized that Terri had finished her detailed comparison of Maytag and Kenmore. I opened my eyes and looked at her. She picked up my hoodie from where I'd placed it on top of the dresser and held it in her hands. "You're surrounded by some pretty tough lives here," she said, glancing at the empty bunks.

"I guess."

"That one girl — what's her name — Bullet?"

"Boone," I said.

"Anyway, she seems to have had a rough time of it." Terri began to fold the hoodie neatly. "Is she nice to you?" She stole a glance at me. "I mean," she corrected, "there's no bad blood or anything, is there?"

I resisted the urge to touch my hair. "We get along fine," I said.

"Good." Terri let out a breath. "I'd hate to get on the wrong side of her."

I didn't say anything. There was no way I was going to gossip about Boone. She would know about it before the words even left my mouth.

Terri prattled on, unaware that I wasn't responding. "And that poor Julie," she said. "Talk about a tragic case."

That got my attention. "What do you mean?"

Terri looked up quickly. Clearly, she thought I knew. "Oh," she said uncomfortably. She looked around the room, down at her hands, anywhere but at me.

"Tell me," I said.

She spoke quickly. "It's really not all that dramatic, and I didn't know it was a secret. I thought you knew; it's probably not my place . . ."

"Tell me."

"Oh, Lida." Terri looked at me with resignation and what? Pity? "Fine." She sighed. "Julie is a sweet girl. She really hasn't done anything terrible. What was it her mother told me? Treasurer of the student body? Something like that." She had folded the hoodie yet again, and she looked down at it in her hands as though confused as to how it got there. "Anyway," she went on, "it's just one of those tragic stories. Julie and her two best friends were driving up to a ski hill for the day last winter and they hit some ice. And, well, Julie was driving too fast, and her mother said something about looking for a song on the iPod — I think — and they went off the road." Terri shrugged helplessly. "A terrible accident. Just terrible. And Julie walked away unscathed. But the other two didn't." She paused to let this sink in. "She didn't go to jail — no one pressed charges — but school, I think, was difficult after that. Either she felt unwelcome, or it was just too much of a reminder, but she stopped going."

"But how did she end up here?" I shifted my weight from one foot to the other. Jules did have a Thing, after all. But unlike the rest of us, she didn't choose hers.

"That's the funny part, if you can call it that. She picked it. Told her parents that this was the only place she'd go. Funny choice, huh." Terri smiled weakly at me.

I didn't stop thinking about Jules as I walked around the school grounds one last time with my dad and Terri, or when I stood by the fleet of vans and waved them off, fighting back a sudden, childlike impulse to cry. There were only a handful of girls standing in the parking lot — it appeared as though the tensions of the morning had not been repaired — but Jules wasn't among them.

Jules. Who had welcomed me to school as though welcoming me to summer camp. Who, with her incessantly cheerful attitude, never seemed to fit the Alice Marshall mold. I had always chalked her admission up to a fluke, but what did I think? That she was blameless? No one was. But I was willing to bet that she was the only girl at school who had decided to enroll, instead of having it decided for her. And while I knew that we all wore our guilt like suffocating garments, hers was made worse by the fact that it was an *accident*. Nothing the rest of us had ever done had been accidental.

She was in the cabin when I returned from the parking lot. She was reading a magazine, but I noticed that she never turned the page.

"Well, they're off," I said. "Good-bye, parental nightmares." It sounded fake even as I said it.

She kept her eyes fixed on the page. "I know," she said. "I couldn't see my parents off. I would have tried to keep Westy. Hide him in my pillowcase or something. It would have been too hard." She looked up. It was clear that she had been crying. "Did you see them? What were they doing?"

I hadn't. I'd been so fixated on enduring the hugs and getting my dad and Terri into the van as quickly as possible, a hard knot forming in my throat, that I didn't notice anyone else's parents. Her mom and dad could have been drinking wine coolers and high-fiving for all I knew.

"Yeah," I said, "they looked pretty pathetic. I think Westy was whimpering. He was trying to get off your mom's lap, but she held on. It was a heroic effort."

Jules smiled. "He's a great dog," she said. "I thought he wanted to stay with me."

I watched her as she looked back down at the magazine and slowly turned the page. Her forehead was creased, and she wrinkled her nose in concentration as she read. She looked fragile, like a glass egg that would shatter if pressed too hard. There was no way I could ever tell her that I knew about her Thing.

Epilogue

Terri comes into my room. They're worried about me, I can tell. They think I don't see the raised eyebrows and tight little frowns that they give each other at the dinner table, as though I'm still nine and only four feet tall, as though they can still shoot looks over my head. They're worried, and maybe they should be.

"You've been spending a lot of time in here," she says, jerking her chin toward the bed, the dresser. "It's almost summer. Don't you want to get outside?"

"I'm fine here," I say. I have my arm across the paper on my desk, just in case she tries to look.

"Jen and Gretchen keep calling," she says. "What happened? Did you fight about something? You're all still going to the graduation party next week, right?"

I can hear the concern in her voice. It's real. Not accusatory, not exasperated. Just genuine worry. I look at her arms hanging by her side, and remember how they used to look just like that before, when we were in the counselor's office or the emergency room.

"I'm just kind of caught up in a project," I say. "I'll call them back later." And I will. I'll call them and we'll load into Gretchen's old Volvo and

head out to Powder Mountain with our bikes, take the chairlift to the top, speed down over the green slopes as the world unfolds below us. *I will do this. But later.*

"You'd tell us if —" She pauses, wanting to be careful. "I mean, Lida, if you felt as though —" She sighs, annoyed with herself. "'No more tiptoeing,'" she says, repeating one of our newer family mottoes. "Just tell me if you're okay. Are you okay?"

"I'm okay."

When she leaves, the door whispering shut behind her, I turn back to the page I was working on. *I'm running out of time, I think. I have to get this down now, before I forget how easily it all unraveled in front of me, like a loose knot of yarn that needed only to be shaken out. No. That's not right. I wasn't an innocent bystander. When it unraveled, I was there, holding the knot, shaking with all my might.*

CHAPTER THIRTEEN

THERE WAS AN INITIAL FLURRY OF GOSSIP ON THE DAY THAT the parents left (Sasha's mom's eyebrows were tattooed onto her forehead; Lindsey's parents wouldn't speak to each other, forcing Lindsey to act as a kind of U.N. translator; Ronnie told her dad to fuck off in front of Bev). Everyone compared notes about their meetings with Bev, and it turned out that *none* of us had been deemed fit to leave Alice Marshall. Surprise, surprise.

But if the theme of Parents' Weekend was Good Clean Fun, then the theme of the week that followed was Pretend It Never Happened. I guess most girls, for their own reasons, wanted to put it behind them. I know I did. Terri's odd behavior, the news about Jules, Gia's absence, and what my dad had told me about my mother — there were too many things to decipher, like paintings on an ancient stone wall.

That's why we ignored it. But it's hard work, pretending to be unaffected all the time. Hard, hard work. No wonder there were some minor fistfights in the cabins (though not in ours) in the days following the visits. Name calling, hair pulling, even the No. 2 pencil that mysteriously found its way into the back of one Fifteen's head, sending her (briefly) to the Infirmary — we knew it was kid's play compared to what we felt like doing.

Needless to say, the Smokers' Beach was crowded after the parents left.

When I finally saw Gia on Monday, she didn't want to talk about the fact that her father hadn't been there; he'd been way-laid by business in Bangkok, she said. I dropped the subject. Jules talked about her parents incessantly for about two days before Gwen asked her (not very politely, I thought) to shut the hell up. Boone didn't say anything about what she'd done all weekend, but she did produce two new bottles of rye whiskey, so no one asked. Regardless of whether the weekend had been terrible or merely tolerable, we all emerged feeling like we'd escaped. At the very least, we all had to stay. And that was just fine with us.

By the time the next Saturday rolled around, everyone was exhausted from the effort it took to forget Parents' Weekend. Most of us stayed in our cabins, holed up on our bunks, not talking to anyone all afternoon. I wrote in my journal, an activity that was becoming rather habitual. I had already written about my Thing, and now that I had shown it to Gia, I felt like the worst was over. What else could I possibly write? Still, I couldn't forget the wave of stillness that passed over me once I had written it down, and so I kept trying, filling pages with my thoughts about the school, about my cabinmates, about Gia. I wrote about what it felt like to be around her, and the fact that I was scared (ridiculously so, I told myself) that she would tire of me.

Eventually, though, I ran out of things to say, so I decided to wander around the school grounds, grabbing a cup of coffee from the Mess Hall first. Flashes of Bob were visible through the trees as I walked, the lake calm and unrattled. I envied the lake its ability to thrash and roil one minute, causing docks and stray life jackets to toss about wildly, and to lie dormant the next, unflappable as a school principal. We thought there might be sturgeon or sharks hiding in Bob's depths, but when we fished, *if* we fished, we only caught lake trout and bottom-feeders, and were disappointed. Winter was another thing, or so I heard. Bob iced over, but not enough to skate across, and the wind cut across the rocks and moved the trees almost horizontally. You had to practically be an action hero to get in and out of Alice Marshall once the first snow fell.

So that Saturday, I was standing by the Mess Hall, having just returned my mug to the kitchen, when I heard the crunch and rustle of someone coming up quickly behind me. I felt a hand on my shoulder. I hadn't seen Gia all day and was hoping that she'd find me.

I turned. "Hi," I said, trying to mask my disappointment.

Boone smiled at me conspiratorially. "Let's get the hell out of here," she said. "This place feels like a sanitarium."

"Where should we go?" I asked, even though I knew damn well what she had in mind.

Boone didn't say anything, but she pointed her finger toward the sky.

I squinted my eyes, peering into the trees. Maybe Gia was in the Rec Lodge with the I-bankers.

"What are you waiting for? A transcendental moment? Come on!" Boone started toward the path to Buckhorn. With one last glance behind me, I trundled after.

By this time, I had figured out that Boone slowed her pace down whenever she was hiking with me. Neither of us ever mentioned it. As we hiked, though, I realized that I was speeding up. Lately, I'd been spending more time watching Gia roll cigarettes than smoking them myself, and I could feel the difference. My legs felt stronger, more capable. Since I wasn't hunched over my shoes in a breathless contortion of pain, I was able to focus on the landscape around me: the dry, naked stalks of grass, the golden crust of pitch on the sides of old pine trees. I breathed in deeply. The thought flew through my mind before I had a chance to check it: *This is the life.* It was a cool afternoon, and I pulled the sleeves of my shirt down over my knuckles as we walked. Autumn, it seemed, was alive and well in the Frank.

Finally, when I felt the need to break the silence, I asked Boone about the book Ben had lent her. "How was *The Dharma Bums*?"

She stopped on the trail with one foot resting on a large rock. "How would I know?" she said.

"Oh," I said, confused. "So you haven't finished it yet?"

Boone laughed. "I've finished it," she said, pulling the book out of the back waistband of her jeans. "You could say I drank it up." She opened the book so that I could see where the pages had been carved out in the shape of a bottle. A small, presumably empty flask rested snugly in the hollow.

"Some book club," I said.

"I find it to be quite inspirational," said Boone. "And refreshing," she added, slipping the book back into her pants.

As we continued up the path, Boone told me that Ben often gave her little "pick-me-ups" like that one, because, she said, "he knows I can handle it." He had always ordered wine and bourbon to be delivered on the back of a burro with the rest of his monthly supplies anyway, and he had taken to ordering just one or two extra bottles for her.

"Ben was wild when he was our age," Boone told me. "He was a jock — a footballer — but he never felt like he fit into that world. So he did other stuff. Lots of other stuff." She skirted around a fallen log in the path, pointing behind her so that I wouldn't trip over it. "He and I are more alike than you'd know.

We're basically the same person." She quickly added, "I mean, as far as that goes."

I wondered about that as we got nearer to Ben's lookout. It was hard to imagine Ben — good-looking, confident — as ever having screwed up. Ben struck me as the kind of person who had *always* had his shit together.

"Why, hello, girls," he said when we finally got there. Boone had let out a long, high whistle as we got near, and Ben was standing in front of the lookout with two glasses of water, waiting. "Glad to see you." He looked at me and shook his head. "Lida, you're looking very rugged these days. Elsa must be rubbing off on you."

I looked down. It was true that my arms were tan and strong, and that my legs no longer threatened to snap under the weight of a backpack. I *had* gotten more fit. I smiled.

"Well, you two are just in time," Ben went on. "I was about to shoot my own foot for something to do."

"I thought you were an avid reader," Boone said, taking a long sip of water and handing him his empty book. "Don't tell me it's gotten that bad."

Ben shook the book gently in front of Boone's face. "This is one of my favorites," he said. "But even so, I need to hear real voices from time to time, not just the voices in my head. Wouldn't you agree, Lida?" he asked, turning to me.

He caught me off-guard, but I nodded. "You must have some pretty serious voices to be able to stay up here for so long."

"You can't imagine what they say." Ben laughed. "It's every lookout's curse: You're always alone, and yet you're never alone. I don't know anyone who has done a stint on a mountaintop without questioning their sanity two, three times a day."

"You wanna talk bat-shit crazy, you should try the school," said Boone. "It might give you a run for your money."

"All those girls? Say no more; I'd lose my mind."

We followed Ben as he walked back to the lookout. The wind had picked up, and it cut across the rocks and scrabble to slap us. I raised my hand to shield my face.

"I was just about to open a bottle of wine," Ben said as he held the door for us. "An early happy hour. It's that kind of day."

"Damn straight," said Boone, plopping herself down in one of the chairs around the wooden table. "It's that kind of month."

Ben walked over and put a hand on her shoulder. He laughed softly. "I think we could all take a breather here. Lida, I hope you won't be offended if we imbibe a little." He winked at me. "You're more than welcome to join us, of course." He pulled a box out from under his cot and reached in, grabbing a dusty bottle of red wine. Wiping it on his shirt, he set the bottle and three water glasses on the table. I guess he took my silence as acquiescence. Ben uncorked the wine and poured generous amounts in each glass. "To your health," he said, raising his glass in a toast.

"To your liver," Boone said, before tipping her glass and taking a long drink.

To be honest, I hadn't had much red wine before. Liquor, definitely. Beer, sometimes, those few instances when I stood outside of the 7-Eleven and asked dirty men to buy it for me "and my friends," imagining what it would be like to carry the six-pack triumphantly back to a waiting car full of laughing girls. Truth was, I hardly ever finished all of the beer before throwing the remaining cans in the trash and walking home.

Wine was different. It was smooth and full, and it cut through the cool afternoon to settle warmly in my stomach. I felt distinguished. Maybe it was the feel of the heavy water glass in my hand, or maybe it was the way that the wind carried the smell of pine needles and moss through the thin walls of Ben's house. Whatever it was, I wanted more. I felt like I could stay up there forever, drinking wine and half listening to the banter between

Boone and Ben. Everything else — Gia, the school, my dad and Terri, my mother — slipped away. The afternoon grew sweetly hazy and muddled.

"So, what's happening with the Princess?" Ben's voice broke my reverie. We were finishing our second large glasses of wine, and the bottle was nearly empty. He leaned forward, resting his forearms on the table. "She up to more tricks?"

Boone narrowed her eyes at Ben and nodded toward me. "Let's drop it," she said.

"Who are you talking about?" I asked. "Who's the Princess?"

"You must know her," Ben said. "Some little lady who thinks she owns the school, right, Elsa? I don't know her name, and I don't really care. She's the Princess to me."

"Ben, seriously. We didn't come up here to bitch and whine. Drop it."

"Why?"

"Because Lida and I don't agree on everything," she said, looking at me.

"Oh," I said slowly. I knew who she was talking about now.

Ben turned to me. "Don't tell me you and this Princess are friends," he chided. "She sounds like a real piece of work."

I looked at my empty glass. "She's different when you get to know her," I said quietly.

"Yeah, I'm sure Hitler's wife said that about him too," Boone snapped.

Ben raised his hands in defeat. "Simmer down, ladies," he said. "I was just making conversation. I'll stick to safer subjects from now on."

"Good idea," said Boone. "You don't want to mess with catfights."

"Wise words, wise words," Ben agreed, pouring the last of the wine in our glasses. "Let's wipe the slate clean with another toast." He lifted his glass once more. "Lida? You do the honors this time."

I raised my glass and looked at Boone. She shrugged. "No more drama," I said.

"No more drama."

We didn't talk about Gia on the way back down the mountain. We didn't talk much at all, actually, because we were too busy walking carefully, our feet cautious and slow. I wouldn't say that we were drunk, exactly, but the mountain seemed much larger and the trees less familiar. Boone had given Ben his copy of *The Dharma Bums* when we first arrived, and before we left, he handed it back to her with a wink. She kept checking to make sure it hadn't fallen out of the waistband of her pants as we walked. I could imagine the liquor inside of it sloshing around with each step, and it made me dizzy. I had the odd sensation that I was walking at an angle, and I kept straightening my back and rolling my shoulders to correct it.

At the bottom of the trail, Boone patted me on the back, and I raised my shoulders protectively. "Scared much?" she asked. "God, you always act like I'm going to hit you or something. Anyway," she continued, "I was just going to say that today was kind of fun." I turned around to catch her customary smirk, but it wasn't there. She was nodding at me. "Seriously." She walked quickly toward the cabin.

I watched her leave. I thought back to the first time I met her, and how she had looked at me like she could have just wadded me up and thrown me away. I didn't know which side of her I could trust: tough and hard, or earnest, almost kind.

Everything around me was still a little fuzzy, like I was constantly squinting, so I decided to head down to the dock. There were still twenty minutes before dinner, and I wanted to give my head a chance to clear before making conversation with the other girls. I was pretty sure that Margaret would be able to tell exactly how many ounces of wine I had drunk just by glancing at me from across the Mess Hall. Plus, I wanted to be by the lake.

I stood on the beach and looked out across Bob to the mountains beyond. I let the breeze tousle my hair, and I planted my feet firmly on the sand. Raised my arms up over my head and swung them in lazy circles, copying some of Margaret's morning exercises. Brought my arms down before bending at the waist and rolling my torso from side to side. I felt like an acrobat, a yogi. I swung my head first in one direction, so that I could see the top of Buckhorn, and then I swung it the other way. My eyes locked on Gia's. She was standing just behind me and to the right. Knowing my luck, she'd been there the whole time.

"Shit," I said, "you scared me." I laughed. My laughter sounded too loud. "I was just . . . exercising."

Gia stared at me for a moment. I knew how stupid I looked, how ridiculous I sounded. I wouldn't have been surprised if she had laughed at me and walked away. But she just kept her gaze on me until I blushed. I crossed my arms over my chest and stared at the ground.

"I looked everywhere for you," she said. I glanced back up at Gia. She shook her head. "Where have you been?" Her eyes were lit embers. "What were you and Boone doing?" She pronounced Boone's name as though it was fake, with a little pause before the *B* that could just as well have been quotation marks: *If that's her REAL name.*

"We went on a hike," I said. How did she know I'd been with Boone? How long had she been watching me?

"Where?"

"Up a mountain."

"Which mountain?"

I shouldn't have paused then and shifted my weight from one foot to another. Nothing says Outright Lie like a pause before speaking. "Up Vespers Summit," I said.

"For three hours? You took your time," Gia said coolly.

I kicked myself mentally for not thinking of a different mountain. Vespers was an anthill compared to Buckhorn. I could have been up it and back in the time it took to have a morning shower.

"I had no idea you were friends with her," Gia said. She waved her hand in the direction Boone had gone. "I mean, I didn't know you guys hung out. What else have you kept from me?" For a moment, her mouth trembled, then she pursed her lips together. Her voice was hard. "Lida, look: I'm not your babysitter. You can do anything you want with anyone you want." She waited a beat and continued. "But you *know* how much she hates me."

I nodded.

"So you can imagine how much this hurts my feelings." She scuffed the toe of one shoe in the dirt. "I mean, can't you?"

I nodded.

"I don't think I've asked much from our friendship," she went on, "but I never thought I'd have to ask for your loyalty. You know, just plain respect. Now I see that I should have. I guess you must think of me as kind of . . . I don't know, temporary."

"No!" I said. "God. I mean, you could never be temporary. Boone just —"

Gia interrupted, speaking softly. "Sometimes," she said, "it feels like you just don't have time for me."

"I'm sorry," I said. My face was burning. I felt about three years old.

"You always say that." She shook her head and turned to walk away.

There was something about the finality of her back as it moved away from me. The words were out before I felt myself open my mouth. "Boone is friends with the guy in the fire lookout. We were up visiting him."

Gia turned slowly back around. "Guy?" she asked.

"Just a ranger," I added lamely. I was trying to backpedal but couldn't figure out how. "Just some guy."

"And you two visit him often?" Gia straightened her shoulders and narrowed her eyes at me. "You weren't going to tell me about this." A statement, not a question. "Your best friend."

I felt a warm bubble pop somewhere down low in my chest. I tried to keep from smiling.

"You're a different person than I thought you were." Gia wasn't smiling at all.

"No." I couldn't think of anything else to say. *Best friend best friend best friend.*

"I don't keep anything from you."

"No." *Best friend.*

"I would never."

"No." I wanted so badly to reach out and grab her hand, touch her face, rest one palm on that cool cheek.

Gia sighed, long and low, like she was giving up on something. Finally and irrevocably. "Well. I guess I know where I stand." She looked away.

"No!" It was a high-pitched shout. I'd never heard a sound like that come from my own throat. "It's not like that!" I was shaking. I knew she was going to leave me if I didn't come up with the right combination of words. I had to say the right thing, had to make her understand. "He's Boone's friend, not mine. I've only been there a couple of times with her. I think . . . I think she doesn't like to hike alone. And we only stay for a little while. I hardly know him at all."

Gia watched me as I floundered through my excuses. "Right," she said finally.

I pressed on. "I mean, he's not even that exciting. It's pretty up there, sure, but he's just kind of sitting around with his maps and his books. You'd probably think it's boring."

"How old is he?"

"Twenty-five," I said.

"And are he and Boone . . . ?"

"I don't think so."

"Huh," Gia said quietly, studying her hands. She picked casually at a fingernail. "Well, then, there's only one thing to do."

I knew what she was about to say, and mentally willed her to say something else, something like, *We just have to pretend this conversation never happened,* or *You have to stop going up the mountain with Boone.* I would agree to any of it, if only she wouldn't say what I knew she was about to.

"You have to take me up there."

There was no arguing, of course. Gia spoke as plainly as though she was telling me to screw the cap back on a tube of toothpaste.

CHAPTER FOURTEEN

IT WAS HARD TO FIND A TIME TO GO. I'VE LEARNED THAT YOU can always find obstacles to keep you from doing the things you don't want to do, but that these things ultimately have a way of imposing themselves on you anyway, so you find yourself singing in church choir or babysitting the neighbors' kids or eating a slice of fruitcake at an old person's holiday party. Taking Gia up Buckhorn was like that, but worse. For a week or so, I managed to be busy. Too busy. We were reading *Tender Is the Night* in English class, and I spent a lot of time in the cabin, trying to finish it before the discussion. Miraculously, our science teacher finally gave us homework. That kept me occupied for an afternoon as well. Lots of things, really.

But could I tell you what *Tender Is the Night* is about? Nope. Do I even know what we were studying in science? Huh-uh. What I was really doing during all those boring hours was hiding. Hiding and thinking about Gia, and how she'd looked at me when I told her I'd been up Buckhorn with Boone. I could see how that might cut her, make her wonder what kind of friend I was, whether I might be some kind of double agent, a disloyal companion who goes around telling secrets and playing both sides. I had never talked to Boone about Gia, not in any real way. And I never would. But Gia couldn't know that, could she?

These things swirled around in my head as I listlessly turned the pages of my book or jotted down notes. And amid this maelstrom, one thought appeared again and again, elbowing its way to the front of the line and blocking out the others. *Best friend.*

As though on cue, the weather started turning. Less than two weeks after Parents' Weekend, we woke to the sight of our own breath fogging up the cabin. The pine needles still crunched underneath our feet as we walked, but now the crunch was more brittle, as though the frost that would inevitably blanket the woods with infinitesimal icicles had already taken up residence. Boone started wearing a skullcap to bed at night. Gwen wrote to her mother and asked her to send a box of skiers' hand warmers. I spent more and more time in the Bathhouse shower when no one was there, just letting the hot water run over the top of my head.

One morning, I headed to the Bathhouse before the rest of the school awoke, crossing my arms over my chest and clutching my shoulders like a saint or a mummy. I had always liked showering at this time. The sun was just beginning to rise, and the air around me was soft and gray. In this light, even the trees looked indistinct. Though the landscape seemed completely still, a sepia-toned photograph, there was yet a low hum that resonated through the woods as the birds awoke and called out to one another: chickadee, flicker, tanager, warbler. We'd learned to identify birdsong in Margaret's class, and I'd realized quickly that I had an ear for the nuanced patterns of their calls. I felt comforted by the thought that the forest was like this every morning — impassive, beckoning, alive — whether I awoke to see it or not.

Showering alone was a gift I gave myself. I never showered in front of the other girls anyway, but those mornings when I was able to drag myself out of my sleeping bag and tiptoe across the cabin without waking anyone else, my feet whispering across the floorboards, were when I most appreciated the school. Walking alone to the Bathhouse, opening the door, stepping into its humid warmth — at those times, I could pretend that I had chosen all of it. That it had been my decision, like it had been Jules's. I allowed myself to love it. Now that it was so cold out, these mornings were even more precious to me.

I spent a little more time showering that morning, lost in the same thoughts that had plagued me all week. It was so warm in the Bathhouse that I felt comfortably drowsy, and I was in no hurry to leave. Finally, though, my fingers began to resemble dried cranberries. I stepped out of the shower, wrapping my towel around me.

Gia was standing across the room, watching me. Had she just gotten there? Had she followed me all the way from my cabin? No, that was crazy, I told myself. Her arms were crossed as she leaned against one of the sinks, studying me.

"You sure have a way of surprising a lady," I said awkwardly, and then, when she didn't respond, I added, "I didn't know you were a morning person." It was as good a greeting as I could manage.

She still didn't say anything. She came toward me softly, almost floating. There was a look on her face that was the strangest blend of curiosity and conviction. I remember thinking that if I moved one muscle, if I even shifted my weight, she could hear my bones knocking against one another.

Gia stopped with only about six inches between the two of us. She reached out and hooked a corner of the towel with her finger, pulling it so that my left side from my thigh to my ribs was exposed. My scars were red and puffy from the heat of the shower, cutting across the skin in a pattern decipherable only by me. I had sketched it myself during still, solitary afternoons, my school books outside the bathroom door where I dropped them, no sound but that of my labored breath.

Gia let the towel hang open and traced the crisscrossed lines on my hip with her finger as if she was reading a newspaper. "Oh, Lida," she said sadly. Very slowly, she let the towel drop. We stood eye to eye, our inhalations and exhalations in harmony with one another. The only other sound in the room was the rhythmic *drip, drip* of a leaking showerhead. Then she leaned forward until her mouth was hot against my ear.

"I'm sorry about the other day," she said, her voice a throaty whisper. "I should never have doubted your loyalty." She took one step backward, turned, and walked out of the Bathhouse.

"What's wrong with you?" Boone leaned over and hit my plate with the side of her fork. "Still having nightmares about Parents' Weekend?"

I shook my head. "Sorry. Lost in thought, I guess."

Breakfast was almost over, and I couldn't stop looking aimlessly around the room. It must have seemed aimless, I mean. I would look over toward the door first. Then my gaze shifted slightly to the other table of Sixteens. Then over to Margaret, where she was eating oatmeal with a gusto traditionally reserved for refugees or starving orphans. Then, ever so slowly, I would glance toward Gia's table. And just as slowly, I would look away. My eyes had been making these rounds ever since we sat down.

"My ass."

"What?"

Boone stared me down. "Lost in thought, my ass."

"Don't worry," Jules chimed in. "It's early. You're allowed to be disoriented."

Everyone else resumed digging into their bowls of oatmeal and orange slices. I resumed my careful study.

She hadn't said anything to me when we saw each other in the Mess Hall, only one hour after she had whispered in my ear. I hadn't known how to act. Cool and aloof, like her? Should I have winked or nodded my head, acknowledging whatever moment had passed between us? *Had* something passed between us, or had I imagined it?

I looked down at my fingers, which were pale and dry from the steam of the shower. Remembered the way her finger had felt on my skin. I hadn't imagined it.

After breakfast, I stood up to join my cabinmates in our chore for the day, cleaning up the Waterfront. It was really too cold to swim, so there wasn't much to do: pick up driftwood that had floated onto the beach and throw it behind us into the trees, scour the thin strip of sand for whatever scraps of paper were hidden there. I was walking toward the door when I saw Gia standing next to the industrial-sized coffeemaker, gesturing at me with one hand — an almost-wave.

"I'll catch up to you guys," I said.

Boone looked in the direction I was headed. She shrugged. "Suit yourself," she said.

I made it over to Gia just as she was stirring cream into her coffee. She spoke before I had the chance to blunder through some greeting.

"My math class is canceled today," she said, her voice low. "Miss Flynn is sick. What class do you have at one?"

It took me a full minute to remember what my schedule was for the day. Finally, I said, "English."

"Can you get out of it?"

I had no more excuses. "Yes. I can meet you." At that point, I would have agreed to anything to be alone with her again.

"The trailhead at one o'clock. Just the two of us." Gia gave me the slightest smile — a thin, brightly colored ribbon. "We'll have lots of time to talk, then, and . . . you know . . . Continue the conversation we started this morning." She laid her hand on my arm. Her cheeks glowed a dusty pink. Then she picked up her coffee cup and headed toward the door.

One o'clock couldn't come fast enough.

When I met her at the trailhead, Gia had changed her clothes and was wearing an outfit I had never seen before: a tight plaid shirt, equally fitted jeans. She'd pulled her hair up into a messy twist, and was wearing heavy mascara and perfectly smudged eyeliner that made her look unkempt and tousled, like a French actress. She looked, I thought, ten years older.

"Wow," I said as she walked up, pulling on some fingerless gloves. "You look . . . great." I'd gotten there early, my stomach fluttering wildly.

"Thanks," she said. "You do too."

I looked down at my outfit: same old jeans, same gray hoodie. I was wearing her T-shirt again, nestled underneath the sweatshirt, but she couldn't have known that. I smiled uncertainly.

"Shall we?" She nodded toward the trail.

I led the way, but I felt as though I was following clumsily behind. I was breathless with anticipation and anxiety, those friendly cousins. We hiked steadily upward, neither of us speaking. I could hear Gia's breath at my back as we wound our way along the switchbacks. I was waiting for her to say something first, to start a conversation I'd been hoping to have with her, I realized, since the day she arrived. But she didn't say anything. We reached the spot where we could see the school quite clearly, like a miniature town, and I paused, hoping she'd understand that I was ready to listen. To do anything. But she just smiled at me, raised her eyebrows, and lifted her chin in the direction of the trail, urging me to keep moving.

So I said, "This way," and started around the back, moving toward the boulders. Once we reached the final ascent, I could hear Gia's footsteps quicken behind me, imploring me to move faster. There was an urgency in each footfall that I couldn't place or name. Was I imagining it? Was she just as eager as I was to get up there, see what I'd been doing with Boone all this time, and then head back down the trail, where we could be alone together again? So I sped up too. The fact is, I couldn't have stopped if I tried, and as long as Gia was with me, I didn't want to.

When we rounded the final corner and the lookout appeared before us, Gia touched my back so that I stopped and turned around to face her.

Now, I thought.

"Lida," she said.

Now.

"Why don't you let me handle this one."

I looked at her.

"Follow my lead, you know? I'd just feel better if I introduce myself." She waved one hand dismissively. "I mean, what with Boone and all . . ."

I was about to ask her what she meant by this, but Ben's voice floated down from the lookout.

"Lida!"

We glanced up in time to see him waving from the narrow deck. He was pulling on a long-sleeved shirt over his T-shirt. I heard Gia's sharp intake of breath. I tried to shake it off, but my skin grew clammy underneath my hoodie.

We trudged up the last few yards to where Ben was standing with a pair of binoculars in his left hand.

"Hey," he was saying to me when we reached him, but his voice trailed off when he saw Gia. He cleared his throat. "Well," he said. "Someone new. My place is becoming the locals' hangout, I guess. I'm Ben," he said.

"Georgina."

Ben smiled at Gia and turned to me. "Where's Elsa?"

"Boone had a class," said Gia, surprising me. I didn't know she knew Boone's first name. "I pulled Lida here out of English so that she could bring me up to meet you." She took her time with each word. "I thought it was time that one of us met the man on the mountain." She laughed lightly, never taking her eyes off him.

One of us? I thought. *Who is she talking about?*

"Ah," said Ben. "So you're checking up on me."

"Exactly. We have to make sure they're not up here getting into trouble. We wouldn't want anything *untoward* to be happening." Gia's smile was a wink.

Ben laughed. "Of course," he said. "Frankly, though, I'm surprised that Elsa would have said anything to you or anyone about her visits. I always gathered that they were rather illicit."

The way that Ben said "illicit," almost as though he thought it was funny, made me feel suddenly infantile.

"Oh yes," said Gia, "very illicit. But these girls can't keep much from me." She smiled at me in the way that a mother smiles at an adorable, drooling baby. "I'm something of their confidante, I suppose."

"Sure," said Ben. "I can see that."

Gia started to ask Ben about himself, standing close to him on the deck as though she was having a hard time hearing, and I stood mutely by, staring at the side of her face, willing her to look at me and explain herself.

But I knew exactly what she was doing. I should have known since the minute she asked me to bring her up to the lookout. Ben was a smart guy, way too smart to get involved with a teenage inmate at a wilderness school. If he happened to meet one of the instructors, on the other hand . . . Gia looked like she was twenty-five, she acted like she was twenty-five, and most important, judging by the way that Ben was gazing at her, I knew that he wanted to believe that she was twenty-five. The whole thing had been settled before they even introduced themselves to each other.

Gia leaned back, her hands behind her on the deck's railing. "That's interesting," she was saying. Ben's eyes were soft and yielding, and I knew exactly how it would be, how the lies would accumulate, wrap around one another in a great, tangled mass with me in the middle.

And yet, strangely, I wasn't mad. Not at that moment, at least. I felt frozen, unable to feel anything other than pure, stunned amazement. How did she do it? How did she know when to smile and tilt her head in just that way so that Ben would step closer, as he was doing, and touch her once, just above her elbow? How did she know when to talk and when to say nothing, communicating only with her eyes? How did she know how to *be*? If I learned how to be, would she look at me like Ben was looking at her?

"Lida, why so quiet?" Ben was looking at me strangely, a faint smile on his lips. "I don't think you've even said hi to me."

"Oh," I said. "Hi."

Ben laughed. "'Oh, hi,'" he said. "That's it?" He paused. "Okay, okay, I see how it's going to be here. You want to play the ingenue. Quiet Lida. I get it."

Gia smiled at me. She might as well have reached over and tousled my hair.

"No I'm not," I said. "I'm not that quiet." I looked out over the railing, scanning the distant peaks for some sign of assistance. Obviously, there was none. "Boone knows that." I looked over at Gia in time to see her eyes sharpen suddenly, as though frozen in ice, and then she blinked and laughed.

"Oh, that's probably true," she said to Ben. "You can feel as though you know these girls so well, and then they end up surprising you."

"I'd guess you've got quite a few stories," Ben said, smiling. "I'd like to hear them sometime."

She's got stories, all right, I wanted to say. *You're starring in one of them right now.* But I couldn't.

Gia touched Ben's elbow and steered him away toward a corner of the deck. I knew what she was doing: They were making plans to meet again. A time when they could talk away from the kids. What was it my dad used to say? Little kernels have big ears? They walked back to me, both of them smiling, though each smile held a different quality of happiness.

"Well, Lida, shall we head back down the mountain? We don't want Bev to send the cavalry after us, do we?"

Ben reached out and rather formally shook my hand. "Pleasure doing business with you, Lida. Perhaps at our next meeting you'll say more than ten words." He laughed, sticking his hand out for Gia's. "And very nice meeting you, as well." Ben held her hand just a second longer than necessary. "I'm sure I'll see you around."

"I'm sure." Gia's voice was almost a whisper, close to a purr.

There was a heaviness like sand in my gut.

We walked silently away from the lookout, Gia leading the way. The sun was just starting to move toward the tops of the peaks. We hadn't been visiting with Ben that long, but it had felt like hours. Once we rounded the bend in the trail and could see Bob again, Gia spoke.

"That was nice."

I said nothing.

"I don't know how a person can stand to be alone up there."

Nothing.

"He must get cabin fever."

Nothing.

"I'm sure he's just desperate for company, don't you think? I mean, his only visitor is some half-wild cowgirl." Her laugh was light.

I spoke quietly to Gia's back, because if I raised my voice I thought it would come out in a scream. "He and Boone are friends because he *likes* her, not because he's desperate." I stepped heavily, hoping that she would speed up. She kept on walking unhurriedly, though.

"I didn't say that, Lida. I'm sure he finds Boone quite . . ." She paused, looking for the right word. "Amusing."

"No," I pressed, "you don't get it. They're friends."

She stopped so suddenly that I almost knocked into her. She turned and smiled at me sadly, as though she was sorry for something I had done. "Sure. Maybe they are." Gia reached up and touched her hair. "But I doubt that Ben talks to her about *everything*." She continued descending toward the lake.

"You mean you," I said loudly, hurrying behind her. "You don't think he'll talk to Boone about you."

"I don't know what you mean, Lida," said Gia. She sounded farther away than she was. "I just think that Ben probably doesn't talk to Boone about his very personal business. Only that."

"And you're going to be his personal business, right, counselor?" I don't know where it came from, but it hit me like a Mack truck: a rage so hot I thought I might be glowing. "Or should I call you camp director?"

Gia turned to face me. "Lida, calm down. It's not like I'm going to kidnap Ben or anything. I just want to get to know him better, and I can't do that if he doesn't think we're on a level playing field." She sighed. "You're making a big deal out of nothing."

"No!" I almost shouted. "This *is* a big deal! You can't do this! You can't just go around collecting people like — like — they don't matter! They have to mean something to you! They have to!" I grabbed her arm.

Gia recoiled, trying to shake me off. "Let go of me!" Her voice was high and thin, like a young girl's.

"Why did you lie? Why can't you just let it go?" I shook my head, ashamed at the tears that had sprung to my eyes. "Why do you have to have everything?" I released her arm.

Gia wheeled around and faced me. Her eyes were burning and bright. "I don't have to have *everything*. You know me well enough to know *that*. But this is something I need. There's a difference. I would have thought you'd understand."

"But Ben is Boone's!" *And you are mine*, I wanted to add. "You can't take him away!"

"Don't be stupid! People aren't commodities. They can be with whoever they want."

My rage was tumbling over itself, spilling into despair. "But they have to know the person first, and everything you said up there is a lie! Everything you ever say is a lie! It's as fake as that stupid drawing you showed me. No one will want to be with you if they don't know you!" I shouted this last part, and then froze, my mouth partly open. I hadn't meant to say that. I didn't even know it was what I thought.

Gia had two crimson patches on her cheeks. Her eyes glinted, and I thought at first that she was about to cry. She was shaking, her hands stunned birds at her sides. I was shaking too. I wanted to swallow the words that I had just spoken, stuff them in my mouth like incriminating pieces of paper.

She took a deep breath, steadying herself. "Lida, I've tried with you. I really have." Her voice wavered but got stronger as she went on. "I guess it's easy, in a place like this, to think a friendship is different, you know — special — when really it's just based on necessity." A calm had descended over her face again, and she spoke evenly. "I thought, at first, that you were . . . *more* than you are. I see now that I mistook loneliness — *your* loneliness — as something deeper, more mature."

She looked straight into my eyes.

Cold, then cold, then nothing.

"I'm sorry," I said. I spoke so quietly that I wasn't sure she heard me.

"There's nothing to apologize for. You are who you are. I'm only sorry that I didn't recognize this sooner. You're just not . . ." She paused. "You're just not *right*. And I should have seen that."

Gia turned and began walking down the trail, leaving me cemented there. I couldn't breathe. I listened to her footsteps as they receded around a bend in the trail, and then the breaths started coming, shallowly at first, and then quickening, speeding into one another, each inhalation more frantic than the last. I'd felt this way once before, and the memory of my dad's voice collided with the wretched stillness around me. *She's not coming back.*

I knelt on the ground, curling my arms around my knees, sticking my face into the dark space they created. I closed my eyes as tightly as I could, until orange and yellow spots appeared behind my lids. The pain — the pain rose from somewhere beneath my ribs, blooming up through my throat, down to my gut, spreading heat like a disease to my fingers and toes. If I rocked back and forth, or if I moved at all, I'll never know. The silence was absolute, an emptiness that only made room for the terrible heat pulsing relentlessly through my body. I wasn't thinking, not really. Just one phrase kept repeating in my head until it lost all meaning and became a mother's soothing lullaby. *All wrong. All wrong. All wrong.*

When I finally stood again, I had no idea what time it was. Five hours could have passed just as easily as five minutes. My nose was running, and my cheeks were wet; I wiped my face on my sleeve. I walked down the trail toward the school, more certain than ever before that I was the one girl at Alice Marshall who couldn't be fixed.

$\mathscr{C}$HAPTER $\mathscr{F}$IFTEEN

A WEEK PASSED. TWO. AND THEN IT WAS THE FIRST WEEK OF October, that sharp and cold month up in the mountains, when the aspen grove along Red Dot Trail became a bunch of naked stalks and even the fir trees seemed to shiver far above us. If you strained your neck, you could see where the tips of those trees bent under pressure of the wind, a wagging finger: *Oh no you don't.*

It was October, and I couldn't imagine November. Time had stopped for me on the trail from Buckhorn.

I hadn't talked to anyone about the fight with Gia. Hadn't talked to anyone, really, about anything at all. Not Jules, who kept shooting worried glances in my direction, even though she had stopped asking me what was wrong after a week of my silence. Not Gwen or Karen, who seemed to accept my reticence as easily as they'd accepted my sociability. And definitely not Boone.

Look: I'm not stupid. I knew that what Gia had done was wrong. I knew it the way you know *Parents were once my age too!* and *I'll be glad I have these math skills one day*: a fact with no substance. She'd used me; she'd lied and was lying still. But that wasn't what made me cry in the shower in breath-crunching gulps, the pounding water my alibi for anyone who might come into the Bathhouse. It was the sudden lack of her, of *me with her*, a dancing cluster of shooting stars and then — suddenly — nothing, the sky black as dreamlessness. I missed who I was when I was with her: I was *someone*, a photograph in focus. And now I'd lost it all. I spent nights tracing the scars on my hips with the jagged end of a fingernail.

I don't know why it is that, whenever there is one person, only one person, who it pains you to see, she happens to be within your line of vision at all times. That's how it was with Gia. She was *everywhere*. Laughing with the other Seventeens as they walked toward their morning chores. Whispering conspiratorially at her table in the Mess Hall. Standing regally with a secret smile whenever her name was announced during Mail Call. Most often, though, I saw her walking toward, or coming from, the path up to Buckhorn Peak. Once, she caught me watching her go. She didn't smile. Instead, she glanced at me casually and then tossed her hair over her shoulder and glided on, as though I was a deer or squirrel she had momentarily surprised on the trail. My heart swung on a string.

I knew it was only a matter of time before Boone caught Gia heading up to see Ben — or worse, met her up at the lookout. That's why I was through with talking. Nothing good had come of it so far. I had ruined everything the minute I told Gia about Ben. I dreaded what I might say next.

Not that Boone would have listened to me, had I wanted to tell her what happened at the lookout. She had bigger things on her mind.

Boone was going home.

She got the news after a grueling day hike with our Outdoor Education class. The long-awaited Solo Trip was coming up, and Margaret was putting all of her classes through what felt like a training for gladiators. We'd just gotten back from bagging Townsend Peak in less than three hours. That's what Margaret had said — "Let's bag this one" — like it was a cantaloupe at a grocery store.

I felt like a baby giraffe by the time we got back to the school, my legs still wobbling from the effort, and I was in such a hurry to get back to the cabin with the other girls and lie down before dinner that I didn't notice Bev waiting for us near the Outdoor Ed building, and didn't hear her ask Boone to hang back for a chat.

But I heard what she said soon enough. Boone came bursting into the cabin, her face red, eyes wild.

"Bitch thinks it's that easy?" she said, almost snarling. "Thinks she can just take or leave me?" She slammed her fist against the wall. The cabin rattled around us. "You can't do that! You can't just take it back!"

"Take what back? What's going on?" asked Jules. She was the only one with the guts to say anything.

"Fuck you," said Boone. She hit the wall again. "Fuck this." Boone marched to the door and opened it. She paused there, and I could see through her polypropylene shirt that the muscles on her back were flexing, as though waging war with whatever was roiling inside her. She slammed the door without going out. She took a deep breath and sighed it out heavily. Then she turned to Jules. "Looks like my sentence is up," she said. "The Great and Powerful Oz has instructed me to go home."

"Impossible," said Gwen from her bunk. "You're an institution."

"No," said Boone, "you're wrong. The Department of Juvenile Corrections is an institution, and the good folks there have decided that they've spent more than enough of the taxpayers' dollars on the rehabilitation of one troubled Minster girl. They're ready to start fixing another. Probably already told the Mormons to pick someone new. Good-bye, scholarship." She sounded more like herself, her voice oozing sarcasm, but I could hear a different bass note thrumming underneath the words.

"Oh no," Jules said sympathetically. "What are you going to do?"

Boone laughed once, loudly, like a clap. "I didn't know I had any options." She sat down heavily on her bunk.

"Sorry," said Jules, blushing. "I guess I mean, do you have people to stay with? Does your family know you're coming home?"

"They'll know when they see me," Boone said.

I wondered whom she was talking about. I knew her brother was in the prison in Kuna, over in the western part of the state, because she'd talked about having visited him there. She still had yet to mention her parents, though, and no one had gathered the courage to ask.

"I leave in two weeks. Two weeks."

I heard her kick her legs up onto the mattress.

"God," said Gwen. "Bev is going to start filling our cabin with new girls." She paused. "And who's going to welcome them to school?"

Boone laughed drily along with the other three. Even I smiled, though my hand flew up to my hair automatically to check its progress, like it always did whenever someone mentioned Boone's antics.

"Someone else will have to take up the mantle, I guess," said Boone. "What about Townie, here? What do you think, Lida? Can you put on a mean face?" Her relaxed tone sounded forced.

"Lida couldn't be cruel if she tried," said Karen. "Plus, she's all but stopped speaking, haven't you noticed?"

"That could work in her favor," said Gwen. "She could never be confronted."

"Now *that's* tough," said Boone. "All explosion, no fire."

"Shut up," I said, and they did. I didn't even glance to see whatever look Gwen was probably throwing at Karen. *Lost cause*, it probably said. *What a baby.*

I hated the fact that my silence was so dramatic. I didn't want to be the center of anyone's attention. I certainly didn't want their pity. I just wanted to sit quietly, huddled into myself. I didn't want to have to say another word. Ever.

"Really, Boone, what are you going to do?" Jules looked concerned. She pulled at the zipper of her sleeping bag: zip up, zip down. "I mean, maybe this isn't ideal, but you know, you could always stay at my house."

Boone looked at her as though she had just suggested we all drink acid and throw ourselves off a peak. "What, in Denver?" she asked.

"Yeah," said Jules. "It's kind of a nice city, and there's plenty of extra room in my house." Her eyes brightened. "You could take care of Westy!"

Boone shook her head angrily. "Don't be stupid," she said. "I'm not going to take care of your damn dog. Think about it. Can you really imagine me at your house? With your parents? Can you?"

Jules blushed. "They're nice people," she said softly. "I'm sure they would be very welcoming."

Boone moved until she was standing directly in front of Jules's bunk. She leaned forward. "You're here," she said quietly. "How welcoming is that? Parents who really love their kids don't toss them into the woods for months or years. No thank you. I don't think I need your kind of family."

Jules looked down at her sleeping bag. I knew that she could have told Boone the truth, that *she* had sent herself to the school, but she didn't say anything.

Boone ran her hand over her face. She suddenly looked very,

very tired. Slowly, she reached down and touched Jules on the shoulder. "I'll go back to Minster," she said. "They'll hear me coming from a mile away." She left her hand on Jules's shoulder for another minute, and then she walked over to her bunk and lay down. I could hear her feet kick at the wood at the end of the bed, and I imagined Boone on a horse, hurtling over dirt and rocks, the sound of the hoofs louder than whatever she could scream.

It was funny — everyone at school was upset about Boone's encroaching departure. Even people like timid Miss Flynn moped around with a halfway devastated look on their faces, like we were losing our star player, which I guess we were. Apparently, everyone had forgotten the mice in their beds, stolen clothes, and toothpaste in their shampoo bottles. They were willing to forget everything, I think, if she just wouldn't leave. I could still recall what Chandler said to Macy on our overnight. *She's fierce.* Boone was the bad one. She set the bar high. Maybe everyone was afraid that we'd become *good* if she left.

The hand on my shoulder shook me awake. This was a couple of days after Boone got the news. I was bleary-eyed and groggy, but I could still make her out as she leaned over me. Her braid slapped me gently in the face.

"Get up, Townie," she whispered.

"Nungh," I mumbled. "Go 'way."

"Let's go have some fun."

"Don't wanna."

"Get. Up." This time, it wasn't her braid slapping me.

"Jesus!" It wasn't a shout, exactly, but it was close.

"Shhhh." Boone stepped toward the door. "I'll wait."

I figured I lost nothing by getting up and following. It wasn't like I'd been enjoying my beauty sleep, anyway. I hadn't had a solid night of sleep since Gia left me on the mountain.

I was still shrugging into a sweatshirt when I met Boone outside the cabin. It must have been three in the morning, a moonless night. I could barely see her hand as she waved it in front of me, snapping her fingers in the cold.

"Wake up," she said. I could see the clouds of her breath more easily than her face in the dark. "It's time to bid this place adieu."

"What do you mean?" I rubbed my eyes, hoping that I'd be able to see better. Still nothing. "You're not leaving tonight, are you?"

"No, Einstein. You heard them — I've got two more weeks. And when I do go, they'll be pulling me by the ankles. No, what I have in mind is more like a parting gift. Lots of parting gifts." I couldn't see, but I knew she was smiling. Boone grabbed my arm to pull me after her, and I yelped.

"What the hell?" she whispered, letting go. "You're going to give us away."

I rubbed at the place where she'd grabbed me and said nothing. Scabs were just beginning to form over the two raised lines on my forearm. I may not have had my knife, but nature had provided other implements. A stick. A chiseled rock. The sharp, pointed end of a pinecone. The pain, when I felt it, had been a relief.

There was a scuffling sound to our left, and Boone whipped out a flashlight and turned it on quickly, illuminating a porcupine as it shuffled quickly into the trees.

"Shit," she said, flicking the flashlight off again. She marched ahead. I exhaled heavily through my mouth and followed.

The Rec Lodge was unlocked, which was odd. Bev made the rounds herself each night, making sure that the school buildings were impossible for us to break into. "How —" I started as we entered, but Boone shushed me.

"Mysterious ways," she whispered, pulling something out of her pocket and jangling it in front of my face. "I've been awake much longer than you. Done some prep work. We'll just leave these keys here for Bev to find, shall we?" She set them down on the fireplace mantel, and shone the flashlight around the room.

Prep work indeed. Boone had amassed a small arsenal in the middle of the room. There in front of me, heaped in some places and spread out thinly in others, were hundreds of weapons of questionable destruction: flasks, pizza cutters, pipes, bottles of Wite-Out and Robitussin, butter knives, steak knives, needles, bags of weed and one small bag of white powder, tiny airplane portions of vodka, tequila, and rum, and one lone hammer, its handle weathered from use.

"Recognize anything?" Boone shined the flashlight into my face and I turned away, blinking. "Look closer." She handed me the flashlight.

I walked around, peering down at every object. Some of them seemed harmless. A walkie-talkie, for instance. A stuffed rabbit. I picked it up and squeezed its plush body. Tiny plastic bags inside crackled against one another. When I turned it over, I could see the seam along its back that had been opened and then sewn hastily shut over the bunny's new narcotic organs.

I continued looking. Crouched down and moved away a plastic bottle of gin. There, looking fairly innocuous among the other items, was my X-ACTO knife. I rocked back on my heels, keeping the light trained on the knife. "Where did you get all this?"

Boone's laugh echoed around the lodge. "Didn't you know? Bev doesn't trust throwing anything remotely dangerous in the garbage. She's got a little padlocked shed behind her cabin where she stores it all."

"Maybe she keeps it for a reason," I said. "Maybe she offers it back when we leave, just to test us all."

"Not a good idea. I bet there'd be some takers."

We laughed quietly and then fell into silence. I kept my eyes on the knife.

"How did you know I'd have something here?" I asked finally.

Boone knelt beside me, tracking the direction of my gaze. She picked up the knife. "I didn't know for sure," she said. "I just assumed that you, like the rest of us, would have brought something . . . useful . . . with you."

"What'd you bring?"

Boone put the knife back down. She reached over and rummaged around in the large pile, pulling out a child's toy gun. "Lame, isn't it?" she said. "It was kind of a joke. I had a feeling there would be a bag check. There were matches too, but Bev threw them away."

"Why a gun?" I asked.

"Playing to type," she said. "I knew what they expected me to be — some sort of outlaw, I guess. Minster's had its share of bar brawls, and the ones with guns involved tend to make the state newspaper."

Like the one your brother was in, I thought.

"Bought this at the dollar store on my way out of town. They lapped it up. Bev took it very seriously. What was it she said? 'I don't know what you're used to, but we strive for civility here.' Civility? What — was she afraid I was going to ride in on some horse, wearing chaps or some shit? Hold up the town bank? Jesus. They wouldn't have been half as upset if I'd packed a purse full of coke, like some of the I-bankers."

"Yeah," I said, though I was thinking about all of the times when I had pictured Boone exactly like that: the wild cowgirl, straight out of a picture book. "So what *was* your life like in Minster?" I asked cautiously. "I mean, what were you like?"

Boone's eyes pierced me cleanly. "Just like you, Townie." She twirled the gun in her hands like an outlaw. "I saw it in you the first day you got here: You feel the same way about Bruno as I do about Minster. That town was no home to me. You gotta belong somewhere before it's your home."

I knew exactly what she meant, but I pressed the issue anyway. "But your family —"

"The only thing that ever kept me in Minster is currently locked up in the state pen on a twenty-year sentence, twelve if he's good. And I doubt he'll be good." Boone turned and stared into the pile of weapons and drugs, and I could see what she was thinking as though it was lit up on a freeway billboard. *This is child's play.*

Outside, an animal snapped twigs as it hustled past the building.

"So," I said finally, "what are we going to do with all of this?"

"We're going to show Bev that her little school isn't as safe and clean as she thinks it is."

It struck me that neither Bev nor any of the teachers ever heard about Boone's "welcoming" activities, and that this probably frustrated Boone. When you're an artist of any kind, you want to show off your skills to the world.

We began by decorating the fireplace mantel. I brought all of the liquor bottles over to Boone, where she arranged them by height, forming a semicircle with the largest bottles on each end. She garnished the spaces around the bottles with little buds of weed, and placed the keys to the lodge in the center. It looked like a holiday wreath, and I said so.

"Just like Christmas at your house, eh, Townie?"

Next, we set up the folding chairs in the middle of the room, as though preparing for Circle Share. In the seat that Amanda usually took, Boone placed the stuffed rabbit. We peopled the other chairs with a good variety of items. Some of them looked pretty impressive. The chair that I was most proud of had a stick figure lying on the seat, with steak knives for arms, butter knives for legs, and the pizza cutter for the torso and the head.

"Nicely done," said Boone, as we walked around the circle together, looking at each finished chair. "You're quite gifted."

Finally, we piled the remaining objects together in the center of the circle, like a bonfire. I had been scanning the items for anything that could possibly be Gia's, but none of it seemed to fit her. I was disappointed, and then ashamed. What was I doing, still looking for clues, ways to understand her? It was useless.

We stood back and looked at our work. For the briefest moment, I was afraid that Boone was going to light it up, and I wondered idly if I would do anything to stop her. Instead, she walked to the pile and pulled two objects out of her back pocket, laying them gently on the very top.

I stepped closer. The first object was a pair of large crafting scissors with a red plastic handle. Boone chuckled. "They've been under my mattress this whole time," she explained. I touched my hair and shook my head.

The second object was the one letter she had received, the one everyone had said was from her brother. It lay there, fluttering softly in the draft of the old lodge, its blackened lines impossible to read. The only word that was legible was the name at the top, the letters thin and gangly. *Elsa.*

"They'll know," I said.

"What are they going to do? Kick me out?" Boone didn't laugh. "Come on. We're finished here."

She turned and walked toward the door of the Rec Lodge. I followed, though not before I reached into the pile and slipped the X-ACTO knife into the back pocket of my jeans.

Boone's interior decorating skills were common knowledge by breakfast the next morning. The word spread stealthily from cabin to cabin. Everyone knew that, as soon as Bev heard about it, the Rec Lodge would be off-limits. But before it was completely light, each cabin had toured the Rec Lodge and seen for themselves what Boone was capable of. These tours were made silently — reverently, it seemed — often with someone standing guard by the door. Jules reported back that some girls were even leaving additional items around the pile: empty cigarette cartons, a pipe that someone had made out of a toilet paper roll. It was as though they were leaving offerings — not only to the shrine itself, which was a testament to our collective badness, but to Boone specifically. *Here is what we've done in your honor,* the offerings seemed to say, *and here is what we will continue doing in your name after you have left.* There was another reason for these gifts, as well: Because there were so many new items on the pile by the time Bev saw it, she wouldn't be able to pick out Boone's letter and definitively say that it belonged to the person who was responsible. And she couldn't just punish us all.

I'm sure girls took things from the pile in the middle of the room, little keepsakes from their time before Alice Marshall, but for the most part, the decorations in the Rec Lodge remained intact. No one wanted to mess up the mantel or the chairs that we had so lovingly adorned; it would ruin the thrill of Boone's victory. Still, I was pretty sure that the next random bag check would be more fruitful than most.

As for me, I kept the X-ACTO in the front pocket of my hoodie all day, wrapping one hand around it from time to time, feeling its reassuring shape and promise.

Breakfast itself was a giddy affair. Each table buzzed with the anticipation of a showdown between Bev and Boone. No one came by our table; it was one thing to know who was responsible, but it was quite another to publicly identify her. (From what I could tell, no one else knew that Boone had an accomplice. And that was just fine with me.) Our cabinmates were impressed too.

Gwen said that the chairs in the middle of the room looked like a wagon train circled around a campfire for the night, and I agreed. It was the first remotely pleasant thing I'd said to the cabin in a while, and I watched as Jules lit up like a streetlight.

The Seventeens' table seemed just as excited as everyone else. From the few glances I stole in that direction, I could tell that they were whispering fervently, their heads all inclining toward one another like secret-sharers. Gia's head was lowered too, but I couldn't see her expression. She never turned toward our table.

When Bev entered the Mess Hall, Margaret trailing behind, we all held our breath. Finally, *finally*, we were going to see Bev get mad. Really mad. We couldn't wait to hear what Boone would say in retort.

She walked to the front of the room, where the coffeemaker was located, and poured herself a cup. She was wearing her signature pressed slacks, which looked freshly ironed and stiff as cardboard. She stirred in the milk and sugar slowly. There was no way she couldn't have known that we were all staring at her, but she did a good job of pretending she was unaware that there were other people in the Mess Hall at all. Bev carefully carried her drink to the staff table, where she sat down with a pleasant expression and began making small talk with the other teachers. She didn't look around the room once.

I glanced at Boone. Her eyes were narrowed, and she was staring at Bev intensely, as though trying to teleport herself to the staff table.

"Maybe she hasn't been in the lodge yet," offered Jules.

"Oh, she's been there," said Boone. "Bet you five bucks everything's cleaned up by the time breakfast is over. She's just not going to mention it."

"Ever?" Karen looked disappointed.

"That's her game."

"How do you know?" I asked.

"Because she's an adult. It's always a power struggle with them. Bev subscribes to the *If I Ignore Her She'll Go Away* school of thought. In this case, of course, she'll eventually be right."

"So you thought she might act this way before you ever . . ." Jules began.

Boone interrupted her. "Of course. See, the thing is, Bev doesn't get it. This doesn't have anything to do with her. It has to do with us. She can ignore it all she wants. What matters is that no one else will."

And Boone was right. After a few minutes of quiet conversation, during which everyone came to terms with the fact that Bev wasn't going to say anything, the room returned to its initial state of excitement. People started laughing. I heard one girl exclaim from across the room, "No, guys, seriously — did anyone see my bong?" Girls started looking in the direction of our table. I think someone even gave Boone a thumbs-up. I guess they figured that, if Bev really was going to pretend nothing had happened, she couldn't very well punish the perpetrator.

And just as Boone had predicted, the Rec Lodge was as clean and sterile as a conference room by the time breakfast was over. I peeked in the window first, and then Boone edged me aside with an elbow and looked in. Nothing. No evidence that there had ever been a Christmas altar of liquor and weed, or that a stoned rabbit had sat in Amanda's seat.

"Just as I thought," said Boone.

"Yes," said a voice from behind us. "A shame, isn't it. And after all that careful work too." It was Margaret, standing there in a lopsided cap, cradling the stuffed bunny in her arms.

Boone played dumb. "What's that you're carrying?"

"This?" Margaret held the bunny out and shook it. I thought I could hear the baggies wrinkling together inside its belly. "Some toys are not safe for children between the ages of one and one hundred." She looked around. "Some, like Bugs here, are downright illegal. I'm going to perform a minor surgery and send his . . . goods to the proper authorities."

"Ah," said Boone.

Everyone else was in the cabins already, or still finishing up their chores. Bev could have been anywhere, but I guessed that she was sitting in her cabin, sorting through the pile of crap that Boone and I had left in the lodge, making an inventory and trying to figure out which items were missing. My hand instinctively found its way into the front pocket of my hoodie.

"It was an artful decorating scheme," Margaret said quietly, a faint smile on her lips. "Too bad no one claimed it." She paused, and then continued, staring at Boone. "I have a feeling that Bev won't hesitate to punish the responsible parties, however — *if* they seem too proud of themselves." She glanced down at the rabbit and shook it once more for emphasis. "And that would be the real shame, wouldn't it?"

"Point taken," said Boone. Just as she began to push me toward the cabin, I heard Margaret call out.

"Lida," she said, "a word?"

I shrugged at Boone, who raised her eyebrows at me and continued on toward the cabin. I stayed and turned toward Margaret.

"I've been meaning to ask if you'd help me lead this afternoon's hike with the Fourteens," she said.

"Oh," I said. Why had she kept me behind for this? Why not just ask me in front of Boone?

"You know your way around a mountain," Margaret continued, "and I'd love it if the younger girls could take a page or two from your book."

"Fine," I said. "Whatever."

Margaret gazed at me calmly. "Lida," she began, but I didn't want to hear it.

"I said fine."

"I know you did. And you said it like I'd just asked you to clean the toilets with a toothbrush. That's not the Lida I've gotten to know. What's going on with you?" Her look was compassionate, but her voice, as always, was commanding.

"Nothing."

"I don't think so."

I shrugged.

"Something's been bothering you these past couple of weeks. I'd like to know what it is." Margaret stuffed the bunny under one arm and stuck both hands in her pockets, rocking back on her heels. "You know you can always talk to me — about anything. You know that, don't you?"

I shrugged again.

Margaret was undaunted. "You've done a lot of work here," she went on. "I'd hate to see you throw it away."

"I'm not throwing anything away." I stared beyond her at Bob.

"Nothing concrete, Lida. You know what I mean. You're on the road to sliding back from all the progress you've made." She shook her head. "And that would be a shame."

"Well, I'll try not to disappoint you," I said, my voice almost a snarl.

Margaret sighed heavily. "Do that," she said. "In the meantime, I'll talk to your other teachers and let them know you'll be with me this afternoon." She walked away, humming softly to the rabbit in her arms.

Boone was waiting for me outside the cabin.

"Leading a hike, huh? Clearly, you're doing something right," said Boone. "Don't worry, Townie," she added, "we'll breathe some life into you yet."

It was true that I hadn't thought as much about Gia in the past twelve hours. This was both a relief and a sadness. I had grown accustomed to thinking about her constantly — like having one eye always fixed on a certain spot while the other has to take in everything else. I couldn't imagine her smile, the warm weight of her hand on my shoulder, without also hearing her voice: *Not right.* The thought that I *could* feel better — that maybe, with time, her words would become muted in the back of my brain — was somehow just as painful as the words themselves. I followed Boone into the cabin, wanting equally to hear the sound of Gia's voice and to forget it.

The knife was cool and smooth in my hand.

Epilogue

My hand is cramping from writing so fast. I need to slow down, to get it right. *"Precision, precision," I tell myself. It's the only way.*

The telephone rings down the hall. Terri's voice floats my way. "Lida, for you!" I can hear the radio in the kitchen, her favorite NPR program trilling away as she makes another pot of coffee. Always with the NPR. It's like having a gaggle of boring professors and a string quartet sandwiched in the living room all day.

"Take a message!" I yell. "I'll call them back!" I turn back to the paper. For some reason, writing this on my computer was never an option. I have to get it down the way I learned how: with ink and sweat. And besides, it's easier to lie when there's a keyboard between you and the truth. When it's your hand forming every letter, finishing every sentence — well, it keeps you honest. As honest as possible, anyway.

Terri's standing in my doorway, the phone in her hand. "Lida —" she says, and I cut her off.

"I'll. Call. Them. Back," I whisper, since I can see that she's only loosely covering the mouthpiece with her hand.

"It's Margaret," she says, and holds out the phone.

I take it from her wordlessly and wait until she's gone and I can hear her banging around in the kitchen. Then I put the phone up to my ear. "Hello?" The word catches in my throat.

"Lida. You're a tough woman to get a hold of. I've been leaving you messages for six months." Margaret's voice, still so familiar to me, crackles over the school's emergency radio phone. She keeps talking, says she's got a question for me — "a big ask," she says — and explains that she wants me to come back and share my story with the other girls.

"What?"

She continues as though she hasn't heard me, and maybe she hasn't. "We don't normally bring in speakers, you know, but this batch of girls could really benefit from hearing your story," she says.

"Why?" I ask, and this time she responds.

"Because they're looking for a quick fix, Lida. An easy out. Because we've been talking about patterns, and how they're hard to break, but they don't believe me."

"I don't see how —" I start, and then stop. "I mean, what would I say?"

But the phone connection weakens. It sounds like there's gravel in the receiver. Margaret says something, but I can't make out the words. I tell her I need more time to think about it, that I don't know if I can go back, but she doesn't hear me.

Then she says, ". . . both sides of the story." Her voice sounds distant and hopeful. "I think that . . ." The phone fades in and out of service. ". . . two of you," she says.

"What?"

"Just . . . You both . . . explanation."

"I can't hear you," I say, panic pulsing in my chest. "Am I . . . Are you inviting anyone else?"

Static. Then: "I hope you'll both come," she says. "Just the two of you."

I know who she's talking about. There's really only one person it could be.

"She hates me," I say. "You know how much she hates me. I don't know

242

if I can see her again without —" Without what? Falling back into it? Wanting to hurt myself as much as I hurt her? "How can any of this be helpful?" I ask, my voice wavering.

I wait for Margaret's response, but it never comes. All I can hear is static, a rushing sound like wind or water, and the bell's thick chime, striking once like a warning. Then the line goes dead.

$\mathscr{C}$HAPTER $\mathscr{S}$IXTEEN

BOONE TOOK MARGARET'S NOT-SO-SUBTLE SUGGESTION AND didn't advertise her role in the defamation of the Rec Lodge. There was too much to do, too many "last" activities to accomplish before her departure; she couldn't afford to waste her time talking about something that had already gone down when there was still so much that needed to happen.

For one thing, our Solo Trips were coming up.

We'd been hearing about them from time to time over the past few months, but Margaret finally spelled it out for us when she popped into Circle Share and asked Amanda if she could make an announcement.

"It's really the most celebrated program here at Alice Marshall," she said, "as in, this is one of the reasons parents choose our school over others. You will head out with a group, but each of you will have your own campsite away from the others. The expectation is that you'll use your time to meditate on your progress here, face some fears, identify solutions."

Gia was sitting five seats to my right, so I couldn't see her face, but if I glanced casually at my knee from time to time, I could see her foot as she crossed and then uncrossed her legs. Now she jiggled her foot around in the air.

"Basically, it's a wonderful chance to reflect," Margaret continued. "Some people call it Solo Meditation, though I think that puts too much pressure on the art of meditating." She smiled around the room. "And another thing. Instead of dividing you up by cabin groups, we thought it best that we send you out with your fellow Sharers. Amanda and I have some activities planned that will help you process what you experience out there, and she'll guide you through them together when you return."

The foot had stopped jiggling. Now it was moving in slow, deliberate circles, as though working out a cramp in its ankle. She'd been wearing more makeup than normal when she walked into the Rec Lodge, and I wondered if she'd just come from Ben's, or if she was about to head up there.

"Everyone's doing it, guys, so don't think about opting out. Amanda's Monday group is heading out Wednesday — tomorrow, in fact — and you all are scheduled to go a week from then." She took a deep breath. It had been quite a speech. "Any questions?"

A girl named Heather raised her hand. She was a quiet Seventeen from Chicago with buckteeth and curly black hair. "Yeah. What if we don't want to spend the night in the woods? Can we just do, like, a solo night in the guest dorm or something?"

There was laughter. Margaret shook her head. "You know the answer to that one. But thank you, Heather, for reminding me of one important fact. The 'overnight' is actually two nights, not one. We wanted to give you a full day by yourselves."

The cursing and complaining started off loud and got louder.

But Amanda and Margaret both put on their grim "This is not a preschool" expressions and made eye contact with each of us. The room calmed down quickly after that.

"Yes, Heather?" said Margaret.

Heather let her hand fall back into her lap. "Yeah. Do we get to bring guns? Or are you gonna send us out there with nothing to protect ourselves?"

There was nervous laughter. The foot started jiggling again.

"No guns." Margaret smiled at us conspiratorially. "I don't know if any of you have noticed, but I like to sleep outside, once, maybe twice a week. Just hike up Red Dot a ways, bed down . . . It's only me and the trees and the stars. And let me tell you, not once have I felt as though even my pinkie finger was in danger." She waggled her hand in the air to prove it, and then nodded at Amanda. "Okay. I think that's about it. Sorry to take so much time — if you have more questions, I'm around. I just wanted to let everyone know what to expect before the Monday group spilled the beans."

Amanda smiled serenely. "No problem," she said. "It sounds lovely. Now," she said, as Margaret made her way out of the lodge, "where were we?" She called on a raised hand, and Circle Share resumed, but I'm not sure how many of us were very "present" for the next thirty minutes.

Gia was gone before I had even gotten out of my chair.

Just as Margaret had said, the Monday Circle Share left for their overnight the next day. Almost everyone was terrified by the prospect of sleeping under the stars with nothing to protect them from what Margaret often referred to as the Awesome Power of Nature. I wasn't one of them, though. A couple of nights out in the cold sounded just about right to me.

Karen was in the first group. When they arrived back at school right before lunch on Friday, she came into the cabin to set her stuff down, wearing her pack and looking like she'd just rolled down the side of a mountain. Jules pounced on her first.

"How was it? Did you see a bear? Were you scared? Were you able to light a fire all by yourself? Are you glad to be back? Did you —"

"Hi, Jules," Karen said, interrupting her with a smile.

"Give the woman some room," said Boone.

Gwen jumped off her bunk to help Karen with her pack. I was lying on my bed, pretending not to listen. Jules drummed her fingers on her pant leg in a nervous rhythm. Finally, Karen sat on her bunk, stretched her arms, and told us about it.

"It really wasn't that big of a deal," she said. "I mean, we were all together for a while, hiking along this path. Margaret gave each of us a map."

"Was she with you?" Gwen asked.

"No. It was just us. But on the map, you could see where everyone would be camping, so it wasn't like we had to, you know, *find* a campsite or something. So we hiked along, and every once in a while, someone would see the little spur — you know, like a side trail — that she had to take to get to her site, and she'd wave and head down." Karen fluttered her hand and smiled.

"Where was your site?" asked Jules.

"Oh, I was somewhere in the middle, I think — maybe nearer to the beginning. It was magical: There was a little creek, and a nice log to sit on, and a little campfire circle." Karen smiled wistfully, like she was already nostalgic. "I mean, guys, it wasn't that scary. I just set up my tent, read a book until it started to get dark, and then made a little fire, heated water on my stove for this soup mix that Margaret gave us, and went to bed. Yesterday, I pretty much read and meditated and walked along the creek. It was transcendent, actually." She smiled serenely.

"Did you hear anything either night? Like, wolves, or foot-steps?" I think that Jules might have been more afraid than anyone.

Karen laughed. "I wouldn't know. I've always been a sound sleeper."

"You're no help." Jules sat back on her bunk and crossed her arms. "I need direction here! I want to know what to expect!"

"I've told you what to expect," said Karen patiently. She paused, as though weighing what she would say next. "But one of the Fourteens — Lindy — she heard something the second night. She swears it was a bear at her site. But on the ride back, Margaret told us that she probably heard a raccoon or deer and imagined it was a bear."

Jules's face turned white. "Great. A bear." She turned to Boone. "You've gotta tell me how to scare them away."

Boone rolled her eyes.

Karen turned to Gwen. "It's awesome," she said. "You'll see. I wish I could go again." Gwen's group was heading out the next day.

"Well, I can't wait," said Boone. "It'll probably be the last chance I get to commune with nature for a long time."

"Isn't there plenty of nature around Minster?" said Jules. "It's not like you live in Chicago."

"Nature." Boone mulled this over. "If you mean old railroad ties and piles of sawdust, the occasional feral dog, maybe some horse shit, then I guess you're right. I live in a wonderland. Can't wait to get back."

She laughed loudly. It was a new kind of laugh for Boone, one that she had taken up ever since she found out she was leaving. It had a sharp, hollow snap, like the sound that a branch makes under the weight of snow right before it begins to fall.

The next day was rather quiet. Gwen's group went on their Solo Trip, and the rest of us pretended not to notice. I guess the girls who had already been on their overnight were jealous and wanted to go again. Everyone else was just in denial.

It was cold on Saturday afternoon; there had been real frost blanketing the ground for the first time that morning. One of the teachers hosted a movie marathon in the Rec Lodge, and almost everyone piled in, jockeying for seats on the two tattered couches that usually rested against the back wall but had been moved closer to the fireplace. They were watching some old G-rated, feel-good movie. *The Journey of Natty Gann*, I think. That, or *The Incredible Journey*. Not hard to get the two mixed up.

Boone opted out, which means she opted me out too. I knew this by the hard knock she gave the back of my head as she made her way out of the lodge. I was only too happy to go. Anything was better than waiting for Gia to walk in at any minute. Plus, because Boone refused to talk about Gia, I found it easier to think about other things when I was with her. Sometimes, I even surprised myself by having fun. We could hear Jules calling after us as we walked away: "You guys! This is the best movie ever!" We let the door swing shut behind us.

"What do you want to do?" I asked, once we were outside. I wrapped my arms around myself. "Man, it is *cold*."

Boone was wearing a faded black T-shirt that said *Renegade* across the front. She didn't even have goose bumps. "Sissy," she said. "Fine. Let's get you in some swaddling clothes."

Back in the cabin, I chose to layer my hoodies, one on top of the other, so that I looked like a puffy gray marshmallow. Boone smirked at me.

"Don't laugh," I said. "Winter is no time to worry about style points."

"You sound like a mom."

"Shut up." I did my best motherly voice. "*The best protection is prevention,*" I said in a singsong. "Where are we headed?"

As soon as I asked, it hit me. If Gia wasn't in the Rec Lodge by now, there was only one place she could be. I mentally willed Boone to suggest anything other than visiting Ben.

"I don't know," said Boone. "I guess we could walk around the grounds, pop a squat in the Mess Hall. Waste time, you know?"

"Fine," I said.

So, we wandered. Boone took me on her "Greatest Hits" tour of the school. "Here's where I got into a fight with a Seventeen, right after I arrived," she said as we passed the stump of a large pine tree near the Bathhouse. "She didn't know what hit her. I'll tell you what hit her: my elbow. Of course, it was an accident," she added, glancing at me slyly. "I just turned quickly, and gosh, I hadn't known her face was so close by."

"Right."

"And here's where I caught my first mouse," she said, pointing down at the ground as we walked.

I was about to ask her why, but then I remembered her way of "welcoming" the I-bankers. "You must have been so proud," I said drily.

She pointed out where she once hid the decorative flag that hung outside of Bev's door. The hole that she had dug in the ground near the Infirmary where she had stashed a Fourteen's candy, covering it with a rock, until she could find time to take it up to Ben's place. Where she smoked a joint with a girl, long gone now, who had somehow managed to get through check-in without Bev finding nearly an ounce of marijuana in her shoes.

"She had these fancy insoles," Boone told me, "because of her arches. Everyone knew it. What no one knew, though, was that they were hollow. She didn't need arch support. She needed herbal support."

We walked all around the school, and I learned more about the time that Boone had spent there than I had learned in almost six months. Finally, we made our way back to the Mess Hall. The wind had picked up, and I could see that there were jagged white-caps all across Bob. The warmth of the hall was comforting. Boone went straight for the coffee, and I sat down at one of the tables.

"You sure have spent your time productively," I said. "No one could say otherwise."

She brought us both a cup, and started to pour mounds of sugar in hers. "I know," she said reflectively, "but my work is never over. There's still so much to be accomplished."

"You sound like a superhero," I said.

"Thank you."

"Hey," I said cautiously. "Why didn't you want to go visit Ben today? I mean, you don't have that many more chances to see him."

She looked at me, then down at the table. "Oh, it just wasn't a very good day for him," she said. "I snuck up and saw him on Wednesday during that history lesson, anyway. But he had some map work that he had to do today or something. I guess I'll go tomorrow." She looked back up at me and smiled awkwardly. "Hey. You can't fault the guy for working from time to time, can you?"

"No," I said, though I knew exactly what Ben was doing, and it had nothing to do with maps. "Boone," I said, "there's some-thing I've always wanted to ask you about."

Boone stared at me. "This sounds promising."

I didn't know how to start. "There's this rumor I've heard . . ."

I said, hoping that she'd pick up where I left off. But she didn't. She just raised her eyebrows and waited for me to go on. "About, you know, before you came here. A fight with another girl?"

"A fight with another girl," she repeated. "Hard to say. There've been so many. I'll need a little more information."

God. Why had I started in on this?

"Just that, well, I heard that you actually, um, did some serious damage. Back in Minster?" Everything I said sounded like a question.

Boone stared at me for a long while. Then she leaned forward. "I know what girl you're talking about, Townie," she said in a low voice. "The one I killed with a steak knife. What do you want to know about it?" She kept her gaze level.

"Uh." My mind was blank. "Nothing. I mean, sorry, nothing. I just —" My voice faltered and I looked into my coffee cup. Did I really want to know what she'd done?

Boone laughed loudly and slapped the table, causing me to look back up.

"Jesus! You really believed me!" She kept laughing as my face turned red. "Steak knife! How cliché!"

"Thanks," I said. "Now I feel like an ass."

"That rumor's been going around since I first stepped foot in this place. I've never killed anyone. Not that I wouldn't, if the circumstance called for it. Not that I didn't try once. I guess that's where the rumor comes from." She shook her head.

"What?"

"Oh God, you know. I threatened a girl once. Bitch asked for it. Maybe there was a knife in my hand at the time. I couldn't say." There was a sly smile on her face. "At least, no knife was ever reported."

"What'd she do to you?"

The smile disappeared and a shadow crossed Boone's face. "She was one of those girls, you know. The kind who think their spit's finer than champagne. In Minster, that's a tough act to maintain. But this one did. And she treated everyone — I mean everyone — like they'd be lucky to share a sidewalk with her."

"That doesn't sound so uncommon," I said. "What about the I-bankers?"

"Oh, big difference. The I-bankers stick to themselves, like a little colony of bees. They just make their honey and ignore everyone else. This girl was dangerous. She'd find some older guy, string him along, treat him like shit, make him do things for her. She wanted a car? He'd steal one. Someone offended her? He'd beat them up. I mean, we're talking jail time here."

It struck me quite suddenly with perfect clarity. "Your brother."

"Damn skippy." Boone looked out the window. "Oh, she was a doozy. Guy in a bar hits on her — with no flirtation on her part, I'm *sure* — and suddenly he's annoyed her, tarnished her honor or something. So she gets her latest toy to fight the asshole, and what does my brother do? He accidentally kills the guy. Complete bullshit."

We were quiet for a minute, then I said, "You must have been a lot younger than her."

"Yup. But I was strong. What's a few years between enemies, anyway? After my brother went to jail, I stopped by her house to show her how it felt to lose everything. Got the knife all the way up to her throat before I chickened out." She paused. "I do regret that."

"Threatening her?"

"Chickening out." Boone turned away from the window.

There didn't seem to be anything else to say, and it was clear that she was done talking about it. We drank our coffee in silence for a few minutes, and then Boone got up. She walked to the door that separated the dining room from the kitchen and pulled a safety pin from the back pocket of her jeans. The cooks would be coming in shortly to start dinner, but for now, we were the only people in the building. Boone worked on the lock until it popped, and she disappeared through the door. She came out soon enough with a plate of leftover cookies.

I raised my eyebrows as she plopped the plate down between us.

"We better eat quickly," she said. "You never know when someone'll decide to come in for a refreshing beverage."

The cookies were delicious — peanut butter and M&M — and we scarfed them down in less than two minutes. Finally, Boone wiped a crumb off her chin and looked down at the empty plate.

"Congratulations," she said. "We are official gluttons." She sighed contentedly and leaned back in her chair, closing her eyes.

The sun was starting to go down over the trees. From where we sat, we could see through the windows to the lake. I stood up. "Let's get back to the cabin," I said. "The movie is probably over. We can see if Jules still thinks it's good, twelve years later."

"Good idea," said Boone. "My guess is that she likes it even more now. Especially if it's that one with the talking dog."

We were laughing as we left the Mess Hall, and I was still laughing as I pulled one of the hoods from my sweatshirts over my head, so I didn't notice, at first, that Boone had gone silent.

"What?" I said, when I realized that she had stopped making any noise at all. I had to turn my whole torso to look at her, since the hood obscured my peripheral vision. When I could see her, though, I was also able to see what she was looking at.

Gia. Coming down off the trail from Buckhorn, jacket cinched tight, makeup in place. She was pulling her messy hair back into a ponytail.

The wind, frosting through the boughs of the trees.

The staccato chatter of a chipmunk.

The distant, rhythmic pulse as the water lapped at the shore.

These were the only sounds.

I didn't move. Neither did Boone. Gia hadn't seen us, and I wondered whether it would matter even if she had, or if she would just continue smoothing her shirt and putting one foot in front of the other.

Finally, I heard Boone take a deep breath. She was preparing herself. She was going to cry out, ask Gia where she'd been — and Gia would tell her, of course, and then it would all be known. My treachery, Gia's lies, everything. She took another breath, but no sound came out.

Gia kept walking, and soon rounded a tree and disappeared from sight.

I looked at Boone. Her eyes were half-closed, like she was remembering a dream she'd had the night before. Her mouth was set in a tight line, but I could see how it quivered at the edges.

"That little bitch." She opened her eyes and glared at the trees where the trail to Buckhorn began. Her voice started off flat, void of emotion, but it got louder as she spoke. "That slut." She turned to me suddenly, her eyes narrowing. "Did you — ?"

"No." The word was out of my mouth before I even thought it. "I swear I never told her." I couldn't stop. If there had been a roll of duct tape lying around, I would have taped my mouth shut.

Boone nodded slowly. "Okay." She let out a long exhalation. I waited for her to ask me more questions and uncover my lie, but she didn't. "Then she must have heard us talking about Ben. And now she's . . . what? She's *visiting* him? What else is she doing? BITCH!" Boone yelled the word into the trees.

I heard a noise behind me and turned to see one of the cooks letting herself into the kitchen. She had paused at the door when she heard Boone shout. We looked at each other now, and I shrugged my shoulders. She raised her eyebrows, opened the door, and went inside.

"What are you going to do?" I didn't know what else to say. She assumed that Gia had done this on her own. How was I supposed to tell her that it was my fault, now that I'd already lied? My mind knew that she would find out soon enough, but my gut wanted to believe that she might not, that I could be absolved by omission.

"I'm going to kill her."

The words rocked between us like an abandoned swing.

"Don't joke." I tried to come off dismissive, carefree, as though I already knew it *was* a joke, but my voice sounded thin and scratchy.

"Who's joking?" Boone didn't pull her gaze from the trees. She seemed to be speaking only to herself and those ancient pines. "I'll kill them both."

And then she started to cry. One tear pushed angrily down her cheek, willfully paving the way for the others to follow. Boone didn't sob — she didn't even catch her breath — but the tears came steadily, falling together in a thin stream from each eye. She didn't brush them away. She seemed incapable of it. Her arms hung uselessly at her sides, and she just kept staring into the trees as though looking for something she had lost, as though it might be there yet: a way out.

Finally, she swiped at her face with the sleeve of her shirt. She laughed once, loudly, and then began to walk toward our cabin without acknowledging my presence. I stepped quickly after her. Just as she was about to open the door, she spoke quietly, without turning to face me. "I'll tell you one thing. Ben'll have some explaining to do." Then she went inside.

The next day, Boone disappeared after breakfast. I knew where she was going, and my plan consisted of hiding from her for as long as possible. The problem was, of course, that I was also trying to hide from Gia. It would only take one glance in my direction, and she would know everything. This complicated matters. I decided to stay in the cabin until I thought Boone would be coming back, and then hide out in the Infirmary until dinner. Nurse Whitfield would let me sleep off an imaginary stomach bug for a few hours at least. Nurses have a sixth sense for bullshit, but I was willing to test my luck.

I didn't know whom I was more scared of. On one hand, Boone would probably kill me when she found out who had introduced Gia to Ben. Then again, that might be preferable to what Gia could do. It didn't take a mathematician to see that first Boone would find out about my little "introduction," and then she would tell Ben that his new girlfriend couldn't even smoke legally, not to mention everything else she was doing. And Ben would break it off with Gia. If A, then B, then, eventually, C. And that's where the equation circled back to little old me. Gia would assume that I had told Boone everything.

I lay on my bunk, staring at the ceiling, trying to remind myself that Gia couldn't really blame me for any of this. Except for the things I had said to her on the mountain, I hadn't done anything to harm her. But I knew she wouldn't see it that way. Somehow, I knew, she would find a way to believe that this was all my fault. And she would be right. If I hadn't wanted so badly to be alone with her on the mountain, maybe I would have been able to see what she really intended. But even as I thought about that, I couldn't silence the voice that still whispered to me in the back of my mind, reminding me of the way she'd looked at me in the Bathhouse. The touch of her finger. The fact that, despite everything she had done and said in the past week, I still knew — still wanted to know — the girl beneath the lies. I'd glimpsed her before. She was the one I wanted.

Right before lunch, Jules popped her head into the cabin.

"Still sick, huh?" She cast a worried glance at my prone form on the bunk. "Maybe you need some fresh air. Wanna go down to the beach?"

"Why?"

I had spoken sharply, and Jules looked confused. "I don't know," she said, "just to, you know, get outside?"

I pulled my arm over my eyes. "No thanks," I said. "I'd rather lie here."

"Okay." I expected to hear the door shut and the sound of her retreating footsteps, but I didn't. Instead, she walked softly over to her bunk and rifled around in her dresser drawer.

"What are you doing?"

"I want to show you something. I didn't get a chance to tell you yesterday, because you and Boone were gone all afternoon, but my parents sent me another picture of Westy."

"Great." My voice was flat. I didn't want to see a picture of her ridiculous dog. I wanted her to leave.

Jules either didn't hear me or pretended she hadn't, because she pulled out a photograph from her drawer and looked at it for a long minute.

"Wanna see?" she asked.

"No thanks," I said.

"Oh." She sat down. "God, I miss him," she said. "He would do this thing where —"

"And what else do you miss?" I interrupted.

"What?"

"What else do you miss from home?" I felt a hard knot in my chest, pushing its way through the layers of skin and bone.

Jules glanced over at me. "The usual things, I guess," she said. "Friends, family, good coffee. You know."

"You miss your friends." The knot was turning, twisting, getting hotter.

"Sure I do." Her voice was hesitant.

"That's got to be hard, being away from your friends for so long. I bet you're a good friend to them." I swallowed, and then continued in a voice that was unrecognizable to me. "I mean, you've been here a while. I'm surprised that Bev hasn't let you leave yet. It's not like you *chose* to come here or anything, like you could just *choose* to leave . . . is it?" Quickly, frantically, the knot began to unravel. I felt the heat spreading across my chest; all the anger, fear, and loneliness of the past week — of the past sixteen years — washed over me in a burning flood. I was so, so tired of hurting myself. I wanted to hurt someone else.

Jules looked up slowly. She had heard the accusation in my voice. Her eyes were bright with defeat. "Who told you?" she whispered.

"Terri. Your mom told her." I felt like I was tumbling down a hill: faster, faster. "You might tell your mom to keep her mouth shut if you want to preserve your little secret. You wouldn't want everyone else finding out that you're a tourist here."

"I'm not!" Jules cried. "I'm just as bad as the rest of you — I'm worse! There's no other place for me!" Her face crumpled. Tears started to pour from her eyes, but she went on, taking shallow, skipping breaths as she talked. "I would have done anything to get sent here. I begged the police to charge me, but there's no punishment in the world for what I did. You can't know what it feels like to kill — to have killed . . . in an instant. In one fucking second! I was looking for a Beatles song on the iPod, and I ruined everything." Jules put her face in her hands, dropping the photograph to the floor. She started sobbing loudly, her shoulders shaking, breath ragged and fierce.

My chest was empty. There was nothing left: no heat, no knot, no anger. Instead, I watched Jules cry, the enormity of her mistake rocking over her again and again, and I knew with a wrenching clarity that this was one of the worst things that I would ever do in my life. I saw myself for what I could be — what I had just been: cruel, bullying, intentional. Jules was right. There was no punishment for this.

"I'm sorry," I whispered. "I shouldn't have said that."

I didn't think she heard me, if she remembered that I was in the room. I had never heard anything like the sound that Jules was making. It was the kind of noise that you imagine mothers make when their children die: the sound of a heart rending. Tears stung my own eyes, and I focused on the foot of my bed, blinking.

Finally, Jules lifted her face from her hands and looked at me through puffy eyes. "You're not," she said.

"What?"

She was still choking back the occasional sob, but she breathed deeply and continued. "You're not sorry."

I nodded. *I am.*

"Then why did you say all of that?" She swiped at her cheek with the back of her hand.

"I didn't —"

"I don't understand you, Lida." Jules's voice got stronger as she went on. Her eyes were still red and teary, but they focused on me as she spoke. "You've never been a friend to me. From the moment she got here, you've only had time for Gia. Sometimes — *sometimes* — Boone. Like the rest of us are too *average* for you. Do you think I haven't noticed that you only come to me when you need information — or when you're bored?"

"I haven't!"

"Please. Think about it."

She gave me a long look, shaking her head, while I sat there, the fire in my chest replaced by a cold stone of shame.

"It's like you've got this blind spot. You can't even see the rest of us. Instead, you just keep chasing after a mirage. And it's making you mean." She reached over and grabbed a Kleenex off the dresser, wiping her eyes delicately. "I might have killed my friends," she said, taking a deep breath to steady herself, "but at least I knew they loved me." She stood up and walked to the door, pausing by my bunk. I couldn't even look at her, but I could still hear her.

" 'Blackbird,' " she said. "That's the song I was looking for."

I awoke to Boone's hand on my arm, shaking me again.

"Lazy ass," she was saying. "Wake up. It's almost time for dinner."

I struggled into a sitting position, rubbing at my eyes. I knew how they must look: swollen and guilty. "I fell asleep."

"No shit." Boone looked like she had been running. Her braid was disheveled, stray hairs crowding her face, and she was breathing heavily. "Get up."

"Where have you been?" I asked, even though I knew the answer.

"Ben's. I went up there to get some answers."

She leveled a gaze at me, and I knew it was over. He had told her everything. Their first meeting. My role in it. I scooted back toward the wall protectively.

"What's wrong with you? You look terrified. Hey — have you been crying?" Boone's eyes turned soft, and she leaned over the rail of my bunk toward me. "You okay?"

"I'm fine," I said nervously. Why hadn't she hit me yet? "Bad day."

"Hmmm." Boone kept looking at me, but she went on, "Fine. Okay. Guess who else is having a bad day?"

"You?"

"Always. Who else?"

"Ben."

"Not just Ben. You won't believe what she did." Boone looked wild, almost happy. "She told him she was a teacher here. A counselor. And poor, simple Ben believed her. Men." She snorted, and went on. "Of course they've been at it like rabbits."

"Did he tell you that?" *What else did he tell you?*

"Didn't have to. Ben didn't have much to say for himself. He was surprised that I was upset. What was it he said, at first? Oh, yeah — *But Georgina is your favorite teacher!* You should have seen the look on his face when I set him straight. Like I'd just told him his father was a horse or something." She tried to laugh, but it came out mangled. From far off, I could hear the sound of the dinner bell, and of cabin doors opening and slamming shut.

"So you guys are okay, then?" If she was waiting to spring it on me, I could play along.

"Okay? No, I wouldn't say we're okay. I never want to see him again." I thought I heard her voice crack. She cleared her throat. "But at least he knows what he's done. He can just sit up there in his bird's nest and think about that."

This was too much. I had to ask. "What else did he say?"

"Nothing. Frankly, I didn't give him a chance to get a word in." There was that mangled laugh again. Boone's eyes flashed with sadness, but cleared to slate just as quickly. "Asshole."

"What are you going to do now?"

"Now?" Boone looked at her hands. "Now I'm going to wait for that little bitch to visit him again. She'll have quite the welcome, I'm sure."

My stomach sank. Gia didn't know that Ben knew. It didn't take a psychic to see that this wasn't over yet.

"Oh, but hey — I scored us some spoils." Boone reached into the backpack at her feet and pulled out two bottles of wine. "I took them on my way out. What was he going to say? *You're too young?* We can take them on our overnight. One for me, one for you."

She held out a bottle, and I took it, tucking it into my sleeping bag like a stuffed animal. Somehow, confiscating the wine didn't feel like a victory.

"Thanks."

Boone swung her head back and forth like she was releasing a demon. "Screw him," she said finally, though her voice wasn't convincing. She rested her forearms on the rail of my bunk. "So, are you going to tell me why you're being so weird? You look like you just robbed a senior center."

"Ha," I said flatly. "Just tired. It's a bad day. That's all."

Boone straightened. "Fine. Wallow if you want in your . . . whatever. But come on. Let's go to dinner. This cabin is making me crazy."

I was terrified to face Jules again, but I knew that I'd have to, sooner or later. I swung my legs over the side of the bunk.

The Mess Hall was already packed when we got there, and we scooted into our seats just as Margaret started counting heads.

"Just in time," Karen said.

I stole a glance at Jules. Her face was still a little blotchy, but I'm not sure you'd notice if you weren't looking for it. She had tucked her napkin into the collar of her shirt (we were having spaghetti and meatballs), and she looked like a little kid, holding her utensil in her hand like a pitchfork.

"I'm starving," she said to the rest of the table. Our eyes met briefly, and she nodded at me — not with malice, but with something more like pity, I thought.

Jules had my number. She'd seen straight through to my twisted, rotten core. Everything she'd said back in the cabin was right. Six months at Alice Marshall, and I hadn't learned a damn thing. I certainly hadn't learned the two simplest things: how to keep a secret or be a friend. But unlike me, Jules *had* learned these things, and more. She wasn't going to hold a grudge — that wasn't her way. In fact, I could see that Jules wasn't mad at me at all. She was just sorry for me. And in some ways, that was worse.

"Hey," she said to me, "pass the salad?"

And I did.

$\mathscr{C}$HAPTER $\mathscr{S}$EVENTEEN

I'D ALWAYS HAD A HARD TIME KEEPING MYSELF FROM watching Gia. There was something about her that just seemed to demand that I watch — something magnetic, unarguable. Over the next couple of days, though, I became the master of not-looking. Every mealtime, every large group activity became a test of my ability to keep my eyes averted. I have never been a fan of horror movies, and this was no different. When the monster jumps out of the bushes, wielding its chain saw or brandishing its talons, I cover my eyes or look at the ceiling or just stand up and leave the room. Then it isn't really happening. Why couldn't the same approach work with Gia? I didn't want to be the first thing she saw once she visited Ben.

And I did just fine, all the way until Tuesday morning.

It was a Bad Breakfast day to begin with: oatmeal and canned peaches. We sipped our coffee and sluggishly stirred brown sugar into our bowls, only occasionally taking a bite. It was freezing that morning, and getting out of bed had been an almost heroic act. No one wanted to eat, but no one wanted to leave the warmth of the Mess Hall either. Gwen and Karen were arguing over whose turn it was to refill each other's coffee cups when they were interrupted.

"Elsa, a word." Bev stood next to our table, one hand on her hip. She looked like a statue, unsmiling and perfectly still. I hadn't even noticed her as she walked over.

Boone looked at the rest of us. She raised her eyebrow. "Sure, Bev. Should I meet you in your cabin later?"

"No, I'd prefer we speak now, please." She didn't sound angry, exactly, but her voice had the calm precision of a high-end kitchen knife.

Boone stood up slowly, folding her napkin and resting it next to her plate. She slipped into her jacket and followed Bev outside without another word. The rest of us looked at one another.

"What do you think happened?" asked Gwen. "Did Boone do something last night?"

"Wouldn't we know?" said Jules. "I mean, I think we'd know."

"Do you know anything about this, Lida?" Karen looked at me.

I shrugged. "Huh-uh." I looked nervously at my lap. There was no way that Gia wasn't involved somehow. She had to be.

Five minutes later, Boone and Bev came back inside. Bev walked back to her table, and Boone sat down, blowing on her hands to warm them up.

"Well?" Gwen leaned forward in her seat. "What?"

Boone looked at me and shook her head. She spoke to the group, but her words were directed only to me. "I've been caught. The whole scene in the Rec Lodge last week? I did it." She spoke in a monotone so calm it could have been a recording.

"Um, yeah, we know," said Gwen. "Everyone knows that."

"Yeah," agreed Jules. "Even *Bev* knows. What's the problem?"

"Well, that was all fine, I guess, until someone made it clear to her that everyone knows, and that everyone knows that she knows."

"You're losing me here," said Karen.

"Bev has it on good authority" — Boone paused to make sure I got this — "that I have been bragging to the whole school about it. That I've been bragging about how powerless she is to do anything to stop me from doing whatever I want. And she *can't abide pride*, she says." She never took her eyes off me.

"Who told her that?" I asked, though we both knew who it was.

"She wouldn't say."

I turned in my seat. I knew I shouldn't, but there was nothing I could do — I had to look. Sure enough, Gia was watching our table, her chin resting on one hand. Her face was completely blank, like an old-fashioned portrait.

"So it was okay until you *allegedly* started bragging." Gwen looked thoughtful. "Well, now what? What's she going to do?"

"The wicked must be punished," said Boone. She took a deep breath. "No mystical overnight journey for me."

Karen's spoon clattered onto the table. "What? She can't do that! Everyone's going on their Solo Trips! It's the most important thing we've done! You *can't* miss it!"

"Thank you for making me feel better," said Boone. "That's just what I needed to hear."

"Sorry," said Karen quickly. She busied herself by lifting a glob of oatmeal onto her spoon and then dropping it back into the bowl.

"Whatever," said Boone. "Look. I knew what I was doing when I did it, right? I was ready to get in trouble then — why not now?"

She was being way too calm about this. She sounded like Margaret, in fact: Zen. What was it Gia once said? *Cool as a cucumber.* But with Boone, cucumbers were never just cucumbers; they were pickles. Something was up.

Jules reached over and patted Boone's hand. "I'd let you go in my place," she said, raising the corner of her mouth in a smile. "I'd *pay* you to go in my place."

Everyone laughed at that, Boone the loudest, and I spent the rest of breakfast listening to Karen and Gwen extol the virtues of the Solo Trip to a doubtful Jules. I didn't look at Gia again.

We had kitchen patrol that morning, which basically meant cleaning the tables after everyone else left. The cooks were listening to the Grateful Dead as they began prepping for lunch, and they propped open the door between the dining room and kitchen so we could listen. (They probably knew that we were the ones who stole food when they weren't there, and I think they respected us more for it.) I was walking around the tables, picking up the salt and pepper shakers and putting them on a tray, watching Gwen and Karen dance to "Friend of the Devil" as they wiped down each table with a damp cloth. Karen waved her arms around her like a genie or a belly dancer, and Gwen stomped her boots and jerked her head from side to side. Jules stood near them with a bottle of Windex in her hand, moving her shoulders in time to the beat and smiling self-consciously.

"She's going to pay." Boone was standing behind me. I hadn't heard her come over from where she'd been sweeping by the door. All of the anger that she'd kept at bay during breakfast seeped out through each word.

"You sure it was her?"

"Come on, Lida. Who else?"

I picked up a pepper shaker and placed it carefully on the tray. "She must've gone up there yesterday."

"Bingo."

Now Karen had grabbed Jules's arms and was pulling them back and forth in a strange couple's dance. Jules started laughing. "Stop!" she said between gasps. "You know I can't dance!"

"What are you going to do?" I still hadn't turned around to face Boone. I spoke to the tray in my hands instead.

"I don't know," she said. "Maybe she's already had her punishment. Maybe that's enough." She paused just long enough that I started to believe her, and then she slapped my back, hard, with the palm of her hand. "Kidding! That bitch is going down."

I listened as Boone moved away, back toward her broom. Gwen, Karen, and Jules were all dancing together. Jules spun around with her arms outstretched. The cooks turned up the music for the last refrain. I could hear them singing along in the kitchen. *Set out running, but I take my time.* Jules was spinning faster and faster now, her head thrown back, nothing between her and the music but the dizzying world. *A friend of the devil is a friend of mine.*

We had Circle Share later that morning. It was our last one before the Solo Trips. I walked to the Rec Lodge slowly, head lowered and chin tucked against the cold that had moved down the mountain overnight and hadn't dissipated after breakfast. It nipped at my fingers and carried with it the unmistakable scent of snow.

All I wanted to do was get through Circle Share and get out. I had thought briefly about opening the bottle of wine that Boone brought down from Ben's place, but I didn't have the stomach to be a morning drinker. And besides, being drunk wouldn't change the fact that Gia had declared war.

I slouched in, wishing for some sort of crisis — a flood, maybe — so that Amanda would be forced to cancel the session. Gia wasn't there yet. I sandwiched myself between a Fifteen and Heather, the Seventeen who had asked Margaret if we could do our Solo Trips in the guest dorm. I started counting the minutes until the meeting would be over. Boone shot a look at me from across the circle, raising her hands in a "What gives?" gesture, but she didn't come over, and I stayed where I was.

Amanda had lit a fire in the large fireplace, and it crackled near us as we began. I sat on my hands to warm them.

"Okay," said Amanda. "Everyone have everything they need?"

A few girls raised their cups of coffee in confirmation.

"Good."

"Sorry I'm late." Gia stood in the doorway, leaning against the frame as she pulled a cashmere glove off her hand, finger by finger.

"Well, come on in. You haven't missed anything." Amanda smiled warmly at her. All my life, my dad had been telling me that there would come a time when I realized that grown-ups are just people, prone to the same weaknesses and embarrassments as the rest of us. At that moment, seeing Amanda so blissfully igno-rant, smiling in that benign way of hers, I knew that my dad had been right. The grown-ups were useless.

Gia stepped lightly into the circle. She sat herself next to a shy Fourteen who blushed and shifted her chair to give her more room. "Thank you," she said to the Fourteen, to the room in general.

"All right," said Amanda. "Let's start again."

We chanted together. Some of the girls held hands while we said the incantation. Others, like me, looked at the floor.

Amanda began the session by asking us to close our eyes. "Picture the best moment of your life. Try to remember what that felt like. Where were you? What were you doing? What made it the best?"

Nothing came to me, at first. I squinted my eyes shut tight. I thought, *My best moment.* I pictured the letters of each word, watch-ing them dance in front of my eyes: red, yellow, orange, blue.

B-E-S-T. I opened my eyes again and looked around. Everyone else, apparently, could conjure up fantastic memories at will. They all had their eyes closed. Some girls were smiling, and one even covered her mouth with her hand as she giggled at a particularly wonderful moment. A half smile played across Boone's face, and Gia looked like she was either napping or recalling something peaceful and serene. I looked around the circle until I got to Amanda. She raised her eyebrows at me; I quickly closed my eyes.

Images started developing slowly in my mind, like old Polaroid photos. The view of my bedroom at home from where I usually sat, my back against the door. Saying good-bye to my dad and Terri in Hindman. The look on my mother's face, right before she left. The morning after I got to Alice Marshall, when I looked in the mirror for the first time and saw what they had done to my hair. I could see my face perfectly, how my mouth had hung open like a trout's as my eyes filled with tears. No one else had seen me at that moment; I had been alone in the Bathhouse.

I shook my head, tried again. Amanda had said *happy* memories.

Dinnertime in the Mess Hall. I could almost hear the ambient sounds of chattering girls, the clatter of silverware. I tried to place the memory, because all I saw were the faces of my cabinmates around the table. Jules, laughing. Boone with the look she got right after she told a funny story, chin lowered, a "Believe me if you dare" look in her eyes.

Another picture floated in, covering up the dinner scene like a drop cloth. Gia's back, turned to me, as she riffled through her dresser drawer for something. This was a memory I could place. I watched the scene in my mind as she turned around with the T-shirt. Her smile was genuine. *It'll look better on you*, she said in my memory. *Take it.*

I tried to talk to her. As though stepping through a sheet of water, I entered the memory. *What happened between us?* I asked. *Can we get it back?*

She reached over and laid the T-shirt in my open arms. She smiled at me still, her head nodding slightly, and opened her mouth to speak.

"All right, open your eyes now." Amanda spoke softly, but her voice was jarring nonetheless.

I snapped my eyes open with the alacrity of a window blind. The other girls were stretching, yawning, glancing around themselves hesitantly.

Amanda leaned forward in her seat. She took a sip of coffee and placed the cup on the ground. "Did everyone think of some happy times?"

Happy times. Were we in preschool? Nevertheless, some girls nodded. Someone, I don't know who, said, "I thought about prom."

"That's great," said Amanda. "We'll share those memories in a moment. But first, I want to ask: Did anyone have a hard time remembering the good times? Did anyone find themselves remembering tougher moments?"

This time, no one wanted to nod. Oh, we'd get to the Happy Times soon enough. But first: Addressing Our Mistakes. I should have known Amanda would do something like this. No matter that she was right; I'd had to slog through the bad memories to get to the good. And from the certainty in Amanda's voice, I guessed that other girls had too.

Amanda looked around the circle, waiting for someone to speak up. There was a long silence. I looked at my lap, which is why I didn't see her raise her hand. I only heard Amanda say, "Yes?"

"I'd like to share."

I looked up so quickly that my neck twitched. Gia sounded nonchalant, though maybe a little nervous. She had her hands clasped on her lap, and she looked at Amanda as she talked. "I was just remembering something I'd done right before I came here." She glanced down at her lap. "It's silly, really."

Amanda sat quietly. She nodded encouragement. I don't think she noticed the electrical current that had swept around the circle as soon as Gia spoke. Her Thing. It was what we had all been waiting for since the moment she'd arrived. Every single one of us.

Gia took a deep breath. "The first thing you should know is that my mother's not dead." She spoke quietly, and half of the room leaned forward in their seats.

I knew it, I thought, but then she went on.

"She's not dead, but I don't know where she is." She looked down at her hands. "It'd be so easy to say it doesn't matter. To say, maybe, that an eight-year-old can't know her mother that well anyway, and that kids heal — they're resilient. But I did know her."

Wait. I shook my head as she kept talking. This was sounding familiar. No. Not this.

"But it was like she was reminding herself that I was still there. Still a burden, still the one wrong thing in her life that she couldn't get away from."

Gia had told me she had a photographic memory, but I had sometimes wondered if she was exaggerating so that she could embellish the letters that she received from her admirers, repeat them back to me as she would have liked them to be written, not exactly as they were. Now I saw that, regardless of whether or not she had remembered those letters accurately, she really was able to quote something word for word. And there was nothing I could do but sit there as she told everyone my Thing.

272

"— that other person in the room right here, right now, every single day, breathing in my ear, looking past me, telling me good-bye."

The room was silent. Even Amanda looked like she was listening to something strange and beautiful, a far cry from the everyday complaints and regrets of Circle Share. I knew it wasn't what Gia was saying, but the fact that *she* was saying it, and that made me feel even worse.

She went on, repeating everything I'd written in my journal. All of it. "My dad isn't a bad person. I can say now without smirking that he really has tried. But there's only so much one person can do with a kid who acts out, doesn't want to play well with others, hates any new woman you bring home. I don't blame him for remarrying. I don't blame Terri either."

I watched as Gia looked around the room after she said Terri's name, worried, perhaps, that she'd given herself away. But no one had noticed. They were too enthralled.

Reassured, she kept going. "The fact is, I had no one. I was no one. So, when I saw the nail on my dad's workbench in the garage, I decided to see what it felt like to inflict the pain myself, to be in charge of how and when I hurt."

There were some nods, a few sighs of agreement.

"And I liked it. I liked the way the nail (or razor, or knife — I'm an equal opportunity cutter)" — she paused for the light patter of laughter — "pierced my skin. I liked the way it looked clean for the briefest moment before beading up, and the way I felt so calm after I cut myself, like I could just float away from all the crap in my life for a few sweet minutes. It was such a relief.

"I used my forearm the first time, and the second, but I cut too deeply and Terri noticed." This time she didn't even blink when she said the name. "Three stitches and an emergency family session later, I'd learned to be more discreet. From then on, I stuck to places no one would see. I was my own art project. And I felt like an artist too. Sometimes, looking at the lines on my hips, I could imagine that they were red roses, that they were beautiful."

There was a strange sound coming from somewhere in the circle. I looked around, caught a few glances thrown my way, glanced down. My chair was rattling back and forth on its legs, the movement caused by my shaking body. Boone stared hard at me, her eyes a pair of question marks. I sat on my hands, closed my eyes, willed myself to stop. Gia must have noticed too, because she spoke a bit more quickly.

"Like all secrets, I couldn't keep mine forever. I wasn't trying to kill myself, but I cut too deeply into my side one day, and I fainted. When we got back from the emergency room, my dad and Terri practically babysat me. And when the stitches came out and the scars started to heal, they began talking about moving me to a *different environment*, one where I'd be *less inclined to harm myself*. That's how I ended up here."

She paused, smiling, and then leaned forward. "But for a couple of years, I owned myself. I decided when, I decided what, I decided if I'd had enough. And I know this sounds wrong now, but I've never felt so healthy. I was in control of my body. It was mine to cultivate or destroy." She looked at Amanda, let out a long breath. "There. That's all I wanted to say."

Amanda swallowed heavily. "Thank you for sharing, Gia," she finally managed. "I wonder if you'd like to talk about how it felt when your mother left. Can you tell us more about your relationship with her?"

Gia answered her, but the air around me had taken on a fuzzy quality so that everything was indistinct, barely audible. I had never *spoken* about my Thing. It was my secret story, and I had protected and nurtured it like a wounded animal. I felt as though

Gia had ripped off my clothes in front of everyone there and spun me around, asking everyone to look, *look* at what I had done to myself.

But it wasn't just that. It was the way she told it. She was comfortable, speaking easily. She took my story and made it hers. She might as well have stolen my name. Grief flooded my body, my face, but I couldn't move. My arms and legs were useless bricks.

I could feel Boone's gaze from across the circle. She was putting it all together from my expression. I didn't make eye contact. *Do not cry*, I told myself. *Do. Not. Cry.* But that was all it took. As soon as I thought the word, one tear escaped and rolled down my cheek. It was followed by another, and then another. I didn't make a sound. I didn't wipe the tears away because I felt that even lifting one hand might draw attention to me. Surprisingly, no one noticed. No one but Boone. She moved her head back and forth, looking between me and Gia, and I could see the realization spread across her face. I sat there, my face burning, crying silently as Amanda asked Gia question after question. And Gia had answers for them all.

"I don't know," she was saying, "I guess that's just how it is when your mother abandons you. I mean, think about how little she must have loved me to just leave like that, you know? I must have done something terribly wrong. Or, rather, I just wasn't right enough to keep her." She looked toward me indifferently.

"Oh no, I don't think — Lida, are you okay?" Amanda had finally noticed, and was looking at me with concern. "Do you —"

Boone interrupted her. "Hey, Gia, that's a pretty sad story." She wasn't even pretending to sound sincere. She leaned forward, resting her forearms on her knees. "I've got a few questions, though, if you don't mind."

"Of course not."

"First, I'd just like to know: Are you even capable of telling the truth?"

Everyone had turned to look when Amanda addressed me, but no one was watching me now.

"Boone —" Amanda started to interrupt, but Gia held her hand in the air to silence her. *I've got this one*, her hand said.

She shifted so that she sat even taller in her chair. "I don't need to lie. And I think it's odd that you'd choose this moment to attack me, Boone." Murmurs of agreement. "Can't you just respect the fact that I've shared something that is, actually, quite painful to relate?" She cast her eyes down at her lap.

"She's right, Boone. I think —"

But Boone cut Amanda off again. "Okay. Sure. My apologies. But just one more thing, then. Where specifically were you, again? I mean, where was that hospital that your dad and *Terri*" — she paused, looking around meaningfully — "took you to?"

"Out near my home. Kind of downtown." Gia smiled.

"What town?" If Boone had leaned farther any more, she would have fallen out of her chair.

"I'd rather not go into the specifics."

"Of course not," said Boone. "But then again, you've just really opened up to us. You've shared a lot. I don't know why you wouldn't divulge such a trivial fact at this point. It would be . . . suspect." She paused for emphasis. "So tell me: What. Town. Are. You. Talking. About?"

I'd seen Boone look at girls this way before, but never with the same steel and flint in her eyes. She held Gia's gaze.

Gia's smile faltered. She bit her cheek to cover it up. "Des Moines?" she said finally. Her voice lifted up at the end of the last word, so that she sounded like she was asking Boone's permission.

Des Moines? Iowa? Was that where she was from? Or was she still lying? Some of the other girls exchanged questioning glances.

"Des Moines," said Boone. "How odd. I think I speak for all of us when I say we thought you were from somewhere more . . . *interesting* than that."

"Now —" began Amanda, but Gia cut her off.

"You don't have to be *from* somewhere interesting to *be* interesting," she said evenly. She rested her hands carefully on her knees. "Though in your case, I suppose it would help."

A murmur rippled over the circle. We might as well have been the bystanders around a boxing ring. I brushed at the tears that were drying on my cheeks, tamping down my urge to get up and run.

"Girls, that is enough," said Amanda sternly. "I don't know what you're playing at here, or what difficulties you're having in your friendship, but Circle Share isn't the place to publicize them. At least, not this way."

"Friendship?" Boone laughed. "Believe me, Amanda, if we were friends, I would have told her long ago what a colossal bitch she is."

Amanda opened her mouth, but Boone kept going. "See, Gia, Des Moines sounds about right for you. It sounds like the only honest thing you've said since coming here. Everything else has been as real as Styrofoam. Do you want to tell everyone about your latest lie — aside from the one you just told us, that is — or should I?"

Gia still looked composed, but when she spoke, her voice sounded strangled. "Don't you dare."

Don't, I thought. *Please don't start this.*

277

"You'll be interested in this one," Boone said, addressing Amanda. "Turns out Gia is not just a student; she's a teacher too. At least, that's what she's been telling the ranger who lives up at the Buckhorn fire lookout. The one who thinks she's twenty-three."

This time, it wasn't a murmur; the sound that cascaded around me was more like a collective yelp. All of the tabloid magazines that the girls had been smuggling into school couldn't compare with the drama they were watching.

Boone continued. Her voice was casual now. She could have been giving directions to a misplaced tourist. "I wonder, Amanda, if this isn't a bit of a liability for Alice Marshall. Troubled girls coming up here, causing more problems than they would down in the real world. Sets a bad precedent, doesn't it?" She leaned back in her chair and crossed her arms. "Well. Bev'll have some thoughts, I'm sure."

Amanda said nothing. She looked down at her hands, as though they might tell her something new, give her an idea of what to do with the situation.

Gia just looked at Boone. I don't think she ever believed that Boone would actually tell on her. I hadn't believed she'd do it either.

Boone wasn't finished. "You just don't know how to play well with others, do you, Gia?" She smiled horribly.

Gia stood up slowly. She smoothed the front of her jeans, and pulled her gloves out of her back pocket. She held them loosely in one hand, dangling between finger and thumb.

"Gia, we are going to need to discuss this." Amanda's face was flushed, and she raised herself halfway out of her seat before giving up and sitting back down again. "Stay," she added, with no conviction.

Gia hardly glanced in Amanda's direction as she crossed the circle toward the door. Just as she was about to leave the circle, she spun on one heel. She was in front of Boone in less than a second. Maybe it was because I'd imagined something like this so many times that I substituted the scene in my head for the one in front of me, but I heard the slap before I saw it: the hand pulling back, the expert swing. The sound echoed off the Rec Lodge walls like the knocking of joists at a construction site.

Epilogue

Sometimes I'm afraid that life is just a series of Things, that we keep fucking up and making up and learning nothing and doing it all again and again and again. Those are my darker moments, when I see her face before me and remember how it looked the last time I saw her. No — how she looked at me. Those are the times when I want to slide back into the gray cave of not-thinking, not-hoping, not-caring, not-being. It would be so easy, even now.

I love how people say, "If there's one thing I learned . . . ," like they're able to sift through the complexities of a conversation or situation and choose what they want to take away from it. What lesson they want to say they learned. Please. Maybe in retrospect it seems clearer. But what about all the things they didn't even know they were absorbing?

Still. If there's one thing I learned, it's that you will always have to deal with yourself, whether you like what you're doing or not. And if you do screw up again and again, you will have to deal with it again and again. And if that sounds exhausting, that's because it is.

You get it now, right? This is my Thing. Every single page.

Chapter Eighteen

AFTER THE SCENE AT CIRCLE SHARE, AFTER GIA HAD WALKED languidly out of the Rec Lodge, after Amanda had calmly told us all to take a breather and come back new again and she kept Boone behind for twenty minutes, they almost canceled the overnight hike. I guess it was because a younger girl heard Gia whisper something to one of her cabinmates before breakfast the next day, and though she didn't catch it all she thought she heard the word *blood* or maybe it was just *bitch*, and she couldn't be sure who Gia was talking about. But they looked through all of our bags, and even took Gia aside for a more thorough search of her clothing, and all they found was a blue pen that didn't even have its metal clip in some other Sixteen's daypack, so they let us all go because, they said, this was the world we created and didn't we have to learn to live in it?

What was surprising, of course, was that they still let Gia go at all. She must have given Amanda an elaborately convincing explanation when they spoke alone in the Rec Lodge. That, or there hadn't been time for Margaret to climb up to the lookout to find out from Ben if the story was true. Or maybe they just simply didn't believe Boone. But the fact remained that, when it came time to load up the van with our packs and boots and water bottles, squeezing ourselves in between the gear where we could, Boone was nowhere to be found, and Gia got in. She sat up front, of course. Didn't so much as glance at me.

Margaret drove out of the parking lot and headed down toward Hindman. We'd only been in the van about ten minutes before she turned onto an old fire road that was edged with the brittle skeletons of whortleberry bushes, tangled and brown in the October light. From there, we continued to drop down a few hundred feet. Margaret stopped the van at the trailhead long before I was ready to get out.

To say that I didn't want to be there would be a serious understatement. It had been just over twenty-four hours since Gia had slapped Boone in Circle Share. I hadn't talked to either of them since then. Boone had been in the cabin the night before, of course, but she'd been uncharacteristically quiet and — perhaps in deference to her — the other girls didn't ask too many questions about what had happened. I caught Jules looking at me strangely a few times, but I'd gotten into my sleeping bag early, turning toward the wall and pretending to sleep. Boone hadn't hung around in the morning to watch Jules and I stuff our backpacks with the requisite crap. In fact, I hadn't seen her at all since right after breakfast, when she left the Mess Hall, a pack of cigarettes clearly visible in the back pocket of her jeans. It was obvious that, since she had nothing left to lose, she was going to leave nothing left undone. Smoking in plain daylight was just an afterthought.

"Here we are," Margaret said to a silent audience. No one moved. She swiveled in her seat so that she could see most of the van's occupants. "Ahem. Ladies. I said, here we are."

The look she gave us was persuasive. People started moving, though slowly. Boots were laced, shirt layers added. One by one, we piled out of the van and huddled next to it in the cold, looking around at the austere scenery. This was not one of those pristine mountain days that photographers seem to capture so well for outdoor magazines. The muddy abundance from earlier in the summer had given way to desiccation in some places, rot in others. The smell that rose from the ground was heavy with decomposition: leaves, soggy pinecones, limp and wilted flower stems. The air was dry, though, so cold it burned the backs of our throats as we stood there breathing nervously and taking it all in. Margaret had stopped at a trailhead that wound away from the old fire road and disappeared into the trees.

"You'll want to hold on to these," she was saying as she handed out photocopies of a crudely drawn map. "Each of your camping spots is marked here with an X. If you run into trouble during the night, find your closest neighbor. You won't be so far apart that this would be difficult." She paused, glancing around the group mildly. "And you'll also want these." She reached into her coat pocket and pulled out a tangle of red whistles. Gwen and Karen hadn't mentioned the whistles, and I wondered if they were a new addition to the overnight. "I've given a walkie-talkie to three of you." Margaret pointed to a Seventeen and two Fifteens who shuffled their feet importantly. "If Betsy, Katia, or Jennifer hears you whistle, they will contact me immediately. Okay? It's not like you're totally alone out there." She smiled.

I didn't feel especially comforted by the bright red whistle in my hand. Even so, I slung its thin rope over my head so that it lay across my chest. I felt like a lifeguard. Jules caught my eye and pointed her finger at me.

"Hey, you! Out of the water!" She laughed.

We began putting on our backpacks, testing their weight, adjusting the shoulder straps. Margaret had handed out Ziploc bags before we left the school that were filled with two nights' worth of pasta and dehydrated sauce, instant oatmeal, and energy bars for our lunch, and we each had a small cooking pot and a miniature camping stove. Somehow, these items made our packs feel twice as heavy. There was, I'll admit, quite a bit of groaning.

"Buck up," said Margaret as she helped a petite Fourteen into her pack. "This is nothing compared to what some folks bring for weeklong trips. Be thankful it's just two nights."

I was.

"All set?" She looked around the group, taking in the spectacle. Margaret put her hands on her hips. "Enjoy yourselves out there. Take some time to reflect on your journey so far. Ask yourself the hard questions." She looked at Gia. "Make sure you're the person you hope to be in this life." Then she paused, and I could tell that we were going to get another one of Margaret's Life Lessons. "The wilderness doesn't judge, ladies. When you're out there alone, you have the unique opportunity to think about who you are and what you want — from yourself and others. Try not to just go through the motions. *Use* this time. *Own* it." Margaret was quiet for a moment, then she put her hands on one girl's — Betsy's — shoulders and gave her a slight push in the direction of the trailhead. "Now go."

We started shuffling toward the trail in a single-file line. I was near the back, and right as I picked up one foot to start moving, I felt Margaret's hand on the strap of my backpack.

"Don't be afraid to explore the shadows," she said quietly to my back. "You might find some hope within the hurt."

I nodded and, without looking at her, moved forward. The last thing I heard before we rounded a corner and fell into silence was Margaret's voice, shouting one last direction to all of us.

"And be safe!"

It was hard to tell just by looking at our maps how far we were going to hike. Clearly, Margaret hadn't been attempting any feats of topography as she was drawing. There was a very clear squiggle that was meant to be the trail, I guess, and little, lighter squiggles that shot off it in intervals and ended at Xs with our different names attached. My name was next to the very last squiggle. Gia's was closer to the middle. There was also another long line that wove around all of the other lines, crossing the trail a few times. This line had pointy caps scattered across it like party hats. I guessed they were supposed to be waves, and I assumed that the line was a river.

Some of the girls chatted while we hiked, comparing the locations of their campsites, exchanging fears about snakes and bears. Gia was somewhere near the front of the procession, and I was happy to stay at the end, as far away from her as possible. Part of me wanted to grab that long mane of hair and pull until she explained how she could hurt me so badly. Part of me wanted to explain myself, to tell her that I hadn't been the one to tell Boone about Ben, that her secret had been safe all along. But that part of me had seen the casual way in which she slapped Boone the day before — like she was chiding a disobedient puppy — and I didn't want to tempt fate. It just felt too irreparable.

The trail curved up for a while, and then we dropped down and followed the river. Excuse me: Did I say *river*? I meant creek. It was hardly worthy of the poorly drawn whitecaps that Margaret had allotted it: The creek pushed gently over rocks, waving moss visible in its shallows. We had to cross it a few times, and each "crossing" consisted of stepping onto whichever rock was prominently sticking out of the water and hopping lightly to the other side. Not quite the harrowing experience that I used to read about in my old Oregon Trail history books. Even so, there was a muffled ocean roar in the trees above us, and it was so cold that we breathed heavily through our mouths and only smelled the deliberate sharpness of the air when we stopped to drink water from our bottles. Our packs, which had felt heavy and encumbering when we first set out, started to feel like an extra layer of protection against the elements, and I welcomed the weight on my shoulders and back.

We'd probably been hiking for about forty minutes when Jules hung back to talk to me.

"Lida. Hey." Jules fell into step beside me.

"Hey."

We walked quietly for a minute or so. Watched as, up ahead, one girl hugged her friends dramatically and then turned off the trail toward her campsite. "Good luck!" one of her friends called. "You'll need it!"

"That was your Thing that Gia was talking about yesterday, wasn't it?" Jules spoke suddenly, her words coming out in a rush. "I mean, it had to be. She was looking right at you."

"No she wasn't."

"Yes, she was. At one point I saw her look straight at you. And that's when Boone started up. It had to be your Thing, or at least, something having to do with you."

I didn't say anything, but sped up a little instead. I guess Jules took that as an affirmative. She sped up too.

"Look, I want you to know —" She sounded out of breath, and I slowed down just a bit. "You should know that I don't hate you for what you said to me in the cabin. I don't. I guess I didn't have any idea what was going on between you and Gia." She stopped walking suddenly, grabbing my arm and forcing me to stand still too. "But what *is* going on? Why did she —"

"It's too complicated," I said. I peered toward the group in front of us, trying to discern where Gia was. I didn't want her overhearing any of this.

"Try me," she said.

I looked at Jules — really looked at her. She was willing to forget all of the hateful things I had said to her, all because she was worried about me. I could see it in the way her eyes widened, her eyebrows knitting together with concern.

"It was my Thing," I said softly. I started walking again, though slowly.

Jules matched her pace to mine. "Yeah, I thought so," she said.

I took a deep breath. "I used to hide in the bathroom at high school at the end of the day." I looked at my feet as I talked. The tops of my boots were gray with dirt. "I know most people hide during lunch hour, when everyone is eating together and all that. I didn't. But after school, when everyone was at their lockers and talking about what they were doing that afternoon, making plans, exchanging numbers, just being normal, really — I couldn't stand it. So I would hide in the bathroom until most people had left. And then I would get my stuff and go."

"That sounds horrible," Jules said. "Didn't you have anyone?" I expected to hear pity in her voice, but I didn't. She sounded sad.

I kicked a pebble out of the path with the toe of my boot. "I didn't try." And the funny thing was, I could still remember exactly how it had felt to not try anymore, as though I had decided to sell a broken-down car that had been rusting away. How useless it had all felt.

"And so you started to hurt yourself?"

"Yeah. I just needed to escape, you know? I had all these thoughts whirling around in my head all day, every day, questions with no answers, and it gave me a release. I mean, when I was . . . cutting, I wasn't thinking about school, or my mom, or anything, really." I paused. "I didn't feel alone, because I didn't really *feel*."

Jules shook her head. "That's shitty. That's really shitty." She sounded almost indignant. "I mean, not what you did, but why you did it. Because, Lida, you can be . . . fun. I know that's a lame word," she added quickly, "but it's true. Maybe not at first —" She threw me a sly smile. "But once you warmed up, you could be funny. Kind of caustic, but in a good way. And people should know that." Her footfalls became heavier as she spoke, as though she was trying to stomp on the past, grind Bruno High and everyone in it into the dirt. "Damn it, your mom should know that."

"Thanks," I said. I meant it too.

There was a moment of silence before I felt Jules's hand on my arm.

"But that doesn't explain why, in Circle Share . . . why did Gia do that?" Jules's eyes searched mine. "What's going on, Lida?"

I knew that I could tell Jules. She wouldn't judge me; she never had. Maybe if I had recognized this earlier, and hadn't written her off as a flake, someone I didn't have to take seriously . . . maybe if I'd taken the friendship she'd offered on my first day at Alice Marshall, none of this would have happened. I could start now. I could tell her everything.

"You're a good friend," I said instead. "Anyone is lucky to have you on their team. Anyone." I meant this.

Jules blushed and smiled; she couldn't help it.

"But it's really, really too complicated," I went on. "Even just talking about it now makes me tired." I took a deep breath. "Can we talk about it later?"

"Sure," Jules said slowly. "But I'm here, you know, if you need anything." Suddenly, she turned toward me and enveloped me in a hug. Her arms reached around so that her hands landed on the sides of my backpack, and she spoke into my shoulder. "People like you, Lida. Maybe in Bruno it felt like you didn't have a choice about who you were, but you do now. You're Somebody here."

She squeezed me, hard, and then let go. We started walking again, our boots scuffing against the dirt.

I saw a Fifteen slow down up ahead, falling back so that she could walk with Jules. It was Lucy, the sullen girl who had been Jules's canoe partner when we paddled to the waterfall across Bob. She stopped and waved at us as we caught up. I could see for the first time that Lucy had an interesting face, with lively eyes that shimmered when she smiled, as she was doing now.

"Julie!" she said as we caught up. "You slowpoke." She hit Jules playfully on the shoulder. It was clear that they were closer than I'd known, and I recalled that Lucy usually sat on the other side of Jules in Circle Share. "Hi, Lida," she said carefully.

"Hi," I said. I thought I would hang back a bit, and let them walk together. I stopped and knelt down under the pretense of tightening the laces of my boot. "You guys go ahead," I said. "This might take a while."

"You sure?" Jules looked down at me. "We can wait."

"Yeah, go ahead," I started to say, and stopped myself. I remembered what it had been like in the bathroom stall at Bruno High, waiting for everyone to go so I could gather my things. The way my shoes sounded as I walked down the empty hall alone. Jules was right: This wasn't Bruno High. I didn't have to hide. "I mean, yeah. I'll walk with you. If you just hold on a sec, I'll be ready to go." I finished tying the laces quickly and stood back up again. "Ready."

"Good."

I walked down the trail with Jules and Lucy, listening to their comfortable patter, chiming in when I had a chance. I stood there as Jules hugged the younger girl good-bye, and waved as Lucy headed down her allotted spur. Our group was thinning. Gia had left the trail while I was talking to Jules, so I hadn't watched her disappear into the trees. Too soon, it was Jules's turn to depart, and she hugged me fiercely again before squaring her shoulders and trudging off to the left. The sun had settled itself behind a low, bleak cloud, and the trees appeared bleached and defeated. Even though I was wearing a jacket and sweating heavily underneath my pack, my wrists and hands were chapped with cold. I stuffed my fingers into the front pocket of my jeans, scraping knuckles against denim.

My campsite was last, and I hiked on alone, clutching the map in my hands and looking again at the X that designated my camping spot. I didn't want to think about Gia, about what her face looked like when she was telling everyone my Thing. If I hadn't known it was mine, I'd have never guessed that she was lying. What else had she lied about? I shivered in the cold air.

I tried to fill my mind with other things. Breathing, for instance. Taking one step, and then another.

Finally, after what felt like miles, I saw the spur that I was supposed to follow. It looked narrower than the trails the other girls had gone down, and it plunged steeply toward a cloak of heavy pines. I looked behind me once, and then left the main trail, stepping deliberately as I descended into the woods.

My site was located about a quarter mile in, and was crowded on three sides by trees. I put down my bag, stood in the center of the site near the campfire circle, and looked up. The trees leaned over me like inquisitive bears. I took that image as a sign of protection. I was intent on feeling optimistic.

The fourth side of the site opened onto a side path leading down to the stream, which was lined with rocks and coarse grasses. This, then, was the first order of business. I grabbed the collapsible water bucket from my pack and tromped down to the creek's edge to fill it.

That was basically how the first night went. See a need: Fill it. It was the kind of hard work that was easy to do, and it kept my mind occupied with its rote demands. I took it in steps. First the water, then the firewood. I gathered kindling, looking for bigger logs along the way to bolster the large half-burnt log that the previous girl had thoughtfully left in the campfire circle. I found enough heavy logs for a massive bonfire, and I stashed some next to a tree, away from the fire circle. *Who knows?* I thought. *I might be too busy tomorrow to get more wood.* Yes, busy indeed. I tried not to think about the next day — all those hours to fill. I thought it might be as excruciating as filling a bucket with sand, using only an eyedropper.

Back to the tasks at hand. The tent was easy enough; for someone who had always thought of herself as a fairly useless student, I had sure picked up the apparently elusive skill of fitting two poles together. (On the van ride in, I'd heard a number of girls quizzing one another on how, exactly, to set up a tent, like it was a chemical compound whose elements they could never remember.) I thought about that first overnight with Boone, and was careful to look for tiny rocks that I knew would feel more like nails when they were pressing against my back or shoulders during the night. Then I put the tent together over what appeared to be the flattest stretch of flat ground.

Next, I walked into the woods around the campsite until I found a high branch where I could hang my bag of food overnight. I tied a rope around a rock and tossed it easily over the branch, letting the rock pull the rope toward the ground. That would make it easier to attach the bag in the dark and shimmy it up toward the branch, hoisting it with the other end of the rope before tying it around a tree. "Don't even think about it," I said to the bears in my best Dad voice.

When all of that was done, I looked at the sky, which was the color of a dirty shell. That was when I realized that I'd forgotten to pack a watch. I was hungry, sure, but that didn't mean it was dinnertime. What time was it?

Panic knocked on the door; I opened it an inch. Without a watch, how was I going to know when to go to sleep, when to get up? What if I ate my lunch too early the next day and then had to wait eight hours for dinner? Would I sleep all day and wake up at night, restless and jittery? How would I know when to leave in two days so that I met up with the other girls along the main trail and made it to the van by eleven, like Margaret had said? What if —

I took a deep breath and looked at the sky again. Thought about the sky over Bob, the way it changed the lake's colors and patterns as the day wore on. If I could read the sun over Alice Marshall, I could figure out what time it was here, at least roughly. Boone, I reminded myself, never wore a watch, not even when we hiked to the fire lookout. I could do this.

And I knew something else too — very clearly. It was definitely time for dinner.

My hunger, which had politely waited in the wings while I set up camp, had emerged like a maniacal tap dancer, buffalo-stepping all over my stomach. Waiting for the water to boil was torture. I struggled to keep myself from cooking both nights' dinners at once. Starving, I devoured my pasta. Approximately two minutes later, when I was done, I washed my pot and congratulated myself on my various successes of the afternoon. I chalked my initial discomfort up to stress. Now I smiled, comfortable with the silence.

At first. But the evening, as all evenings will, eventually turned into night. I started the campfire. I put on another sweatshirt, and zipped my whistle into the front pocket of my backpack so I wouldn't lose it. I listened to the nighttime sounds, which were at once similar to and utterly different from the sounds at Alice Marshall. I snapped on my headlamp, picked up the water bucket, and headed down to the creek to fill it again. I wanted to be ready when it was time to put out the fire and go to bed. Sitting by the creek, holding the bucket at an angle in the water as it filled, I *felt* how alone I was. My aloneness had contours. I felt strange, disembodied. I carried the bucket back to the campsite, wondering at this.

And this feeling didn't go away. I wasn't scared; it wasn't that. I was just watching myself. I watched my Self sit by the campfire, warming her hands. I watched her stand and walk into the woods to hang the bag of food. I watched her squint up at the carousel of stars and then poke at the fire with a stick, separating the logs so that they lost some of their flame. I watched her pour the water slowly over the fire, listening to the hiss of the coals, stepping away from the smoke. And I watched her unroll her sleeping bag and curl into the tent, zipping it shut behind her. My Self was good at these things; she was capable and smart. But I didn't want to *watch* her; I wanted to *be* her. What was it Margaret had said during one orienteering class? *You're no more you than when you're alone.* If that was true, then I was long overdue for an introduction.

·

CHAPTER NINETEEN

I SHOULD HAVE KNOWN THAT A WATCH WOULD BE UNNECESsary. If the sun hadn't woken me, the cold sure as hell would have. My fingers were clumsy and slow as I set about making another fire. I could sense my feet moving beneath me, but they felt like ice skates, hard and sure and totally unrelated to my body. I knew that, as they warmed up, I'd feel them plenty. And I did.

I crouched next to the fire, fighting the impulse to stick my feet in it, boots and all. I watched as the light shifted across the campsite, gaining traction, getting brighter. *One night down*, I thought. *One more to go.*

I untied the food sack from the tree where it had hung unmolested all night. Digging through it for the instant oatmeal, I found a glorious surprise. Margaret had snuck in some brown packets of instant coffee, with a Post-it note attached that said, *Some addictions are worth feeding.* I wondered what Bev would say to that. Probably wouldn't agree. The note sailed effortlessly into the fire.

The coffee tasted like dirt, and I lapped it up. The oatmeal had the consistency of paste, and tasted about the same. But I dutifully shoveled it in anyway, knowing that everything I ate was one less ounce, one less pound that I had to carry out of there in my pack.

I rinsed my bowl and mug. I hung the sack back up in the tree. I straightened my sleeping bag in the tent. By this time, the sun was canting in the sky, and the fire had died down. I no longer felt like I was walking on swizzle sticks. The day had officially begun.

Sit down. Stand up. Sit down again.

What do you do, when there's nothing to do and no one to hold you accountable for doing it? That's right: a whole lotta nothin'.

Margaret hadn't told us about this part. She hadn't said, *Oh, hey, make sure to bring some knitting or a 2,000-piece puzzle or that copy of* War and Peace *you keep meaning to read. Because YOU'LL HAVE TIME.* Nope, she hadn't mentioned it at all. And what had I brought? Two hats and an extra pair of socks. If it snowed, I thought, I'd at least have a well-dressed snowman, though by then I'd probably have died of boredom.

I glanced back up the spur that I'd come down the day before. The trail we'd all been following didn't end at my turnoff, I remembered. It kept going. Might as well go on a little hike, I thought. See where it leads.

I grabbed my water bottle and the crude map that Margaret had given each of us, and I took off.

The trail roughly followed the creek that ran past my campsite, gaining elevation slowly so that I was far above the water before I ever felt short of breath. I looked down at the tiny stream below, peering for some sign of my tent. All I saw were rocks, moss, a chipmunk scurrying for cover. From there, the path turned away from the water, and I followed it, winding in and out of dense forest.

Now that the day had wedged itself firmly between the cold of morning and the cold of night, I was comfortable, almost too warm in my fleece. I hiked along, letting thoughts come and go at random, remembering pieces of conversations from the past five months and then trying to forget them, paying attention to the world around me without focusing on it entirely.

And that's how I surprised the mountain lion.

The trail had leveled out again so that I was following long, flat switchbacks, gaining only a few feet with each turn. Margaret had said that the Forest Service created these kinds of paths from time to time in an effort to cut back on the erosion that tight, short turns on a trail could sometimes feed. From the crumbling "alternative" shortcuts that I could see connecting each switchback, just about as wide and deep as a boot heel could make them, the Forest Service hadn't done a very good job of convincing rushed hikers to stick to the path. But, honest hiker that I was, I stayed on the trail. And when I rounded one of the long bends, looking up from where I'd been vacantly staring at the tip of my shoe, the mountain lion was right in front of me, frozen with one paw slightly raised in a not-step.

It wasn't quite as big as I'd imagined, just the size of one of those large breeds of dog that I always picture giving toddlers rides at county fairs. Its tail was almost as long as its body, and hung lazily off a soft tan hide that winked as the sun and early afternoon clouds moved across it in patches. It had the innocent face of a household pet. An extremely large, very deadly household pet.

I should mention that, by this time, I was no longer moving.

Margaret had told us about mountain lions during one of our Outdoor Ed classes, of course, adding to the scant information I'd gotten from Ben. Here's what she'd said:

"Most people live their whole lives in the West without seeing one."

"If you see one, you can be sure that it saw you first."

"If a mountain lion is stalking you, however, it'll be on your neck before you ever see it."

"Do not look away. Do not lean over. And Never, Ever, *Ever* Run."

All of this ran through my head in the five seconds or so that I was looking at the mountain lion and it was looking at me. I wasn't sure Margaret had been right when she said that, if you do see one, it's because it *lets* you see it. The animal seemed just as surprised as I was.

And then it opened its mouth and kind of growled — the sound was a mix between a roar and a hiss. When I saw its teeth — all two billion of them — I realized that now would be a good time to do something.

I squared my shoulders, raised my arms above my head, and waved them around. I made myself look as big as I could. And I yelled — loudly.

"NICE TO MEET YOU!" I thundered aggressively. "OH, NO, NO, *NO*," I answered myself, "THE PLEASURE'S ALL MINE!" It was the most ridiculous thing in the world to yell, but it was what came to mind, and my voice didn't sound polite at all. I sounded like a quarterback.

It worked. The lion started, turned, and ran soundlessly into the woods off the side of the path, just a flash of gold from its long tail, and then it was gone.

I stood for a long time on that trail, my feet unable to think for themselves. I was sweating. I didn't move.

I was waiting, of course, for it to come back.

It didn't.

After about ten minutes (which could have easily been an hour; the sun wasn't very helpful at this point), I turned cautiously and started back the way I had come. I spoke out loud to myself, to the mountain lion, to the bears and trees and dead leaves and anything else that might be listening.

"Well, I'll just be going. Yep, here I go. Down the trail. Just walking down the trail." I inhaled and exhaled, kept talking loudly, and walked as quickly as I could without breaking into a run.

Needless to say, I paid more attention during my hike back. The whole forest was lit up like a Technicolor car lot at night. I saw a small grove of aspens that I had missed before, dried golden leaves hemming the stand of bare trees like fans at a rock concert. I heard the rustle of branches breaking as a squirrel jumped from one tree to another. I watched two juncos making lazy eights around each other before lighting soundlessly on the same branch. And all the while, I took deep, calming breaths, feeling the sharp air sting my nostrils and soothe my throat.

"How much can you control?" Amanda had asked us in Circle Share soon after I'd arrived at Alice Marshall. I hadn't given it much thought at the time, but now I did. "How much of what you might feel the world has done to you can you change? What can you direct?" She'd asked us to think about the way that we thought people saw us. And I remembered thinking, *They don't.* See me, that is. Then she asked us if there was anything that we might be doing to nurture — her word, of course — that perception. "Sometimes," she'd said, "it can be a self-fulfilling prophecy."

If I had come around the corner at any other time, the chances are that the mountain lion would have been hidden in the trees along the trail. Mountain lions are elusive; they can make themselves invisible both day and night. Back in Bruno, I knew how to be that animal: Make as little noise as possible, even when eating your lunch. Never raise your hand in class. Wear sweatshirts like flour sacks, in colors that blend into the walls. Don't strike up conversations. Hide your face behind your hair, your smile behind a scowl. Whatever you do, don't make any friends. Oh yes, I knew how to be invisible too. But what about now? There had been no hiding today.

My dad and Terri and I had gone on vacation in northern Idaho once when I was twelve. We stayed in a tall hotel in Coeur d'Alene that looked out onto a small portion of the twenty-mile-long lake. There were entire towns scattered around the lake, little places with one or two stores, a lakeside bar and grill, and a place to fill up the gas tank of a boat; and there was a terrible boating accident while we were there. Three teenage girls were driving across the lake at full speed one stormy night, and didn't see the buoy with its flashing red light, warning them of the rocks ahead. They hit those rocks at full speed, flipping the boat and flying into the cold, black water. One broke her arm but managed to climb onto a rock, where she waited, shivering, for Search and Rescue. One swam a full mile to shore and eventually got help, though she was so disoriented that it took the sheriff an hour before he realized the other girls were still in the lake. The third girl held on to a cooler of beer for the entire night as she floated farther and farther away from the wreckage. When they finally found her the next morning, she had died of hypothermia, one hand hooked inside the handle of the cooler.

This is what I thought about as I hiked back toward my campsite. I thought about that girl in the lake, how cold she must have been as the knowledge of her death crept slowly up her legs. The cold, unyielding fact of it. And how unfair it must have seemed, how ridiculous, to be able to look across the lake — *right there* — and see the lighted cabins. To know that people were enjoying the *Late Show* with a glass of wine, safe and oblivious on their couches, or standing over the sink and brushing their teeth, thinking about the day to come. Any one of those people could have saved her, and none of them would, and this realization probably made her cry out in fear and anger. She had to watch from the chilling lake as the world went on without her.

Back in Bruno, I'd felt that way all the time. It was a loneliness that defied solace. Each day in high school had been a dark night in a freezing lake with no one there to pull me out. As far as I was concerned, all those other students were as inaccessible as lights on the shore.

But hiking back along the trail, I wasn't so sure. I had always believed that I had no people, that no one ever looked for me. And maybe that was true. But maybe, just maybe, I wouldn't have noticed if they *were* looking. Maybe I walked down the halls with my eyes closed, terrified of what it would be like to try, to stretch out my hand and see if someone took it. Maybe those lights had always been within reach. Maybe they still were.

Margaret had asked us to reflect on our journeys so far at Alice Marshall. Not to judge ourselves, but to acknowledge the ways — big or small — in which we'd grown. So I thought about that girl and I thought about my mountain lion, because he was quickly becoming *my* lion, in the way that anything that you experience alone becomes irretrievably *yours*. I replayed those five seconds on the trail in my mind. Would the old Lida have yelled at him? Nope. Would the old Lida have even been on a trail by herself, hiking along for the damned pleasure of it? Hell no. In the past five months, I had found myself buoyed countless times by the pines, the firs, the wind, the calming scent of mud and moss. And it was in those moments that I felt most like myself.

I breathed in the fresh air, letting my lungs expand and contract, and I thought, for the briefest moment, that I wished my mother could see me like this. For the first time, I just let myself think that, instead of adding a litany of self-recriminations crowd my head. I didn't judge her; I didn't think about the *why*s and *what if*s and *wasn't I enough*s. I just thought: *My mom should see me like this. She'd be proud.* And then I kept on down the trail.

300

By the time I got back to my campsite, it was midafternoon. My hike had taken longer than I thought. I spent what was left of the day sitting next to the creek, looking for tiny fish or frogs and calming down. After the initial fear had subsided, I felt almost giddy with the excitement of having seen the animal. I pictured the way I would tell the story to everyone back at school. I could imagine the look on Jules's face: She would be just *thrilled* to hear (once she was indoors, that is) that bears were the least of her worries. And how I would impress Margaret and Boone, when I told them about the way that I stood up to the mountain lion — literally! — and did exactly what I was supposed to do. And Gia. I tried to ignore the excited flutter in my stomach when I imagined telling her about it. I didn't *want* to want to tell her. But oh, I wanted her to look at me the way I knew she would when I told her.

I boiled water and let it cool, pouring it back into my water bottle for the hike out in the morning. I took a short nap, and when I woke, the sky had darkened to a deep gray. Just like that, the day was over. I'd done it. I'd been alone with myself, and I had survived.

I pulled a hoodie out of my pack, layered it under my fleece jacket, searched for the mittens that Margaret had given each of us before we got in the van, found one of them, put it on, and contemplated the fire circle. For some reason, the idea of building yet another fire exhausted me. I sighed dramatically, since no one could hear me, and then said, "It's just you and me, partner."

I tried to get it done the old-fashioned way. After all, it had worked the night before. I leaned the smaller branches against one another like a pyramid, with the log in the middle. When that collapsed, I tried structuring it log-cabin style, laying the twigs over one another in a crosshatch. That didn't fall down, so I tried to light it with the small lighter that Margaret had given each of us. (*And, ladies,* she'd said, *I'll be getting these back at the end of the hike. Be sure of that.*) Nothing took. I remembered that I'd woken the night before to the sound of light rain. I'd thought that it was a dream, but maybe it rained just briefly enough to dampen my sticks. My one naked hand was red in the cold, and I stuffed it in my jacket pocket. I tried again, throwing in some dried moss and pine needles as kindling. Nothing.

I don't know how much time had passed at that point, but I do know that I was freezing, and hungry, and so focused on my goal that a Sasquatch could have snuck up on me and I wouldn't have heard. The thought of spending the night in the cold without a fire made me feel reckless, almost hysterical. I riffled through my pack wildly, tossing out items as I went: flashlight, extra socks, knit cap. Finally, I found what I was looking for.

I held my journal in front of me, peering through the dim light at the unicorn on the cover. It had always seemed to be mocking me, I thought. It certainly seemed to be doing so now. "I wouldn't look so smug," I said to it, my voice echoing and loud. I opened the book and turned to the last empty page. I ripped it out quickly, wadded it up, and threw it in the fire pit. I did the same with the page before, and the page before that. And the paper, when I held the lighter to it, began to blaze.

I kept adding to the flame, working my way backward through the journal. Some pages were blank, some had doodles on them, some had little notes that I'd written to myself. It was like watching a movie in reverse. I knew what scene was coming up, and even though I didn't want to see it again, I kept getting closer and closer.

Finally, I was there. The fire's long flames reached with furtive fingers toward the night sky. I didn't have to turn the next page. But I did. And I looked at where I had written down my Thing. The page wasn't wrinkled or dirty; only two people had ever touched it. My handwriting looked foreign to me.

I ripped it out. And the two pages before it too. Ripped them all out and sent them sailing into the fire. I watched as my words took flame, the paper curling around itself as the edges browned, then crisped black, and finally disintegrated into ash.

At first, I felt nothing. They were just words, after all. Sure, they were *my* words, but were they still? Gia had stolen them, claimed them for herself. She'd taken my worst moments, my biggest secrets, and treated them like they were hers to twist and tell and forget. I watched the pages burn, and felt the familiar hollowness that I had been trying for so long to fill open up inside of me, gaping like a yawn.

"No," I said.

I had worked too hard. Those weren't just words. They counted for something. I'd let go of my Thing when I wrote it down, and Gia couldn't take that from me. She couldn't take what I felt as I was writing it, the painful release and the compassion that followed, filling the spaces between the words. The peace that I'd felt when I was done writing.

There was so much that I had done wrong. I had been a bad friend — to Jules, Boone, even to Gia. But at least I had done this: I had looked my demon straight in the eye and I had recognized the eye as my own. By sharing my story — even if it was just on paper, even if no one else read it — I'd owned my actions. I closed my eyes now and breathed deeply. When I opened them again, the words had all disappeared in the smoke.

Epilogue

I've been doing so well with this project of mine. I've managed to keep it secret all this time, work on it mostly when no one's home or I know they won't bother me. Usually, that means late at night, after the news is done and my dad's turned off the TV and I've heard the sounds of their bedtime routine as they brush, floss, flush, close doors, and finally go to sleep. And now I'm nearing the end, and I have to fight the urge to throw down the pen and dive under my covers, where my world is safe.

I don't want to tell the rest.

But I know I need to.

There are those things you can't bear to live with, and those things you must live with. And between the two, like the translucent liquid that protects the brain from the skull, are the things you do in order to live. For me, writing is one of those things. I know that now.

So I have to keep telling this. And I have to do it soon, because the clock is ticking. I'm going to see her again in just a couple of weeks. Of course I told Margaret I'd go back. What else could I say?

Will she even agree to go? Will she want to see me?

Hurry, Lida. Hurry.

CHAPTER TWENTY

ONCE I GOT THE FIRE STARTED, I SAT HUNCHED NEAR IT FOR a good ten minutes, just warming my hands. Then I made dinner, and scarfed it down so quickly that I didn't even taste the pasta sauce's dehydrated goodness. Man, I had earned that meal. I did my dishes, sat back by the fire, thought some more. I knew what I needed to do.

I walked over to where I had leaned my backpack against a tree and pulled out another book. It was far too dark at this point to read, but I carried it over to the fire and sat down, scanning the familiar cover. *The Dharma Bums*. I opened it and looked at the X-ACTO knife that was resting in the hollow, pillowed by Kleenex so that it didn't make a noise when Bev checked the contents of my bag. The knife was like a sibling, a freckle; in a crowded airport full of harried X-ACTO knives, I would recognize mine immediately. It knew pieces of my life that no one else had witnessed.

"Well, hello again," I said to it. I picked it up.

"Hello."

The voice breezed out of the shadows in the trees, and I almost fell into the fire. It was so dark that I couldn't see past the campsite, and I stood quickly, dropping the book but holding on to the knife. "Who's there?" I whispered, like some horror movie heroine.

I heard a familiar laugh. "You'd better drop that before you do something rash, Townie, like whittle a *real* weapon out of wood." Boone stepped closer to the firelight. "That knife is as handy as a sponge. What are you going to do, tickle a bear with it?"

I watched as she walked over to the fire, holding her hands out in front of her to warm them. She was wearing a light jacket and a skullcap that she'd pulled down low over her ears. Her shoes were covered in dirt, and there were some pine needles stuck in her hair. She had a small backpack slung over one shoulder.

"What are you doing here?" It was the obvious question.

Boone squatted next to the fire, setting her backpack down next to her. She glanced up at me. "Thanks for the gracious welcome." She clenched and unclenched her fingers as she held them close to the flames. "You forgot something in the cabin, and I thought I'd bring it for you." Boone reached into her backpack and pulled out one of the bottles of wine that she had taken from Ben's place. "I assumed you wouldn't try to smuggle it in, not with all of the bag checks they were subjecting you to." She grinned wickedly. "But then, I guess you're wilier than I thought." She nodded at the knife, which I was still holding.

I set it back inside the book and shut the cover, laying it on the dirt next to where I was sitting. I reached out and took the bottle. "Thanks," I said. "But, I mean, really — what *are* you doing here? And how did you get this far, anyway?"

"What the hell else was I going to do? You all left, and I couldn't very well sit around with everyone feeling sorry for me." She mimicked the high, Valley-girl voice of some of the I-bankers. *"Poor Boone. She doesn't get to have her own Special Nature Time. We should cheer her up. I know! Let's dress up a pinecone in silly doll clothes and give it to her as a gift!"*

I started to laugh. "What?"

"Admit it — they'd think of something like that." Boone shook her head. "I just couldn't abide the shitstorm of sympathy that I was getting. So, you know . . ." Her voice trailed off.

"No, I don't."

"Well, I happened to be in Margaret's cabin while she was getting ready to drive you to the trailhead."

"Oh."

"And I happened to see a copy of the map that she'd been looking at on her desk, and where each of you would be," she said lightly. "And it really wasn't that far from school, so I just, you know, started walking."

I stared at her. "Was that where you went yesterday?"

"Roger that."

"You know how pissed they're going to be," I said. "Bev especially."

"Lida, I've said it before, and I'll say it again: What are they going to do? Nothing! There's nothing they *can* do to me now. So what does it matter?" Boone stood up and started pacing around the fire. "I'm about to head back to a place where nothing like this" — she waved her arm around — "exists. Nothing. So I think I deserve a little slice of beauty for just one goddamn night, thank you very much."

I looked into the fire, which was flickering weakly in the dimming light. "You're right," I said. "Whatever. I'm glad you're here." And I was. Kind of. Under normal circumstances, I would have been grateful for Boone's presence. Nothing says safety like a girl who could probably scare Bev just by narrowing her eyes. But something wasn't right. Her voice had an oddly chipper tone, almost too friendly. I was on edge, but I couldn't put my finger on the reason why.

Boone slapped her palms on the sides of her pants and sat down by the fire, which crackled weakly. She sniffed the air. "It's going to snow tonight."

"No it's not," I said doubtfully. But I glanced at the sky anyway. There weren't any stars out, but it wasn't exactly pitch-black either. The clouds had a kind of silvery glow to them. "It's not," I said again, more forcefully.

"If that's what you want to believe, Townie," said Boone. "I just hope there are some snow boots in that pack of yours." She smiled. "Hey. Let's crack open that wine, eh? Little toast to the good ol' days at Alice Marshall?" She walked around to my side of the fire, and sat next to me on a dusty rock that someone had set there as a makeshift chair.

"Sure." I handed the bottle back over to her, and Boone produced a corkscrew from one of the deep pockets in her jeans.

"Took this from Ben's too," she said by way of explanation.

Boone opened the bottle with the deftness of a seasoned bartender. She took a deep swig, and handed it to me. I did the same. The wine was vinegary and tart, and it numbed my tongue.

"This is terrible," I said.

"Yes. Yes it is." Boone took another gulp. "Just terrible."

We drank in silence for a few minutes, passing the bottle back and forth, listening to the hiss of the fire. I still couldn't name the uneasy feeling that lay in the pit of my stomach, but the wine did a pretty good job of muting it, at least for a while.

"What a week," Boone said finally. "As the I-bankers would say, 'drama-rama.'" She held the bottle out in front of her as though studying the label. Then she turned to me. "You okay? I mean, after Circle Share?"

I nodded.

She glanced at the book near our feet. "I wondered where my book had gone," she said. "Any reason why you happen to have brought your knife up here?"

"Not really," I said. "Protection, I guess." That wasn't true. I was going to use it just the way I always had. At least, that's what I'd been planning when I'd packed it. But after the day I'd had, it all seemed a little silly. When I'd taken it out of the book, the knife had felt uncomfortable in my fist, like a pair of too-small shoes.

"Huh." I hoped that was the end of it, but she went on, circling back to the topic at hand. "What I can't figure out is, why did Gia do that to you? I mean, why *you*?" I didn't turn to face her, but I could tell that Boone was looking at me expectantly. "What does Gia have against you?"

I shrugged. "Maybe she was just in a 'take no prisoners' kind of mood."

"Maybe." Boone kept watching me. "But it's strange. I mean, aren't you her little pet? You must have *really* pissed her off." She shook her head, then reached down to the ground and picked up the book, opening it and examining the knife. "So this is what you used," she said, her voice quiet.

I shifted around on the rock. "Yeah."

"And she was the only person who knew?" The question came out weakly, and I wondered — just for a moment — whether Boone was jealous. She didn't even have to look at my nod of assent. "Why did you trust her? I told you not to. I can't believe you shared something so private with someone so . . ." Her voice trailed off, and she stared angrily into the fire. "I mean, what was going on with you two?" She turned suddenly and grabbed me by the shoulder. "Lida. If she knew something so private about you, what did you know about her?"

I shook my head too quickly. "Noth —"

"What secrets did you keep for her?" Her fingers dug into my shoulder. "What did you know?" she repeated.

"None! Nothing! I didn't know anything!" My throat constricted, making my voice sound thin and girlish. It was the voice of a liar, and I was sure that Boone knew it. I stared into the fire, blinking furiously.

Boone released her grip on my shoulder and leaned back. She pulled a new pack of cigarettes from the same pocket where she had stored the corkscrew. She hit it forcefully against the palm of one hand, packing it, and then ripped it open and pulled out a long white cigarette. She stood and leaned so far over the fire that the flames could have licked her eyelashes. When she straightened again, the cigarette was lit. Boone stood there silently, smoking. At one point, she held the pack out to me, and I shook my head. Finally, she looked off into the trees, blew a perfect smoke ring, and said, "Okay."

"Okay?"

"Yeah." She looked down at me. "Sure. Okay."

The fire glowed fiercely. From where I sat, Boone's eyes were obscured by the interplay of light and shadow.

She dropped her cigarette into the flames and stepped toward my pile of extra logs. "Your house is going to lose its foundation," she said.

"Huh?"

"Plain English: All these logs won't do much good without more kindling. Otherwise, we're going to freeze overnight."

I laughed uncomfortably. "I guess."

"Clearly, you didn't absorb what I taught you, Grasshopper." Boone reached into her small backpack and pulled out some gloves, which she slipped on. "I'll be back in a few."

"Where are you going?"

"To bolster our reserves."

I watched her walk into the trees. She hadn't taken a flashlight with her, but the light in the air was still that strange shade of silver, so I thought she'd probably be fine. Plus, I half believed that Boone could see in the dark.

I sat on my hands to warm them as the fire crackled. Boone was right; it wouldn't last long. Already, the flames were dying down, red coals pulsing with heat.

I had to admit to myself that I was glad she'd come. What did I think I was going to be doing out here alone all night, besides fending off frostbite? And she'd seemed to believe me when I told her I didn't know about Gia and Ben. I kept repeating this to myself as I stared into the coals, the way an addict imagines innocence, insists that no one knows. She hadn't pushed the issue. She'd really seemed to drop it. She believed me. Still, I felt nervous, unmoored. *Explore the shadows*, Margaret had said. Shadows were all I could see.

When I heard the snap of a twig behind me. I said, "Just in time. The fire's almost out."

"I hope you're going to put some more logs on it, then."

The voice behind me wasn't Boone's. It was smooth and even, with the faintest trace of an unidentifiable accent.

I didn't turn around. Closed my eyes for a beat and said, "Why are you here?"

"I wanted to see you."

My heart tumbled over itself, but I didn't say anything. Instead, I pulled my hands out from under me and laid them on my thighs. I heard the whisper of dried pine needles as she walked closer. She was right behind me, but still I didn't turn to face her.

"I can understand the unwelcome welcome, but you could at least look at me." She walked around my left side and sat on the rock in front of the fire. Her hair had fallen out of its ponytail so that it hung down, framing her face like a halo in the firelight. She was wearing the cashmere gloves that she'd had on in Circle Share two days before, but I could see that her hands were shaking with cold. "Lida. We need to talk."

"Really?" I asked. "It feels a bit late for that." Sarcasm coated my tongue like syrup. I hoped I could keep it up despite my traitorous heart.

"Lida —" Her hands were still shaking, and I wondered if she really was cold, or if it was something else — anger, maybe, or fear. "I want to explain why I did what I did."

"You've got nothing to explain," I said. "It was crystal clear a couple of days ago." My scalp shivered, and I glanced behind me. Nothing. But I knew I had to get Gia out of there before Boone came back.

"I thought we could discuss it. Maybe talk it over? I've had some time to think about it. I'm not mad anymore," she added, as though that meant anything.

"*Talking it over* would have been helpful before Circle Share. It feels a little late now." I stared into the fire. I wasn't going to make eye contact with her. I knew that if I did, I might bend.

"Oh, just listen to me, will you?" Gia's voice began to rise, sounding younger, less sure. "I was really upset. I'd just come down from visiting Ben, and he told me — Well, you can guess what he said. Lida, I really liked him. And he just —" She turned to me, staring at the side of my face until I was forced to look at her. When I did, I could see that her eyes were bright with tears. "He wasn't like the other guys I've been with. He was . . . interested in me."

"He was interested in who he thought you were, you mean." I was pulling from a place behind my lungs, where anger had been simmering all along.

She was quiet, but her expression moved from sadness to anger to sadness to shame. "Maybe," she finally said, "but I didn't think of it that way."

"So you thought you'd punish me, right? An eye for an eye?" I wanted to scream that I had a pretty good idea of how it felt to like someone, to have them think I was interesting and wonderful, and to lose them in an instant. Why couldn't she see that?

"Kind of." She glanced down.

"Well, maybe this will help. I didn't tell him anything. I didn't tell Boone, and I didn't tell Ben."

"What do you mean?" She looked up sharply.

"*Boone* saw you coming down the trail. *She* put two and two together. *She* told Ben, not me."

The fire crackled and sparked. I heard Gia's breath shudder uncertainly as she tried to control it. Finally, she said, "I didn't know that." Her voice sounded so small that I had to glance at her. Her face held the regret of a child who, in anger, has destroyed some little gift or trinket. Her jaw trembled.

"No," I said, "you didn't." I was saying all the right words. I was doing just fine. I remembered, suddenly, the way I'd felt when I'd called Jules out in the cabin. Powerful. And ashamed. Expansive. And small. Good, for one whispered moment, and bad, for all the long hours after. And I realized that Gia had probably been feeling this way for the past couple of days. A wave of sympathy coursed through my body. I looked away.

She didn't say anything for a while. Eventually, I glanced over again. I saw the streak of tears as she sat quietly, crying without making any sound at all.

Gia raised her eyes to mine. "Oh, Lida. I wouldn't have done it if I'd known. In all honesty — I've never . . . had a friendship like yours."

I'd heard Gia lie. Over the past couple of days I'd thought about it, and I'd realized that she'd probably lied to me plenty of times. But she wasn't lying now. I believed — I still believe — that she was serious. My heart, that disloyal sidekick, flipped again. I'm sure Gia could see the hope that dashed across my face like a thief.

She shook her head. "Who am I kidding? You're probably the only real friend I've ever had. And that made it worse when I thought that you'd —" Deep breath. "I thought you'd given me up. That you'd given up on me. It was the worst feeling in the world. There's no word to describe it." She laid one of her cashmere gloves on my knee.

I couldn't stop two fat tears from rolling down my own cheeks. I wanted to tell her that I knew how that felt. I knew exactly how that felt. But I didn't get a chance.

"I believe the proper word for it is *bullshit*."

Boone was standing next to the tent, her arms filled with pinecones and tiny sticks. I didn't know how long she'd been there. She walked over and dropped the wood unceremoniously next to what remained of my earlier forage. Then she turned to Gia. "Welcome to our humble home. Now get out." She crossed her arms and stood across the fire from us. She stared hard at me.

Gia didn't even blink at Boone's sudden appearance. "No, thank you. I came to see Lida." She turned to me. She lifted her hand and wiped away a tear with her index finger. "I really am sorry," she said. "You have to believe me."

"I've asked you once, politely. I'll ask you again. Leave." Boone stepped closer to the fire, pulling off her gloves and holding her hands out in front of her like she had nothing better to do. She never took her eyes off me.

"I'm not going anywhere," Gia said to me. "Lida," she continued, pretending as though Boone wasn't even there, "I should have given you more credit."

"Credit for what?" Boone asked.

"This is a private conversation."

Both girls were addressing their comments only to me.

"Lida."

"Lida."

They were waiting for me to say something. But what?

"I'm sorry," I said to the coals.

"No need," said Gia, just as Boone asked, "What for?" Then there was silence.

And here's what I wanted to say, what I was screaming in my head: *For pretending that I'm not responsible for any of this. For lying to each of you, and to myself. For wanting you to look at me the way you looked at Ben, Gia. Most of all, for being unable to control my chaotic, heedless heart.*

Here's what I said instead:

The fire was hissing, just coals and the occasional intrepid flame. Boone bent down and reached for some sticks. I wasn't looking at either of their faces, but I watched Boone's arm as it floated over the fire, placing a log on top of the small pile of branches. Her arm retreated and then reappeared moments later with another log in hand. The flames caught quickly. A thick wall of heat stretched out toward us all, and — I know this sounds crazy — I felt safe. No one had said anything for at least a minute. I don't know what I thought was going to happen, but I do remember this: I thought the worst was over.

That is, until Gia said to me, "I should never have doubted your loyalty."

Boone's hand reappeared over the fire with a stick.

"I should have talked to you, instead of assuming you'd betrayed me."

The hand shook, dropping the stick. It hovered there too close to the flames.

I looked up, and turned my face toward Gia's. I shook my head, hoping that she could read the message in my eyes. But she couldn't — or wouldn't — understand what I was asking of her.

Boone's hand withdrew from the fire. I heard the whisper of her feet as she walked around the pit to my other side. She squatted down on her heels next to me, saying nothing.

I stared at the fire until my eyes burned and tears sprang from their corners. Then I took a deep breath. "I —" But I couldn't finish. I didn't know how to explain.

Boone's voice was low and soft, as though she was coaxing a feral dog with a piece of meat. "What did you do, Lida?"

Gia shifted so that she could peer around me at Boone. "What do you mean?" I could almost hear the snap of each puzzle piece as they fit together in her mind. "Or maybe you don't know. Is that it?" I felt her gaze settle on the side of my face. "How did you think I met Ben in the first place?"

I heard the sharp intake of breath from my other side.

"I thought you were dumb, *Elsa*, but I didn't think you were oblivious." Gia wasn't talking to me anymore. Everything she said was meant for Boone now. Each bladed word.

Boone raised herself to her feet. "Go," she said again, though her voice was raspy and thin. "Leave." She sounded far away, as though the words came from someplace remote, inaccessible by car or conversation. It scared me.

"No," said Gia.

Snow began falling, gauzy in the firelight. Tears mixed with the flakes as they hit my face. I had to make them understand. I had to make them see that this was all my fault, that it was *my* fear, *my* weakness, *my* desire that had gotten us all to this point. "I —"

Gia's hand was on my arm, squeezing. "Lida, listen. I *didn't* know," she was saying. "I'm sorry I blamed you — you can't know how sorry." Her voice broke. Then she added, "Lida, I need you."

I yanked my arm free with a sharp twist. "No!" I was out of breath, shaking, tears and snot running down my face and into the collar of my jacket. I stood quickly, backing away from the fire. Even then, at the moment when I most wanted to be free of her spell — even then, I could still feel the imprint of her hand on my arm like a yoke, pulling me toward her. But I kept backing away. I could feel the snow tingling my bare hand as each flake landed and dissolved.

Boone watched me. Her face held a mixture of regret and understanding, but not anger. She didn't move as I kept stepping backward until I stood equidistant from both of them, the three of us making a perfect triangle. Then she spoke in a voice so calm and certain that she could have been a school counselor.

"I should have known," Boone said to me. "I mean, I had a feeling you might have . . . I guess I just hoped . . ." She raised her hand and pointed her finger at me. It was shaking slightly. "Don't think you're off the hook," she said quietly. "You'll have to . . ." She broke off suddenly, let her hand fall to her side, and drew a deep breath. Then she directed her words at Gia, never losing the lucidity of her tone. "But you. I've known people like you before. You all think you're unique, but you're not. There are too many of you, and you play the same games. And you're charming; I'll grant you that."

Boone took a step toward Gia, who stood up.

"But charm isn't enough. Everything you do is a facade, a performance. And it won't be enough to get you through life unscathed." She took another step. "It can only mask who you really are for so long. And what you are, what you really are," she took another step, "is rotten. If I cut you open right now" — she was only a few feet from Gia, so close that she could have reached out and grabbed her by the neck — "I'd find a gaping, festering, black hole where your heart should be." Boone drew her shoulders back. "Wouldn't I?"

Gia lunged. While I was clothed in shadow, the two of them were backlit by the fire, and I could see Gia's face as clearly as if it was a photograph: Her eyes were wild and dark, and her mouth had turned into a wavering line so that she looked like she was about to either laugh or scream. She grabbed Boone's shoulder, digging her nails in, and swung at her with the other fist. The impact was dampened by the fact that Boone's hand had come up suddenly and wrapped itself around Gia's face, holding her chin as though in study. Then Boone shoved her back, and Gia stumbled, taking three steps before regaining purchase. "Hate you!" Gia was shouting. "I have always hated you!"

But Boone said nothing. She just advanced. The palm of her hand snapped across Gia's face once, twice. And with a primal scream, Gia dove forward and wrapped Boone in a vicious hug. She was pinning Boone's arms, pushing her closer and closer to the fire. Boone stepped back, her foot landing so close to the flames that I was sure she could feel the burn before it started. She lifted the leg and swung it around, catching Gia's knee and sending them both tumbling forward to the ground, their heads only inches from the fire. They started hitting each other then, fists flailing wildly so that I couldn't tell their limbs apart.

"Lida!"

That was when I felt my own feet moving beneath me. I had been watching it all from my place in the shadows, everything unfolding in front of me in slow motion, the fists moving through the air as though pushing through taffy, but when I heard my name, it all sped up. I ran toward them both, my arms waving stupidly like an air traffic controller's. I don't know if I was making any sound; the only noise I heard was a rush, like wind gusting through trees, that seemed to emanate from my own ears. The snow had quickly picked up momentum, and I had to push my hair back from my face so that I could see past its frozen white veil.

That's when I saw the book.

It was lying near the fire, so close to Boone's and Gia's feet that either of them could have easily grabbed it. But they hadn't seen it. They were too focused on choking, punching, pulling at each other's hair. I still couldn't hear them, though I'm sure now that they must have been making noise, something animalistic and primitive.

I ran to the book, opening it and relieving it of its cargo. Then I turned to Boone and Gia. I stood over them, holding the one thing that had ever given me strength and control. I felt its smooth contours in the palm of my hand, remembered what it was like to draw it slowly across the skin, leaving a faint crimson line. I looked at the tangle of muscle and bone that writhed on the ground below me. And I glanced up, once, to see the snowflakes as they made their way toward the earth, fat and heavy with purpose. Then I knelt to the ground.

In the morning, snow would blanket everything, covering all evidence of the night before, revealing nothing until the thaw of spring. And the permissive woods would keep their secrets, veiled in a white so clean it looked like forgiveness. But in that moment, I wasn't thinking of absolution. I looked at the two reaching, grasping hands: one rough, one smooth. One finger with the smallest lint of cashmere in the nail bed, one finger callused and raw. I looked at them both, and then I placed the knife in her outstretched hand.

Epilogue

I've come too far to turn back now.
Fact. Later, I wanted to die.
Fact. Much later, I wanted to live.
Fact. For over a year, I wanted to forget.
Fact. I knew exactly what I was doing when I handed her the knife.

$\mathscr{C}$HAPTER $\mathscr{T}$WENTY-ONE

AFTERWARD, NO ONE COULD FIGURE OUT HOW WE ALL ENDED up at the same campsite. Bev wanted to know because the parents wanted to know. The parents wanted to know because the cops wanted to know. I imagined a team of Alice Marshall trustees who looked at the situation, saw a lawsuit, and wanted answers. How did three girls who clearly had issues with one another end up on the same patch of ground on a moonless, snowy night, miles from the nearest authority, a weapon in their possession? Who let this happen? They looked at Bev, who looked at Margaret, who looked at me.

"What happened?" she asked, and I told her, there in the cold green plastic bucket seats in the Hawkins Memorial Hospital emergency waiting room in Boise. When I was done, she looked at me and asked again, "But what happened?" And I started all over again.

I had already told Bev everything, after they came for us in the waning dark and hauled us off the mountain in the snow. Katia heard my whistle first, and she'd apparently radioed

Margaret immediately, even as she was running down the trail toward the sound. I don't know how Margaret and the others got there so quickly with the makeshift stretchers, but they did — when they arrived, I was still holding the whistle in my hand, staring at the pocket in the backpack where it had been all along. Katia had done what she could with the small first-aid kit that we'd each packed, but I don't remember anyone saying anything. I don't remember any words at all until I heard Margaret's voice. There hadn't been time to drive to the hospital, so we'd flown in from the airstrip at Runson Bar, the tiny plane skidding once before takeoff and then rising above the white peaks and turning toward Boise. Margaret had been grilling me since we landed, and I hadn't changed my story yet. What did it matter? It was all settled now, anyway.

"I just don't remember much," I said for the twentieth time. "I mean, it must have been the firelight. It was in my eyes."

"You really didn't see anything. You didn't see who had the knife, or where it came from."

"No. After she hit her the first time, I couldn't see anything else."

I stared at the sliding glass doors, beyond which lay the nurses' station. Doctors were crowded around it, passing a pink file back and forth. Most of them were frowning, though one doctor said something and opened his mouth for what must have been a self-satisfied laugh. Even from that distance, I could see his teeth glinting in shiny white rows.

Margaret placed her palm lightly over my hand, which had been tapping a disjointed rhythm against my jeans. "Lida," she said quietly. "Stop. You don't have to do this anymore."

I stood quickly. It was suddenly too hot, and I needed air. So I started walking around the waiting room, refusing to glance back at Margaret, whom I couldn't look at. No, that's not true: I couldn't bear to have her look at me. I looked around the room, instead. One woman cradled a baby in her arms, singing softly. An old man slouched in his bucket seat, sleeping, his mouth opened wide like a bass. Some kids crouched on the ground with a set of dominoes, constructing a long row of black-and-white tokens before knocking one over and sending the whole line toppling.

I stopped by a corner table and picked up an old copy of *Highlights*, flipping through it restlessly. There were the familiar exercises — rhyming games and hide-and-seek picture puzzles. How easy it had been, I remembered, to pick out the incongruous elements: the basketball in the kitchen, the sailboat in the jungle, the tiger in the apple tree. The picture blurred suddenly, and I put the magazine down, wiping my eyes with the back of my hand.

What could I have possibly told Margaret that would have made any sense? What was the truth in all of this? Somehow, I didn't think she would understand if I told her that a fire, once lit, will consume everything. It will turn abruptly if you try to contain it, and will dissolve even the water you throw at it. And that's not all, I wanted to say. The smoke is as dangerous as the flame.

I walked back and sat down again.

Margaret didn't say a word.

We sat there for what seemed like hours. We were both waiting, though for different reasons. Margaret was waiting for a doctor to walk past the nurses' station, step through the glass doors that divided the healthy from the hurt, and stand in front of us with a verdict. She kept going outside to call Bev on her cell phone — I guess just to let her know that there hadn't been any updates so far. I got up once to get another magazine and saw her outside, sitting on the curb where the ambulances parked, smoking a cigarette that she must have bummed from some paramedic or lab technician. I stepped away from the exit doors before she had a chance to see me.

I was waiting for my dad and Terri.

Of course I was going home. Right back to where I started. We all were. Dad and Terri had been on the road, I imagined, since about five minutes after they got Bev's phone call, which meant they would be arriving within the hour. But no other parents had shown up, and I was beginning to wonder if anyone would.

Finally, I asked Margaret about it. She'd come back from a phone call with Bev, and had been reading a magazine from cover to cover. She was on the last page. I watched as she finished reading, closed the magazine, and then opened it absentmindedly to the first page again.

"Um," I said.

She looked up.

"Are the other parents coming too? I mean —" My voice trailed off.

Margaret sighed and placed her index finger halfway down the page to mark her spot. "They've been called. Boone's guardian . . ." She paused as though trying to decide how much she could tell me. "Well, someone'll turn up at some point, I expect. And Gia's father couldn't get out of a meeting in Des Moines, so he'll be here tomorrow." She looked back at the magazine.

"Des Moines? What does he do?"

"Something with taxes," she said, and glanced at me. "IRS. I'm surprised you didn't know that."

I mumbled something noncommittal and studied my fingernails. There was still dirt and grime embedded under each one from the day before. Taxes. *My father works for the government.* Of course. I let it sink in. Then I asked the question that had been worrying me the most. "If they — I mean, if the doctors can —" I swallowed the fear that was making my mouth dry, and tried again. "What's going to happen to them?" What I meant, of course, was *What's going to happen to us?* But I couldn't ask that.

"I don't know." Margaret looked away. "Lida, we don't know anything yet. The doctors weren't sure if . . ." Her voice trailed off, and she blinked. "Boone's brother was her guardian, and he's in jail. If she . . . She'll probably become a ward of the state, at least for another year. Then . . ." She cleared her throat. "Alice Marshall was the best place for her. Bev and I were devastated when we learned that her scholarship had been discontinued."

"Bev?"

She nodded. "I know she's prickly. But she cares more about you all than you'll ever know." She stared absently at an old woman in a seat nearby who was tapping her cane rhythmically against her chair leg.

"And Gia?" One of my hands was shaking. I covered it with my other hand, hoping she hadn't noticed.

Margaret took a deep breath. "I don't know if Gia . . ." She exhaled loudly. "She'll probably go back to the Juvenile Detention Center in Des Moines."

I started. *"Back?"*

Before Margaret could respond, the sliding doors hissed open, and a doctor with a stack of manila envelopes in her arms stepped through. Her eyes roved over the motley assortment of waiting room inmates until they rested on Margaret. She walked over.

"Margaret Olsen?"

"Yes." Margaret stood so quickly that the magazine slithered off her lap and onto the ground.

"Let's speak privately," the doctor said, gesturing with a free hand toward an unoccupied corner of the room.

They walked away together. I bent down and retrieved the magazine. There was an elderly couple on the cover, beaming as they held a squirming toddler between them. "The New Wave of Nontraditional Households," the text read in bold lettering. I set the magazine facedown on Margaret's seat.

When Margaret returned, the doctor at her side, she was pale. She wouldn't make eye contact when she said, "Boone's awake. She'd . . . like to talk to you."

"What about Gia?" I asked.

"She's still under sedation," the doctor explained, her tone perfunctory, "and she previously expressed a desire for solitude when she wakes up." She looked over at Margaret. "She will be speaking with you and the police, of course. Her wishes only extend so far."

"Is she okay?" I couldn't keep the pitch of my voice from rising.

"Her arm is broken," said Margaret, "and they'll have to reset her nose. But yes, she'll be fine."

I let the air out of my lungs and nodded.

"Lida. Boone's not . . ." Margaret's voice broke suddenly, and she took a couple of deep breaths before continuing. "Go see her."

I followed the doctor through the doors and into a world completely at odds with the one I had just left. Gone were the anxious faces, the smell of people who have been sitting in one place for too long. This part of the hospital smelled like antiseptic and citrus. The halls were bright and noisy, with doctors and nurses speaking to one another in a clipped, abbreviated sort of language. The floor was made of white tile that squeaked underneath my hiking boots.

I followed the doctor down first one hall and then another. The hospital was much bigger than it appeared from the outside. I would never be able to find my way back alone. Finally, she stopped in front of a room and placed one of the manila folders in a file holder that hung on the door.

"I'll give you about ten minutes and then send a nurse in to escort you back to Ms. Olsen." She twisted the knob on the door and pushed it open a crack. Then she turned to me. "Don't overdo it in there," she said. "Your friend can't handle much right now." She walked away.

I looked at my feet as I entered the room. Watched as first one foot and then the other squeaked across the tile, passing the wheeled base of a rolling table, inching past the foot of the hospital bed, making their way toward the head. Only when my feet had nowhere farther to go without crashing into what appeared to be a makeshift nightstand did I look up.

Boone lay propped up on four or five white pillows. A thin sheet lay over her waist, and she was wearing a threadbare hospital gown adorned with hundreds of pastel stars. Her arms were bruised, claw marks cascading from elbow to wrist. Her lip was cracked, and a yellow-and-green flower blossomed above it. A black patch covered her right eye, attached to an elastic band that circled her head. From beneath the patch, I could see a thick red line that stretched toward the middle of her cheek, black stitches forming a crosshatch all the way down.

"Well," she said. "What should we call this scene? How about: 'The Troops Come Back from Battle.'" She coughed weakly and cleared her throat. "You should probably come over to my other side. Otherwise, I'll get dizzy from the effort of trying to figure you out."

I walked around the foot of the bed and stood on her left.

"Quiet today, aren't you?" She studied me with one eye. "You might want to say something about now."

"Is that —" I couldn't finish. My hands gripped the metal bar on the side of her bed until my knuckles turned the color of the bone beneath.

"It's as permanent as sin," she said, and then laughed abruptly. "The eye's gone. I'll be able to work around it, sure, but it's never coming back." She nodded. "There's an upside, though."

"What?" I whispered.

"I'll only be able to see half of what's waiting for me in Minster. And that's worth something, wouldn't you say?"

I shook my head.

"Come on, Lida. Let's cut the crap. You can play the penitent later. Just tell me why you did it." Boone spoke without malice; it was as if she had been preparing for her injury all her life, waiting for the inevitable. She seemed calm, unhurried. "What was going through your head?"

"I don't know."

"Bad answer."

"I don't know!" And the truth was, I didn't know — not really. Whatever it was that had compelled me to hand over the knife in that moment had disappeared as soon as I'd done it, like a figure retreating into shadow. Now I just felt empty.

"Look. You'll be going over this in your head for the rest of your life. The rest of your life. You might as well start to make sense of it now, before you forget what really happened, or you begin to change the facts so you can live with yourself. Here: I'll help. You picked up the knife and . . ." She waited, crossing her arms over her chest and staring at me.

I started to cry. What do you say when there is no explanation for what you've done? "It was the firelight," I said, as I had to Margaret, the tears washing down my face. "I couldn't see."

"Bullshit."

"I didn't —" I started to say again, and then gave up. I couldn't fool myself any longer. Until that moment, I'd been able to pretend it was a dream, some sort of nightmare that I'd erase in the daylight. But looking at Boone's face, I got it. I finally got it. I'd created this nightmare, and now I had to live in it. My legs shook under me. "Oh my God, I'm so sorry," I said.

"Your apology is all I need. Thank you. No, really, thank you. That and a nickel will make up for all of this." She swept her arm up, cringing as she did so, and pointed to the patch over her eye.

"Save your fucking apology. How about saying this, instead: 'Gee, Boone, I meant to give you the knife. Really, I did. I just got confused and gave it to Gia, instead. Whoopsie-daisy. My bad.'" Her eye narrowed, but not before a tear slipped out, inching its way down her face. "You chose her. After everything she did to you."

I couldn't catch my breath. Every inhalation felt like a mountain ascent.

"Lida! Tell. Me. Why." She raised a fist in front of her face and held it there. The knuckles were white, the veins popping out like raised riverbeds.

I tried to wipe the tears away with the heel of my hand. "You were always so much stronger." My voice trembled with the truth.

"Double bullshit! I don't need your excuses."

"Boone, I'm trying to tell you. I thought I'd gotten over her. I hoped I had. Hoped I was all better. Fierce, like you."

"But."

"But something —" I stopped. Took a breath. Tried again. "Something wouldn't let go. Not when I needed it to." There was no stopping the tears now — they swam down my face, stinging. A sour wave of despair rose up through my stomach and into my throat and I bent over, heaving drily. When I straightened, I was breathing shallowly. "I love her." I closed my eyes and shook my head. "I loved her."

And that was it, exactly.

I listened to the hospital bed squeak and settle under Boone's shifting weight. I thought I could hear it creaking with every labored breath she took.

Finally, she said, "You were just her reflection. That's all you were to her." She leaned forward. "And no one can love a reflection. Not really."

A nurse knocked on Boone's door and stuck her head in.

She had a crown of dyed copper curls that rested on her head like a bowl. "I hate to break this up," she said perfunctorily, "but it's time Elsa rested." She had a stack of papers in one hand, and she pulled one out and placed it in the manila folder on Boone's door.

Boone rearranged a pillow behind her back. She looked at me for a long time. When she spoke again, her voice was tired. "You never thought anyone understood you, Townie. But I did, all along. Too bad you didn't realize that sooner." She closed her eye. "Good luck living with this," she said. "You'll need it."

I walked mechanically to the door. Just as the nurse was about to close it behind us, Boone called out. "Hey."

The nurse opened it a bit wider.

"You know, Townie, it occurs to me that maybe I should be thanking you." She was choosing her words carefully, each one a tight bullet of sarcasm.

The nurse looked at me. I looked at Boone in confusion.

"I guess you did me a good turn, in a way." Her laugh was hollow. "If you'd given me the knife, I would have killed her."

The nurse raised her eyebrows, but she shut the door softly and started to lead me back to the waiting room. Right before we reached the sliding glass doors, I stopped.

"Can I go to the bathroom?" I asked, pointing to the unisex restroom on my right.

The nurse glanced from me to the bathroom. I could see her trying to decide if it was a good idea to let me go.

I pointed at the glass doors, through which I could see Margaret in her chair. "I think I can find my way out," I said. "Really."

She nodded once. "When you're done, go back to the waiting room. You're not allowed to be in this area unattended." She shuffled the papers in her hands.

"I promise," I said. My fingers were already turning the bathroom knob.

I shut the door behind me and waited until I heard the nurse walking away before turning the lock and sliding down onto the tile with my back against the wall. I placed my head between my knees, willing the nausea to go away. I sat like that for a long time, wanting so badly not to think, not to remember Boone's face, the set of her jaw, the sound of her voice, but knowing that it was useless. I'd never forget.

Finally, I stood and walked to the sink. I splashed water on my cheeks, trying not to glance up. I didn't want to see the face looking back at me. But I had no choice. As I straightened and turned toward the paper dispenser, I caught a glimpse of my cheek, my hair. I stared at myself in the mirror and wished there was someone else there instead.

Was that what Gia wished for as well? The question came out of nowhere, as clear as if I was reading it on a billboard. I could hear Boone: *You were just her reflection. And no one can love a reflection. Not really.* Gia didn't love me; she loved how I loved her. I'd been so eager for her friendship — for whatever she could give me — that I hadn't stopped to wonder why she'd picked me. Why she needed me.

I'd never know what Gia really saw when she looked in a mirror. No one would, I expected. But just as Ben's Gia was a perfect, sexy woman, mine was fearless, stunning, brilliant, and thrilling. Gia needed me to be her mirror, to reflect that version of herself back to her, the version that I loved.

I knew I'd take that Gia with me, whether I wanted to or not. And I know this is crazy, but it felt like I was stealing something precious. Because I knew that my Gia, *that* Gia, would live on only in my memories, nowhere else. And the real Gia wouldn't be able to get her back, to be that person ever again.

And what about Boone? What would she see in the mirror? I asked myself the question, but I knew the answer already. She saw what I saw — what everyone saw. Boone was herself. Irredeemably, unabashedly, ferociously herself. She lived in her skin the way we all wanted to live: without excuses. And I hadn't seen that. Or, if I had, I hadn't cared. I'd wanted what Gia offered instead. I'd wanted to be chosen over and over, no matter what, no matter why. No matter who.

That's when it happened. I grabbed onto the smooth lip of the sink and sobbed. My knuckles were white against the porcelain, veins protruding as my hands shook with every gasping breath. From some deep, black cavern inside of me came a sound that I'd never heard before and haven't heard since, a sound that contained the sudden, piercing knowledge of what I'd done to Boone, what I'd done to her life. And worse: that I could never, ever take it back. It was there in that bathroom in the Steele Memorial Hospital, faced with what I'd done, that I felt my heart truly break for the third time in my life. And this time, I knew *I* had broken it.

Margaret stood when I came through the sliding glass doors. She had a concerned expression on her face that turned to a deep sadness when I came closer and she could see the splotches and tearstains on my cheeks. She enveloped me in a hug that surprised me with its warmth. Pressed up against her shoulder, my face buried in the flannel of her shirt, I cried again. I thought, perhaps, that I might never stop. She held me there, and she didn't say anything. Finally, I pulled away and wiped my face messily on my sleeve. We sat down again. I took a deep breath. I thought I would speak loudly, forcefully, but my voice came out in a whisper.

"It was my fault."

Margaret was very still. "I know you feel that way."

"I handed Gia the knife."

She was quiet, and then she said, "I know."

"How could I do that?" I was speaking more to myself than to Margaret. "After everything . . . What's wrong with me?" I stared emptily at the nurses' station.

Margaret answered slowly, as though weighing each word against another before she spoke. "Lida, listen to me. Alice Marshall isn't a place where people 'get cured.' What ailed you when you came to the school wasn't an illness; it was a sadness that was rooted so deep that you didn't know how to address it." She paused, started again. "I'm not excusing your part in this. You'll have to answer for your role in what happened last night. If Boone decides to press charges, you'll have to deal with the police." Margaret's eyes plainly said, *And maybe she should.*

But then her expression softened and she added, "But I want you to hear me. I think a greater tragedy would be for you to forget how far you've come."

I almost laughed, the idea was so ridiculous. *Greater tragedy?* Hadn't she seen Boone?

She must have seen the look on my face, because she smiled sadly. "Your life will be shaped by this, Lida. Absolutely. But you'll have to decide *how* it's shaped. One of those ways is by not forgetting the good things that happened at the school. And Lida —" She grabbed my hand. "Good things *did* happen." She let go and leaned back in her chair, studying me. "None of us are superheroes," she said. "These sadnesses that we have never fully go away. And sometimes they rear up, and if we're not careful, if we don't find ways to remind ourselves of what we know — who we know we can be — they make us forget what we've learned, and take us back to the dark place where we started. The place where every decision is a wrong one." She nodded at me. "We can end up repeating these patterns of unhappiness and hurt forever."

"But Boone —"

"What happened to Boone *is* a tragedy," Margaret interrupted. "But it would be a tragedy as well for you to go back to that dark place again and again. You will have to work hard — very hard — not to let that happen." She looked at me steadily, and then said, "Boone lost something. But, terrible as it is, it's something she can live without. She didn't lose herself."

I wanted to tell her that she was full of shit, that nothing I could ever do or not do would make up for what had happened. But I could hear just the faintest peal of truth threading throughout each word. "What if I'm not strong enough?" My voice quavered.

Margaret shook her head. "You are, Lida." She paused. "But strength doesn't have to define you," she said. "It can be a decision. It can just be what you choose to do, day after day."

The word *choose* bobbed between us, and I thought again of the girl in the boating accident, the one who was left in the lake after her friends were both gone. I thought about how she held on to the cooler in the freezing water, floating, as she let the water carry her far from the wreckage. How she waited for death to take her. I knew what Margaret was saying. That girl didn't have to float. At any point, she could have let go and start swimming, could have reached out one arm and then another, pulling herself through the water. She still might not have made it, might only have gotten a few yards before her muscles seized and she dropped soundlessly through the depths, but she could have tried.

"Your parents are here," Margaret said, nodding to the emergency room entrance. I could see my dad and Terri walking swiftly across the ambulance parking lane toward the doors. "Why don't I go out and talk to them first?" She stood. "Then you can tell them the rest."

"The truth?" I whispered.

"The truth." Margaret headed toward the doors, which slid open. I watched as she stopped my dad and Terri outside, making comforting gestures with her hands as she began talking.

A man walked through the entrance, carrying two babies, one in the crook of each arm. Before the doors hissed shut behind him, I could hear my dad's voice. ". . . worried, so worried," he was saying. Beside him, Terri was crying.

I stood very still for a moment, watching them through the glass. They hadn't seen me yet, and I paused, waiting, my breath tight in my throat. I let the sounds of the hospital wash over me: lives beginning and ending, accidents and intentions, a wrong step, a swift response, a tragedy realized or avoided. If you're lucky, a second chance.

I walked toward the doors and stepped outside.

Epilogue

I couldn't tell you who called out to me first, when I was watching Gia and Boone fight by the fire. I'll never know the answer to that question. I only know how still it was in that moment when I put the knife in her hand, how the forest pulsed once around us and was silent, and that I knew even then that this was what I would remember: that stalled drumbeat, that pierced skin.

And Boone was right. If I weren't careful, I would start to believe myself as I changed the story over time, piece by piece. I would do it so slowly that, by the time I had to tell myself the story again, the way that we do when our lives contain essential memories that are nonetheless unaccountable, I wouldn't even know what was or was not true. And I might remember that it was Boone with the knife in her hand, Boone raising it high above her head, not Gia with her arm slicing the firelight like a scythe, not Gia with a look in her eye like she was counting the strokes. One. Two. Three.

"You own it," she said, "and then you leave it behind."
This is mine.
It's the truth.
Take it.

336

Prologue

The Hindman Diner looks exactly the same. What did I expect? That the rickety wooden tables would be replaced by glass and steel? That they'd have any new songs on the jukebox? Nope. Same old Hank Williams. Same old Patsy Cline. And is it a freak coincidence that my dad, Terri, and I are seated at the same table where we argued and I threw a glass on the floor over two years ago?

Feels like decades.

We've been here twenty minutes. Three burgers sit in front of us, untouched. Three glasses of water, two of them drained. My dad watches the door like a nervous security guard, his hand resting on his butter knife in a way that I'm sure he doesn't even recognize as being threatening. I want to tell him that he doesn't have to protect me from anything, but it wouldn't matter. He's afraid that she'll come at me, spit on me, scratch my face with unforgiving claws. Terri is looking at me. Every once in a while she reaches across the table and rests her hand on one of mine. I jerk away the first couple of times, but I eventually let her do it; it gives her comfort, I can tell.

As for me, I'm staring at the antler chandelier, which appears to have lost a bulb in one of its lights since the last time we were here. I'm pretty sure that if I tried I could memorize every grain on each of the twenty or so antlers that make up the fixture. So I try. I stare so long and so hard at the chandelier that when the door opens, I register the noise only faintly, realizing who it is by the way that Terri grips my hand with sudden pressure and then lets go.

I swing my head around, slowly, and there they are, standing just inside the door. Margaret looks the same. Her hair's a little longer, I guess, sprouting up out of her head in a slightly less manageable way. She's smiling bravely, like a general who's about to command an army to swim through a crocodile-infested swamp because there's just no other way to get across. She does a quick sweep of the room, sees us, and turns the smile onto me.

"Lida," she says, "I'm so glad to see you." Margaret steps forward and I stand up, and she envelops me in a hug. "Thank you for coming," she whispers into my shoulder. Then she lets go and steps back, nods at my dad and Terri, and turns to me. "Well, ladies," she says, "here we are."

I know I can't put it off any longer. I have to look at the person who has followed Margaret over to our table and now stands just behind her and to the right. And when I do, she's looking at me, and she looks exactly as I've been picturing her all this time: same long hair, same chiseled jaw, same look just as sharp and as piercing as it was the last time we spoke.

"Hi," I whisper, and she nods.

"Hey," says Boone. She's still wearing the patch over her right eye, and she looks a little like a pirate, though not as much as you would think. She sticks her hands in the pockets of her jeans and steps from one foot to the other, as though she's standing in a cold doorway.

"Sorry we're late," says Margaret, addressing my dad and Terri. "Bee got a flat on our way up from Boise."

"Boise?" asks my dad.

Margaret jerks her thumb back at Boone. "That's where I picked up this one," she says. "She's a big-city girl now." I wonder for the first time whether Margaret might be nervous, maybe even scared. After all, she set this whole thing in motion; if everything combusts, it's on her.

"Well," says my dad, "that's quite a drive." And suddenly he and Margaret are off on some long-winded discussion of road conditions and weather forecasts, with Terri chiming in every once in a while with "Oh, for sure," or "You wouldn't even believe it."

I look at Boone, wondering if this is all it's going to be: she and I standing quietly like centerpieces as the adults talk over and around us. Then she shakes her head just as my dad says, "And the rain this spring! Torrential!" And I widen my eyes, and her mouth twists, just for a second. I quickly look down at my hands.

It's a funny thing. I haven't smoked in over a year now, but I suddenly want a cigarette more than anything. And I'm guessing Boone does too. I glance at her. She reads my expression and jerks her head toward the door.

"Hey," I say casually, interrupting my dad's recitation of annual rainfall statistics, "we're going to walk down the street, take in the sights." It comes out more like a question, and I watch Margaret's face dissolve into the bland expression that she wears so well around parents who are just about to get duped for the three thousandth time.

My dad laughs. "Good idea!" he booms. "Let us know what you find!"

I reach down and grab my backpack, swinging it over one shoulder. Outside, it's warm. No, not warm. Hot. Uselessly hot. Especially for early September. My armpits start sweating almost as soon as the door shuts behind us. I pull at my T-shirt, holding it away from me as though that'll help.

"Jesus," says Boone.

"Hot."

"Yeah."

We start walking in the direction of the pawnshop. Boone pulls a pack of cigarettes out of her back pocket and holds it out to me. I take one, and she gets hers going first before handing me the lighter.

When I inhale, the smoke clogs my throat. I want to puke, but I don't know if it's because of the smoke or because of the nervousness that's been swirling around in my gut all week. I hold the cigarette down by my side as we walk, hoping that it'll burn itself out before Boone notices.

"So, how's shakes, Townie?" Boone takes a short drag and looks over her shoulder at the diner. I notice that she has to turn her head farther around to get a good look at it, and I wonder what else has changed, what she has to do differently in her daily life. I feel sick again.

"Good," I say, swallowing. I glance at her. "I mean, good. You know . . ." I let my voice trail off. How do I say what I need to say?

"Looks like one big happy family."

"Sometimes." Then, I risk it. "How're you?"

"Free," she says. "As of May twentieth, I'm my own agent. Government cut me loose."

"You mean — ?"

"I outgrew the interest of the state, the missionaries, even the juvenile corrections officers. It's official, I guess. We're adults." She kicks at the ground, sending a rock skittering ahead. "I'm starting school in a couple of weeks at Boise State. Seems like they've got a soft spot for Mill Casualties too."

"That's great."

"What about you? Off to college? Some East Coast breeding ground for I-bankers?" She puffs on her cigarette once more before dropping it on the ground and grinding it down. Then she bends and picks up the butt, slips it in the front pocket of her shirt. "Margaret's influence," she says when she catches me watching.

"Not the East Coast," I say, pausing to put my own cigarette out on the sole of my shoe. "Not any coast. I'm taking a year off." I drop the butt in my back pocket. "Actually, I'm going to spend a couple of months up at a fire lookout in the Sawtooth Mountains. It's kind of a volunteer internship." I watch the side of her face for a response, but I don't see one. If she thinks about the lookout on Buckhorn Peak or anything else, she's not letting me know.

"Sounds nice," she says instead. Her voice is flat, painfully civil.

If we were still at school, I'd let Boone take the lead, as I always did. That way, I wouldn't be responsible if the conversation turned a corner and disappeared. But we're not at school anymore, and I know I have to do this.

"Boone," I say, and my voice sounds different.

She turns to me.

I've been thinking about what I'll say all week, but suddenly, each of my well-practiced lines sounds childish in my head. *I'm sorry. Forgive me. You can't know how terrible I feel.* Worse than childish — they sound courteous.

It's not going to be perfect, I say to myself, and then I say this to Boone. "It's not going to be perfect."

"What's not?"

"What I need to say. I need to tell you how sorry I am —" My voice catches, but I continue. "But I don't need you to forgive me. I just need you to listen." I don't look away from her the whole time I'm talking, so I see her nod slightly. "I've had time to think about this — believe me. So I know there's nothing I can do to —" I run my hand through my hair. "I can't change anything that happened."

"Tell me something I don't know." Boone turns her gaze to the road.

"I'm trying," I say, breathing through my nose as I attempt to quell the anxiety that rises in my chest. "I'm trying to tell you what it's been like. I didn't want to believe it then, but I get it now. I know that Gia —" Boone shakes her head at the mention of Gia's name, but I keep going, afraid that, if I pause, I'll lose my nerve. "That she could only have ever hurt me. She wasn't like you."

"No shit."

She needs to hear this. "Boone. Your friendship was the most honest thing I'd ever had." I'm speaking more quickly now, and I remind myself to slow down. "And Gia . . . Sometimes it felt like, for all the good I found at Alice Marshall, there was still the bad, you know? Like, no matter how hard I tried, there was still this piece of me that wanted to hurt." I pause, swallowing. "To be hurt. You can't know how much I wish I'd been stronger for you. To at least have been able to see Gia for who she was."

We're standing in the middle of the road, the heat heavy on our shoulders. I reach up and dash my arm across my forehead, trying to wipe away the tears that are threatening to spill.

Boone turns on her heel and starts back toward the diner. I think she's ignoring me, and my breath jerks in my throat. But then she raises her hand over her shoulder. She curls her fingers together, calling me. I catch up with her, and we walk slowly, neither of us in a hurry to get back to my folks and Margaret. I'm waiting for her to say something. Anything. She does.

"Get over yourself," she says.

"What?"

"Get over yourself," she repeats. "I had to." She kicks at the ground. "I hated you for a long time," she says. "A long time."

"Oh." I feel it all collapsing, and I steel myself for what she'll say next.

"But it turned out that hating you was almost worse than learning to live with this." Boone points up to the right side of her face, and the pink fault line extending from either side of the patch. "I mean, it was toxic, spending all that time thinking about what I would say to you, what I would do . . ." Her voice trails off, and then she adds, "Like something poisonous was just festering inside of me. I had to deal with it." She gestures toward the diner. "Margaret helped."

"Margaret? How?"

"She visited me every few months. Said it was part of the job. What bullshit. But she came anyway. We did some heavy lifting, let me tell you." There's almost a smile. "I mean, God! The talking! Sometimes I wished it would stop, that she'd just go away." This time, she laughs, though it sounds a little forced. "And I will say this: I got to a place where I could understand where you were coming from, how you might have felt about Gia — no matter what she did, no matter how thoughtless she —"

Her voice catches and she looks away, starts again. "If Ben had apologized, called me back, asked me to . . . I would have done anything for him. I mean, it's so stupid." She's kicking up so much dust with the toe of her shoe that a small cloud has formed around our feet. "But, yeah," she says, "pretty much anything. I guess when I think about it that way, I can see how, in that moment . . . Sometimes the line between love and desperation is damn thin." Boone shakes her head. "You just have to hope you don't have a knife in your hand when you figure that out." She throws a smile my way that almost cuts me with its sadness. But there's understanding there too.

We've stopped walking, and are near enough to the diner that I can hear the clattering sounds of lunchtime. The sun is so bright that I can't see past the windows' glare to where my parents are probably still standing with Margaret. I wonder if they can see us.

Boone continues. "I guess what I'm trying to say is, after all that, after the months and months of ridiculous soul-searching, I at least got to a place where I no longer wanted to kill you."

"I'm so sorry," I say now. "I —"

Boone holds up her hand. "Don't want to kill you," she says. "Doesn't mean I forgive you."

I nod, blushing at the tear that makes its way down my cheek. I'd hoped, hoped, hoped. But, I remind myself, I didn't expect.

She reaches out a hand and grabs my shoulder, squeezing tightly, in anger or compassion, I can't tell which. "Margaret's got this thing, this mantra," Boone says. She makes her voice low and throaty, a good approximation. "*Forgiveness is a work-in-progress.* And you know Margaret. Full of shit half the time, karmic genius the other half."

"I'll take those odds," I say.

"I thought you might." This time, the smile is real.

"So did you and Margaret cook this up, then?" I wipe at my face with the hem of my T-shirt as I fight the briefest blaze of envy. Margaret never visited me. Maybe that was my punishment: to struggle with this alone. Maybe she knew that was the only way I'd work through it all, anyway.

"This trip back to school? No. I mean, it was all Margaret's idea. But I knew about it before you did. I doubt she'd put us in a room together unless she was sure I wouldn't gut you or something." Boone lifts her palms up. "See? Nothing, not even a pair of scissors."

There's something about the way she's looking at me. Now, I think. It's time. I swing my backpack around and unzip it. "I have something to show you," I say. "I made it."

"Oh, Jesus. Tell me it's not a macaroni necklace or another lanyard." Boone exhales and laughs drily, clearly ready to lighten the mood, but she stops when she sees the thick manuscript, bound by an industrial clip. "What's this?"

"It's my Thing," I say.

Boone looks down at it for a long time. When she looks up again, her cheeks are flushed. "You wrote about it?"

"It's all in there," I say. "Everything. Gia, and Ben, and . . . you." Maybe she'll laugh, but I don't care. "I want you to have it."

Boone looks at the first page. Reads the epilogue as I stand there, staring at the diner's weathered door. "Damn," she says. "You really did write it all down." She swallows, and I can see that she's trying not to cry. "Okay, then. Okay." She exhales and looks up at me. "Thanks."

We both laugh, awkward and relieved. We were never good with moments, and now it has passed.

"Maybe we should just read excerpts to the girls at the school," I suggest, trying to keep things light. "Take on different voices. Give them some theater."

"Hmmm," she says. "Somehow I think it might be more beneficial coming straight from us." She points to the patch over her eye. "You know — more 'in your face.'" Her laugh is soft.

"Yeah," I say. "Probably."

Boone nods toward the door, and I grab the knob, but before I've had a chance to turn it, she says, "Hey. Wait." She holds out the manuscript, points to the first page. "Looks like you took some creative liberties, Townie," she says, frowning. "It's missing a prologue."

Behind her, a gust of hot wind sends a holdover from last year's leaves skittering down the road. I inhale deeply. There it is: the distant, familiar scent of the mountains. We're almost there.

"I'll write it," I say. "I'm writing it now."

Acknowledgments

When I think about an acknowledgments page, the list of people to thank begins to spiral backward, my relationship with each person dependent on an introduction by another, or a conversation, or a situation in which others were involved. So, with that in mind:

My parents and my sister have always supported and encouraged my desire to write, even when I was penning stories with titles like "Sally Needs a Friend." Thanks, Mom and Dad, for settling in Idaho and forcing me to go to Girl Scout camp with Morgan Cole, whose father, Steve, took me on my first backpacking trip in the Frank Church Wilderness eight years later — an experience without which this book would never have been written. Ruffneck Peak was always in the back of my mind as I wrote. Thanks to Jennifer Purvine, who knows Ruffneck well, and who, as a wildlife biologist for the Salmon-Challis National Forest, answered all of my questions about flora and fauna. Any mistakes or liberties I've made or taken are in no way indicative of her limitless knowledge of the Frank.

There are so many people with whom I've shared experiences in the woods and who've taught me different ways of appreciating wildness: Carrie, Emma, Catherine, Marcus, Mike, Kim, and a Girl Scout camp counselor who went by the nickname Twizzler — you're all in here somewhere. Bradley and Frank Boyden, fearless stewards of the Margery Davis Boyden Wilderness Writing Residency, provided the priceless gift of getting off the grid. I finished the novel at their secluded cabin and encountered a mountain lion, not exactly in that order.

A big thank you to Denise Shannon, my wonderful agent, and to the other first readers of this novel: Morgan, Alexa, MJ, Polly, and Sierra — and to the readers before them, when this novel was just a story in a graduate school workshop: Chris, Drew, Will, Matt, Elaine, and Todd. And speaking of readers and writers, I extend heartfelt gratitude to my college professors Susan Jaret McKinstry and Gregory Blake Smith. I got to know Cheryl Klein in their classes, and long after we'd graduated, she wrote to me in Africa and suggested that I write a book for young adults. Now she's my fantastically insightful editor. Thank you, Cheryl, for sparking the fire of this book over a decade ago, and for tending it with such care and wisdom.

First and finally, my deepest thanks go to Rob, with whom I'll enter any wilderness.